Broken Allegiance

OTHER BOOKS BY MARK YOUNG:

GERRIT O'ROURKE NOVELS:

Off the Grid

Fatal eMpulse

TRAVIS MAYS NOVEL:

Revenge

Broken Allegiance

A Tom Kagan Novel

by Mark Young

Mass market © 2013 ISBN: 978-0-9832663-8-9
EPub Edition © 2013 ISBN: 978-0-9832663-9-6

Library of Congress Cataloging-in-Publication Number: 2013917850

To all my friends in law enforcement

fighting this ongoing war against gang violence:

Stay safe. Stay strong.

May God have your back!

Acknowledgments

Writing a novel like *Broken Allegiance* takes more than putting words down on paper. It is an accumulation of experiences. I would like to acknowledge those who worked alongside me in law enforcement and those in the editorial and book-publishing field. Without them, this novel would never have existed.

First I would like to acknowledge all those I served within SRPD's Organized Crime and Intelligence Section. My hat is off to these SRPD officers—George Collord, Brenda Herrington, Jeneane Hood, Jim Lane, Ray Navarro, Ken Pistorio, Andy Romero, and Bob Scott—who waged a war against gang violence. I would also like to thank Chief Sal Rosano, who sanctioned the first gang unit north of San Francisco to be launched, and Chief Michael Dunbaugh—though battered by political and organizational pressure—allowed us to bring Operation Black Widow to its successful conclusion.

A special thanks to our state and federal friends who put jurisdictional issues aside to make Operation Black Widow a success. From the California Department of Corrections, I would specifically like to thank those in the Special Services Unit—Special Agents Louis Holguin, Leo Burgos, and Jefrie Dix. A special thanks to CDC Assistant Director Brian Parry, who paved the way for us to work closely with all the California prisons, parole agents, and SSU units around the state.

From the Sonoma County District Attorney's Office, a special thanks to Andy Mazzanti and Gary Giovannioni, with a special thanks to David Dunn for his legal help and support all those years.. And from Sonoma County Sheriff's Office—Carlos Basurto and Lloyd Hernandez.

From the federal side, I would like to recognize our FBI friends who funded and housed the OBW crew and provided leadership and continuity through the U.S. attorney's office to make this operation a success. Specifically, I would like to mention Special Agents Greg Snider, Gary Joseph, and Mac Crumrine, who willing worked alongside us to make this case happen. Without their money and special equipment, we would have been dead in the water.

I would like to recognize Barney and Kathleen Pedersen for sharing with me the wonders of Lake Tahoe—past and present. The place will always be special to me because of them.

This list does not do justice to all those who worked with us during this five-plus years of investigations. I am sorry I could not include all of you in this, but if I did it might be longer than this novel.

As always, I want to express my appreciation to my great editor, Julee Schwarzburg, who always makes my novels better than they should be. Thanks, Julee, for guiding me through another project. A special thanks to my friend and mentor, author James Scott Bell, who first helped me get this novel on track during his Santa Cruz Mountains writing clinic at Mt. Hermon.

Lastly, I want to thank my family for their love and support. To my wife, Katie, who always pushed me to finish this novel and get it out to the readers because she believed in it. To my daughters Jacqueline, Julia, and Ingrid—thank you for always reminding me what is important in life.

Chapter 1

Santa Rosa, California

A full moon cast shadows of burnt-ochre over acres of dying vineyards. Giant oaks stood like towering sentinels in the gathering darkness along the edges of the vines. As Toby trudged past the tree line and moved into the open, he spied it dead ahead. An abandoned winery, blackened by fire and broken by age, valiantly stood its ground in the middle of yellowing grape vines like a wounded warrior waiting for the end to come.

Toby tugged his girlfriend's hand. "I brought a present." He held up a bottle of wine by its neck. "To set the mood." He flashed her a sensual smile before turning toward the winery, carrying a cumbersome wool blanket under his arm.

She giggled, playfully resisting his tug. "You're sooo wicked, Toby. My momma—"

"Your mommy isn't here to spoil our fun, baby. Come on. I found just the place."

The bleached-blond girl gave him a teasing smile. "I know what you want, big shot. Dream on."

Toby slyly glanced back. "Ahh…and I thought you loved me."

They nimbly sprang up a short flight of flagstone pavers, peppered with overgrown weeds, littered with bits of trash, and coated with dirt. Just as they passed through a charred doorway, Toby thought he heard voices coming from the vineyard.

"Shhh." He let go of her hand and placed his across her mouth. "Someone's coming."

She tore his hand away. "Don't." Her nose flared, illuminated by the blush of moonlight through a broken window. She glanced around. "You call this romantic? It's a dump."

"Please, keep it down. I don't want us to get nailed for trespassing." Toby crouched beneath an open window, glass long-ago shattered, and slowly raised himself to peer outside. Off to his right, a car had been parked on a gravel road leading from the winery to the horseshoe-shaped Round Barn Boulevard. They must've already parked the car when he and Charlotte made their way into the winery, or he would have heard them.

Maybe we've already been spotted.

Through a row of vines, he saw three men dragging a fourth thirty yards away. The moon flashed a cold-white beacon like stage lights reaching across a darkened stage. Toby could see every detail: the victim, mouth taped shut, struggling to free himself; and one of the captors waving a gun as the others fought with their captive.

"Oh no!" Toby dropped down, whispering to his girlfriend as he clutched her arm. "They're coming this way and dragging someone with them." Thoughts of romance fled.

Charlotte wrenched herself from his grasp. "Let me see."

"No. Please stay down." He reached up for her arm again. "These guys mean business. And they're getting closer. They may have seen us."

Ignoring his plea and his groping hand, she peered out the window. Suddenly she squeezed his shoulder. "One of them has a gun."

"I know. I tried to tell you." Toby slowly stood, unable to tear his attention away from this unfolding drama. "Get ready to run."

All four men sported shaved heads—captive and captors. The man with a gun waved it at the others. "Let him be. I'll shoot him if he tries to run."

Without their support, the fourth man fell to his knees, arms bound behind him. Blood rippled from a head wound, a crimson river flowing onto the captive's white T-shirt. The group stopped fifteen yards away. Toby could hear every word, see every movement, every expression. He held his breath, fearful that the least bit of noise might attract these gangsters.

The gunman reached down and ripped the tape from the victim's mouth. "Any last words, Paco?" All of them seemed to be Hispanic, the gunman's voice heavily accented. "Before I…"

The kneeling man stiffened, glaring up at his captor towering above him. "You're making a big mistake, Rascal. This is not sanctioned. Check it out, bro."

"I'm not here to flap my gums about the green light on your ass… bro. I'm giving you an opportunity to say your last words. Maybe shoot up a little prayer to the big guy in the sky."

The other two men, standing next to the bound victim, gave nervous chuckles as if they couldn't decide whether to laugh at Rascal's joke or keep still. They lapsed into silence.

"Here are some last words for you." Paco spit in Rascal's face. "*¡Nos vemos en el infierno!*"

Rascal cursed and wiped his face with a sleeve as he slowly circled behind the kneeling man. He raised the gun to Paco's head and squeezed off two quick shots. Explosions from each shot made Toby involuntarily flinch. The victim twitched and collapsed facedown like a marionette with its strings severed. Deadly silence filled the air as if all nature held its collective breath in fearful anticipation.

Toby stared in horror. He couldn't breathe. A numbing chill spread through his chest as he realized a man just died a few yards away. Toby drew farther into the shadows and tripped over the blanket that had fallen to the ground. Trying to gain his balance, he dropped the wine bottle. It bounced and rolled on the winery's concrete floor without breaking, but the sound echoed loudly in the darkness.

Rascal wheeled around and glanced in his direction. Toby crouched down out of sight, moving farther back, ready to run.

"You guys hear that?" Rascal called out to the others. "Go check it out."

One of the other men laughed. "Getting jumpy? Probably some animal moving around in there."

Toby couldn't help himself. He had to know if he and the girl should run. Slowly, he raised himself and saw the gangsters still standing in a tight cluster over the body.

Rascal peered into the darkened winery. "Maybe you're right." He turned to face the others before staring down at the body at his feet, still grasping the weapon as if it was a part of him. "I'll hand it to Paco. Once he knew it was coming, he sucked it up. Took it like a *soldado*."

The others bobbed their heads in agreement. Another said, "I wonder why they ordered us to kill him? I thought Paco was all good. Was he stiffing the bank? Not paying taxes?"

Glaring at the speaker who dared question the killing, Rascal snapped, "We got our orders. That's all we need to know."

The inquisitive one glanced at Rascal, then quickly averted his eyes.

"No more questions? Good." Rascal gestured toward the car with the gun. "Let's get out of here in case someone heard the shots." They trudged toward the car.

Toby sank to his butt, leaning against a wall. Charlotte huddled next to him, shivering. "They killed that man, Toby, What are we going to do?"

He leaned closer to her, speaking as softly as the night breeze, afraid any sound of substance might give their presence away to the killers. "As soon as they leave—we're outta here. And we can't tell anyone. You understand? No one!"

She nodded as if in a daze. "Shot him like he was…nothing." Charlotte started whimpering, laying her head on his shoulder.

He pulled himself away and rose from the concrete floor to glance outside. Across the vineyard, the killer and his friends climbed into an aging Ford Galaxy facing the paved road ahead. The driver turned the engine over and punched the accelerator, tires spraying gravel as the car fishtailed back to the paved highway. Once rubber grabbed pavement, the driver hit the gas hard and flicked on the headlights as they roared through the darkness.

Toby tugged at his girlfriend. "C'mon." They scrambled down the stairs and ran in the opposite direction toward the edge of the vineyard. As they broke through a grove of eucalyptus and scrub oak trees, Toby saw the comforting lights from the Hilton below. Beyond that, farther to the left, stood the silhouette of the landmark Round Barn. Farther down the hill, low-lying coastal fog captured the city's brightness, muffling the light in a heavy blanket of mist.

Toby led her across Round Barn Boulevard and into the hotel parking lot where he'd stashed a car. He turned to Charlotte. "Remember. Don't tell anyone what we saw — or we're dead."

Her eyes mirrored the shock she must have felt inside. "I'm not stupid, Toby. But that man...left like that. Someone should tell someone, shouldn't they?"

Toby shrugged without answering. As far as he was concerned, silence was the only barrier between life and death.

Chapter 2

Barely a whisper of wind moved through the trees outside, its gentle breath coaxing a few leaves to flitter to the sidewalk. Standing near the window, Tom Kagan searched for any hint of danger. It looked like the city of the damned since he took up his watch four hours ago. No life. No cars. No pedestrians.

Eerily quiet in the neighborhood.

In the palm of Tom's calloused hand—toughened by years of horse-back riding, fence mending, and struggling to keep an aging ranch afloat while still a cop—his cell phone vibrated. He glanced at the caller ID glowing across the screen in the darkness.

Fat Louie.

Tom bit his lower lip. Should he let the call go to voice mail or not? Fat Louie was the supervisor of the Santa Rosa Organized Crime and Intelligence Section, a little Napoleon who enjoyed pushing his men around as pawns on a chessboard. No one took him seriously—except Fat Louie.

The man was not fat—except for his overly wide rear end—and his name was not Louie. Tom and his coworkers had secretly christened their supervisor: Sergeant Art Crenshaw. The man dreamed of making lieutenant, and he sat on his rear end all day kissing up to anyone with rank. Hence, Fat Louie.

Tom raised the phone to his ear. "Kagan here."

"Where are you, Tom? And don't tell me you're at home. I just called there."

"I'm babysitting the grand jury witness for tomorrow's testimony. The one the bikers want to silence. I want to make sure she and her son are safe until we hand them over to the U.S. Marshals."

"Who you got for backup?"

"My .40 cal Glock and a 12-gauge shotgun."

"You know what I mean."

"Art, I'll let Dispatch know if something comes up I can't handle." His supervisor hated it when his men used his first name. Tom sensed where this conversation was headed, and he wanted to get under his supervisor's skin as a distraction.

"I told you no cowboy stuff. Call in Bill or one of the other guys to back you up."

"Don't trust me to do the job…Art?"

"Let's not drudge up old history, shall we? I took a chance letting you back in the unit. After—"

"Don't go there. We've been all over this. I can do the job just fine if you guys will back off."

A door cracked open down the hall, and light spilled into the darkness illuminating Tom near the front window. He moved away from the glass to minimize his silhouette. "Officer Tom, everything okay?" A ten-year-old boy walked toward him, rubbing his eyes. "I heard noises."

"Everything's fine, Bobby. Go back to bed. Give me just a second and I'll tuck you in. Okay?"

The boy gave him a sleepy nod, yawned widely, then retraced his steps and closed the bedroom door.

"Sarge, I gotta go. Let's take this up another time."

"Tom, listen. I assigned you to work with the feds on this Hells Angels case so you can have a break from…the other stuff."

"Go ahead and say it. Afraid I'm going to cap one of those Norteño lowlifes?"

"See, that kind of talk makes me nervous."

Tom moved closer to the window, looking for anything that might be out of the ordinary. He silently counted before responding, giving him a moment to cool down. If he blurted out what was really on his mind, Fat Louie might slap Tom with desk duty. It wasn't worth it. "Look, Sarge. You're covered. I met with the department shrink. She cleared me for duty."

"I'm not saying you're unstable." Crenshaw seemed to be struggling for the right words.

"But…?"

"You wouldn't be back in the field if we felt that way. On the other hand, if it had been up to me, I wouldn't have let you back into the gang unit."

"My biggest fan." Tom glanced out the window one more time. "So why the phone call, Art? Afraid to let me work on my own?"

"No. No. I just feel there's no need for you to be babysitting those witnesses. Nobody knows where we stashed them."

"Then I'm not in any danger."

"I don't want you running up the overtime."

Man, this guy is full of excuses. "I'm doing this on my own dime." Tom rubbed his jaw, clenching the phone in his other hand. The sergeant cared more about his budget—keeping everything in the black and looking good to his boss—than he did about the lives Tom wanted to protect.

Crenshaw sighed. "I can't have you working off the clock, Tom." His supervisor waited for a response but got only silence. "By the way, I talked to Sara when I called your house. She didn't have a clue where you were."

Tom rubbed his forehead. A headache began to send shooting pains between his eyes. Fat Louie had just made Tom's life more difficult. Now his wife would be worried. "I'll take care of it. From now on, I'd appreciate it if you would use my cell phone to reach me. Leave Sara out of it."

Tom disconnected the call and shoved the phone into his pocket as he quietly made his way down the hallway. Opening the door to Bobby's room, he saw the boy lying under the covers facing the door, wide awake. Beyond Bobby, Tom saw the outline of a woman beneath the covers—Bobby's mom. She seemed unaware the boy had left to check on Tom.

Bobby's gaze followed Tom's movement across the room. Kneeling by the bed, Tom lowered his voice. "Everything's fine, Bobby. Sorry I woke you up. Try to get back to sleep." He tucked the covers around the boy and patted him on the head. "It's going to be a long night. You let me worry about the bad guys."

"You promise they won't get us?"

Those words, drawn from the boy's own fears, tugged at Tom's heart. A ten-year-old boy shouldn't have to worry about whether he and his mom might be killed by outlaw motorcycle gang members. But Clarice made "bad life choices"—as one social worker phrased it—and now she and the boy stood in harm's way. Tom just wanted to make sure they made it safely through the night.

"I promise, Bobby. Now, go to sleep." Tom stood as the boy closed his eyes. He eased open the door and crept down the hall. His foot struck a wooden baseball bat lying on the floor as he passed the kitchen. He stooped to pick it up so no one else would stumble over it in the dark and carried it to his chair in the front room.

As Tom clutched the bat, memories flooded in and he clenched his jaw. Memories of better days—maybe even happier days—when everything seemed right with the world. And then like a flash his mind staggered with how his life had changed. Life had become just like this room—dark and foreboding.

He glanced out the window when a vehicle passed by. A dark-colored van with tinted windows crept down the residential street. He watched it disappear down the block. It did not turn around. Still, the van made him cautious. He stood at the window until he was sure the vehicle left the area. He finally sat down, his eyes heavy, and tried to stay awake. For the moment, everything seemed peaceful outside

Fat Louie was right about one thing. Nobody should know where Tom had hidden Bobby and his mother. Only those in the unit knew of this safe house. He felt himself drifting off to sleep.

Maybe this night would pass without Tom breaking his promise to another young boy.

Chapter 3

Tom sat up with a start. He glanced at his watch. Three in the morning. Outside, he heard someone moving slowly. He went to the window, still clutching the baseball bat.

Two men—heavyset, dressed in dark clothing—came down the front walkway toward the house. One man reminded him of the Popeye comics character Brutus, a bruiser with his hair pulled back in a ponytail. Brutus came straight for Tom, a sawed-off shotgun grasped in his right hand. The man was about twenty paces from the front steps.

The other guy—a slimmer version of his partner—carried a large semiauto in his left hand. *Southpaw* broke off, leaving Brutus at the front, and began to work his way to the back of the house, edging around the attached garage until he was out of sight.

Tom started to reach for his cell phone. *No time to dial.* Brutus was almost to the front door.

Stepping to one side of the doorway, Tom waited for the biker to make the first move. He heard a gate open and close beyond the garage. Southpaw was in the backyard. They were making sure no one escaped.

A loud bang shook the front door. Brutus tried to kick his way through the solid-core door. Once. Twice. Three kicks. Still the door didn't budge.

Tom raised his bat.

On the fourth kick, the door frame splintered. The fifth slammed the door open and banged against the wall. Brutus barreled through wielding the sawed-off shotgun in both hands like he was leading some kind of charge across enemy lines.

Tom swung the bat, aiming for Brutus's head. *Crack!* He felt the satisfying crunch of wood meeting bone. A blast from the shotgun sent pellets harmlessly into the living room wall as Brutus fell backward. The weapon clattered to the floor.

The big man crumpled to the ground without moving. Tom knelt to feel the biker's pulse. Still alive. He grabbed the shotgun, emptied it, and tossed it behind the sofa.

One down. One more to go.

Rushing down the hallway, Tom made it to the back door before the second biker. Southpaw booted the door with one kick just as Tom slid off to the right into the shadows of a laundry room. As the back door slammed open, the biker barged through wielding a gun.

Tom lunged and grabbed the intruder's gun hand, twisting it back until the wrist snapped. Dropping the gun, Southpaw yelped and tried to lash out with his other fist. Tom fended off the blow with his forearm, shifted his body while torquing the biker's injured arm, and rammed an elbow into his nose.

Tom followed up with another arm twist to the man's injured arm and slammed the biker's head into the ground in a takedown. He quickly handcuffed the man as Southpaw screamed in pain. Tom searched for more weapons on the man, ignoring the biker's threats.

Finishing, Tom leaned down and said, "You're lucky I didn't just shoot you." He dragged the man to his feet and marched him to the front room where he forced the injured man to sit on the floor, back to the wall. After handcuffing both men together, and searching Brutus—who still lay unconscious—Tom called Dispatch and requested reinforcements. Just as he stood, Brutus began to regain consciousness. "Both of you—stay put or I'll put a world of hurt on both of you."

Southpaw glared up at him. Brutus looked like he was still trying to figure out what day it was.. Then he scowled at Tom and told him what he could do to himself.

"Hey, big mouth," Tom said, "put a cork in it or I tape your mouth shut. We have a kid down the hall with his mom. But I guess you already knew that, didn't you?"

Southpaw still glared. "We heard the boy and mom were in trouble. We just came over to make sure she was all right."

"That's why you guys kicked in both doors? You must be idiots to think anybody is going to buy that story."

Looking at the two prisoners and the damage to both doors, Tom decided to wait awhile before calling Fat Louie. His sergeant would be livid. Everything had to be orderly and safe in his supervisor's world. Otherwise, the man started yelling and his blood pressure started turning his face scarlet. Too early in the day to deal with all that drama.

While waiting for patrol units to arrive, Tom made one more phone call, listening as it rang several times before a female answered. "Sara, it's me. Sorry for calling so early but I wanted to let you know that I won't be coming home tonight. Didn't want you to worry."

Sounding groggy, Sara said, "It's almost time to get up. Are you all right?"

Tom looked at the two bikers in the living room. "Yeah, I'm fine. Made some arrests and have a little paperwork to finish up. By the time I finish, my workday starts."

"Without sleeping? That's crazy."

He started to reply, but Bobby peered out of his bedroom doorway. Clarice yelled at him to shut the door and he slammed it closed. "Look, Sara, I gotta go. Just wanted to let you know I'm fine."

"Your supervisor called—"

"I know. We chatted."

"It didn't sound like he knew where you were."

"Don't worry, honey. He never knows what I'm doing. Safer that way. Talk to you later." He hung up, flicked on a few lights, and walked toward Bobby's bedroom, looking back over his shoulder to make sure the two bikers stayed put.

Standing in the hallway, Tom opened the door and motioned for Bobby to join him. "Hey, little guy. Need you to help your mom start packing. Everything's fine—just like I promised. But I need to take the two of you to another place until your mom goes to court. Okay?"

Bobby turned to leave without comment.

"Tell your mom I need to talk to her, out here."

The boy nodded and disappeared into the bedroom.

The first patrol unit rolled up as the boy's mom emerged from the bedroom. "Is it safe, Detective?"

"It is now. I need to talk to you—privately." He nodded toward where Bobby had disappeared. "Shut the door behind you."

Clarice, wearing a tattered pink robe, nodded and closed the door. As she walked toward him, the first officer on the scene announced himself at the front door. Tom quickly identified himself. As the officer entered, Tom said, "I've got two 10-15s in the living room." He motioned to the two bikers. "Both need medical attention."

The officer nodded and moved toward the prisoners.

"Could you have other units search the area for a van?" Tom gave a brief description of the one he had seen drive slowly past the house earlier. "They might have a driver standing by."

The officer relayed Tom's request to Dispatch.

Tom turned toward Clarice. "Where's your cell phone?"

She glared up at him, jaw jutting out. "Why?"

"I don't need to explain myself. Where's your phone?"

Slowly, Clarice pulled out a cell phone from the pocket of her robe.

Tom snatched it up and searched for recent calls. He saw one call he recognized, a woman affiliated with one of his suspects. The call had been made yesterday afternoon. Tom pointed at the number. "What did you tell her?"

Clarice pursed her lips.

"You put your life—and Bobby's—in danger. Tell me what you told her."

"I was scared, Tom. I just needed someone to talk to. We're good friends. That's all. She wanted to come over and help with Bobby."

Tom motioned to the two bikers nearby. "Your friend just tried to get you killed." He dropped the phone on the ground and crushed it with his boot. "Now, go back there and try to calm Bobby down. I want to move the two of you out as soon as possible."

The women grimaced but followed his orders without further conversation.

Reluctantly, Tom pulled out his cell phone. He'd have to call Fat Louie. He stepped outside so the patrol officer wouldn't witness this call. The faint hue of dawn could be seen creeping over Mount Hood east of Santa Rosa, casting light on the dark city that lay in the valley below.

Tom rubbed his eyes as he heard the call go through. It was going to be a long day.

Chapter **4**

"A 10-55. Suspicious death. Gang related."

Tom knew the call might be unusual just by the pitch and tone of the officer's first words. A death termed *suspicious* covered the full gamut of a person's demise—from suicide all the way to premeditated murder. This call did not sound like a self-inflicted death. The term *gang related* gave him authority to answer this call—at least until Fat Louie found out. He headed toward the door with a jacket, straw Stetson, and portable radio in hand before the transmission squelched to an end.

After relocating Clarice and Bobby into the waiting arms of the U.S. Marshals, Tom had returned to the office to finish in-custody reports regarding the arrests of both bikers for attempted murder. Fat Louie had left for a luncheon with some city official, and the other guys were conducting a probation search of a gang member near Sebastopol, east of Santa Rosa. Tom was the only one in his unit stuck in the station.

Dispatch came over the air, calling for gang officers to respond. Since his supervisor was off the air, Tom let Dispatch know he would be responding. He'd deal with the heat from Sgt. Crenshaw later.

A blistering August sun temporarily blinded him as he searched for his car among a stable of unmarks. His vehicle had been "borrowed" by one of the other officers and left parked somewhere in the back lot. Wincing, he located the car and slid behind the wheel. The dark blue-on-blue Ford Crown Vic baked in the heat like an oven.

As he started the car, he felt like he was sitting in a sauna. A stifling breeze swept over him as he rolled down all the windows. His plaid George Strait shirt, trapped between his backside and the plastic seat cover, became drenched with sweat.

"Six-David-Fourteen. Contact Dispatch by landline."

He jumped as the radio call blasted through the speakers. Someone left the volume on high. He scrambled to turn it down before he lost what little hearing remained. He snatched up the mike and acknowledged the call.

Tom flipped open his cell phone and punched in the number for Dispatch. A woman answered on the second ring and cut him off in mid-sentence as she transferred him to another dispatcher. He listened for a moment to elevator music as they routed his call.

Joy Geraty, a veteran dispatcher, came on line. He relaxed as he recognized her pleasant, no-nonsense voice. Joy would give him everything he needed to know on the way to this call—as long as he didn't give her any guff. She could be brutal to officers with an attitude, but when an officer needed help—even if he was a Dodgers fan—she was one of those you wanted to hear over the airways directing backup.

"Tom, an anonymous female called in the 10-55 near Round Barn Boulevard from a pay phone at the mall. She mentioned the body could be found in a vineyard near an abandoned building. You want to take this or give it to one of the other guys?" She paused, leaving the line open as Tom listened to her acknowledge another caller over the radio. In a moment she came back.

"I'll handle it, Joy. And send me Stevenson."

"You got it. Sorry for the delay. Dispatch is slammed. Patrol's screaming for Violent Crimes to roll as well as the gang guys—that being you, Detective." She filled him in on more details.

Tom cut her off. "I know the location and heard the call go out. I'm on my way. Just give David-Sixteen a heads-up and tell him to eighty-seven me at the scene."

He eyed the air-conditioning switch with disgust as he slid the cell phone back into his pocket. The yard promised to have it fixed in a day or two. That was three weeks ago. At this rate they'd fix it by winter, at which time the heater would take a dump.

He drove east off Mendocino Avenue and began climbing into the hills. Round Barn Boulevard, like a giant horseshoe, began and ended on Fountain Grove Parkway. The crime scene lay in the middle of this gigantic horseshoe.

As Tom adjusted the rearview mirror, he caught a glimpse of a familiar stranger with tired, dark brown eyes. The reflection staring back revealed the harsh truth of his age—gray flecks in otherwise blond close-cropped hair, and the beginning of crow's feet marching across a lean, weathered face. His tanned features still retained that chiseled look of his youth, his muscular body winning the upper hand against middle-age for the moment. He took one more look in the mirror, searching for that young man that still lived in the recesses of his mind. Instead he saw the physical toll this job had taken on his fifty-one-year-old body.

Kagan, you've become an old fart.

He spotted several patrol cars parked ahead as he pulled off Round Barn and followed a gravel road. Tom eased off the roadway and parked between two rows of vines. He walked down a path toward the crime scene. As he drew closer, Tom saw a man in a black sports shirt—*Santa Rosa Police Gang Enforcement Team* printed in white letters across the back—standing twenty yards ahead. As Tom narrowed the gap, the officer abruptly turned and sauntered toward him with a broad smile.

"Took the long way around, Kagan? I beat you by fifteen minutes."

Tom grinned. "Detective Stevenson. I see Dispatch finally tracked you down. Didn't hear you answer up."

A sly grin crept across Bill's face. "They told me you couldn't figure this out by yourself. I guess since you've been off playing with the feds, you needed someone with real gang expertise to bail you out."

"They got their wires crossed. I told them to have you meet me here. You still have a lot to learn. And I have a lot to teach you, rookie."

Stevenson's tanned face carried a deceptive look of youthfulness. He was a decade behind Tom, but he looked even younger.

Tom lifted his Stetson and wiped his brow, sweat beginning to burn his eyes. "How are Mary and Jonathan?"

Bill shot him a smile—the look of a proud husband and father. "They're fine. Mary's busy with Jonathan at his school. I'm supposed to swing by and help him practice for Little League tryouts later this afternoon. They're not until next year, but he wants to get in as much practice as his old man can squeeze in. I can't wait—" Stevenson stopped in midsentence as if his words slammed into a brick wall.

Tom glanced away and gritted his teeth.

"I'm sorry, Tom—"

"Forget it."

The two men stared down the pathway toward the crime scene in uneasy silence. A gust of warm wind caused the canary-yellow crime-scene tape to flutter in the hot breeze like the tail end of a kite trying to reach into the heavens. Charred remains of what once was part of a farm—including a decrepit winery—stood off to the left.

For a moment Tom watched the officers huddled near where the body had been discovered before speaking. "You've seen the body?"

Stevenson cleared his throat. "Not yet. First officer on the scene—Jim Hardy—says he saw gang-related tats on the dead guy. I was just waiting 'til you got here. Didn't want to screw up the crime scene. Least 'til I could blame it on you."

Tom tried to smile. "Always with the jokes." Even though Stevenson kidded around with him, Tom saw a flicker of concern in the other man's eyes. He hated that look—especially from friends. *Focus, Kagan. Forget everything else but the job at hand.* Another dead body beckoned him. Gang members killing gang members.

As he walked toward the body, Tom realized how many years he had been doing this. Then another thought crossed his mind even more disturbing than this crime scene.

This death, like all the others, gives me a reason to live.

He brushed this thought aside, not wanting to deal with what those words implied. "Come on, partner. Let's get this thing over with."

Chapter **5**

Tom glanced to his right and saw the body fifteen yards away. The victim lay facedown in the dirt, hands tied behind his back. Tom returned his attention to the group of officers. One of them glanced his way and then nudged another officer. They stopped talking and watched as Tom and Stevenson walked up.

One young officer gave him a look of impatience. "Hey, detectives. What's shaking?"

Tom remembered this guy from when he taught gang investigations at the academy a couple years ago. The officer was a ball of fire back then, and it appeared his fire was still lit. Tom had mentally tagged this guy *Firecracker*.

The young man gestured toward the others. "If you don't need us, we thought we'd go ahead and clear. Calls are stacking up."

One of the older officers groaned. "Sometimes it's best to keep your mouth shut, newbie."

Tom glared at Firecracker. "Are we keeping you from something important, sport?" The man's face flushed and Tom relented. "This heat's getting to all of us. VCI will be here soon to take over the investigation. Until then, I'll need all of you to lock down this crime scene. We'll be out here for a while. Once the news media gets wind of this, we might have all kinds of rubberneckers showing up."

Firecracker seemed to have recovered his dignity. "What do you want me to do, boss?"

Tom pulled out a clipboard. "Document everyone who sets foot in this crime scene. I don't care if the chief or God Himself crosses that line, record it and get their John Henry on paper."

Dispatch tried to raise Tom on the radio. He keyed the mike and let communications know he heard. The dispatcher continued. "David-Fourteen, be advised, VCI responding and the watch commander's ETA—ten minutes."

Tom acknowledged by clicking the button twice and slipped the portable into his back pocket. He glanced Stevenson's way. "Let's go earn our paychecks."

They made a wide circle around the body, coming at it from the far side. He saw several pairs of shoe prints between the victim and the pathway. He made a mental note to make sure VCI had forensics do eliminations of the officers' boots. VCI always hated to have others tell them how to investigate, but unless this was mentioned and checked off, it would bug him. He wasn't here to make friends.

Looking closer at the prints, he thought he recognized the pattern of heavy boot prints left by the first officer—long, solid strides stopping just short of where the body lay.

His attention was drawn to the number of tennis shoe prints not related to police. "Must have been more than one person." He pointed to the impressions left in the freshly turned soil. "Looks like at least three—not counting the victim."

Stevenson nodded and kneeled beside him. Tom pointed to what appeared to be drag marks that abruptly stopped. Footprints, presumably the victim's, led to where the body had been left.

Tom tried to visualize the victim struggling with his abductors, trying to free himself as the end neared. Tom noticed where the victim had futilely tried to pull his bonds apart. The tape, stretched and rolled together, stubbornly held.

At the base of the victim's head, the hair had been shaved close to the scalp, making his job easier. He bent and scrutinized two entry wounds where the killer's rounds shattered his skull, two shots closely grouped together. The second shot must have been fired quickly before the body lurched forward. Muzzle-flash burns encircled each entry wound where gunpowder peppered the scalp. He didn't need to turn the body over to know what the face must look like. He'd wait for the coroner's office to do the honors.

Stevenson, still squatting, said, "This was a cold-blooded execution, Tom. It looks like they forced him to kneel before they shot him. He must have known it was coming."

Tom squinted at Stevenson. "Maybe there is hope for you yet, Sherlock."

His friend opened his mouth as if to retort and then closed it. Something else appeared to catch his attention as he leaned over the body.

"Hey, I recognize those tats." Stevenson pointed to the side and back of the victim's neck. "This bird, it's an image Norteño gangsters like to copy, slightly modified from the farm worker's huelga bird." He pointed to the side of the victim's neck. "See the tattoo of a sombrero with the knife through it?"

Tom nodded. "Only an NF, a *Nuestra Familia* prison gang member, wears those tattoos. This guy must be connected." Tom stood. "So we have an execution of a prison gang member. Where do we go from here, gang expert?"

Stevenson stared at the body. "I'm not sure. You're the expert, Tom. You tell me."

"Not so fast. Someday, I won't be around to tell you what to do, my friend. Show me your stuff."

"Okay." Stevenson scratched his jaw. "It depends on who killed him. One way or the other, this will spark some major payback. If the Southerners whacked him, if it was blue on red, we'll have the mother of all gang wars on our hands. Innocent people will get caught in the cross fire."

He paused, looking at Tom. "On the other hand, if the NF is cleaning house, red on red, someone within the gang ordered this hit."

Firecracker carefully walked up to them, clutching a clipboard. Tom was pleased that the young man had followed the exact path he and Stevenson used to get to the body.

Firecracker scratched his head. "Red on red, blue on red? Sounds like some kind of game."

Stevenson looked up. "Actually, it's a war, rookie. A war between prison gangs like the Mexican Mafia—whose gang claim blue—and Nuestra Familia with its gang claiming red."

Tom glanced down at the body. "But this guy's not showing any colors, which makes me think it is an internal conflict unless the Sureños already had him in their sights."

"Yeah, I noticed," Stevenson said. "If this was a blue-on-red killing, they must have known he was a Northerner. And with those tats, they knew he was high up in the gang world—an OG with juice."

"Could you translate?" Firecracker asked.

Stevenson scratched his head. "Sorry. OG Refers to *Older Gangster*. Someone who's been around and earned respect in the gang."

Firecracker pressed on. "But what if this was red on red?"

Tom unbuttoned his shirtsleeves and rolled them up to his elbow. An afternoon breeze teased his face with a hint of cooler weather. He stared down at the dead man. "That's not as easy to answer. If it's internal, we'll have a harder time trying to figure this out. A sanctioned hit had to come from the leadership. No one else can lay a hand on one of their members. If this was on orders from NF, we just moved into a whole new ball game. I'm not even sure who the players are. Another consideration is that this was a power grab or a vendetta by one faction of the gang against another."

Tom grimaced. California's Department of Corrections was comprised of enough people to house a small city. He'd focused on white gangs and biker groups for the last couple years, and this killing gave him a good excuse to renew old CDC acquaintances that worked Hispanic gangs. "You know the cases I got stuck with for the last few years with the FBI and U.S. Marshals—thanks to Fat Louie. My Hispanic gang contacts with CDC have gotten rusty. How are yours, Bill?"

It looked like Stevenson was struggling to keep a straight face. "I can't wait until you meet my connection. He runs the SSU here in the North Bay. I'm surprised you never crossed paths with him."

"SSU?" Firecracker broke into the conversation again. "What's that, some kind of college?"

Stevenson turned to Tom. "Would you say the state's Special Services Unit is some kind of college?"

He shook his head. "The guys in SSU graduated from the school of hard knocks. They know how to take and give—with the worst offenders in the state."

He turned back to the dead body. The tattoos, the cold-blooded execution—this was way beyond what they'd dealt with in the past. This killing was different. They may have stepped into a hidden storm within the gang. A killer storm that no one could control—cops or crooks.

Tom felt ancient as he stared at the body. Somewhere along the way he lost count of how many bodies he came across in these gang wars. How many shootings, stabbings, and mutilations one gang perpetrated on another. How many innocent victims had been attacked. He was sick and tired of all the gang violence, going from one human tragedy to the next without any hope that it might stop.

Maybe it was time for him to walk away while there was still a little of him left. Maybe it was too late. He feared this job had already taken everything he had until there was no more to give.

Chapter 6

Pelican Bay State Prison, California

A guard shoved a white envelope into a small, tomb-like cell. The envelope had been cut open before delivery. The prisoner, sporting a pair of boxer shorts and a white T-shirt, turned the wrinkled envelope over in his hands. It bore a woman's name and a post-office box number from Windsor, California, down near Rosetown.

He opened the envelope and withdrew a sheet of lined tablet paper. After placing the envelope on his bunk, the man unfolded the letter. It was written in code. The neatly printed message made reference to "Uncle Rascal." He knew who sent it.

What has my little bird to say? The man, known as Ghost to other gang members, pored over the letter's words. *My faithful Rascal, have you obeyed my orders?*

Ghost rubbed a hand over his shaved head. The smoothness felt good and gave his enemies nothing to hang on to if anyone dared to attack. He grimaced as he eyed the envelope now lying on his bunk. Prison staff read his letter long before it ever reached his cell.

They can read all they want; they'll never break the code.

This was the second letter he received from the outside this week. The first one came under the protection of legal mail—precluding guards from taking a peek inside—directly from his attorney. After a frantic investigation, the attorney reported that gang and VCI investigators were taking a look at Paco's murder. Looking at the attorney's findings—including the fact that a cop by the name of Tom Kagan was assigned to the case—Ghost grimly smiled to himself. What a small world?

Ghost sent a protected letter back ordering the attorney to hire investigators to find out everything they could on Kagan, his family, his residence. Kagan didn't know that he and Ghost had indirectly crossed paths in the past. This cop might be trouble, and Ghost wanted a dossier on this guy just in case.

Know your enemy!

He returned his attention to Rascal's letter. He meticulously studied each word of the coded message, each letter, and each punctuation mark. Ghost noted the number of words on each line and the spacing of each letter. He matched specific letters hidden in this communication to a deciphering code locked in his brain.

It took more than a half hour of labor before the message emerged. The sequence of the code was known only to a handful of gang members, all of whom reported to Ghost. Each deciphered letter he extracted from the text was transferred to a second piece of paper. Once the last letter was transferred, he leaned over and grinned as he read the message. Once read and memorized, he ripped up the letter and its translation into tiny pieces, flushing the evidence down a stainless-steel toilet.

My order has been carried out. Paco is dead and Rascal has earned his bones.

Ghost pulled out a tiny piece of paper and wrote his own message. This note in plain English would be clearly understood by the reader. Ghost smiled to himself. *I'm sorry, Rascal, but soon you too must die for the cause.*

In about a week, his note would be hand delivered to a house in Sonoma County. Assassins would race to obey his command once they understood his orders.

Ghost held the power of life and death in his strong hands. He wrote this simple order and a man would cease breathing a hundred miles away.

Blood in. Blood out.

Tom Kagan. Just thinking the name made Ghost's blood pressure rise. This detective would never give up—just like a pit bull Ghost once owned. The dog would latch on to his victim with his jaws and never let go. Kagan was like that. For ten years the man continued to be a pain in the butt, sniffing around where he was not wanted. If Kagan got too close this time, Ghost would send a note to take this man out. No more dancing around.

Ghost would be watching.

Tom slipped the key into the lock and opened his front door. He was so tired, the keys slipped from his grasp. It had been two days since he'd had any sleep. In the scarlet and pink dawn light, he could barely make out the keys lying on the ground in front of him. His back ached and his feet throbbed in protest.

A rooster crowed from the barn behind him a few hundred yards away. One of the horses snorted a greeting, kicking a stall door trying to get Tom's attention. The ranch would have to wait. While the rest of the world was starting to wake up and start anew, he must crash for a few hours. A few hours before getting up and starting all over again.

Tom closed the door and slipped out of his well-worn cowboy boots. He started to creep down the hallway when he heard a stifled cough. Turning, he saw Sara sitting at the kitchen table.

"Sorry, honey. Didn't want to wake you."

"I've been up all night—waiting." She brushed a strand of blond hair from her face as if to emphasis her point. Her green eyes looked tired.

"I'm sorry. Bill and I needed to follow up on a lead out of the city, and time just got away from me. Meant to call."

"You always *mean* to call. I was worried sick."

Tom let his boots drop to the floor. "Look. Just call me next time if you're that worried. I have a lot of things on my mind."

"I did, Tom. It transferred me to your message center."

He pulled out his cell phone and winced when he saw it had been turned off. "Sorry. I forgot to turn it back on."

"You always have things on your mind. Just once I wish you'd think of me."

"That's a cheap shot. I'm always thinking about you…about us." Tears welled up in her eyes at his outburst and his stomach tightened into a knot.

He walked over and knelt beside her as she turned her face away. He drew her face to his, brushing her tears away with his thumb. "Honey, I'm sorry. I'm just beat."

She turned to face him. "It's not just tonight, Tom. It's…everything. We've become strangers. I don't understand what's happening to us. To you."

He withdrew his hand and stood, crossed his arms and leaned against the kitchen counter. "There's nothing wrong with us. I've just had to work a lot of overtime. Things will change. You'll see."

Sara rose and rested against him. She held his face in her hands, looking into his eyes with such intensity he tried to turn away, her voice as soft as her warm fingers. "We need to talk. Tom. I think we need help."

He bristled. "Here you go again. Wanting to bring strangers into our world. There's nothing here we can't fix ourselves. Just give it some time."

"It's been ten years."

"Look, I've been up for forty-eight hours and I have to be back to work in a few hours. I can't deal with this right now."

"You never want to deal with it."

"Sara—give it a rest." He wrenched himself from her embrace. "We'll talk about this later. I need some shut-eye."

The house seemed cold as he walked down the hallway. Just as he reached the bedroom, he heard Sara crying softly. The sound pierced him like a knife, twisting and cutting its way into his heart. A rush of anger and guilt swept over him, frustration hammering at him until he felt like he might explode.

He closed the bedroom door and slammed his fist into the mattress, striking it over and over. He hated himself for hurting her. He wanted the hurt to go away—for both of them. Instead he felt powerless to do anything, and this helplessness created its own fury inside.

God, where are You?

He listened to the silence of the room, the only answer his prayers received since the accident. The garage door opened and the car started up. Sara leaving again. He was pushing her away, little by little. Like a man caught in quicksand, life seemed to be sucking him down. The more he struggled, the more life—or was it death?—seemed to draw him away from the living.

He slowly succumbed to the fatigue of a tired mind as the shadows of the silent room waged a battle against the light. A part of him wanted to rise from his bed and stop her from leaving. To tell her he still loved her.

Unable to bear the silence, Tom slipped out of the bedroom and walked into the kitchen. He reached for a glass and pulled out a bottle of scotch from the top shelf. He downed one glass, refilled it, and retuned the half-empty bottle to the shelf. He walked back to the bedroom and emptied the glass in one burning gulp. He slipped out of his clothes and stretched across the bed, his brain numbed with fatigue but his body refusing to surrender to sleep. He lay there watching the morning sunlight steal past the window curtains.

His gaze wandered to the nightstand next to him where he just set down his duty weapon, too tired to place it in the safe. What would it be like if he no longer had to carry one? A part of him just wanted to let go. One pull of the trigger and he would be free.

But he always pulled back from the edge, from consciously carrying through on this thought. He remembered the suicide calls he answered on patrol. The damage caused to survivors by this one act of selfishness. The baggage of guilt they were saddled with for the rest of their lives. The thought that maybe there was something they could have done to prevent this.

No, he could never go out that way. He must hang on because, if for no other reason, others relied on him. Sara needed him—and he needed her. Two things kept him alive and forced him to keep fighting—his love for Sara and his burning desire to find out who destroyed his world.

He rolled over and tried to go to sleep. In a few hours, he must get up and keep on searching. Awake or asleep, he must continue to fight the demons.

Chapter 7

Sara Kagan cringed as she edged the car into a tight parking spot. She was late and really didn't have time to find another spot. As the car came to a rest, she sat back and relaxed for a moment. She glanced to the side. Mary Stevenson stood on the sidewalk. Sara climbed out and locked the car before joining her friend.

Mary pointed to a café across the street. "Saved us a table. I almost gave up on you."

"Sorry. I almost decided not to come. Left Tom at home…" Sara stopped, deciding to leave the rest of that conversation for later. "Anyway, here I am."

A large maple tree, its delicate leaves stubbornly fighting the on-slaught of the August heat, sheltered the café's outdoor tables with cool, breezy shade. They ordered coffee and carried their drinks to a table Mary had reserved.

"So, my friend, tell me what's up? You mentioned something about Tom over the telephone."

Sara stirred a spoonful of cream, watching her image in the dark-brown liquid disappear into a swirl of caramel. "He's slipping away. One day at a time."

"Is there someone else?"

Mary's question made Sara laugh. "I wish. At least it'd be something I could get my hands on—"

"Hands on?"

"I mean…oh, I don't know what I mean."

Mary leaned over and hugged her.

Sara placed her spoon on a napkin. "He's slowly shutting me out as if to protect himself from any more hurt."

"Sorry for my comment about Tom seeing someone else. I know him better than that. He only has eyes for you. I see it every time he looks at you."

A memory Sara had forgotten resurfaced. "You know, Tom can be very tender at times."

"Really?" Mary laughed. "We're talking about Mr. Kick-in-the-door-and-take-no-prisoners, Tom Kagan?"

"Yeah, my Mr. Tough Guy." Sara took a sip of coffee. "Don't ever tell Tom I told you this. Promise?"

"Absolutely. Now tell all."

Sara gazed across the street toward a church, its white clapboards glimmering in the late afternoon glow. "Tom was working swing-shift patrol just before we had David. He was grabbing all the overtime he could get his hands on once we knew the baby was coming."

Sara paused, letting those earlier memories return with clarity. "A couple days before Christmas, he was sent to a domestic disturbance. Husband beating on the wife, both of them high on drugs. Tom saw two little ones in the house, two small girls." She stirred the coffee again. "Pain filled his eyes when he came home that night. I asked him what happened."

"I'm married to a cop, Sara. I can imagine what happened. He shrugged and said *nothin'*. Right?"

Sara shook her head. "We were young and he was so excited about his work. Things were different then. He'd tell me everything. Every last detail. It was later when he started keeping things from me. 'Don't wanna bring all that garbage home,' he'd say." Bitterness crept into her voice for a moment.

She set the cup down, then rubbed the rim with her finger. "As it turned out, he had to take those children from their home for their own protection. It choked him up telling me how frightened they were as he drove them to the children's shelter. That look of fear as they were ripped from their home."

"Bill says one of the worst parts of his job is seeing the children caught in the middle like that."

"But this story doesn't end there. As I said, money was tight."

"Been there," Mary said.

"But here's the side of Tom no one sees." Sara glanced at her friend. "He disappeared Christmas eve and returned several hours later with gifts for those kids." Sara smiled as the memory of that night came back. "He went out Christmas morning and played Santa Claus at the shelter."

Sara looked back toward the church. Two stands of giant redwoods dwarfed the buildings, their large, draping branches partially blocking the church's steeple from view.

"Times have changed." She returned her attention to Mary. "Since the accident, Tom shut himself off from everyone. And now, with my job opportunity at the newspaper as a reporter and Tom's schedule…well, I'm afraid where this is headed."

Mary reached across the table and took her hand. "Give it time. I know Tom. He will find his way back."

Sara closed her eyes for a moment. If only she could believe.

Through a telephoto lens, the man could almost read their lips as the two women chatted. Sara Kagan was his target. The other woman he would have to do a little homework on to identify.

From across the street, he clicked off more shots he would later sort through for just the right angle. His main target looked worried as she sat hunched over a cup of coffee, her hands making all kinds of gestures as she spoke.

He looked up and down the street. No cop cars. This would be hard to explain if he was caught. As long as he stayed out of jail, this would be easy money.

Once a month an envelope stuffed with cash was shoved under his door around the first like clockwork. This little arrangement started a long time ago. If he kept shooting photos and mailing to the address he was given, money would appear under his door like Christmas. That and notes on his surveillance of Sara and her husband.

Easy money.

Now her husband was a different kind of target. Following that cop made him nervous, so he usually stuck to the easy job and picked the woman and her friends to shadow. Paid the same and a lot less risk.

What did his *client* do with the photos?

He shot a few more photos before starting up his car. He would park farther down the street and wait until Sara's friend left. Then he would do a little research to add a name to these photos and maybe a residence. His client should be pleased.

Chapter 8

San Rafael, California

A blast from a motorcycle's modified mufflers ripped through the parking lot. Startled, Tom jerked awake to see Stevenson still sitting in the driver's seat, their car wedged between others in the parking lot. His friend pointed. "Here he comes."

The motorcycle's roar erupted once again, drowning out a woman's scream as the bike came to a screeching halt in front of their car. The rider threw his head back, laughing at the frightened woman glaring back. The biker yanked hard on the throttle just as she stepped from her car.

"Garcia, I'm gonna kill you." She slammed the car door. He revved the throttle one more time.

Tom rose up in his seat. "I'm going to put a stop to this."

Stevenson tugged his arm. "No, wait. That's the guy I was telling you about—Hector Garcia."

Tom watched as the biker climbed off and removed his helmet. "That's the gang expert you wanted me to meet? You've got to be joking."

Garcia was built like a fire hydrant, hard as a rock and not much altitude. People wanted to navigate to the other side of the street when they saw him approach. He had ink-black tattoos etched on his forearms, a wickedly crooked nose, and a scar that looked like a knife wound along the right side of his face.

"I'm going to yank those wires off your bike the next time you scare me like that, Garcia." The woman stood with her hands jammed on her hips, her feet firmly planted on the sidewalk. "Why don't you act your age?"

He smirked, revving the engine once more before pulling into a parking space. Silence followed the thunder as he switched off the engine. Tucking the helmet under his arm, Garcia grinned. "Come over here, sweetheart, and I'll show you just how young I am."

She thrust a finger toward him. "Have you ever heard of sexual harassment?" She started to turn away, then looked back. "I'm going to ask the boss to send you back for more training."

Garcia laughed. "Heck, Wilma. I'm the reason they teach that class."

She threw her hands up and stomped away, disappearing into a brick building next to the parking lot.

Stevenson tapped Tom on the arm. "Come on. I'll introduce you."

"I can't wait."

"Hector grows on you. You'll see."

Tom turned to open the car door. "Yeah. Like fungus between my toes."

They walked up just as Garcia pushed the bike's kickstand into place. He turned and grinned as they approached. "Bill, how goes the war?" He thrust out a hand. Stevenson grimaced as Garcia's fingers seemed to crush his fingers.

"Whoa, partner. You trying to cripple me?"

"You're not turning into a sissy are you?" Garcia glanced over at Tom.

Stevenson followed his gaze. "I'd like you to meet my partner—Tom Kagan."

Tom extended his hand and waited for the pain to start. "Agent Garcia, nice to meet you."

The man grasped Tom's outstretched hand with enthusiasm. "My friends call me Hector. How come you're running around with this young pup?"

Tom glanced at Stevenson. "Not sure. My friend fancies himself as some kind of gang expert. But this case we're working stumped him. So he came running to you."

Stevenson shot Tom an irritated look. "I'm not stumped. Just came for consultation, Hector. One expert to another."

Garcia grinned. "Well, Mr. Gang Expert, you tell your partner what we do here?"

"He knows SSU by reputation. I just warned him to be careful. You guys run with a pretty tough crowd."

Garcia gestured toward the building where Wilma fled. "Why don't we take this up to my office, gentlemen?"

He bounded up a concrete stairway two steps at a time, then flung open a large glass-paned door and strode to a bank of elevators on the far side of the lobby. One of the stainless-steel doors started to close as he neared. Garcia thrust out a hand, causing the door to slowly reopen. A man standing inside flashed them a look of annoyance.

He must know Garcia, Tom thought.

They rode the elevator to the third floor, then followed a gray carpet that ran the full length of the hallway, abruptly ending before a pair of stained oak doors. An engraved placard, announcing the offices of the California Department of Corrections, hung to the right of the doors. Garcia ushered the group into a reception area.

Wilma from the parking lot scowled at Garcia from behind a desk, her features still flushed. She pursed her lips without speaking. Garcia smiled back with a look of innocence. "Wanna go for a ride this afternoon?"

She hurled him a look that could have scorched the paint off his motorcycle. "Playtime's over, Garcia. I see you've got visitors. Try to act your age."

He blew a kiss in her direction as he ambled down the hallway. "Down deep, she loves me." He looked back at Tom.

Tom glanced at the receptionist, muttering. "I wouldn't count on that."

Garcia laughed as he ushered them into his office.

Tom peered inside the room, then glanced back at Stevenson. There was no polite way to describe the place. It looked like an environmental hazard.

Stevenson just smiled.

A government-gray metal desk piled high with bulging manila files sat in the center of the mess. An assortment of official-looking forms, some yellowing with age, sat amid pens and paper clips cluttering the desk. Protruding from this mountain of disorder perched a light-gray computer monitor, its CPU probably buried somewhere beneath the desk.

An old Clint Eastwood poster, somewhat tattered with corners peeling back, hung on the wall. Anyone sitting in front of Garcia's desk looked up into the business end of a .44 Magnum Smith & Wesson revolver. Above the gun, Eastwood's scowling eyes and the words "Go Ahead—Make My Day."

The rest of the office looked like the handiwork of a hurricane: a wrinkled raid jacket flung on the floor, a black-leather holster draped over a coatrack where the raid jacket should have hung, and a gaudy Hawaiian shirt pitched over the back of his chair. When Garcia pulled open a drawer, Tom saw an assortment of bullets, handcuffs, pens, pencils, and a partially empty Twinkies package shoved inside.

"Sorry for the mess," Garcia said. "I try to spend as little time as possible in here."

Tom warily eyed the room and found two chairs facing the desk. He and Stevenson waited until Garcia settled behind the desk before sitting. Tom leaned forward. "They call your group the Special Services Unit. I always thought the name was a little vague."

Garcia rubbed his bald head. "They call us by that because they can't decide exactly what they want us to do. A lot of different jobs get thrown our way. Our most important job is to be a link between the prisons and you guys out on the street."

His chair creaked as Garcia leaned back. "As you know, we track and monitor all high-risk offenders who hit the street on parole—prison gang members, sex offenders, whatever. We try to make sure these predators stay contained."

"You guys do excellent work." Tom nodded. "I worked with your predecessor a few years back. Tracking a Japanese Yakuza member, just out of prison, who decided to settle in our area."

Footsteps echoed in the hallway. Garcia glanced toward the doorway and nodded. Twisting around in his chair, Tom saw another SSU agent he vaguely remembered holding up ten fingers.

"My partner just reminded me, we've got to do a special prisoner transport today," Garcia said. "They've asked us to move an inmate from Corcoran down to Calipatria next to the border. We'll be back late tomorrow night. Gotta leave here in just a few minutes."

Garcia unlocked a lower desk drawer and pulled out a small revolver. Not much bigger than the palm of his hand. Garcia slipped the weapon into a leg holster and stood. Tom had seen a larger weapon tucked in the back of Garcia's waistband when they entered the office. Garcia reached for his coat.

Tom glanced up. "Before you run, Bill thought you guys might be able to shed some light on our case." He opened a file and handed it to Garcia. "Our murder victim is on parole."

The burly agent sat back down and eyed the file with interest. "Yeah, I heard about the killing. So you got him identified?"

"Yeah. Name's Javier Valdez. Goes by Paco." Tom pointed to the file. "You know the cliché. He's got a rap sheet as long as your arm. Well, this guy's sheet is as long as both my arms."

Garcia squinted at the file, staring at the dead man's photo. "Yeah, I know this creep. We've been tracking him since he paroled three months ago. A high-priority target for our team."

Tom spotted concern on the agent's face. "What's the matter?"

"I thought this guy was untouchable." Garcia's jaw tightened. "He had all kinds of protection out here, protection granted from the leaders of Nuestra Familia. He was their man on the outside. Whoever whacked this guy is in deep, deep trouble." The agent fingered the scar along his cheekbone. "This might spark the mother of all gang wars. Like inviting conservative talk host Glenn Beck to be the guest speaker at the next Democratic National Convention."

"Look, I know you gotta run," Tom said, "but can you take a few minutes and point us in the right direction?"

Garcia dug under a pile of papers and withdrew a computer keyboard. The agent reached under the desk, apparently searching for the CPU's power button. In a moment, Tom heard scratching noises as the steel-gray monitor came alive.

Garcia's chair squeaked as he straightened up and pecked a sequence of numbers on dirt-stained keys. "Give me a minute." He positioned the monitor so Tom and Bill could see. The grayish drab of the monitor suddenly sprang alive with color. The words *Parole Leads* and the state's emblem for the Department of Justice popped into view.

Garcia gestured toward the screen. "This system helps track thousands of parolees by computerizing their files." He pecked away at the keyboard again with two fingers. The face of the dead man slowly emerged in full color across the computer screen. "Here's your boy, gentlemen."

The scowling face of Javier Valdez sprang into view, along with a series of photos. Each photo a different angle of Paco's face and body, zooming in on each of his tattoos.

Tom and Stevenson leaned forward to scan the information. Garcia clicked the mouse and sent the data to a printer. "You can pick this up on your way out."

Garcia pushed back in his chair. "Paco was one of the highest-ranking NF leaders on the street. Few ever make it back out for any length of time. We have most of these guys locked up in our Special Housing Units around the state—Pelican Bay, Corcoran, some of our level 4 yards."

Tom pointed to Paco's photo on the screen. "I guess he wasn't high enough in the NF to save his own skin."

Garcia hunched forward. "Here's the bottom line. Paco is a validated NF gang member in good standing. He was just released from the SHU in Pelican Bay, and based on what you've shown me here, I doubt this was a Sureño hit. It looks like this might have been sanctioned by NF leadership."

Tom grimaced. "If this was a hit ordered from within the prison: Who ordered it? Why did they order it? And how are we gonna prove it?"

Garcia frowned. "Look, guys, I have to fly. As soon as I get back, I'll give my home boy a call up at Pelican Bay and see what we can dig up for you. Okay?"

Tom nodded. "Thanks. Any information will help at this point. We're working completely in the dark."

"You got it, *amigo*. I'll be in touch." Hector almost ran out of the office.

Bill looked at Tom and smiled. "Now that…is a character."

"I would have to agree with you for once. He reminds me of an old rodeo term—bail out."

"I hesitate to ask, but what's a bail out?"

"It's when a horse charges out of the chute on its hind legs and then bucks like crazy. Hector comes out reared up and ready to create all kinds of crazy."

"Well," Stevenson drawled, "you better hang on tight, cowboy. I think you are in for a long ride with that one."

Chapter 9

Santa Rosa

A gangster, just released from Pelican Bay, knocked on the door. Still prison pale, the parolee glanced around with furtive eyes when Gato had opened the door.

"You Gato?"

His homies called him Gato. His mother called him Juan Diego Sanchez. "What's it to you?"

The man handed him a rolled-up piece of paper. "A kite from Ghost through your dad." He abruptly turned and disappeared into the night without another word.

Gato stared at the note. His father, doing life without at the Bay, helped send this message? A cold tightness squeezed his lungs. Just the sound of the author's name sent a chill down Gato's spine. If Ghost wrote this, Gato knew it came from a man who wielded power over life and death. Gato's father must have been forced by Ghost to send this to his own son.

Before returning to prison several years ago, his father had explained the "Family" business. "It's just a matter of time before you wind up in prison. That's the way of life. Like your uncle and your mom's dad—and the rest of our family. We are soldados, soldiers of the north. We men need to stand up and be counted. It's a matter of honor." His father called it "putting in work."

Now it was time for Gato to put in work for the Family; just like his father and his uncle. This was a family business. And it was time for Gato to pay his dues.

His hand shook as he deciphered the code. It was an order to kill. As its message sank in, he struggled with the *honor* of this order. He must obey. It was a matter of life and death. His life. His death. It also meant the survival of his father.

Even this note was delivered by peons acting on orders. His father warned him the Family might reach out and contact him someday. Through a *wila*, a message, delivered under the noses of the guards. These messages were carried out in an inmate's rectum. They called it "carrying it in the hoop."

Gato gasped as he read the message. The words suddenly blurred as his eyes watered. *No, this can't be!*

With a heavy heart, Gato wiped the tears from his eyes and read the message one more time: *Take the wind out of Mikio.* It was signed: *Ghost.*

This was the second message he'd received from Ghost this month. The first ordered him to kill Paco. Someone else had taken care of Paco before Gato could obey.

Ghost must be sending out duplicate orders. Another gangster was probably holding the same message Gato now held in his hands. Someone else was preparing to kill Mikio.

The race was on.

His hand shook as he folded up the note and thrust it in his jeans pocket. His stomach churned. Blood pounded in his head. Mikio was his father's oldest brother. Gato had been ordered to kill one of his own family members. And his father had helped send this message of death.

The churning in his stomach worsened.

Gato suddenly bent over and threw up. The sickness deep inside spilled onto the kitchen floor. His world became a blur, dizziness causing him to sway in the quietness of his apartment.

Chapter 10

Santa Rosa

As Tom trudged up the stairs to the gang office, he tried to prepare for a confrontation with Fat Louie. The sergeant had been at a two-day leadership conference in Napa Valley. Tom finally got around to telling his supervisor late last night—two days after the investigation started—that he had taken over the intelligence investigation surrounding Paco's murder, working alongside VCI to give them a background on possible suspects and witnesses. Fat Louie went on a rampage. Tom feigned another call coming through and told his supervisor he would brief him the next morning at work.

Now Tom had to face the music and try to persuade his supervisor to keep him on the case. The side tour to meet Hector Garcia made him late getting into the office. Just as Tom rounded the corner into the gang bull pen, he heard his supervisor's irritating whine. "Detective. In my office—now!"

Bill Stevenson, hunched over his desk, shook his head at Tom. His partner shot him a hand signal to *take it easy* and mouthed the word *please*. Tom gave him a quick jerk of his head and took a deep breath before facing Fat Louie.

The sergeant stood behind his desk and gestured at a chair. "Sit."

As Tom lowered himself into a chair, Fat Louie slammed the door and stomped to his desk. "Now, tell me why you didn't call me about this case until almost midnight last night. And why did you think I would allow *you* to work this case with your history with Hispanic gangs?"

"I was going to—"

"I'm not finished, Detective." Fat Louie glowered. "The city attorney warned me that I should insulate you from these kinds of cases. He thinks that if you stir up any more trouble, we might be facing harassment charges. If the chief hadn't stepped in and insisted I give you a second chance, you'd be in patrol right now—probably working Oakmont. That retirement community would be about the only action you'd ever see."

Suppressing a retort, Tom let his supervisor rant on. Opening his mouth right now would only invite trouble. The leadership conference Fat Louie just attended must not have covered issues like Tom.

"I thought you might be a little off balanced after the accident…" The sergeant paused for a moment. "And blaming the NF, well, that's just crazy. But then you started jamming up every gangster you came in contact with. Complaints started rolling in and then that incident where you put one of the gangsters in the hospital."

"He attacked me—"

"That's your story, Tom. It was time for you to cool down, and I gave you a few days off for violating department policy."

Tom started to speak but Fat Louie held up his hand. "Let me finish. Anyway, the chief wanted you back in gangs, and I followed his orders even though I had my doubts. Now, about your meddling in Traffic's investigation…"

Tom tensed. If Fat Louie went down this path any further, Tom might just reach across the desk and give the sergeant a real reason to bring him up on charges.

The supervisor continued as Tom edging forward. "Accidents happen. Our accident investigators did a full-court press and came up empty. If there had been any workable leads, those guys would have found it. I want you to leave it alone. Are we clear?"

Ten years later and still no suspects. How long was he supposed to let this case sit? Tom's stomach churned and he clenched his fists, trying to hold his anger inside. This idiot sitting across the desk wouldn't know a lead if it rose up and slapped him in the face.

Tom forced his mind to stay focused. He must not allow himself to go down this path, to relive a loss that shattered his world and slowly ate away at his marriage. Otherwise, Fat Louie would bench him indefinitely and maybe—if he got backing from above—bounce Tom from the unit.

"Sergeant Crenshaw," Tom tried to change the focus of this conversation, "there was no one available at the time to take the call the other day. You were off taking care of business and in training. I made an executive decision and took the case, telling Dispatch to leave you a message."

Fat Louie gave him a surprised look. "I don't recall getting any messages."

Tom just shrugged. "Those things happened, Sarge. In spite of the difficulties in the past, you know I can crack this case. We're knee deep into this investigation, and to pull me out now would jeopardize our momentum. Time is critical. We let up—this case dies."

Fat Louie stared at him without speaking.

Tom couldn't tell what was going through the man's mind, so he pressed on. "Look, Bill Stevenson and I will partner up. He'll make sure I don't cross any lines, and that way we won't lose any traction by handing it off to someone else."

Fat Louie still did not respond. Tom decided to try one more angle.

"By the way, when I couldn't reach you, I ran into the chief and gave him an update as we passed in the hallway. He seemed pleased with our course of action."

At the mention of the chief, Fat Louie blinked twice and sat up straight. "You talked to the chief?"

Tom nodded. He had set the bait. He waited to see if Fat Louie would bite. It didn't take long.

"If the chief's on board, then I guess we'll see how this plays out. Make sure you have Stevenson with you every step of the way. Understand?"

Tom gave his supervisor as much of a respectful nod as he could muster, then slipped out of the office before Fat Louie could change his mind. Tom walked over to his desk and collapsed into his chair. He'd dodged another bullet. Around here he had to protect himself at all times, never knowing when he might be attacked. He was sick and tired of people like Fat Louie looking at him as if they expected him to do something crazy.

Stevenson, sitting at the desk next to him, leaned over and whispered, "You still working on the case?"

Tom gave his partner a broad grin. "As long as I take you everywhere I go. Your job—if you choose to accept it—is to keep me in check."

"Jeez, talk about mission impossible."

Tom looked over at his in-basket. Among several police reports stuffed in the basket was the corner of an envelope sticking out. He sucked in his breath and reached for the envelope, withdrawing it with two fingers like the paper might be contaminated.

After taking out a letter opener and slipping on some latex gloves, Tom made a slit along the edge of the envelope. Without looking, he knew it was addressed to him without any return address. He tossed the letter opener back in his desk, then slid a finger inside and withdrew a piece of paper wrapped around a single photo.

Glancing at those closest to him, he saw the others busy at their own desks. Stevenson was on the phone with someone from the district attorney's office. Slowly letting out air, Tom opened the folded paper and saw a photo of Sara and Mary Stevenson sitting at a café having coffee. The sender had drawn a bull's-eye around Sara and a question mark over Mary's face.

He glanced at the note. The same three words were printed: *We are watching!* Just like the other photos sent to him. Photos of him and Sara. Of just him.

Looking around once more to see if anyone was watching, Tom placed the note and photo back inside the envelope, then shoved it into his coat pocket. Again he glanced around. No one noticed. Stevenson was off the phone.

Pushing away from the desk, Tom said, "Let's hit the street. There has to be someone—family, girlfriend, a homie—who can tell us something about what happened to Paco."

Stevenson held up a set of car keys. "I'll drive since I have to babysit you. In your state, you might…"

The silence that followed made it clear his friend did not want to carry that thought forward. Stevenson looked uncomfortable.

Tom pushed himself from the desk and stood. "Grab that file with all of Paco's known associates in the area. We won't learn anything sitting around here on our butts."

His partner jumped up with a look of relief, snatched up a file, and headed for the door. "Come on, old man. Try to keep up."

It was eleven at night before Tom finally drove home to his ranch. It had been a day of futile door knocks. As if the gang world mutely watched and waited for the next event to unfold, fear in some of their eyes, afraid to say anything. As Tom walked toward his bedroom, he saw a pale light burning. As he glanced through the open doorway, he saw Sara propped up in bed reading. He stood there for a moment in the shadowed hallway until she glanced up. "The prodigal husband returns," he said.

"I'm glad." She placed the book—Sherwood Anderson's short-story sequence *Winesburg, Ohio*— down on the nightstand. Her blond hair fell across her face, shielding her eyes from his gaze for a moment. "Mary and Jonathan came by today. That boy's growing like a weed."

"Yeah, Bill's very proud of him. How's Mary?"

"She's doing fine. Got her hands full with Jonathan."

Tom walked over to his dresser and carefully pulled out the contents of his pockets, arranging them on top of the dresser. He stood with his back to her, watching Sara's reflection in the mirror. She smoothed the blanket around her, finally glancing up at his reflection in the glass. He averted his eyes, pretending to be looking for something.

She spoke first. "About the other day—"

"Forget it. Look, I'm sorry I snapped at you. It's just…I, I don't want to take this thing outside. To a stranger."

"I know. You want to work it out yourself."

"I want *us* to work it out."

"Tom, how can we work it out when we never talk? Really talk."

He pressed his lips together. "Let's talk about this later." He turned and walked into the bathroom, closed the door behind him. He was doing exactly what Sara just pointed out—procrastinating. He took his time preparing for bed.

Upon his return, the lamp on the nightstand had been turned off. Soft moonlight floated through the bedroom window. Sara lay on her side, her back toward him. She appeared to be sleeping. He gratefully slipped into bed and faced away from her, hoping she'd fallen asleep. A moment later, he felt her arms encircling him as she drew close.

"I love you, Tom Kagan." She kissed the nape of his neck.

"I love you, Sara Kagan."

With a contented sigh, she nestled against him.

He closed his eyes, listening to her breathing, steady and slow, until he knew she'd drifted off to sleep, her arm slipping from his shoulder. She'd found that peace that always seemed to elude him—the sleep of the innocent.

"I love you more than you know," he whispered.

Moonlight seemed to darken, as if clouds had moved in to shield him from the light. His sleep—when it finally came—would not be peaceful. For a moment he was jealous. After all that had happened, Sara had somehow been able to resolve it within herself. She'd made peace with her Maker.

Not so, Tom.

He could never forgive himself. An emptiness inside him never allowed sleep to come cheaply. And when sleep finally came, it brought with it nightmares: the horrors of the darkness, the sounds of twisted metal being cut away, his screams when he realized there was nothing he could do. And finally, the deafening silence that followed.

Sara, if only you knew how much I love you. His mind screamed out the words into the quietness of the room. *Please forgive me.*

Chapter 11

Santa Rosa

Gato felt the metal bulge in his coat pocket. He slipped his hand inside and grasped the gun handle. In his other pocket, a note ordering him to kill Mikio. He peered down the street toward the apartment complex where his uncle lived. His mind flashed to the last time he and his uncle had spoken two years ago—the day his uncle walked out of the shadow of Pelican Bay State Prison.

"Blood in, blood out. You got to spill it to become an NF member." His uncle's words still echoed in Gato's ears. It had been a rare sunny afternoon for that part of California. Gato, his mother, grandmother, and a few cousins squeezed into a minivan and made the long trek to the prison to watch Mikio become a free man.

He never knew Mikio as a free man. His uncle had been in prison longer than his dad, and Gato only knew him through brief family visits to various prisons around the state and through reputation among the gangs. Mikio gave Gato a street rep by the mere fact they were family. *La Familia.* His uncle looked tough and hard, but his voice carried a warmth that surprised Gato. Mikio's lanky body and shaved head made him look like a panther on the prowl, his taut olive skin marked with the ink of prison tattoos on his back, chest, and arms. The prison art on his skin shouted out his allegiance to Nuestra Familia.

At his uncle's request, the whole family piled out of the van on their way home and enjoyed a romp on the sandy beach just south of Crescent City. Mikio told them he wanted to feel the breeze on his face and see the ocean once again. It had been a decade since his uncle enjoyed this freedom—no bars, no iron gates, or walls coming between him and the setting sun.

Mikio pulled Gato aside as the rest of the family walked ahead. "I hear you've become a Norteño. *¿Es verdad?* Is this true?"

Gato nodded. *"Sí."*

Sadness filled the older man's eyes. "Then what? La Familia next. I don't want that kind of future for my nephew. You are better than that, Juan."

"They call me Gato on the street. And why should I not be a part of the NF if they call? It would be an honor."

Mikio just shook his head. "They require you to spill blood in order to be worthy." He stared out to sea, his eyes as dark as the clouds forming on the horizon. "And if you spill blood, they'll always have this over you. You'll never be free. And once they are through with you—they'll send a friend to slit your throat. To stab you in the back. To kill you."

Gato studied his uncle's face intently, trying to understand. He respected Mikio, this legend among gang members. Stories about Mikio's exploits, shared from gangster to gangster, grew over time until his uncle seemed like Superman. Scraps had tried to take him out, only to find out the hard way this man must have been made of steel. Invincible. Mikio's name was spoken with reverence and awe by others in Gato's gang back home.

"Once you're in there is no way out except by death. You'll die a gang member or they'll kill you if you try to step back. If you try to pull out."

"But why'd I want to get out? It's an honor to be one of the chosen."

Mikio clutched Gato's shoulder. "There is no future in this. I beg of you. Please, walk away while you can."

Gato wrenched himself free. *"Tío,* what're you saying! Why should I walk away? I want to be like *you.*"

"Like me?" Mikio's eyes flashed in anger. "Open your eyes. Look where I spent my last ten years."

"But look at the respect you have. Everyone looks up to you."

"Listen to me carefully, Juan. This respect came at a high price. It cost me everything—my freedom, my future. Any hope I had of a family—a normal family—just vanished with the years."

Mikio turned and gripped Gato's arm. "Follow my steps, Juan, before it is too late. I have left Nuestra Familia. No matter what happens, I will not go back."

Gato slowly backed away, his uncle's words sinking in. He looked at his uncle with shock—and then disgust. He saw his expression registered in Mikio's eyes and his uncle let go of him, and as Gato turned his back and walked away.

It was the last time they spoke.

That was two years ago. Today, Gato carried a gun with orders to kill his uncle. With a heavy heart, Gato made his way toward Mikio's front door. Juan's hand clasped the butt of the gun hidden inside his jacket.

He had no choice.

The snub-nosed .38 tucked in Gato's pocket seemed to weigh as heavy as his heart. He plodded down the path leading to Mikio's front door. Gato fought back tears and his feet seemed to move in slow motion. He heard his labored breathing, sweat burning his eyes and mingling with tears. He wiped his eyes with his coat sleeve and struggled to control himself. His hand felt clammy gripping the smoothness of the gun tucked inside his pocket.

Gato rapped twice, waiting for his uncle to answer. Footsteps inside told him someone was home. He held his breath as the door handle turned. Mikio's broad face appeared and a smile emerged for just a second. Then as his uncle saw Gato's face, his smile turned into a knowing frown. *Mikio knows!*

"Come on inside, Juan. It's been too long."

"I go by Gato now, Tío. No one calls me 'Juan' these days."

Mikio shrugged. "To me—you're Juan. Leave that street stuff out there, nephew." Mikio turned and led Gato inside.

Still clenching the gun, Gato followed the broad shoulders of his uncle into the apartment, numbly putting one foot in front of the other. He slowly pulled out the gun and pointed it at Mikio.

Chapter 12

Law Library, Pelican Bay State Prison

Four men shuffled along a concrete corridor, their hands shackled in belly chains, each man linked to the next like a gangly limbed arthropod. Two muscular guards eyed each convict as a potential threat.

Once they reached the law library, guards segregated each prisoner into mini solo-occupied holding cells equipped for one thing—segregated study of the law. Convicts, however, liked to multitask and reading seemed furthest from their minds.

Coming together from isolated housing units, prisoners used the law library to facilitate illegal communication. Through wire mesh and bars, prisoners whispered to each other while pretending to read their law books or waiting for a volume to be delivered.

And they would go fishing.

Using unraveled thread taken from clothing, they'd hurl "fish lines" to each other. Attached to these lines might be cryptic messages or even handmade weapons. Once the line reached its intended target, the line would be drawn in as these objects were moved from prisoner to prisoner.

They all knew the rules of the house, including the cardinal rule of silence. Daniel "DJ" Juarez violated this rule the moment his cubicle door clanked shut and the guard moved out of earshot.

"Snake—you there?"

"Hear you loud and clear, homie," a man whispered from the next cell.

A passing guard told them to shut up as he made a sweep.

DJ ignored the warning, speaking in low tones. "You heard the word? My man Paco's kicking up dirt in Rosetown."

"I heard," Snake said. "This cleared?"

"You know the Mesa never voted. Paco was all good. Someone went off the reservation. I'm ordering an investigation into this thing because someone acted without permission. We need to get on this—fast."

"Ghost's your captain for Santa Rosa, right?"

DJ grimaced. He was thankful Snake couldn't see his face. He hated Ghost and trusted him as much as he trusted the guards. He'd like to spread Ghost on the high-voltage wires surrounding this place. Watch him sizzle. However, DJ reined in his feelings. Ghost, after all, was a brother. One of the Family.

"Yeah. Ghost has been running a tight ship on the North Bay regiment. I'll shoot him a kite to investigate this thing. Paco was my eyes and ears on the street. If I find out who ordered this, I'll..." DJ stopped in midsentence. These walls had ears.

"He'll be missed," Snake said. "A righteous brother. A true soldado."

"Keep your ear to the ground. Shoot me any news coming your way."

"Consider it done, brother."

DJ kept his thoughts to himself. He did not tell Snake everything. An unknown enemy was trying to make DJ go blind and deaf? He had to find out why. It was a matter of life and death. His life. His death.

Moments before DJ and Snake's conversation, Hulk, one of the guards in the library, quietly positioned himself within earshot. He recognized the convicts and decided to seize an opportunity. What he heard made his heart beat a little faster. He could not wait to make his report. The IGI—Institutional Gang Investigator—had taken the time to drop by yesterday to share some of the intelligence his unit collected on the NF. Hulk learned—from updated organizational charts—all the names of suspected shot callers within Nuestra Familia. The IGI asked to be alerted about any intelligence coming from gang leaders—particularly about the murder of Javier "Paco" Valdez.

Hulk, so nicknamed because of the size of his arms, chest, and thighs from weight lifting, intended to give the IGI's office whatever they wanted. He appreciated them taking time to educate the guards about current events within the gangs. He wanted to reciprocate.

Hulk edged as close as he dared, holding his breath as he tried to listen. DJ said a person—without authorization—ordered the killing of his man Paco in Rosetown. This was probably Javier "Paco" Valdez, recently paroled to Santa Rosa, commonly referred to as Rosetown. He also knew Paco had been recently murdered. The guard slipped away and quickly wrote some notes. He wanted it as accurate and fresh as possible before shipping it to the gang guys.

As Hulk returned to his post, he nudged his partner. "See the guy in cell number two? Daniel "DJ" Juarez. IGI says he is the NF's general of street regiments. He's the shot caller for all of the twelve NF captains in the Bay. These captains carry heavy weight and manage gang activity on the street. Ultimately, DJ controls all of northern and central California."

The other guard's eyes opened wide. "Man, that's a lot of juice."

"See the guy next to DJ in cell number three? That's Victor "Snake" Delariva, the gang's general of the Pintas. He controls, directs, and monitors all gang activity going on within the walls of all California prisons and jails. He's responsible for checking the backgrounds on all prisoners coming into the system and to let the gang know who their allies and enemies are. He even keeps a file on us."

"Man, that's a lot of power between the two of them. They have eyes and ears everywhere. Those guys need to be watched."

"Yeah," Hulk said. "Thanks for covering my post. Well worth the effort."

His partner leaned closer. "Get anything?"

"An earful. One of their own boys just got whacked in Sonoma County. DJ and Snake are trying to figure out who did the hit. IGI is going to love this."

Chapter **13**

Santa Rosa

Gato's mind screamed *Kill Him! Kill him!* His heart said something else. And his gun hand didn't know which to obey. Gato pointed the gun at the center of Mikio's broad back as his uncle moved down the hall.

Without turning around, Mikio said, "C'mon in, nephew. I'm on the phone. Let me get rid of my caller." His uncle picked up the receiver lying on an end table and cradled the phone in the crook of his neck. "Call you back in a bit? Juan just dropped by. Yeah, catch you later."

"Uncle — turn around."

Mikio faced Gato and his eyes widened as he saw the gun. His uncle tensed for a split second and then went limp: arms dangling at his side, body slumping like someone squeezing air from a balloon. Mikio stared back without fear as he slowly shook his head. "They got to you, Juan." A heavy sadness weighed down every word Mikio uttered. "I prayed you would not be the one."

Gato shuddered as he slowly tried to squeeze the trigger. Again, his body mutinied. The gun hand began to wave a figure eight as his arm struggled to hold up the weapon. Sweat poured down his forehead and stung his eyes as he doubled-gripped the weapon, trying to steady it.

"You must decide, *sobrino*. Them…or me." Mikio watched Gato carefully, a blend of disappointment laced with sympathy in the older man's words.

A numbing weakness began to work its way through Gato's outstretched arms and he slowly lowered the weapon. The shock of what he almost did caught Gato by surprise. He gasped and let the gun slip from his hand. The thud of metal hitting wood vibrated throughout the barely furnished apartment.

"Oh, Tío!" He choked on the words, fighting back tears. "What is going to happen to us?"

Mikio walked over and put his arms around Gato.

He felt the older man's strength and hated his own weakness. He trembled as he imagined what almost happened. Just a trigger pull away from murder. Gato could not hold back the tears any longer. They came like a flood, his eyes like a weakened dam struggling to hold back the water. Everything crumbled inside. He stood there, ashamed of his tears and shaking with a new fear gripping his heart.

He failed to follow orders. Now it was only a matter of time before his name was dropped into the hat, before someone received a note telling him to end Gato's life.

Who would the Family use? Someone he trusted. Someone he loved. In a single moment, Gato's world became dark and threatening, and he knew he would be all alone when it was time to die.

Gato pulled himself from his uncle's grasp. "I gotta go, Tío."

Mikio reached out. "Stay here. We'll figure it out together."

Gato shook his head. "We are both targets. I need to start running— alone." Hurrying toward the front door, Gato yelled back, "I will be in touch. Don't try to find me." He left the building and walked away, trying to figure out his next move. He never looked back.

Exploding glass shattered the quietness of his study. Instinct forced Paul Lawson to leap from his chair and reach for a gun. Old habits died hard.

He saw a baseball bounce off his bookcase and drop to the floor. *Just kids.* He relaxed.

After twenty-four years as a cop, Paul finally hung up the badge eight years ago and picked up a Bible. They called him Pastor Paul nowadays. He no longer carried a gun.

Paul glanced at the shards of glass across the floor. A baseball lay among pieces of the debris. He peered through the shattered window. Two young boys stood on the grass outside, looks of horror on their faces. One boy clutched a baseball bat, the other a leather mitt.

"Sorry, Pastor Paul. My fastball got away from me," said the boy with the glove.

Inwardly, Paul smiled. Outwardly, he tried to look stern. "You guys have to be more careful. Wait right there. I'll be out in a minute."

He turned off his computer. The sermon would just have to wait. He picked up his own mitt lying on a shelf and locked up the study on his way outside. He followed a well-lit hallway and opened a second door leading outside onto a partially enclosed brick courtyard. The church building wrapped around the courtyard, with the sanctuary to Paul's left and the Sunday school building to his right. His study and other offices were built off a main hallway that connected the two larger structures.

A black wrought-iron fence separated the courtyard from a large parking lot. Paul walked through a gate and circled around to where the boys still stood in shock. They looked like two pint-sized defendants waiting to hear the judge pass sentence.

The boy with the mitt peered up at him. "My mom is in the choir room, Pastor Paul. Do you want me to go find her?"

Paul smiled. "I'll talk to her later, Jonathan. How 'bout I join you for a quick game of catch? Let's just move it farther away from the church this time."

The boys stole a glance at each other. They smiled like a couple of reprieved prisoners. The boy with the bat handed it to Jonathan. "Here—your turn." He grabbed his own mitt and sprinted across the lawn.

As Paul warmed up to throw the first pitch, he studied Jonathan's excited face. His dad, Bill Stevenson, was a cop with the local police department. A good man. A good father.

Paul lobbed the ball toward him, and Jonathan swung hard. A smack of leather meeting wood made Paul cringe. The ball sailed over his head and hung in the air for a moment as the other boy scrambled to get under it. The ball became just a white dot against a blue sky, smaller and smaller until it began its descent. The ball bounced off the outfielder's outstretched mitt and hit the ground.

Paul relaxed. This game would take some time. He was thankful he had the time. His thoughts wandered as he waited for the ball to be returned. At times, his past would come roaring back—like today. Like a few moments ago when shattering glass made him reach for a gun he no longer needed. The past was the past. Now—he lived for the future. Today he found himself playing baseball with kids on a beautiful late-August afternoon. Playing hooky from church. On days like this, he felt like a kid. He prepared for the next pitch. Jonathan's eyes sparkled as the boy raised the bat once more.

Paul relaxed for a moment, met Jonathan's stare, and then let the ball rip.

Sara had a few minutes to spare before they expected her at the office for a follow-up interview. She felt queasy knowing that one of her dreams might be within her grasp—a reporter on *The Press Democrat*. Since the accident, she had used her journalism degree and writing skills to write freelance articles about topics that interested her. But a full-time writing job in this market? She dried her hands on the edge of her skirt.

"Never let them see you sweat!"

She smiled at Tom's homespun words of wisdom as she paused in front of a store window on Fourth Street. The newspaper office was just around the corner on Mendocino Avenue. She looked through the glass at a mannequin inside.

A reflection caught her attention. A man stood across Fourth Street in the park—armed with a telephoto lens—aiming his camera in her direction. She wheeled around and began walking toward him.

He lowered the camera, shot her a smile, and began walking away.

She stepped out onto Fourth Street, trying to keep him in sight, when a car horn blasted a few feet away. Startled, she froze as the car braked to a stop a few feet away.

The driver leaned out and cussed at her.

"I'm sorry," she yelled, not sure her words carried. She looked the other way before continuing across the two-lane road. By the time she reached the other side, she lost sight of the man with the camera.

She dashed in the direction the man must have gone. As she moved deeper into the park, she glanced in all directions but couldn't spot the cameraman. She could see all the way south to Third Street and across the adjoining roadway that divided the park east and west.

The guy simply vanished.

At first she thought the stranger was capturing the area around her with his camera. But that thought didn't square with the way he had smiled at her—and then disappeared. She had been the focus of those shots.

Why?

And then she got a sick feeling in her stomach. A conversation Tom started a few weeks ago came to mind. Out of the blue, he asked if she had seen anyone suspicious hanging around, maybe taking a special interest in her or her friends. She just laughed it off, telling him she did get a call from a talent scout wanting to know if she would like to be a movie star. Tom seemed lost in thought for a moment and then chuckled without a lot of enthusiasm. Now she wondered if his comments had anything to do with what just happened.

She put those thoughts behind her as she walked toward the newspaper office around the corner. Sara would tell Tom about this later and try to pry out of him what was troubling him. She didn't hold out a lot of hope that she might be successful.

Sara laughed as she thought about trying to get Tom to open up. She would have more luck prying a pearl from an oyster shell with her fingernails than getting him to reveal his secrets. A woman could at least wear a pearl. What did you do with secrets?

She frowned. Once secrets were revealed, then you must deal with them no matter the cost. No matter the consequences. Once ignorance had been enlightened and secrets were exposed to the light of truth, there could be no turning back. So what was Tom keeping from her? Maybe a better question might be—did she want to know?

Yes! She wanted to know because the not-knowing was killing their relationship. All she could do was ask—the rest was up to Tom.

Chapter 14

Gato saw Rascal jump like he'd been zapped with an electric prod as someone banged on the front door. It has been like this for weeks since Rascal shot Paco and about that long when Gato failed to complete his own mission—to kill Mikio. After Gato refused to pull the trigger on his uncle, he went on the run and moved into this abandoned house with Rascal since they both shared something in common. They couldn't tell who to trust anymore. They both looked uneasily at the door, waiting for the other to answer it.

Gato wanted to hide because he knew sooner or later someone would come looking for him. Rascal had other problems. Both of them were looking over their shoulders these days, waiting for trouble to rear its ugly head.

Rascal hesitated, then stood and took a deep breath before opening the door. Gato recognized the visitor's voice and Rascal's body relaxed.

The speaker—a gang member who ran with Gato's crowd—slid past the open door, looking around the candle-lit living room. His gaze rested on Gato, slouching on a tattered couch. Seeming surprised, the visitor waved before turning back to Rascal. "Hey, word on the street is you whacked Paco. Man that's heavy. *¿Es verdad?*"

"You know I can't talk about that, man." Rascal eyed the visitor cautiously. Rumors continued to fly, but he and Rascal never brought up the subject about Paco. If Rascal wanted to talk about the killing, he'd start talking.

Someone in Rascal's adopted family had broken a vow of silence. They snitched. It was only a matter of time until Five-O heard these rumors and caught up to him. Or an enemy tried to even the score.

Rascal had become edgy, looking over his shoulder more than he used to as they traveled down darkened streets. Rascal rarely ventured outside during the day. And once the rumors started flying, they searched for a new home, a safe house where they both could hide. They'd found this abandoned dwelling red tagged for destruction. The vacant house, surrounded by weeds as high as the windows, sat off the street nestled under a grove of eucalyptus trees. Only Gato and a few of Rascal's friends knew of this hiding place.

After the gangster left, Rascal turned to Gato. "I'm going to the market for a few brews. Want anything?"

"Nah."

"Okay. Be back in twenty." Rascal slipped out the back door into the night.

Gato thought about their last visitor. Something seemed off. Rascal was taking too long returning. He remembered Mikio's warning: *"They'll send a friend to slit your throat."*

Gato blew out the candles, pulled back rags they had draped over the windows, and stood in the dark watching for any movement outside. Streetlamps cast a yellowish haze across the black asphalt. He saw a familiar shadow down the street. Gato started to relax when he spied Rascal's shaved head gleaming under the streetlight, a twelve-pack of beer tucked under one arm.

Then something else caught his attention farther down the street. A floodlight from a house shone on a car parked on the street. People sat in the vehicle parked at an angle, pointing straight toward Rascal. The car fired up, headlights illuminating Rascal as he rounded the corner.

Gato's stomach tightened. He sensed what might be coming and dashed out of the house toward his friend, waving his hands. "Rascal, run!"

Rascal froze, looking from Gato to the oncoming car.

Gato spotted several heads pop up inside the car as it drew near, the floodlight silhouetting those inside. His heart jackhammered. Running toward his friend, Gato frantically signaled the coming danger. Tires screeched as the car leaped forward, its driver gunning the engine as the vehicle pulled into striking distance.

Gato stared in horror as the car overtook Rascal in seconds. He heard the *pop, pop, pop* of gunfire. Rascal's body grotesquely spun around before crumpling to the sidewalk. The car roared past and disappeared down the block.

Gato reached his friend's side just as the screaming started, a gut-wrenching howl as Rascal writhed on the ground, blood already pooling beneath him.

"Gato. I can't move." He gestured at his legs that lay useless. "It hurts so bad, Gato. Stop the pain."

And the screaming started again. People spilled out on their homes, but fear kept them at bay. Someone must have called the cops. The first siren came their way after what seemed like an eternity.

Rascal's screams almost blocked out the wailing sirens as the first police cruiser rushed down the block, flashing red, white, and blue Christmas lights that cut through the night. He hesitated for a moment before standing, watching helplessly as his friend moaned on the ground.

"Help is coming, Rascal. I have to go."

As he slipped through the high weeds that surrounded their abandoned house, he felt ashamed leaving his friend like that. Nothing he could do. He must look out for himself. He cut through back alleys, trying to put distance between him and Five-O. He could still hear his friend screaming into the night.

At least Rascal was still breathing.

Chapter 15

Mendocino County, California

Tom glanced in the rearview and saw Hector Garcia sprawled in the backseat, fast asleep. Next to Tom on the passenger side, Bill seemed to have dosed off, his head laid back, eyes closed.

As the nose of the car cleared the last mountain range entering Sonoma County, Tom's cell phone vibrated. He quickly tried to fish it out of his pocket before the vibration turned to a loud ring. He was not fast enough. The phone went dead before he could answer the call.

It had been a wasted trip to Mendocino County. They got an anonymous tip that a recently paroled gang member living in Ukiah, an hour's drive north of Santa Rosa, bragged about the killing to another parolee. After all that driving, they came up empty. The parolee broke his leg prior to the killing and had been in the hospital when Paco was murdered. Garcia used the clout of SSU to pressure the gangster to talk. Once the parolee opened up, he could not stop talking. But he had nothing to share about the murder.

Bill stirred in the seat next to him. Garcia snored in the back, his sleep unabated by the phone's shrillness.

With one hand on the steering wheel, Tom flipped his cell phone open and squinted at the screen. A message had been left. He thumbed a series of push buttons to navigate to voice mail. After listening to the message, he closed the cell phone and tossed it on the console.

"Caught a break." Tom glanced in Stevenson's direction. Garcia sat up and rubbed his eyes. "How was your beauty rest?"

Garcia leaned back and stretched. "A little sleep isn't going to make me any prettier."

Tom laughed and returned his attention to the road ahead.

Stevenson leaned forward. "Well, are you going to keep us in suspense?"

"Oh, yeah." Tom looked over at his partner for a moment. "Remember that gangster who got shot up a few nights ago? He decided to spill his guts."

"Rascal is cooperating?" Garcia looked surprised.

Tom nodded. "I left my number with one of the nurses at the hospital. I told him that if he had a change of heart, to give me a call. He just left a message that he is willing to chat with us."

"Finally, a break in the case." Stevenson settled back in his seat.

The last few weeks had been discouraging. VCI had been relying on the gang unit to come up with some viable suspects based upon intelligence. They had combed the streets searching for information, squeezing snitches, conducting parole and probation searches, trying to rattle a few cages to jar loose some information. Then a carload of gangsters tried to kill Rascal.

They followed up with a visit to the hospital, but Rascal remained tight lipped about the shooting. Tom sensed the man might talk, given a little time, and his hunch paid off. Rascal was willing to spill the beans for the right deal.

Now, it was a matter of negotiation. The day before the shooting, Tom and Stevenson learned of an interesting call to Dispatch. The call had been forwarded to the gang unit's voice mail. The caller—a young female who refused to identify herself—mentioned that she and her boyfriend witnessed a shooting. They had been in the old winery making out when someone named Rascal and others shot Paco. That was all she would say before hanging up.

Tom returned to the crime scene, searched the winery, and found an unopened wine bottle lying on the ground. The bottle had been left there recently. He had it processed for prints. That was in the works when Rascal was shot in a drive-by. Tom didn't believe in coincidences. Rascal may have been the shooter.

So far, only the anonymous girl could place Rascal at the scene. And a search of past residences turned up empty. Rascal had disappeared after the shooting and no one knew where he was hiding. So far, they had not found the murder weapon.

Garcia leaned forward, resting his arms on the front seat between Tom and Stevenson. "Maybe Rascal wants to turn his life around. People do change. Sometimes it just takes an event to shake them up."

Tom tightened his jaw, looking down the road ahead without responding. *Yeah, people can change. Just look at me.* Garcia's comment triggered a memory Tom thought had been put to rest. It hit him so hard, it felt like a physical blow to his stomach. One phone call ten years ago, and everything collapsed like a house of cards. The memory was so vivid, it was like the event happened yesterday.

Police and fire units, amid flashing lights and congested traffic, appeared just ahead as Tom rushed to the scene. Moments earlier he had heard his license plate broadcast over the radio, followed by a report that a woman and child were trapped inside. Flicking on his lights and siren, Tom sped to the accident.

Fear gripped him as soon as he heard the words, squeezing him even harder as he surveyed the scene. Tom slammed on the brake and leaped out of the car, racing between stalled vehicles to get closer.

A late-model black Monte Carlo low rider had T-boned his family's car—a four-door Toyota van—just as Sara passed the fairgrounds and crossed the intersection to take the on-ramp to the freeway.

"No, no..." he heard himself say, as if listening from outside his body. Running, Tom knew the outcome could not be good. He prayed he was wrong.

Firefighters gathered around the wreckage, fighting with hydraulic teeth from the Jaws of Life, struggling to separate the front end of the Monte Carlo from the van Sara drove. Metal popped as they separated the two vehicles. On the far side, firemen already popped a door open and extracted Sara, who was lying on a gurney as paramedics feverishly worked on her.

Tom ran to his son's side of the van just as a fireman peeled back the door. David's body lay distorted inside, and Tom couldn't even recognize his son's face. The Monte Carlo had smashed into David's body, crushing him into a mangled heap of torn flesh and bones.

"Oh, God!" Tom screamed and his legs gave out as he sank to his knees. Shattered glass and pieces of metal bit into his knees as Tom leaned forward, hands on his thighs, shaking. "No. No. No!"

A fire captain he knew from Station One came over and knelt beside him. "Tom, there is nothing you can do here. Your wife survived." He pointed toward an ambulance where they were treating Sara. "Go be with her. You need to take care of the living. Let us take care of your son."

Tom gritted his teeth and rose to his feet.

The captain motioned to one of the other firefighters. "Go with Tom and see what he needs."

The fireman nodded and put his arm around Tom's shoulders. "I'll walk you over. She is unconscious—but alive."

"Who did this?" Tom turned to face the firefighter. "Who is responsible for killing my son?"

The firefighter grimaced. "The driver ran off. Witnesses said he looked like a gangster. Police say there was a shooting down the street and this car was probably involved. We have other units responding to assist."

Numbly, Tom just nodded. As he got to the ambulance, one of the crew members was about to close the door. "Where are you taking my wife?"

"To Memorial, sir. We will meet you there. We need to get to the hospital. Code 3."

Tom walked back toward his car.

The firefighter, still tagging along, said, "Maybe I should drive you, Tom. I don't want—"

"I'll manage." He nodded toward where he left David. "Just take good care of my son." The fireman turned and walked back toward the accident scene.

Tom stiffly climbed into his car and headed for the hospital. Nothing left here except evidence of the gangster who had killed his son.

At the hospital, Tom made contact with the emergency staff and learned that his wife was still unconscious. They would not know the extent of her injuries until she awoke. He called Stevenson and his wife once they stabilized Sara and moved her into the ICU. They arrived a few minutes later and stayed with him until first light.

Tom gave his partner the sketchy details he gathered from the firefighters about the possible gang connection. Stevenson promised to find out more upon his return to work that day. After they left, Tom took a seat near Sara's beside. He tried to nod off to sleep, but his mind and body refused to relax. And he did the hardest thing he could do right then—wait.

Waiting killed him. Waiting to see how Sara survived. Waiting until he must tell her their son had been killed. Waiting to see if he could ever recover from this loss. It felt as if his very soul had been ripped apart.

Around noon he glanced at Sara and saw her eyelids move a fraction. One moment her eyes were closed, her body motionless. The next moment her green eyes opened, glancing at him with a look of confusion and pain, her eyes filled with questions he did not want to answer.

He leaned toward her and cupped her hand to his. "You had me worried." He watched her expression. She looked away as if trying to figure out where she was. And then he saw reality sink in. She remembered.

The shock contorted her face as if her body might be wracked with pain. Sara turned toward him. "Where's David?" Her eyes pleaded, searching the room as if expecting to see their son.

He glanced away, crumbling inside. He struggled to remain strong for her, to give her a facade of strength. "Honey, David is...gone."

She stared at him, struggling to understand. Her eyes closed as those words struck home, tears coursing down her cheeks. Her body shook and she clutched herself.

There was nothing he could do to comfort her. He knew the pain she felt, like thrusting a dagger into the heart. The same knife pierced his soul when he saw his son's crumpled body.

Sara wept. Her cries tore him up deep inside, in those places where Tom thought no more pain could reach. He was wrong. It continued to hack away until his heart felt like a wide-open wound.

That night he started drinking, his first since college. The alcohol only dulled the ache, never healed it. He never wanted to speak about David since that moment in the hospital. Not at his son's funeral. Not when he closed his son's bedroom door, never to go back inside. Just the mention of David's name reopened that wound he tried so desperately to cauterize. It had been ten years since the accident. His life changed that night. And this deadness inside became his only protection.

Stevenson had tried to find suspect information on the crash, but he came up empty. Later, Tom searched for the person responsible. Week after week. Year after year. The more time past, the harder Tom pressed. It was his unwillingness to give up that got him into trouble. Complaints came in about how he'd roughed up this gangster or that gangster. He was tough, but whatever he did was within the law.

He wasn't a social worker. In his search he'd angered some in the community who felt the answer to the gangs was to provide a positive and forgiving environment where these little dirt bags could flourish. Gang community workers started to compare notes about him and began a concerted effort to get him removed from the gang unit.

Finally, Fat Louie assigned him to an organized crime task force that worked out of the U.S. attorney's office in San Francisco. Far from the community outreach programs in Santa Rosa. Still, Tom continued his search to no avail. After all those years, he learned two things from rumors and hearsay. First, it was a gang member fleeing the shooting that caused the death of his son. And secondly, that gang member may have been working for or connected to the Nuestra Familia, which was why no one wanted to talk. So Tom continued to search.

And he still felt like the walking dead.

Chapter **16**

Daniel "DJ" Juarez settled into the visitor's booth and grinned through the glass at his wife. Maria guardedly returned his smile. DJ heard other voices echoing across Pelican Bay's visitor's center as he picked up the phone receiver, gesturing to his wife to do the same.

"*¿Qué pasa?*" he asked, looking deep into her eyes. Maria's brown eyes always gave him a hint as to what was going on inside. Over the years they often communicated without words in this place, the less said between them the better for everyone concerned. Unseen ears might be listening. He assumed someone always recorded their conversations.

Maria brought the receiver to her ear, glancing around to see who might be within earshot. DJ watched closely. Her eyes and body language told him she brought bad news.

"Mikio came by to pay his respects."

Anger put an edge to his voice. "Mikio? Maria, he's no good. Why'd you talk to him?"

"I know. I know. But I had no choice. He sent a message for you." She leaned closer as if that would make their conversation more private. "You need to hear this."

DJ glanced beyond Maria at a guard sitting across the room. He thought back on an earlier visit when he'd told Maria how Mikio betrayed everyone by walking away from the gang.

He seethed inside as his mind replayed what else he'd shared with her. This…*traitor*…this filth called Mikio had been in the gang for many, many years. He'd learned the secrets that high-ranking leaders wanted buried, and he knew where the skeletons lay hidden—literally. This knowledge gave Mikio leverage and power. It kept him alive for two years as the leadership overlooked Mikio's treason to protect their own hides.

Mikio dumped more fuel on this fire. He let it be known that if they killed him, all this information would find its way to Five-O. As long as Mikio breathed, those dark secrets stayed hidden. Some leaders hoped Mikio lived forever.

DJ leaned forward. "Be careful." He pointed to his ear and then to the walls. Maria understood.

"Your grandson got a message from here," she whispered. "Some *heavy work*—involving Mikio. He failed to complete this task, called in *sick* and left the job undone."

Maria anxiously studied his face, trying to read what was going on inside his head. He put on a poker face, a look even his wife could not interpret.

Maria leaned forward and began to unbutton her blouse.

DJ watched her fingers release one button after another. He ran a tongue over his lips as he smiled. Maria's face seemed ashen, her fingers shaking. Slowly, she peeled opened her blouse. Across her chest she had written the words in erasable ink: *Ghost ordered both hits—Paco and Mikio.* She quickly erased the letters with the palm of her hand.

DJ squelched a scream, choking on his words. "I'll kill him."

Maria lurched backward as DJ unleashed his fury. She quickly recovered, trying to button her blouse. She watched in fear as he beat on the wall.

The guard across the room charged in their direction. As the guard neared, DJ glanced from one to the other—Maria still fumbling with her buttons, the guard staring at both of them with a puzzled look.

"Keep it down," the guard finally said. He turned to Maria. "And keep your clothes on while you're in here."

Maria lowered her eyes. The guard stalked away.

DJ waited until the guard returned to his seat. "Tell Mikio we didn't order the job on him, or the other thing." DJ mouthed Paco's name.

Maria nodded. She whispered into the receiver, "One more thing. Mikio said he knows many secrets. Call this off or your secrets will see the light of day."

DJ glared back. It took a moment for DJ to regain control. He eased back in his chair. He studied the look of fear in Maria's eyes. Good. Let her be afraid. She knows I can reach beyond these walls.

He leaned forward and whispered, "Here's what I want you to do."

At one point, her eyes widened. DJ spoke in their own private code, giving her a message of death. And it would hurt the ones she loved. He leaned back and looked at his wife's face. "Have I made it perfectly clear?"

"Yeah, I understand." Her face paled and tears glistened in her eyes. "Must it be this way?"

"There is no other way, Maria. You have to do this." DJ felt a glow of satisfaction as he watched her cry, knowing she would obey no matter who the target was. It had nothing to do with love and everything to do with fear.

Chapter 17

Santa Rosa

Diane Phillips loved the law in its unadulterated form. Sometimes the law stumbled and fell just like people. When the law failed, injustice prevailed: Criminal predators were allowed to roam free to hunt their prey; innocent citizens became victims. The law itself did not fail without a push from others: a judge, an attorney, or a cop, each twisting the law to apply it to their own prejudices and goals.

After ten years slugging it out in the courtrooms, Diane still trusted the precepts of the law in all its imperfections. It became her guiding compass through a maze of horrendous injustices. She still clung to a belief that justice prevailed, a belief that weathered many violent hurricanes in her career.

The Sonoma County District Attorney's Office was her church, where she practiced her legal beliefs. Diane joined the DA's office fresh out of law school. Over the years, she'd survived prejudices and old-boy networks trying to enslave her to their biases. She survived, even thrived, slaving her way through misdemeanor filings, domestic violence purgatory, and three years with the sexual assault prosecution unit. It had taken ten arduous years to attain her goal, chief of the Vertical Gang Prosecution team, an assignment she could get her teeth into. And once Diane dived into a case, she always went the distance, never letting up.

At age thirty-five, Diane still had one goal as a prosecutor. She relished putting bad guys in jail. Everything else in her life took a backseat.

A copy of every gang investigation in Sonoma County wound up on her desk.

One of these reports—Enrique "Rascal" Martinez's shooting—caught her attention. Rascal had been in her sights for several years. She cut and pasted intelligence reports and crime reports that identified him as a player among the gangs, someone to watch as he rose through the ranks. It was not surprising a rival gang had put him in their crosshairs.

However, Rascal's shooting troubled her. Pieces did not fit.

She scoured the CalGang intelligence reports in case she missed an entry from one of the other agencies, looking for a connection, a reason for the hit on Rascal, but everything she read failed to make sense. If a rival gang shot Rascal, gang intelligence should have picked that up on the radar. They should be bragging about the shooting. The gang world, however, remained uncharacteristically silent.

Officers knocked on all the doors around where Rascal was gunned down. No one recalled hearing any threats or gang epitaphs, either before or after the shooting. Gang officers regularly scrutinized all fresh graffiti where gang members liked to advertise their exploits. Zilch.

Street snitches—usually eager to please their law-enforcement handlers—came up empty no matter how hard officers squeezed. And not one single retaliation. The streets remained as peaceful as a lull in the conflict between the Israelis and Palestinians. At any second, she expected a war to break out, but it seemed an uneasy truce settled over the city. Maybe the gangs didn't know who ordered the hit on Rascal. Everyone in the gang world watched and waited.

Another puzzling question troubled Diane. The killing of Javier "Paco" Valdez. After all, a well-respected gang leader, supposedly carrying the NF blessing to operate in the North Bay, was tied up and executed. She waited for violence to erupt over that murder. It seemed inevitable.

Again, only silence.

The report on Paco's murder hadn't reached her desk, although she wasn't surprised. The primary gang detective working an open homicide case with VCI routinely hoarded all of these reports and supplements until completing the investigation. If the case was significant enough, investigators from the DA's office and a prosecutor might team up with the primary investigating agency in a joint effort. This would generally kick in if the investigating agency invoked the protocol set up by all the law-enforcement agencies in the county.

In this case, the protocol had not been used. The Santa Rosa Police Department shouldered the investigative load alone. She heard a rumor that VCI virtually shelved the case pending further information from the city's gang unit. If that was the case, it might be weeks before Diane saw any information on the murder. There would be nothing until the investigator chose to seek an arrest warrant, search warrants, or other legal matters in which her office needed to be involved.

Diane was too impatient to wait that long.

She dialed the SRPD's gang office. An administrative assistant with a British accent came on the line. "Detective Kagan is assigned to this case. He's out of town on business. Can I take a message?"

"Switch me to his voice mail. He does check his messages, doesn't he?" Diane heard a click and the sound of Kagan's recorded voice came over the line. His voice evoked memories from past investigations. She'd worked several gang-related robbery cases with him years ago. He was a good investigator—and ruggedly handsome.

The case with Kagan that came to mind had nothing to do with robberies or gangs. While she was serving her time in the domestic-violence unit, she sat next to Tom in an interview with a victim. The frightened woman carried the black-and-blue marks of abuse—swollen eye, discolored face, fractured jaw.

A spousal punching bag.

Diane watched with fascination as Tom slowly gained the woman's trust. He possessed an uncanny way of making a personal connection with those he interviewed. At least victims. The woman shyly glanced at Tom from time to time like a frightened child seeking comfort and recognition as a human being.

Diane sat mesmerized as Tom coaxed this woman out of her world of distrust and suspicion. And then she willingly offered him brief snapshots of her hell that had been stubbornly withheld from others. It was as if the cop and victim spoke their own language of grief.

She heard the phone line click to allow messages to be recorded. "Tom, this is Diane Phillips at the DA's office. Can you give me an update on the Paco killing when you have a chance? Thanks."

Diane returned her attention to an avalanche of reports threatening the order of her desk. She found it hard to release the memory of Tom from her mind. He was one of the few cops she could count on as a friend. She had heard the rumor mill that he might be facing some problems with upper management at SRPD. Tom was never one to duck a fight, but he had a thing or two to learn about compromise. She should check in on him to see how he was doing. Maybe her lawyerly skills of negotiation might make his life easier. If Tom would only accept help. She laughed. That would be the day Tom gave up riding horses. Well, she could try anyway. What were friends for?

Chapter 18

Maria Juarez could not make her hands stop shaking. Her husband ordered her to make contact with Mikio upon her return to Sonoma County. DJ did not care what she thought about this order. He expected it to be carried out. She was tired and exhausted and wanted to go home to hide. She was not ready to face another one of her husband's former soldiers.

Mikio particularly frightened her. She had never known a NF leader brave enough to walk away from the gang. Mikio was family through her daughter's marriage, but he seemed like a stranger.

In spite of her fears, Maria learned to be an obedient wife, even when it put her life at risk. As the spouse of one of the most powerful gang leaders in California, Maria shuddered at the consequences if she failed to obey. In DJ's eyes, she was as expendable as a roll of toilet paper.

She had reached Mikio on his cell phone when she entered the city limits of Santa Rosa. He agreed to meet in a public place. She sought a place that might provide a lot of witnesses to minimize the risk—a shopping mall, for instance—but he insisted on picking the place.

At first, she thought Mikio might be joking when he suggested where to meet. It was only ten minutes away. She parked her car and strolled toward her destination. As she glanced around, Maria smiled at the irony.

Santa Rosa Police Department. Mikio wanted to meet on the front steps of police headquarters.

Surveillance cameras, perched around the building, scanned the walkways with hungry eyes. No need to worry about drive-by shooters threatening their conversation. And if any gang members had the guts to walk up to them with a gun, cameras and nearby police officers ought to discourage any would-be assassins.

Even Mikio might have his own weapon tucked away someplace close where he could get to it fast. This place would protect her against harm. *Maybe.*

Maria heard a sound behind her, shoes scrapping on the sidewalk. She wheeled around to see Mikio looming over her. He materialized out of nowhere. She blushed as he stared down at her with dark, searching eyes. He had not grown soft since his freedom from prison two years ago, still retaining his dark, chiseled features. He still looked like a disciplined NF soldier. She wondered if other women caught his eye.

Mikio turned his attention to the street. He seemed to study everything, scrutinizing every passerby. His body relaxed as his gaze returned to her. She blushed again as he slowly eyed her from head to foot.

"How was the trip?" He raised his eyes slowly.

"Long and hot." She glanced away, uncomfortable. "DJ insisted we talk—immediately."

Maria paused, waiting for Mikio to respond. Searching his dark eyes, Maria looked to see if there was even a hint of interest in what she had to say. His expression read like a blank piece of paper, not a flicker of interest. This from a man whose life hung in precarious balance. She shuddered at his self-control.

Two police officers strolled past on their way toward the station. The older officer glanced at Mikio. A look of recognition appeared in the cop's eyes. The two officers disappeared into the police station without looking back.

"DJ wants you to know that the Family didn't order the hit on you or Paco." She waited for her words to sink in. Mikio did not respond. "He ordered an investigation."

He shrugged. "Big deal! I told you Ghost ordered the hit. Saw filters with his name on them. He works for DJ. He ordered both hits. You saying DJ wants me to believe Ghost tried to take out two NF members on his own initiative? Without DJ's green light?"

Maria stared into his eyes and saw a flash of anger. Fear stabbed her heart. His look of hate shook her to the core.

"I'm telling you, DJ had nothing to do with this. And why would Ghost want both of you killed? Why would he do something this crazy without DJ's approval? It has to be someone else."

Mikio grabbed her shoulders. He looked deep into her eyes. "Maria. It was Ghost."

"How can you be so certain?"

Dropping his hands, Mikio stepped back. He glanced away, watching a mother pushing a baby stroller toward them. One of the stroller's wheels squeaked as it turned. He waited until the woman, her sleeping baby, and the irritating stroller paraded out of earshot. His face was taut as he turned and stared at her. "I know the reason. That is all I can tell you. We both knew one of his secrets."

She persisted. "But why would he risk killing both of you? He had to know it would get back to DJ."

Mikio looked away before speaking. "Ghost knew it was only a matter of time before his secret leaked out. He must have felt it was worth the risk. And that he could cover himself before anybody put it together."

"But why did he wait until now to kill the two of you?"

"I was an easy mark. He did not have to prove I had it coming. But Paco…that was another matter. As far as Ghost was concerned, his hands were tied while Paco was at Pelican Bay. If something happened to me, Ghost knew word would get back to my man Paco. And Paco had juice. No one would make a move on him without clearing it with high command. Once Paco hit the street, he was away from the power base. Using his position, Ghost ordered one of his street soldiers to kill Paco."

"How is Ghost going to make sure the hit on Paco isn't traced back to him?"

"Kill the ones who killed Paco. He already made a move on Rascal the other night. Unfortunately for Ghost—Rascal survived."

Mikio glanced around to see who might be in earshot, then returned his attention to Maria. His eyes narrowed. "If DJ wants to prove he had nothing to do with this, have him order someone to move on Ghost. Take him out. If Ghost remains breathing, I'll assume DJ is behind this."

Mikio abruptly turned and walked away.

Maria shuddered in spite of the warmth of a September sun raining down on her. This had taken a turn for the worst.

Her mind raced. She felt jerked between DJ and Mikio as a messenger of death. She knew DJ wanted to prove his innocence to Mikio. Her thoughts leaped forward to the sobering conclusion.

She must pass on Mikio's ultimatum. Kill Ghost. These men would force her to be an accomplice to first-degree murder for the first time. As Maria walked toward her car, her hands once again began to shake. Anger and fear.

Ghost would die. And she would be responsible. A chill swept over her as she opened her car door.

Another trip to the Bay.

Chapter **19**

Community Hospital, Santa Rosa

Enrique Martinez was *legally* high, thanks to his doctor. But the price of this euphoria was paid in full by waves of pain and discomfort wracking his body. Eighteen-year-old Rascal was a connoisseur of illegal drugs — sniffing glue, head-blowing street weed, fast meth, slow-you-down H, and ice. He had tried it all. And now he was trying the legal stuff.

He might even enjoy this high if it weren't for five gunshot wounds, a torn-up abdomen, shattered wrist, and paralysis from his waist down to his toes. Every time he tried to get comfortable, pain shot through the drug-induced haze and killed whatever good feeling the drugs sent his way.

He tried to figure how he landed in this hospital bed. He'd sensed his world might come unglued ever since he got the filter from Ghost to kill Paco. The moment he read it, fear climbed up his spine.

No one could expect to waste an older gangster like Paco and walk away without all hell breaking loose. On the other hand, Rascal knew he would be a dead man if he refused.

I guess I'm a dead man either way!

Bitterness had begun eating away at him even before he pulled the trigger. His own homies left him out in the cold. Ever since he landed in this hospital bed, not one visitor made his way to see him. *I am all alone.* He looked at his lifeless legs. How would he stay alive? *I can't even get out of this bed without help.*

He tensed as two men entered his hospital room. They had police written all over them. Rascal warily eyed them as they approached. He recognized one of them.

"Mr. Martinez, my name is Tom Kagan, detective with the gang unit. You were kind of out of it the last time we met. I'm the one who left a business card. And this is my partner, Detective Stevenson."

Rascal rolled his eyes. "I've met Stevenson. He arrested me at least twice!"

"Only doing my job."

"Yeah," Rascal said, his face tightening, "and I can't blame you for this." He rubbed his legs for the millionth time, his fingers feeling his lifeless limbs. He could never get used to the absence of feeling down there.

"I'm sorry this happened to you," Stevenson said. "That's what we're here to talk about. We want to catch the ones who did this."

"And then what?" Bitterness wrapped itself around Rascal's words. "You can't make this go away so I can walk again." He gestured at his legs. "You know I'm unfinished business. They'll keep coming at me until I'm in the ground."

Kagan eased himself into a chair next to the bed, then turned to face Rascal. Stevenson leaned against the wall next to him. "That's why we're here, Mr. Martinez."

"Call me Rascal. Calling me Mr. Martinez...that's just weird."

"Okay, Rascal. No one is bragging about this shooting, no tagging from the other side. Nothing but silence. This tells me someone inside Nuestra Familia ordered the hit. Why'd the NF want you dead?"

Rascal shrugged. "Who knows why? Someday, some way, a brother's gonna come alongside with a gat or a knife and do me in. I mean, how hard could it be to do a gimp like me? Piece of cake. Right? So what's it to you?" Rascal glared back.

Kagan ignored Rascal's last question. "I bet your shooting has something to do with the killing of Paco. Am I right?"

Rascal flinched, then swore silently to himself. He knew the detective saw the flicker. Rascal had played enough poker to know the tell signs of other players. Kagan wasn't a chump.

"Before you say anything, let me read you your rights." The cop read off Rascal's rights off some card. "You understand those rights?"

Rascal nodded.

"You have nothing to lose. If you work with us, your future might look a little brighter."

Rascal shrugged, staring back.

Kagan leaned forward. "Remember, you called us. You have had plenty of time to think this through. Did you have anything to do with Paco's death?"

Rascal's eyes widened. He tried to sit up, but the pain made him wince. "Yo, *Holmes*, you don't waste no time. Just jump right on in."

The detective closed in, his gaze drilling inside Rascal as if reading his mind. "I don't think we have time to dance. Normally, I'd stretch this out, yada yada yada about the family, the dog, the girlfriend. Maybe we'd chat about the weather, the Giants, and the man on the moon. And when we got all nice like and wasted a lot of valuable time, I'd finally pop the question." Kagan paused for a moment.

Rascal waited.

"But you're smarter than that. We don't have any time to waste on small talk. Frankly, I don't know when they'll try again—but you and I know they *will* try again. We're both running out of time."

Rascal closed his eyes and leaned back on the pillow. "Okay. Just suppose I did have something to do with Paco. And I am not saying I did. What's in it for me?"

"To put it bluntly." Tom glanced over at Stevenson. "If you killed Paco, we're going to prove it one way or the other." Tom returned Rascal's stare. "If we prove it without your help, you're facing a possible death penalty. Or life without at the very least. You killed a high-ranking Nuestra Familia gang member in good standing. Prison will be a death sentence."

Again, the detective waited for Rascal to respond.

Nothing.

"The only way you'll survive this is to *PC* up. We can get you protective custody while inside. Maybe we can work it out so you see some daylight on the other end of your sentence."

Rascal looked at the detective as he pictured himself in prison. He'd worked hard to keep that fear at a distance. Now, he must face it. Deal with it. No legs, no way to run—easy prey for the vultures.

Relentlessly, Kagan pressed on without giving Rascal any time to think. "We know someone ordered you to kill Paco. If you work with us, then you have something to trade. I can only assume that whoever ordered you to kill Paco has a little more juice than you. Otherwise, Paco would still be breathing."

Rascal looked at his lifeless legs, his mind traveling a million miles an hour. He continued to listen in silence.

"Now—and this is the tricky part—if the NF did not want Paco dead, they'll be coming after you and the person who ordered you to kill Paco. The question in my mind: Did the NF want him dead? And if not, why did someone higher than you have him bumped off?"

"What do you want from me? What if I can't give you the answers you're looking for? You all going to let me do time alone? No protection? No one watching my back?" Rascal knew a look of fear must be on his face. He heard it in his voice. He was scared to death. As weak as a girl. He hated what he had become—useless.

Kagan spoke softly. "What's your answer?"

Rascal struggled with his options. To live, he must travel across that shaky bridge called *cooperation*, a bridge held together by the strings of promises cops offered snitches. For him, there were no options. Only one choice. It was a matter of survival.

Rascal finally broke down and began talking.

Chapter 20

They must not lose momentum. It took Tom and Stevenson an hour to get the video equipment they needed to capture Rascal on tape. Once recorded, the gangster would have a hard time denying his confession. And this testimony played well to a jury once they finally made it into court.

A lot could happen between now and then.

Stevenson helped him set it up. In a few minutes, they had the video ready to run. Tom closed the hospital door after telling the attending nurse they did not want to be disturbed "unless Rascal takes a turn for the worse." The nurse seemed willing to let them do what they had to do.

As Tom reentered the room, he shot a glance at Rascal. "Okay, ready to rock and roll?"

The gangster nodded.

Stevenson, standing behind the camera and peering through the lens, gave Tom a thumbs-up.

Pulling out a notebook, Tom sat next to Rascal so the camera angled over his left shoulder. Glancing back at the camera, he saw a red light blink as Stevenson activated the recording.

"Okay. Let's get started." Tom gave the date, time, and location of the interview for the record. After identifying those in the room, Tom turned to

Rascal. "Before we start this interview, I just want you to verify that I have given you a Miranda warning and that you have agreed to waive counsel and give a statement. Is that correct?"

"Yeah."

Tom asked Rascal to confirm that he was lucid and of a sound mind and capable of giving a complete and truthful account leading up to his shooting. This brought a grin from Rascal.

"You mean beside the morphine?"

"Are these drugs prohibiting you from giving a true and coherent statement?"

The smiled disappeared from Rascal's face. "Nah, I know what you're asking. I'll give you a straight up answer. Okay?"

With that out of the way, let's start with a few background questions. For the record, are you a member of a criminal street gang?"

"A criminal street what?" Rascal looked perplexed. "Oh, you mean, huh, yeah."

Tom shifted in his chair. He needed this guy to give a statement that a jury could relate to in their *straight* world. Something that would turn a lightbulb on inside their brain.

"What gang do you belong to?"

"VSRN."

"Varrio Santa Rosa Norteños. I saw that tattooed on your right forearm. Why did you do that?"

Rascal rubbed where the VSRN tattoo had been peppered into his skin with black ink. "To show I'm down for them. That I belong to the gang. To let *scraps* know they can't mess with me."

"And who are scraps?"

"The enemy, southerners, those claiming blue."

"And what does VSRN claim?"

"We claim red; we're down for the north."

"What does that mean?"

"That means that we protect each other from the scraps, the Sureños trying to take over our territory."

"What do you mean by *your territory*? Santa Rosa?"

Rascal gave Tom a look of exasperation. "Yeah. Santa Rosa and the rest of Northern California."

Tom leaned forward in his chair. "Now, what are you protecting your territory from? What might the Sureños want to take over?"

"They want to take over our drug trade, our protection of drug dealers, our money from whores—all the action we make money on."

"And what do you do with this money?"

Rascal's eyes lit up. "Party, man. Party big time."

Tom smiled. "Besides party, what do you do with the money? Do you invest it?"

"Oh, you mean what business do we put the money back into? Well, we buy more drugs and weapons to protect ourselves from the scraps. We set up safe houses, places to store our weapons, and we pay taxes."

Tom's eyebrows shot up. "Taxes? You mean like the IRS?"

"Sort of. We gotta pay taxes to the NF, man. If we don't contribute to the bank, they'll come down on us."

Tom wrote a note on his pad. "What is the Nuestra Familia, and why do you pay taxes to this organization?"

Rascal sat up and gave him an incredulous look. "You gotta be kidding."

Tom shook his head. "Remember, others will be listening to this conversation and trying to understand your world. We have to make it clear for them. School them down. Understand?"

"Oh. Okay." Rascal leaned back, then recoiled in pain. That movement must have triggered his wounds. It took a few moments before he could answer. "The Nuestra Familia is a gang every Norteño wants to hook up with someday. The NF are the shot callers for all us Norteños on the street. They give us protection if we wind up in the joint, and they hold the power on the street."

"And what happens if you don't pay taxes or you don't follow their orders?"

Rascal looked down at his hands. "Then they'll take your wind."

"Kill you?"

"Yeah."

"Tell me about the note you got from prison. What do you call it?"

"A filter. A willa."

"How did you get this filter?"

"From a guy just released from Pelican Bay."

"He hand-carried it to you?"

Rascal smiled. "Sort of. He carried the filter out of prison stashed up his butt. But yeah, he handed it to me when he got to Santa Rosa."

"Do you know who he was?"

"No. He was on his way down to Salinas, just passing through. He didn't want me to know who he was."

"Did he tell you who the message was from?"

"Yeah. Ghost."

"And who is Ghost?"

"Ghost is an NF captain in charge of the regiment for this area."

"Was there another reason you knew the filter was from Ghost?"

"Yeah. He signed it."

"What did Ghost order you to do?"

"To kill Paco."

"That's what the note said...*exactly*?"

"No. It said *Take Paco's wind.*"

"Meaning?"

"To kill Paco. To make sure he doesn't breathe anymore."

"Why would you consider obeying this message, this filter?"

Rascal looked at him with sullen eyes. "I already told you. If I don't obey their orders, they'd kill me. Simple."

"Who would they send to kill you if you disobeyed?"

"Probably one of my friends. Someone I trusted."

"Did Ghost pick you to kill Paco because you're his friend?"

Rascal nodded, a look of shame in his eyes.

"Please speak up for the camera."

"Yeah, because I was Paco's friend." His voice seemed hoarse, his words broken up, forced. Rascal looked at Tom and Stevenson with pleading eyes. Like he was begging them to understand. "They knew I was tight with Paco. I looked up to him, respected him. They knew I could get close and take care of business because we...were close."

"How did you set it up?"

The gangster's voice quivered slightly as he continued. "I knew Paco played basketball with some of the boys. They always got a game together in South Park. Same place every Friday."

He coughed. Tom reached over and handed him a glass of water. Rascal took two sips and handed it back. "I took two guys from my gang to back me up. I told them what's up. They knew the message came from the NF. They weren't excited about hitting Paco, but they'd been tapped. They had to obey. Like me—no choice. One of the guys I pulled for the job goes by Tweaker."

Rascal coughed again, trying to clear his throat. Tom started to reach for the glass of water, but the gangster waved him off.

"What was the other guy's name?"

The gangster seemed to waver for a moment before coming up with the other suspect's name.

"How did this go down, Rascal?"

"It was late. We parked on Hendley Street, near the fairgrounds, where trees blocked the streetlights. We walked into South Park from there and made our way over to the basketball courts. Paco spotted me and came over to chat. I told him we had some weight in the car and needed to get rid of it quick."

"What do you mean by *weight*?"

"Drugs. I made it sound like we had a lot. Enough weight to be profitable all the way around. I told Paco I'd give him a percentage if he'd give us an intro to one of the bigger buyers. I knew he'd jump at the chance to make a little green. He's greedy like the rest of us."

"And what happened next?"

"Paco told the other guys on the court he'd be back in a while. We started walking toward my car. Just as we left the park, Tweaker thumped Paco on the back of the head with a tire iron. Not hard enough to kill, just hard enough to knock him out. We threw him in the trunk and taped him up."

"Then what happened?" Tom felt he needed to pry out every detail. Rascal made him work.

"Then I stepped on the gas and got the hell out of there. We circled around the fairgrounds and took the on-ramp to the freeway."

"Who drove?"

"Me." Rascal paused for a moment. "We drove north and pulled off the freeway and drove up to Bicentennial, up where the rich folk live. I know a little vineyard where we could take care of business. I wanted to make it quick and get out before anyone came looking for us."

"So you took Bicentennial to Fountain Grove and—"

"You know," Rascal blurted out. "Past the Round Barn where you found the body."

Tom just nodded, letting the gangster tell the story.

"We pulled Paco out and used more duct tape to tie his hands and feet together so he couldn't move. He was starting to wake up but still out of it. Tweaker must have clocked him harder than I thought. We put tape across his mouth so Paco couldn't yell for help."

Rascal motioned to Tom for another drink of water. After sipping, he clutched the glass. "We dragged him into the vineyard."

Tom leaned over in his chair, looking intently at the gangster. "Was he awake when you opened the trunk?"

"Yeah." Rascal squinted in pain. Tom could not be sure whether it was from Rascal's injuries or from the memory of killing his friend. For the first time it looked like Rascal might cry. "He was awake. When we got him out in the field, I yanked the tape from his mouth. He called me every name in the book, saying I was a dead man and there was no place on this earth I could hide where they wouldn't find me. He knew what was coming."

The glass shook in the gangster's hand as he tried to pull himself together. "I told him I had no choice. That Ghost ordered me to kill him. I was just obeying orders. That just set him off more. He screamed that Ghost would be dealt with for giving out this order. That Paco was all good. That he had the respect of the Family."

"Rascal, did Paco mention who might take revenge on Ghost? Or why Ghost might have ordered him killed?"

"No, he gave no reasons or names. He just looked at all three of us and said we were dead men walking. After that, he seemed to run out of steam."

"And then what happened?"

Silence hung in the air as heavy as the guilt in the gangster's eyes. Tom held his breath and waited for the story to unfold. He wanted it in Rascal's own words.

Hoarsely, Rascal continued. "We forced him onto his knees. I asked him if he had any last words." He peered at Tom with a look of anguish, remorse.

Tom looked back with as much sympathy as he could muster.

Rascal glanced down at the bed. "He just looked at me and laughed. It was like he was mocking me. He talked about dying with honor. Like a true man, a true soldier. Not like us—*cowards*. Then he spit at me."

Rascal's voice broke. "He looked at me like I was garbage. That ticked me off."

Tom shifted in his seat and glanced back to make sure the tape was still running. He returned his attention to Rascal. "And then?"

"Then I shot him. I walked behind him, took out my gun, and pointed it at the back of his head. I pulled the trigger—twice."

"Did you hit him both times?"

Rascal scowled at Tom. "How could I miss? You're damn right I shot him. Two quick shots, one right after the other. His head kind of lurched forward and the second shot caught him just before he fell. Landed with his face buried in the dirt."

"And then what happened?"

"What do you mean what happened? Then we left." Anger flashed across Rascal's face.

"I mean, did anyone do anything to him before you walked away?"

It was a second before it registered. A look of shame returned to the gangster's face. "Oh, yeah. I spit on him. He made me mad. I guess I just lost it for a second."

Tom closed his notebook and placed it in his pocket. "The time is 0200 hours. We're going to take a break." He heard the camera turn off behind him and Stevenson moving around the room.

The gangster handed the glass back and clutched his hands together. His eyes—bloodshot and brooding—carried the look of a man without hope.

Tom stood. "I'll need to go over the details once again. More about the other guys who helped you, where the weapon was stashed. All that stuff. But let's just relax for a while. Can I get you anything?"

Rascal shook his head, his facial muscles working overtime. He was clenching and unclenching his jaw apparently in time to whatever was rolling around in his mind. Rascal looked at Tom with eyes filled with pain. "Find out why I had to kill my brother...my friend. I gotta know why before I die."

Tom nodded. "I'll do my best."

Chapter 21

After leaving Rascal's hospital room at eight o'clock in the morning, Tom headed to his friend's office, ADA Diane Phillips. He wanted a face-to-face briefing with her since he learned she might be prosecuting the case. She called a few weeks ago for information on Paco's killing and later Rascal's shooting. She seemed to be on top of this case and he welcomed her involvement.

While Stevenson drove the unmarked, Tom used his cell phone to connect with Garcia from SSU. The agent agreed to meet them at the district attorney's office within the hour.

Immediately after the interview, Tom called Dispatch and had them send a patrol unit to provide guard duty until further details could be worked out with the watch commander. Next, he met with a harried hospital administrator to make sure Rascal would be listed under an assumed name. There would be an officer on guard around the clock until they could move the injured gangster somewhere else for Rascal's protection.

Security would cost the city a bundle.

Tom glanced at the message screen on his cell and saw someone called and left a message. He activated voice mail and heard Hector Garcia's booming voice. The SSU supervisor sounded jazzed. As he listened to Garcia's message, Tom whistled under his breath and pounded his fist on the dashboard.

"I just love it when things come together. Garcia says a guard at the Bay was listening to a monitored conversation in the visitor's center between an NF general and his old lady. Goes by *DJ*. The gal's name is Maria."

Tom paused as Stevenson continued to weave his way around several cars during rush hour.

"And…?" Stevenson raised his eyebrows. "You want me to guess?"

"Anyway, their conversation was about a gangster named Mikio here in Santa Rosa. Maria told DJ that Mikio's nephew, a youngster known as Gato, got a message from the Bay for some *heavy work*. Garcia thinks that's a euphemism for a hit. That Gato called in sick and left the job undone. Garcia can't figure out whether this meant a planned hit on Mikio's life or Paco's murder. Later in the conversation, Garcia thinks DJ said the NF didn't order a hit on Mikio or Paco."

Stevenson scratched his head. "That was what Paco was trying to tell Rascal. That he was all good with the NF." Stevenson stared out the window. "You know, Tom, I'd forgotten about Mikio. He's an OG—an old gangster. Been out of the picture for a few years. And I remember a gangster with the handle of Gato. If they're related, I think we got something."

"You think?" Tom looked at his friend, placing a hand on his shoulder. "My man, all the pieces might be falling into place. DJ is an NF general. One of his subordinates, Ghost, gives out an order to kill Paco and probably Mikio without telling his boss. So, if DJ didn't authorize the hit, we got Ghost by the short hairs. DJ's not going to take kindly to someone killing one of his subordinates, at least not without permission. Ghost is in the toilet, my man."

Tom peered ahead, seeing the distant outline of the Hall of Justice. "I wonder why Ghost wanted these two guys killed. He's risking everything. Maybe it's some kind of power play. If we give him a glimpse as to what we have on him, maybe he'll be inclined to talk."

Snarled traffic made a ten-minute drive a half-hour marathon. Tom sat impatiently as Stevenson tried to weave a path off Mendocino Avenue and onto Administrative Drive. Finally reaching the courthouse—a complex

shared by the county sheriff's office, the district attorney, among others—
Stevenson wedged the police car into the last parking space assigned to law
enforcement. He placed the police placard on the windshield and tossed
the red emergency light onto the dash for good measure.

The two detectives made their way into the Hall of Justice through an
unmarked door leading through the sheriff's office. They waved at a friend
but did not stay to chat. They left the sheriff's office and walked down a
public hallway where they caught the stairs to the second floor.

Tom led Stevenson into a hallway that ran the full length of the building, a wall of glass to the left, showing an inner courtyard. On the opposite
wall, he saw the gilded words *Sonoma County District Attorney's Office.*
They opened a pair of glass doors and made their way into a no-nonsense
anteroom closed off by a second set of doors. The receptionist recognized
Tom and gave him a wave and a smile as she buzzed them in.

After passing the secured doorway, they turned right and walked
down a long corridor. The hallway was awash with fluorescent light. Small
cocoon-like offices with worker-bee attorneys branched off the hallway
to their left and right. Garcia leaned against the wall outside one of these
offices.

As Tom and Stevenson approached, Garcia pointed toward the office
next to him, shaking his head. "I was waiting in her office. I got claustrophobic in there. She's got nothing but books and files. It's a mess."

"I heard that." Phillips popped her head through the doorway. "I'll
give you a break. Follow me to the boss's office since he's out of town. You'll
be more comfortable."

Tom turned to the SSU agent. "You're calling her office a mess? When's
the last time you took a look at your own?"

Garcia chuckled. "Hey, at least I got some art on the wall."

"A poster of Dirty Harry pulling out a gun? You call that artwork?"

Garcia watched Phillips walking away and then glanced back at the
two detectives, eyebrows dancing like Groucho Marx. "No, I call *that* art."
He turned back to face Phillips scowling at him.

Tom shook his head. "How do you manage to step in it all the time,
Hector?"

Phillips turned and led the group a few doors down the hallway and into a small reception area. An administrative assistant sat behind an expansive L-shaped desk guarding the doorway into the inner sanctum.

Phillips waved to the woman as she entered the unoccupied office. "Would you feel more comfortable here, Hector?"

The agent looked around the office in appreciation. "Man, if I had digs like this, I might even stay in the office more. Suits me just fine."

Phillips sank into the chair behind a beautiful mahogany desk. The men made themselves comfortable in thickly upholstered captain's chairs positioned in a semicircle around the desk. Phillips pulled out a pad of paper and a pencil. "Okay, gentlemen. Where do we begin?"

Everyone turned toward Tom.

"Well, let's start with Paco—the Javier Valdez killing," he pulled out a notepad, "and what we know so far." Tom laid out Paco's relationship and position in the NF, details they'd picked up at the crime scene.

Phillips listened intently, occasionally jotting down notes.

Tom continued. "Just before this meeting, Hector got a call from one of his contacts up at the Bay, an IGI officer by the name of Terry Lentz. He got a message from one of the guards regarding a visit between DJ—one of the NF generals—and his wife." Tom quickly recapped the information.

Garcia stood and walked over to a bank of law books, then leaned his back against the bookcase. "I know Mikio. He stepped back from the gang. We thought he'd be killed a long time ago—but nothing happened. It's not like them to let someone like Mikio walk away. Here's the question in my mind, Tom. If DJ didn't authorize the hit on Paco—who did?"

Tom smiled. "I can answer that question for you. Remember that drive-by shooting from the other night? Enrique Martinez, known as Rascal?"

Phillips and Garcia nodded.

"Well, he's seen the light and decided to tell all. He confessed to killing Paco."

Phillips slid forward, arms on the desk, clasping her hands together as if to pray. "Tell me you got it on tape. Tell me you Mirandized him."

Tom and Stevenson looked at each other with blank expressions. Then Tom learned over and whispered to Stevenson, "Did you read him his rights before he spilled his guts?"

"His rights? That's your job, Tom. I stepped out for a minute. You asked all the questions."

Phillips's face contorted. "For the love of..." Then Tom smiled and she threw the pad of paper at him. Tom protected himself as the yellow paper flew by. The other men laughed as Phillips looked from one to the other. Then a smile crept across her face. "Okay, you got me! Payback is a—" She shook her head. "Tell me what you learned."

Tom stood and walked over to the window. "It's all on video but here's a quick summary. Rascal told us the order to kill Paco came from a guy with the moniker of Ghost. We know this to be James Hernandez." He turned toward Phillips. "Ghost is an NF captain under DJ. Ghost runs the regiment in this area."

Garcia glanced at Tom, a puzzled look on his face. "So how'd Ghost think he could get away with Paco's killing? Mikio was already on the hit list since he dropped out of the gang. But Paco? DJ's right-hand man on the street? It doesn't add up."

Tom shrugged. "We know who ordered the murder and who carried it out. Now we need to learn why before a bloodbath breaks out on the street. Before innocent victims get caught in the cross fire."

Stevenson and Garcia left together as Tom jotted down several thoughts in his notebook. Phillips watched him for a moment and then walked around the desk and closed the office door. Tom glanced up when he heard it click shut.

Phillips smiled and moved closer, leaning on the desk next to him.

"You had me going on that Miranda warning. That was kind of cruel."

Tom smiled. "You're right, counselor. Won't happen again."

She reached out and touched his arm. "How are you doing, Tom? It's been a while since we...talked."

He glanced at her hand resting on his arm. "Talk? We talk all the time."

She edged closer. "About…you know, the accident. It has been a long time and I understand the investigators came up empty. I'm sure it must still be hard. I can't image—"

"You're right, Diane. You can't." Tom slipped the notebook in his coat pocket and stood. "I'd better get going."

"Look, all I meant was I wanted you to know that I'm here. As a friend. Anything I can—"

"Thanks, but I got it under control." He turned to leave. "It's not something I talk about."

She pursed her lips, folding her arms across her chest. "Anyway, we're so focused on the case, I thought—I just wanted to let you know I'm here. I'm a good listener if you need one."

"Thanks. And…likewise. Anytime."

Phillips straightened. "See ya later."

"Yeah." As he opened the door, he turned back for a moment. "Everything okay with you?"

She seemed puzzled by the question. "Yeah. Things are just fine. Thanks for asking."

Tom nodded at her one more time. As he walked down the hallway, he tried to figure out what just went on back there. *Women, who can figure out what they're thinking?* As he reached the lobby, he decided to focus on the case. Gangsters were a lot easier to grasp.

Chapter 22

Santa Rosa

Mikio watched the two men approach from across the street. They'd knocked on his apartment door earlier in the day, but he refused to answer. They followed up with a phone call, which he finally answered. He picked this spot because it was neutral ground.

He sprawled on the bench in the shade of a large tree and warily eyed the two cops. The park was full of people enjoying the cool shade of autumn trees. A chalky-faced mime drew children to him like a Pied Piper at the edge of a concrete fountain. Childish screams of excitement and chatter filled the lazy afternoon.

Large fountains and pools graced both sides of Courthouse Square, with Santa Rosa Avenue slicing it in half. Mikio had seen old pictures of this downtown area and knew he was sitting where the old courthouse once stood, before the 1906 earthquake. This city suffered the same damage as San Francisco when the big one hit. Time had a way of tearing down everything, the good and the bad. As far as Mikio was concerned, he just wanted to live a little longer on this green earth. These two cops just might complicate matters.

Mikio chose the east side, sitting under a stand of Redwood trees, with an eye toward the street and all walkways leading through the square. A kid riding a skateboard cut a path between Mikio and the two detectives as they approached. They waited for the skateboarder to move on before coming closer.

Mikio rose to meet them. "Detective Kagan, Detective Stevenson." Mikio motioned to the bench next to him. "Step into my office." He started to sit down but the cops remained standing.

Detective Kagan moved within an arm's length of Mikio. "I'm glad to see you're alive and well."

The detective's closeness made Mikio edgy. In prison, he'd never allow someone this close. It cut his reaction time down to zero and narrowed the chances of surviving an attack. Even if the cops meant him no harm, he deeply resented them moving into his personal space. "I'm doing just fine, Detective. Thanks for your concern." Mikio stared at him, uncertain where the conversation might be headed.

"I won't beat around the bush, Mr. Sanchez," Kagan said. "Mind if I call you Mikio?"

"Not at all...*Tom.*" He smiled when Tom's face tightened.

The detective seemed to force a smile. "We've just learned someone's ordered you killed. Someone from Pelican Bay."

A child's sharp cry made Mikio glance toward where the mime stood entertaining. A parent grasped a child who had almost taken a nosedive into the fountain. The distraction gave him a moment to collect his thoughts. He turned and stared at the detective.

Kagan waited. Getting no response, he continued. "We're obligated to warn you of this threat."

"Yeah, like you guys give a rip. You know this is old news, Tom." Again, the detective's face tightened. *Score one for the team.* "I've been on a hit list since the day I left prison. You're just getting around to telling me two years later?"

"This threat against you is fresh and it was not sanctioned by the NF. It came from within their ranks—but it seems...personal."

The two men glared at each other, any pretense of civility evaporated in the warm afternoon breeze. The sudden backfire of a motorbike made Mikio jump.

Kagan smiled. "Jumpy, are we?"

"Who put the order out?"

"I think you know. Our money's on Ghost."

Mikio glanced to his right to watch a young woman saunter past. She caught him staring and gave him a coy smile. He returned it, buying time to think. These canines already knew about Ghost? What else did they weasel out of their snitches? Had they seen him meeting with DJ's old lady in front of the police department? Kagan's face told him nothing.

They waited for him to say something. Anything. He was in serious trouble if they knew about the message he sent to DJ. And if Ghost got whacked, Mikio might face a solicitation for murder charge. His jaw tightened as he pictured himself back inside prison without protection. "I appreciate the information, Tom, but I don't know what you're talking about." He looked at the two men, forcing a bland expression to dominate his features.

Stevenson spoke for the first time. "There's a question I've been dying...sorry, wrong word. A question I've wanted to ask."

Mikio turned to stare at Stevenson. "What's that?"

"How'd the NF let someone like you walk away? I mean, you knew all their dirty little secrets."

Mikio just stared.

Stevenson pressed on. "All these youngsters coming up through the ranks are watching. How will the gang hold power if they allow you to walk away without consequences?"

Mikio looked away in silence.

"Makes me wonder what you have up your sleeve. For two years, you've kept the powerful NF at bay. How'd you manage that?"

Mikio looked up at the detective with a smirk. "I guess I'm lucky."

Stevenson laughed, and then his face turned serious. "Of course, you heard about Paco? He wasn't so lucky. Someone got to him."

Mikio's smirk vanished.

Tom handed Mikio a business card. "You can reach me here if you change your mind and want to talk. Twenty-four/seven."

Mikio took the card and slipped it in a pocket.

"See you around, Mikio," Tom said. "Stay healthy."

He watched as the detectives walked away, talking to each other just out of earshot. Their warning hit him harder than they realized. Was he reading the situation right? What if Ghost got DJ's approval to do the hit on him? He felt uneasy that he'd not heard back from Maria since their meeting.

He trusted no one. He rehashed his ties to the NF, the work he'd put in over the years. The loyalty he'd given to the Family without question. And what had he got back in return? He spit on the ground. *Honor, trust, and brotherhood. What a joke!*

Tom and Stevenson strolled away without looking back. Tom glanced over at his partner. "Well, the bait's set. Let's reel him in."

"Hey, speaking of reeling it in. I have a friend who has a friend who has a cabin up at Lake Tahoe. Said we could use the place anytime we want. I think we've been working way too hard. How 'bout a couple of days fishing?"

Tom smiled. "I'll have to take a rain check, pal. We're going to be up to our eyeballs in paper and evidence in the next few days."

Stevenson laughed. "You know what they say. All work and no play…"

"What'd you think about Mikio?"

"I think he was surprised we knew about Ghost."

Tom slipped out of his coat and slung it over his shoulder. "Let's give it time, let him mull it over. We'll take another run at him later. Come on, we need to follow up on those warrants."

A half hour later, Tom and Bill walked into the district attorney's office. They scrambled up a flight of stairs and found Garcia waiting inside Phillips's office. He was perched behind her desk, his boots firmly planted on a stack of files.

"Let me guess," Garcia said. "Mikio blew you off?"

"We just planted the seed." Tom unbuttoned his collar. "We'll go back later and see if anything grew."

Tom glanced at the doorway just as Phillips walked in with a stack of papers in her hand. She glared at Garcia, eyeing his boots still parked on top of her desk. "Comfortable?"

Garcia shot out of the chair and wiped off flicks of dirt his boots left behind. "Absolutely, Counselor. Thinking of getting a chair just like yours for my office."

Tom stifled a grin, watching Garcia trying to clean up after himself.

Phillips glowered at the agent before sitting down. Garcia skirted around the desk and joined the detectives facing her.

She shifted her attention to Tom. "How'd it go with Mikio?"

"We think he knows more than he's letting on. Stevenson struck a nerve when he mentioned the murder of Paco. We'll just have to wait and see if anything pans out."

"Okay," Phillips said. "While you guys were out enjoying a walk in the park, I left the arrest and search warrants sitting on a judge's desk. Based upon what Rascal gave us, these warrants should give us the physical evidence we need to support his testimony in court." She gestured toward Tom. "Let's get over there at noon and have the judge sign off on them. Then you guys can get to work."

Tom nodded. "Thanks for pushing this through so fast. We'll put a raid plan together this evening and hit them first thing in the morning." He looked over at Stevenson. "And you wanted to go fishing?"

Stevenson threw his hands up in the air. "Hey. You need to balance things out, pal. I've seen that look on your face before. It means we won't sleep for the next couple of days."

"What'd you mean *we*, my friend? Just let me know when you've put this all together—raid plan, number of bodies needed for the sweep, the whole nine yards. I'll be home getting a little shut-eye."

"Oh no, *Thomas*. We're both going to lose sleep over this."

Chapter 23

"Police. Open up! We have a search warrant!"

Tom pressed his back against the wall to the right of the front door. It was a single-family shack on the edge of the freeway. White noise of pre-dawn traffic hummed in the background as Tom strained to hear anything inside the house.

No lights were on. No one came to the door. Nothing moved.

Tom motioned to the SWAT leader standing behind him. The man glanced at his entry team and gave the signal. The team leaped into action, a symphony of well-orchestrated moves: Point man slamming a metal ram into the front door, causing it to splinter open as another teammate broke the glass of a side window and hurled a flash-bang. An explosion blasted from within the house.

The deafening roar broke the peaceful quiet of a gray dawn, a blinding light flashed inside to disorientate any occupants. The team swept into the house in a choreographed movement that only took a matter of seconds. In a minute, Tom heard the team leader yell, "All Clear." He walked inside to an empty house.

"Looks like your guy flew the coop." One of the helmeted officers slung his assault rifle over a shoulder.

Tom activated the radio mike. "Six-David-Fourteen. Location 1 clear. Status on two and three?" He waited for a reply.

Dispatch did not disappoint. A woman's voice came over the air. "Three-David-Fourteen, Location 2 and 3 are secure. One in custody at 6-David-Sixteen's location. He requests a 10-21."

Tom acknowledged the information and promised he'd give Six-David-Sixteen a call in a few moments. Stevenson probably wanted to brag about their success. Stevenson and Garcia agreed to supervise the other two locations—Rascal's shack and the third suspect's residence. Stevenson had a suspect in custody. Tom and Garcia came up dry.

Where had his bird flown?

He directed the search team as they combed through the residence, painstakingly looking for evidence of Paco's killing.

Rascal snitched! Galen Roman, known as "Tweaker" on the street, angrily listened to his cousin on the telephone. The punk was giving him a play-by-play account of the police trashing Tweaker's house. The cousin was within eyeshot of the front door.

"They're surrounding the place now," his cousin said. "Some loud-mouth canine is yelling something about a search warrant." Tweaker heard an explosion in the background before his cousin continued. "Whoa, dude. They just exploded something inside your house and busted your door wide open. Man, this is just like TV."

Tweaker swore and slammed the phone down, his head pounding from a hangover and the thought of cops going through his place. A naked teenage girl lay next to him, snoring through his telephone conversation. She'd been fun last night after a twelve-pack and a few joints, but this morning she disgusted him.

He threw the bed covers off and instantly regretted it. Biting cold air sent him scrambling for something to wear. As he tried to slip into his trousers, he stubbed his toes on the metal bed frame. Cussing, Tweaker glanced toward the girl as he finished dressing. Her blissful slumber and wet sloppy snores only fueled his anger.

Details filtered through Tweaker's hungover brain. The cops got a search warrant for his house. Rascal in the hospital. *They must know I was a part of Paco's killing and the attack on Rascal.* Tweaker crawled back under the covers to get warm.

I've got to lay low, maybe run. No, I can't do that. Still have that job to finish.

Tweaker felt in his pants pockets for the crumpled message he'd received from Ghost. He touched the wadded-up note. An OG traveling through town had slipped him this message just before Tweaker helped Rascal take care of Paco.

Skin still pale from the Bay, the older gangster gave Tweaker the old it's-an-honor bull he had heard since joining the gang. That if Tweaker obeyed and put in work, he'd earn respect and honor. And if he landed in the joint, he'd be able to cash in on those chips because he'd earned his bones. Blah, blah, blah.

One thing was true. One day he would wind up in prison. They all would—sooner or later. And the Family supposedly looked out for the faithful who'd been unquestionably obedient.

It came down to a matter of survival.

Tweaker desperately wanted to survive. He knew he'd have to obey these orders—above family, above friends, above any loyalty he had for his homies.

Obedience trumped everything.

Rascal had shown up at Tweaker's front door only minutes after the gangster had delivered the note and disappeared into the night. Rascal—all jacked up about getting Ghost's order to take out Paco—jabbered about all the important stuff the NF would do for him once he'd taken care of Paco. He told Tweaker about a guy named Ghost.

That had been Rascal's first mistake.

As Rascal ran off his mouth about what a big man he would become, Tweaker held Ghost's crumbled note in his pocket, a note telling him to take out Rascal after Paco was killed. That Rascal could not be trusted. That he'd betrayed his brothers and needed to be dealt with by Tweaker.

And yet, somehow, Rascal escaped his execution. Tweaker put together the hit on his friend and personally pulled the trigger. They'd left him for dead in the street, but the damn chump survived.

In the eyes of the Family, Tweaker failed and had to make amends. Failure was never tolerated.

Sleep eluded Tweaker. He lay in the cold dawn, shivering. Fear and anger engulfed him as he tried to figure out his next move. He must act quickly or disappear forever.

Fear had become a way of life for Gato. After watching Rascal gunned down in the street, Gato thought of running but there was no place to run. Fear made his hand shake when he got the message to kill Mikio. Fear mixed with love caused him to freeze as he held the gun on his uncle. And now? Fear forced him to look over his shoulder every time he walked down the street.

There would be retribution for his failure to obey Ghost's orders. Mikio tried to reason with him. "Juan, I'll take care of this. Ghost should not have ordered you to kill Paco. That man was all good. Ghost has another agenda, and the NF will deal with him. Trust me."

Gato wanted to trust Mikio. But his uncle's eyes told Gato he was not telling him everything. Holding something back.

Gato had to earn the NF's respect. Maybe if he conducted himself as a soldier, he might be deemed important to them. Maybe they'd just give him a beat down for his failure.

Like a death-row prisoner, Gato waited for his sentence to be handed out. Until then, he'd try to earn his bones. He'd run with his own gang and act as if nothing had happened. As if he was all good. But after the thing with Mikio, Gato kept a wary eye on everyone—especially his own friends. Any one of them might get a message from Ghost ordering them to take care of Gato. Just like the order he received.

Gato wanted to keep on breathing. There were only two things that might help keep him alive: fear and his own will to survive.

Another lesson Gato learned early was how to gain respect on the street. To prove yourself. If anyone doubted your toughness, your ability to take care of yourself, you'd find yourself in trouble. He must prove himself once again. To go completely whacko at just the right time.

And this was the strategy Gato would follow at the next opportunity.

The downtown mall was the center of attraction for anyone under the age of twenty. It was where all the babes came to shop. And it was where all the young males, hormones raging, came to gawk. Gato and his friends became a part of those gawkers.

The mall was a two-story self-enclosed retail extravaganza. Everything teenagers wanted could be found within these walls. The food court offered every tantalizing dish under the sun: Mother's cookies to pig's feet; strawberry milkshakes to Java Juice. And the shops were bulging with everything that could possibly make a teenager happy.

Gato saw his opportunity in the food court between the Panda Express and McDonald's. It started with a look. A quick one-second stare that inflamed Gato. It was the spark he would use to start a fire. A violent one!

The look came from a boy younger than Gato, strolling with a pretty girl on his arm. The boy was wearing blue. Not truly a Sureño blue, but close enough for Gato to move in and challenge.

"Who you looking at, punk?" Gato approached the boy with closed fists, anger heating his face.

The boy glanced at Gato with fear in his eyes. "I wasn't looking at nothing."

"You calling me nothing?" Gato screamed. "What you claiming?"

The boy's eyes widened like two silver dollars painted white. "Hey, man, I'm not claiming nothing. I'm not into that stuff." He glanced at his girlfriend. She had frozen in place.

"I say you're a lousy scrap!" Gato hurled himself at the boy. Gato's first punch caught the boy in the jaw and spun him around. The second punch landed in the kidneys.

The boy stumbled to the ground. He cried out in pain, doubling over, trying to protect himself.

Gato's friends moved in like a hive of angry wasps. They pelted the boy with their fists and kicked at the victim with their boots. The victim lay on the ground curled up in a ball, howling in pain. Gato caught the boy in the face with the heel of his boot. The boy's head made a sickening crunch against the tiled floor.

The girlfriend screamed. "You're killing him. Stop! Please leave him alone."

One of Gato's friends slapped the girl across the face. "You're a *puta* hanging with this scrap." Suddenly, he reached over and ripped open the girl's blouse.

The girl hugged her chest in shock, trying to hide herself from on-lookers. A group of teenagers gathered around Gato's friends. One of them leered at the girl. "Take it off, mama, take it all off." Others in the group started laughing and cheering. A few stood by in shock.

Gato continued to lash out at the boy on the ground. His kicks and punches were no longer rewarded with screams of pain. The boy lay silent blood running from his mouth, nose, and ears. There was a gash on the back of his head.

Gato looked up as if in a stupor. He caught his breath, watching his friends continue to whale away at the lifeless body. He saw a blur of white shirts coming their way. Private security racing along the upper level of the mall, moving in fast.

"Let's get out of here," he yelled. "Cops are coming!"

In an instant, the attack ended. Gato and his friends scrambled through the food court to a large department store. They dashed through the store and into a multilevel parking garage. They raced down the stairway to the street and jumped into a parked car belonging to one of Gato's friends. The driver fired up the engine and burned rubber on the pavement as they made their escape.

Once clear of the garage, they traveled west toward Mendocino Avenue. Gato looked north toward the shopping mall. Flashing lights of the first patrol car shot through the darkness as it pulled up to the front entrance. The officer dashed inside the mall as other patrol units began to arrive.

"Man, did you see that guy's face when Gato jumped him?" the driver asked, his face flushed. "That *cholo* took a dump in his pants."

One of the other gangsters laughed and slapped Gato on the back. "We put a hurt on that scrap."

Gato leaned back in his seat. Perspiration ran down his neck and under his arms as he basked in his friends' praise. The fear he hid inside was still there. Lurking. But for a moment, he enjoyed this admiration showered upon him. For the moment, his loyalty to the brotherhood was not questioned. A jolt of adrenaline made him feel alive and powerful. Made him feel like he belonged.

For the moment.

Chapter 24

Community Hospital, Santa Rosa

Hospitals were always places Paul Lawson tried to steer clear of—unless duty called. Pastoral duties, however, made this place a regular haunt. At the moment, duty called. He approached a nurse leaning over a pile of charts at the nurses' station next to a computer. The sound of his footsteps caught her attention.

"Hi," Paul said. "I'm looking for the room where I might find Stephen Avery? He's a patient. Stephen's mom called me. I'm their pastor."

The nurse's eyes slightly narrowed, then a spark of recognition lit her face. "Pastor Paul. I haven't seen you in ages. Lilly. Lilly Springfield. Came to your church when I worked day shift last year."

"It's been a while." He hoped that if he stalled for a moment, he might remember her. So far, he came up empty.

"I'll try to get back one of these days. This crazy schedule." She gestured around her. "Never know what shift I'm going to be working next. Oh, let me check that name for you." She peered at the computer screen, scrolling to the information she sought. "Let me see. Here he is." She gave him the room number. "Just down the hall to your left."

"Thanks, Lilly. Hope to see you soon."

"I will, Pastor, I will. Lord willing. This graveyard shift makes it kind of tough."

Paul found the room without difficulty. The door was open and Stephen's mother, Teresa, saw him approach. She met him at the door, her eyes red from crying, dark smudges from streaked mascara shadowed her eyes.

"Thanks for coming at this hour, Pastor."

He clasped the woman's hand. "I'm so sorry to hear about Stephen. How can I help?"

Her eyes brimmed with tears as she glanced inside the room. Paul followed her gaze and saw the boy lying motionless on the bed, tubes and monitors attached to everything not bandaged up, his face wrapped in white gauze.

Paul turned toward the mother. Wrinkles of time swept across her face. It was as if she'd aged ten years since last Sunday. "What happened?"

She glanced at her boy, wringing her hands. "Stevie and his girlfriend were walking through the mall. Just being kids. You know—just window-shopping. They didn't have much money."

She clutched his hand as if it was a lifeline. Her fingers tightened. "The police say some gang members attacked him. His girlfriend saw the whole thing. She said they just kept hitting and kicking him as he lay there on the ground—helpless."

She let go of Paul's hand and hugged herself. Her body swayed, giving evidence of the agony trapped inside. "The cops came knocking on the door. Said they couldn't give me any more details. They're investigating the assault."

She hunched over. "I just went cold inside when the police told me what had happened. I just can't get warm."

Paul put his arm around Teresa. He found a chair near the bed and eased her into it. She was shivering. He sat next to her in silence.

"The doctors don't know how much damage has been done. They won't know till he wakes up…if he wakes up." She looked over at her son. The *beep, beep, beep* of a monitor was the only sound cutting through the gloominess. She looked at Paul again, her eyes pleading. "He's a good boy.

A good student. Works hard, never gets into trouble. Everyone loves him. Who'd do something like this?"

Her eyes searched his face as if he might be able to make sense of this travesty. Paul could not bear to look into her eyes. God must have a reason for all this pain, but Paul was at a loss to try to explain it to her.

"Let just bow our head and pray for Stephen," Paul said. "We must put it in His hands."

Ghost's trip to Pelican Bay's law library had him worried. It was his turn to get a filter—a message directly from his boss, Daniel 'DJ' Juarez. A half hour later, Ghost figured out the code. *"I want to raise you up in our thing, give you more responsibility. I'm sending you a brother to help share the load. He is instructed to do whatever you order. With much respect, DJ.*

Ghost tore the tiny slip of paper into shreds and flushed it down the toilet. *Respect my ass!* Like a caged animal, Ghost paced around his confined cell, trying to read another man's mind. This message appeared to be cordial and encouraging, but it only fired off warning signs to his brain. He ground his teeth, feeling cornered, trapped by this polite command. If he refused, Ghost ran the risk of disrespecting his commanding general. If he consented, he ran the risk of having his throat slit from ear to ear.

DJ sent this new cellie for one of two reasons—to keep a close eye on him because DJ no longer trusted him; or worse, to take Ghost out because DJ learned he had ordered Paco killed.

This transfer request, initiated by DJ, only took a couple weeks. DJ carried a lot of juice in the Bay, a lot of power because of his NF position. Did he have someone in his pocket? Ghost wouldn't put it past him. The warden depended on guys like DJ to keep the peace among the gangs.

The swiftness of this transfer amazed him. At times, it might take a year or more to hook up with a cell mate of your choice. Many times, it was simply denied. The prison staff completed an exhausting threat assessment on each prisoner to make sure they were compatible with each other. In short, the two prisoners were not expected to kill each other.

Ghost's new cell mate would be transferred here in just a few days.

He had not heard anything from Sonoma County. Had Mikio been taken care of? Had Tweaker offed Rascal? This lack of information tortured him because his own life hung in the balance.

Ghost started preparing for the worst the moment he received DJ's note. He took inventory of his paperwork. Some information he could not risk falling into DJ's hands. He must treat this new cellie as a spy. He must not leave any evidence around that could implicate him.

Ghost carefully tore each page of incriminating information into tiny pieces and flushed them down the pipes. He bet the bulls, those watchdogs outside his cell, were not likely to put a trap on his toilet. But even if they did, they would be hard-pressed to try to put all these wet pieces of paper back into a readable document.

Next, Ghost had accumulated a weapons stash in his cell in case he was ever attacked. Several months ago, a raid by the security goons uncovered his metal shank inside a mattress and a razor blade hidden inside a large envelope filled with legal mail. Those had cost him some privileges. They missed a tiny wire hidden behind his sink that he had glued inside a groove in the concrete. The illegal wire, coated with gray paste, blended perfectly with the concrete. The weapon strengthened by multistrands of wires wound tightly together made a perfect garrote.

Each day he stripped down to his shorts for physical training, a routine he followed several times a day. He started with push-ups and sit-ups, hundreds of each, and then a variation of each. The thought of an opponent within arm's reach each day spurred him to push his body to its limit. He had been following this workout for years, but now he must intensify his efforts. His five-foot-ten frame needed a tune-up.

A mountain of legal papers—appeals and charges filed by Ghost with the courts—lay stashed on his top bunk in boxes. The tolerance of the courts finally ran out, and they returned his appeals with a stamp marked *Denied* in big, black letters. Ghost found a use for all these rejections. He painstakingly glued and bound reams of paper together into crude weights. He used these as dumbbells for his homemade weight machine. At least he'd get some use from all these court actions.

For all his physical and mental preparedness, there was something that had not plagued him for years. He felt like he had become the hunted instead of the hunter.

Ghost continued to push himself, waiting for the day when that cell door popped open and he faced his potential killer face-to-face.

When that day came, Ghost was determined to become the hunter once again.

Chapter 25

Santa Rosa

Mikio heard the rub of metal on metal as the slide pulled back on the semiautomatic. He heard the sound before he saw the gunman lurking in the shadows several apartments away. That was the gunman's first mistake. Mikio stood three steps from his apartment door.

Trapped.

In a split second, he made a move.

Mikio wheeled around to attack. He zigzagged toward the gunman. He heard the loud pop of one gunshot and saw the muzzle flash as he ran. Something struck his arm.

He kept charging.

He waited for the next blast from the gun as he dashed toward his attacker. It never came. He hurled himself at the gunman as the attacker seemed to be struggling with the gun. He tackled the assassin with a bone-splitting crunch, then fell to the ground. Mikio beat him with all the terror and rage pent up inside.

The gunman screamed in pain.

Mikio continued to whale on him, hitting, kicking, and kneeing his attacker in the groin. He used all the tricks he'd learned from a life spent in prison. He grabbed the man's throat and pounded his head into the pavement. The *thunk-thunk* of his attacker's head hitting concrete sounded like someone thumping a watermelon with a hammer.

Suddenly, Mikio did not feel any resistance. The man lay motionless. Quiet.

Sirens wailed in the distance. He sat back and waited. No use running. They would know it was him. Too many eyes and ears. He would just have to play the victim and hope they bought it. He heard what must have been a patrol car squealing its tires down the driveway leading to the apartments.

Slowly, Mikio's fear and rage subsided. His breathing was hard and ragged.

A sharp pain like a swarm of fire ants chewing on his flesh swept across his upper arm. He grasped where it hurt and a stickiness warmed his fingertips. Withdrawing his hand, he saw his fingers stained with blood. His blood.

A young police officer bounded toward him, gun drawn. "Put your hands in the air." The gun shook in the officer's hands.

Mikio slowly raised them. "I've been shot."

"Just stay where you are." The officer's voice lacked confidence. The officer's eyes shifted from Mikio to the gunman lying on the ground. Mikio breathed slowly without moving.

Footsteps pounded across the pavement. Several more uniformed officers converged, weapons drawn, aimed at his head. The first officer relaxed as other officers came alongside. Neighbors poked their heads out of doorways.

The young officer lowered his weapon and holstered it. "Lie on the ground, face away from me."

Mikio obeyed. He winced as the officer yanked his injured arm behind and handcuffed his wrists together.

"Hey, man, I'm shot. Take it easy."

The officer glanced at the arm, as if to verify whether Mikio might be telling the truth.

"I need a paramedic here," the officer yelled to no one in particular. "This guy's shot." One of the officers disappeared and came back a few minutes later with two EMTs. One of them, a woman, approached and kneeled next to Mikio and examined his wound.

"Gunshot" she called back to her partner. "Need to transport him." Someone wheeled a gurney toward them. The woman helped Mikio to his feet and had him lay faceup on the gurney. The young officer unlocked one of Mikio's cuffs and then clicked it closed on a metal bar running the length of the gurney.

"Hey, I'm the victim here." Mikio glared up at the officer.

Defiance loomed in the officer's eyes. "Until I know for sure what happened—you're a suspect."

Another officer, flashlight in hand, searched where Mikio's attacker lay on the ground. The man was also handcuffed, still unconscious. The officer appeared to find something of interest in the brush. He knelt down. A moment later, he stood with a firearm in his gloved hand. The officer closely examined the weapon, then sauntered over to Mikio, holding up the gun by its trigger well.

"You're lucky, pal! The semi stovepiped. Looks like the casing jammed up." The officer walked off with the weapon, shaking his head. "The luck of these guys."

The first officer reached down and unlocked the handcuff around Mikio's wrist. "Since you're the one who got shot and we can only find one gun, I'll assume you're the victim—for now."

As the woman worked on his arm, Mikio watched the male EMT working over the unconscious gunman. The medic asked the officer guarding him to uncuff the shooter.

"Not on your life," the officer shot back.

The EMT's face flashed with anger. "We need to get him to the hospital ASAP." As another ambulance crew arrived, the officers helped them lift the unconscious gunman and place him on a second gurney. As if to make a concession, the second officer unlocked one of the handcuffs of the shooter and then clicked it onto the gurney. They pushed the gurney down the sidewalk with the officer tagging behind, then disappeared out of sight.

The female EMT jutted out her jaw in Mikio's direction and glanced at the first officer. "He looks stable, but we want to get him to the hospital as soon as possible."

"It's going to be a few," the officer said, and walked out of Mikio's eyesight.

"I'm not waiting around for that kid to tell me when I can transport my patients," she muttered to her partner. She pushed the gurney toward the ambulance.

"Hold up just a minute!" A familiar voice cut through the darkness. The female medic glanced up with a look of irritation.

Mikio raised his head and peered in the direction of the voice. Two familiar faces emerged from the crowd of uniforms and onlookers.

Detective Kagan. Detective Stevenson. Mikio lay his head back, grimacing. *This night just keeps getting better.* With luck like his, the ambulance crew might get in an accident and kill him on the way to the hospital.

Tom Kagan, wearing a raid jacket over his street clothes, glanced at Mikio's wound. Stevenson stood off to one side.

Kagan peered at Mikio. "You know they'll keep coming after you until they finish the job. Your only option is to work with us. Let us help you."

Mikio glanced away and watched the female EMT talking to one of her coworkers.

Kagan motioned her over. He pointed a chin in Mikio's direction. "What's the damage?"

The woman bent over and tightened a roll of gauze around the wound to help control bleeding. "It looks like he's got a through and through, no bones, no major arteries." She turned her attention to Mikio. "You're just going to be really sore tomorrow. It blew out your muscle a bit, but you'll be all right. You're lucky."

Mikio turned back to the detectives standing next to him. "Yeah, I can't believe how lucky I am." He looked down at his bandaged arm.

Officers were beginning to push back the gawkers. One officer stretched yellow crime-scene tape across the walkway, from building to building, creating a protected inner and outer perimeter around the shooting scene.

Mikio tried to figure out the angles. Kagan's words rang true, but he'd never let on to the detective that he agreed. Was this DJ's doing? To have him killed? Was Ghost actually taking orders from DJ, or was this Ghost's own handiwork? Was the visit from Maria just a stall until they could take him out? Time was running out and Mikio had no answers.

Shooting pains worked their way up his arm to the base of his skull. The pain started to impair his ability to think clearly. He must protect himself. And Gato. Without Mikio's help, his nephew was left to fend for himself because he failed to kill his uncle. Now, they both were in the hat—the NF would make them open targets for any gangster to kill on sight.

"You guys working with Agent Garcia on this?"

Kagan nodded.

"Okay, here's the deal. Get Hector in here. I trust that old geezer. Tell him I want immunity and protection to be provided by his unit for me and my nephew. No local cops calling the shots."

A shooting pain caused him to grab his arm. He waited until the pain eased. "No offense, but some of you locals can't find your butt with both hands."

Tom smiled. "Now why would we take offense over that? We'll give Agent Garcia a call."

Mikio shrugged, causing more pain to his arm. "It's my rear end. Got to protect it the best way I can."

Tom glanced over at Stevenson for a moment before turning to Mikio. "We'll follow you to the hospital. Set up a security detail until Agent Garcia and his men can take over. But you have to give us a quick rundown on what's going on. So we know what we're negotiating for. Fair enough?"

Mikio glanced down at his bandaged arm. "Deal."

Chapter 26

Time to become a deal maker. In order to cut a deal with Mikio, Tom needed Hector Garcia's support to get the Department of Corrections to go along. Without Garcia, Mikio would balk and Tom's case would be back to square one—searching for another witness.

Timing was critical if he wanted Mikio to continue to cooperative. It was getting late, but Tom had to chance it and call Garcia anyway.

The SSU agent sounded like death warmed over the phone. "I'm getting too old for this." He coughed into the phone. Garcia's voice sounded as tired as Tom felt. "I just got home and fell into bed. Man, I'm feeling lousy."

Garcia and his team had been running nonstop all week helping to serve search warrants on Rascal and his playmates, catching a prisoner transport from San Quentin to the Bay, and tracking down an escaped convict loose somewhere in the South Bay. Now, Mikio wanted Garcia's protection.

Tom negotiated with Garcia over the phone. "I'll make it worth your while."

"Sorry, pal, you're not my type," Garcia said.

Tom heard a bed creak, and Garcia whispered something in Spanish. A female mumbled back. A moment later, Garcia came back on the line. "My wife says you can have me. Just let her sleep. I'll be there as soon as I can."

An hour later Garcia strolled into the Santa Rosa gang unit office with bleary eyes and a rumpled Hawaiian shirt that had seen better days. Tom glanced at his watch. Four in the morning. Phillips and Stevenson sat near Tom's desk sipping coffee. Garcia slumped into a third chair he wheeled from a nearby cubicle and looked at Tom with bloodshot eyes. "Any of that java left?"

Tom nodded. "I'll get you a cup." Garcia gave an appreciative nod and Tom returned a few minutes later with two brimming cups. "Hector, before you got here, the three of us talked about the importance of Mikio and his nephew to our case."

Garcia shifted his feet. "Can you guys start from the beginning? Need to hear what Mikio told you and what he's prepared to offer. Then I'll have a better handle on what kind of protection we might be able to come up with."

"Fair enough." Tom looked over at Stevenson. "Why don't you fill Garcia in on the details from tonight?"

Stevenson stood and stretched. "Mikio had just returned to his apartment when he got attacked. We identified the shooter and found his hometown is down near Salinas—Soledad, to be exact. Runs with the red in that part of Monterey County. Just paroled from Corcoran. He got orders from somebody to take out Mikio, but the creep won't tell us who. This shooter is felony stupid. He got off one shot that winged Mikio in the arm before his gun stovepiped. Mikio beat the living daylights out of him. The guy finally woke up, but he lawyered up fast."

Garcia nodded. "Makes sense. Guy knows he's headed back to the joint whether he gets convicted for shooting Mikio or being a felon in possession of firearms while on parole. Doesn't want to go inside with a snitch jacket."

Stevenson continued. "We made contact with Mikio at the scene, before they moved him to Community Hospital. He's stable. Tore up muscle but nothing vital. Anyway, Tom told him this would keep happening until they got it right. First Gato, now this banger from Soledad. We offered to help him if he helps us."

"So Mikio took you up on the offer?" Garcia asked.

"Well, in a way." Stevenson smiled, watching Garcia's face just as the agent started to take another sip of coffee. "He said he trusted that 'old geezer Garcia' and no one else."

Garcia spewed out coffee. "Old geezer! Where does he come off? He's as old as I am."

"He had some unkind things to say about us local cops."

"Well, I can see his point there." Garcia smirked at Stevenson and set the coffee on Tom's desk.

Tom folded his arms across his chest. "We followed the ambulance over to the hospital. Wanted to find out what he had to offer before we got 'the old geezer' out of bed."

"You're so kind. So what did he cough up?"

"He wouldn't give us much until he got immunity."

"And this is where I came in," Phillips said. "By the way, they weren't worried about getting me outta bed at this ungodly hour. I guess I should take that as a compliment. What do you think, Hector?"

"I think I have grounds for an age-discrimination suit here. What's the term, lawyer? Hostile work environment?"

Phillips laughed. "Mikio and I went back and forth for almost an hour. Had to get my boss out of bed to clear it. But he'll get his immunity in writing. I hope we didn't make a deal with the devil."

"So what did the devil have to say?" Garcia looked intrigued.

Tom leaned over and looked Garcia in the eyes. "He gave us the whole enchilada, my man. Every little detail—Paco, Rascal, and the hit called on him."

"And years of dirt on the NF," Phillips said. "He gave us a brief run-down on a dozen killings, robberies, where banks of money might be kept, weapons, safe houses. He's going to keep us busy for years."

Tom spotted mounting excitement in Garcia's eyes. "The downside to this is we have to keep Mikio, Gato, and Rascal alive. Once word gets out these guys are talking, all hell will break loose."

Garcia grabbed his coffee cup and stood. "Can you give me the down and dirty on the shootings? Paco and the other hits?"

Tom pulled a tape recorder toward him. "Here, listen to what Mikio said about Ghost." Tom punched the Play button and Mikio's voice started in midsentence.

"Ghost, Paco, and I go way back." Mikio appeared to choose his words carefully as if he was treading through a minefield and each word might ignite an explosion. *"Paco and Ghost were in reception in San Quentin 'bout ten years ago—before either of them became Nuestra Familia members. Once they cleared reception, they were to be shipped up to the Bay. One day, Paco came in from the yard a little early and looked down to the tier below. He saw four or five Mexican Mafia members corner Ghost and drag him into an open cell. The Mafia members took their turns with Ghost, one after another. Paco yelled down but it did not seem to deter them, and he was cut off from going to help Ghost. At one point, he heard Ghost whisper, "Just don't kill me."*

Tom's voice broke in on the tape. *"You mean...he never—?"*

"Yeah, Ghost never stood up for himself. He just took it without lifting a finger." Mikio took a deep breath before continuing. *"As soon as Paco hit the Bay, he shot me a kite about Ghost. Somehow Ghost learned Paco had snitched him off to me. Paco was holding this information in the bank until he needed a favor from Ghost. Something he could hold over Ghost forever. And Ghost knew it."*

"But why did Ghost wait 'til now to kill Paco?"

"Simple. Paco had power. He was a leader in the NF. Ghost was just coming up and his little secret that he got punked out by the Mafia without a fight—that would kill any chances of him gaining rank in the Family. So he used his new position as captain of the regiment that covered Sonoma County to take care of his witnesses. He must have made younger gangsters think Paco violated the rules. Those street thugs wouldn't question Ghost on this. At least not from the street."

Tom reached over and hit the Stop button.

Garcia took a deep breath. "I can imagine how Ghost will cover all this up—his big secret, Paco's death, and all the other stuff."

Tom glanced at the others. "Frankly, I am surprised Paco and Mikio kept quiet about it this long."

Garcia whistled under his breath.

Tom continued. "Mikio believes that Ghost also arranged for Rascal to be hit so Paco's murder would not be linked back to Ghost."

"What I can't figure," Garcia said, "is why Ghost waited until now to come after Mikio—a man who has been in the hat since he walked away from the NF several years ago. He could have ordered a hit on Mikio at any time."

"Maybe the order to kill Mikio came from desperation. Ghost might have thought Paco might be trying to gain more power. Taking Ghost out by letting this San Quentin information leak to the leadership would give Paco more power in the North Bay. And Ghost—frustrated that DJ and the others were holding back killing Mikio because of what the man might be able to tell the cops—decided to move ahead and do the job himself. Or at least his people."

Garcia picked up his coffee cup. "Man, Ghost is walking a tightrope and there's no safety net if he slips."

"I think he's already slipped," Tom said. "Mikio turned over to us filters his nephew received from Ghost to take out Mikio and Paco. Those are in evidence. We have Racal's testimony about his orders from Ghost to kill Paco. Apparently, Ghost was sending out duplicate filters to make sure the jobs got done. He was taking no chances."

Garcia shook his head. "He's got to be crazy to think the Family won't put this together. It is only a matter of time."

Phillips grasped Garcia's arm. "They already know. Thanks to Mikio."

"You mean the NF knows Ghost sent out these orders without their approval?"

Phillips nodded. "Mikio had a meeting with the wife of Daniel Juarez—DJ—right here in front of the police station more than a week ago. Mikio passed all this information about Ghost to DJ, knowing DJ would be forced to put Ghost out of commission. But after tonight's shooting, Mikio's not sure. And since he stepped down from NF, he feels they may come after him anyway. He's hedging his bets by cooperating with us."

Garcia's face lost some of its excitement. "What if the NF decides to whack Ghost? Mikio would be an accomplice, wouldn't he?"

"Yeah, I thought of that," Phillips said. "That's why you need to contact the Bay as quick as possible and let them know. We need to make sure Ghost is placed in protective custody. He's doing life. But if he knows they're coming after him…maybe he'll roll like Mikio."

Garcia reached into his back pocket and pulled out a thick black wallet. He started pulling out a wad of small pieces of paper. "Ah…here it is. Got just the number to call. Terry Lentz works gang intelligence up at the Bay. There's no reason why I shouldn't wake him up. If I've got to be up this early, I want Terry to be just as miserable."

He picked up a phone and started dialing.

Phillips turned toward Tom, her brow furrowed. "We have enough to charge Ghost with the murder of Paco, the attempted murder of Mikio, and who knows what else. Ship whatever reports you can get to me on all this information and I'll draft up a complaint. I was thinking that we might use the grand jury to keep some of this under wraps. And if Mikio can get Gato to talk to us, with what Rascal gave us, we'll be looking good."

Phillips had a hint of a smile on her face. "And remember. Make sure you *Mirandize* him."

Tom pointed in Stevenson's direction. "Right that down, junior. Make sure to *Mirandize* Ghost."

Phillips started to laugh, then caught herself. "Tom, maybe you and Garcia ought to take a run at Ghost. Bill, I could really use you here to help pull this together. Mikio and Gato will have to be relocated until we know all the threats against our witnesses have been neutralized. Rascal will need protection too.

Garcia caught the tail end of Phillips's comments. "Lentz has been warned. He'll work to isolate Ghost from the gang." He looked over at Stevenson. "I'll give you a couple of my guys to help move Mikio and his nephew. There's a military base near Sacramento we've used in the past. I've got a connection with federal housing people there. They have helped us in other relocations. It will be temporary, but it will do until we have everything else in place. In fact, Tom and I can help get them over to Sacramento, then we'll shoot up to the Bay from there."

"That works for me," Stevenson said. "I'll start on that today. I'd rather not have to investigate another shooting if we can prevent it." He looked at Tom. "If Diane's suggestion works for you, it works for me. I've been spending way too much time with you. Mary's starting to get jealous."

Tom looked down at the floor. It was what he needed to keep moving, keep pushing at this case until something broke wide open. Going home meant he'd have to deal with other matters that he just couldn't face right now.

"I guess a few more days away from home won't make much difference to me." Tom looked up to see Phillips give him a curious glance.

Tom stood. "Hector, how long before you're ready to travel?"

Garcia stuffed his notes back into his wallet. "I guess taking my motorcycle is out of the question?"

Tom laughed. "Now that'd raise some eyebrows around the office. Me hugging your backside all the way to Crescent City. I need to protect my reputation. Let's take your van."

Garcia smiled. "And I thought our relationship was ready to go to the next level, Thomas."

Tom glanced at the others. "This is going to be a long trip."

Phillips gathered her things. "Hey, just make Ghost roll. Then if we play our cards right, we can go after DJ and the other NF leaders."

Garcia faced Phillips. "I love it when you talk prosecution."

She just shook her head, laughing.

As they gathered their belongings, Tom tried to figure out what needed to be done next. This case might blow open the whole Nuestra Familia gang structure. *What would they do to stop us if the NF had an inkling about our case?*

Just how far would they go to protect themselves? And if Ghost didn't roll, would he be crazy enough to send gangsters—with whatever power he had left—after Tom and his friends? He shrugged off the thought. After all, what could one man do locked up in a high-security prison? Once they learned what he had done, Ghost's own people would soon be coming after him.

Still, Tom could not seem to shake that sense of danger. He did not share his thoughts with the others. Let them enjoy the moment. Everyone had a job to do and there would not be much time for laughter in the coming days.

The others had not seen the look Ghost shot him. It was the look of a killer, an animal with only one goal—to kill its prey. Tom knew Ghost—somehow, some way— would be coming for him. As if it was genetically written into the gangster's DNA. And Tom would be waiting.

He just hoped no innocent blood would be shed.

Chapter 27

Sacramento

"Pack up, my man, we're going to find you and your nephew a new home."

The sun was just starting to inch across a gray skyline as Mikio struggled to wake up. He had been released from the hospital only hours earlier and was just getting to sleep when he heard banging on his door.

Garcia hit him with the news. A team of SSU agents had pulled their caravan to Mikio's front door. His first reaction was to tell Garcia to come back later. Then it hit him. This was what he asked for—protection. Garcia was just trying to comply.

Mikio was glad he kept his mouth shut for once.

"Where's Gato?" Garcia peered over Mikio's shoulder into the darkened apartment.

"He's sleeping in there." Mikio pointed down the hall. "I told him that we're to be relocated, but I don't know if that sunk in. Time will tell."

Garcia brushed past Mikio without waiting for an invitation. "We'll get him up. We got to get going."

Mikio trailed behind Garcia into the living room. A brown-plastic sofa dominated the sparsely furnished room. Mikio eyed a large bump smothered by a mountain of well-worn blankets. Muffled snores emanated from beneath the pile. Mikio stuck his foot somewhere in the middle of the mound and nudged the bump.

"Rise and shine, Juan. We've got company."

His nephew slowly emerged, first an arm, then a leg, then a shaved head. A pair of blurry brown eyes peered out from under the protection of the blankets. The young man took one look at Garcia and let out a long belch.

"Show some respect," Mikio said. "And get your butt out of bed. We're moving."

Juan rolled his eyes as he stood. He moved with belligerent slowness as he gathered his clothes. He dressed and filled two paper sacks with his belongings. It was all he needed for the trip.

For a moment Mikio watched his nephew and then impatiently strode toward his own bedroom. Garcia tagged along.

"The prosecutor has okayed some witness protection money for you and your nephew. It's not a bunch, but it will do for now. Till we can get you set up somewhere else." Garcia explained the terms of relocation. "It's important you never directly contact any family members or friends once we move you. If you need to get a message through to someone, give my office a jingle and we'll make it happen."

Mikio listened as he slowly packed a duffle bag. "Before we leave, I wanted to call some family to come and take care of what I leave behind. I'll explain we're out of here and not to come looking for us."

Garcia shook his head. "Absolutely not. No one must know you're leaving until we're gone. I just don't want you or Gato ending up in the morgue while we screw around trying to figure things out."

Mikio glanced over at Garcia without speaking. It had been a long time since he trusted anyone. The verdict was still out on Garcia.

"As soon as you're settled, you can call from one of our cell phones and let your family know what's happening. After that, we'll get whatever messages you need to them. Even take things back and forth if you want."

"I understand. Juan will be the difficult one. He is still adjusting to all this change. What if he makes a mistake and winds up in prison? He'll have a snitch jacket even though he never said a word."

"We've got to make sure he cleans up," Garcia said. "So he doesn't wind up in prison."

Mikio glanced at Garcia. He knew it was a long shot. Cleaning up his nephew might be an impossible task. But he had to try. Mikio lifted the duffle bag from the floor and swung it onto the bed. "We used to try to slip sleepers in the PC yards, pretending they wanted to cooperate. The sleepers were sent in to kill those who ratted us out. Now I'm one of those rats. And so is Juan."

"They forced your hand, Mikio. They used your own family to try to waste you. You owe those cowards nothing."

Mikio folded the bag's ends together and clippied it shut. "It started out so different. We took an oath, an allegiance, a bond for life. We talked about honor and code, brotherhood and family. In the end, I realized it was a sham. What I committed my life to was nothing but a lie. I tried to get out with honor. But they wouldn't even let me do that."

"You're doing what needs to be done to protect your family and yourself. You can hold your head up on this one, partner."

Mikio shrugged, a sudden wave of dejection eating away at his heart. "Part of me feels like a traitor. That's how deep they cut into my soul. Even when they tried to kill me, a part of me felt like I had to keep my trap shut."

Garcia grabbed the duffle bag. "Here, let me."

They walked back to the living room and found Juan dressed and watching television. He glared up at Garcia and scratched his groin.

Mikio looked away in disgust. "Come on, Juan. We have to get out of here. Now."

His nephew pulled himself off the couch, grabbed his bags of clothing, and followed the two men.

Kagan and Stevenson stood with a couple of SSU agents near the vans. The windows of both vehicles were heavily tinted. Garcia pointed at the men. "They'll follow us over and get you settled in your new place. I'll be out of town on business for a day or two. I'll check on you when I get back. Here's my card. I've written my cell phone number on the back. Call me—anytime."

Mikio slipped the card into his pocket. He waited until Juan climbed into the passenger side of the van that would carry them to Sacramento. An agent slid into Mikio's car and pulled behind the two vans.

Garcia looked at the agent driving Mikio's car. "Don't worry, he'll take good care of your car. We'll leave it with you once we get there, but until then, we thought it might be safer if one of my guys drove it over just in case a gangster wanted to take a shot. My agent is armed to the teeth, and the rest of us are backup."

Mikio nodded. "I'd like to talk to you when you get back. I'm going to need help getting Juan turned around. The call of the street is strong. If he runs, I'll lose him for good. He won't survive."

Garcia patted Mikio on the back. "I'll do what I can to help. Just keep your own head down."

The trip to Sacramento seemed to last forever. Juan sullenly stared out the window the entire ride. The two hours seemed to take an eternity.

Once the caravan reached the air base, one of the agents climbed out and approached two airmen manning the security gate.

The guards glanced at the tinted vans with interest. Mikio could only guess what they might be thinking. A few minutes later, a military police unit approached the guard shack from inside the base. The driver leaned out and spoke to the group next to the shack. The SSU agents turned and waved.

Mikio leaned over and tapped Juan on the shoulder. "Here we go." The caravan meandered around the military base and past an inner fence that protected the runway from vehicular and pedestrian traffic. They finally neared a cluster of housing units on the far side of the air base.

They pulled up to one of the houses and the agent driving Mikio's car pulled into the driveway. Mikio climbed out and glanced around. It looked like a ghost town. Many of the houses were boarded up with warnings against trespassing glued to the front doors. Not a soul in sight.

"I guess we don't need to worry about disturbing the neighbors," Mikio said.

Garcia nodded. "Part of downsizing government. Just like they did at Fort Ord and elsewhere. The only people you will see on this side of the base are MPs on routine patrol. No one will find you here. There's security

360 degrees around the place, and everyone who comes through the gates gets checked."

A scowl crossed Juan's face. "It looks like a prison to me, man. I didn't sign up for this."

"It is just temporary, Juan. Until Garcia and his guys get a handle on what's happening back home. Then we move on."

Juan turned away from Mikio, his hands clenched into tight fists. "Move where? We can never go home, Tío."

"Let's take this one day at a time. We'll figure things out as we go. Patience, Juan."

His nephew stormed off. Mikio grabbed his duffle bag, slung it over his shoulder, and trudged to the front door of the house. The place had two bedrooms. At least he would not have to put up with Juan's snoring in these new digs. His thin-walled apartment in Santa Rosa vibrated every night since his nephew moved in.

Mikio wandered around the house to familiarize himself. There was a dining room off the kitchen and a living room. The place came modestly furnished, including a television that worked. At least they would have a distraction from each other.

Garcia followed Mikio around the small house. "Here is a disposable cell phone. You got two hundred minutes to burn. Don't get chatty." The SSU agent handed Mikio the phone. "You have my number. Again, we just ask that you not call home or anyone who might be able to track your number. It is GPS equipped, so be careful."

Garcia pointed toward the kitchen. "There's food in the fridge. If there's something you need, make a list and give me a jingle. We'll drop it off in a few days when we return."

After a few minutes, Garcia and the others climbed back into the vans. Mikio watched them drive away. His car, parked in the driveway, was the only vehicle in sight. At least he'd have wheels to get out of here if he had to escape.

Stillness settled on the ghost town as Mikio gathered his thoughts. The hum of white noise from the big city, beyond the sprawling military base, was occasionally broken by the rude whine of an aircraft or the roar of a jet taking off from the airstrip. Frogs chirped to each other through the darkness.

He retreated into the house and heard voices from the television. Juan was slouching in an easy chair, a leg draped over one of the arms, sitting in darkness except for the flickering of light from the show he was watching.

Mikio turned on a light. "You hungry?"

Juan glanced up. "Yeah." He returned his attention to the television.

Mikio made his way to the kitchen and flicked on an overhead light. A yellow glow illuminated the dreariness of the room. A dirty-white linoleum floor, worn or torn in spots, was matched by whitewashed cupboards that held empty shelves. As he started to open up the refrigerator, he heard someone talking quietly in the living room. The sound was not coming from the television.

Mikio turned on the faucet above the sink to full blast. He grabbed a skillet and silently retraced his steps to the living room.

His nephew was hunched over the telephone, quietly talking. His hand covered his mouth as he spoke. The young man gave a furtive look over his shoulder just as Mikio let loose with the skillet. It bounced off the young man's chest just as he wheeled around to face Mikio. The skillet hit the floor with a thud.

Juan yelped and dropped the phone. He turned toward his uncle as Mikio stormed toward him.

He grabbed the phone and jabbed the End button to sever the connection. "Who you talking to?" Mikio clenched his teeth.

"Just my woman, man."

Mikio grabbed the boy by his throat. "Are you trying to get us killed? Didn't they tell us not to call *anyone*?"

"No harm talking to my woman. She won't snitch us off."

"How do you know she won't?"

"Cause she loves me."

"She loves you?" Mikio slapped him upside the head. "You fool. She'll forget all about you by tomorrow. Did you tell her where we are?"

"No. I just told her we'd be out of town for a while. I'd check her out when we get back."

"She can get the number off her phone, you moron. They can track us that way."

"Nah. She won't tell nobody. She's all good."

Mikio threw the young man onto the couch. He started to lash out with his fist but caught himself, letting his fist drop. "You fool. I'm not willing to bet my life on one of your little whores. You pull a stunt like that again and I'll personally let them know where to find you. Am I making myself clear?"

Juan looked at Mikio. Fear and hate filled his eyes. "It won't happen again. Promise."

Mikio strode back to the kitchen. He leaned over the kitchen sink and watched the faucet gushing into a rust-colored drain. His hands were shaking as his anger slowly subsided. Now that it was over, a sick feeling welled up inside that anger always left behind. He pictured his hands wrapped around Juan's throat. It would have been so easy to squeeze out the life between his fingers, to snap that young neck.

Mikio saw his own reflection in the window and thought about what he was just fantasizing. He hung his head. What was he thinking? Choking his nephew? The old Mikio sneaked inside. He was better than this, but now—Juan would never know. The young man just saw what Mikio used to be in prison. He vowed to try to do better. For Juan.

His nephew turned up the television volume.

A drop of redness fell into the sink. He glanced at his right arm and a trickle of blood oozed from beneath the bandages. He must have torn the stitches loose. He pressed on the wound, trying to get the bleeding to stop.

Mikio made his way outside to get some fresh air and try to calm down. Just as he stepped outside, a fighter jet screamed as it lifted off from the airfield. The giant bird roared overhead, bellowing into the dark sky as it flew to its unknown destination.

Mikio watched darkness settling over the military base as he mulled over the events of the day. Had he made the right choice bringing Juan with him? He felt like a drowning man being sucked downward by forces beyond his control. Dragging Juan along with him was like trying to run a footrace against world-class sprinters with a 150-pound bag of sand wrapped around his neck.

For the first time in his life, Mikio did not have a plan. He was not in control. Even in prison, locked in a cell, he'd always felt that in some ways he controlled the situation. He could always get what he wanted.

The tables had turned, and now Garcia was in charge of Mikio's life. His future. His survival. Garcia had tossed a lifeline into Mikio's outstretched hands and solemnly promised to help Mikio escape, to help him walk away from the only life he had known—a life that threatened to kill him if he stayed.

But this lifeline came with strings attached. There was always a price to pay.

For everything.

Chapter 28

Humboldt County, California

Hector could not shake the look on Mikio's face as they drove away from the base in Sacramento. It was the look of a man caught between two worlds. Would Mikio be able to walk away—and still save his nephew?

Hector glanced over at Tom stretched out on the passenger side of the van, apparently still sleeping, then returned his attention to the road ahead. "You asleep?"

Tom moved next to him and stretched. "Trying for a little shut-eye. You need me to take over the wheel?"

"Nah. I'd rather drive. You drive like an old lady."

Tom sat up, rotating his neck to work out the kinks. "Then why'd you interrupt my beauty rest?"

"I was thinking—"

"Now there's the first sign of trouble."

"Nah. Seriously. It's going to be hard enough for Mikio to break free. To start clean. He wants to drag Gato along with him." Hector shook his head. "Mikio might have a chance, but his nephew? That boy worries me. I don't trust him."

"Frankly, I'd be surprised if either of them make it. I mean, I hope they can find their way to a different life. But I'm not a social worker. I'm a cop. What will be, will be."

Hector jerked the steering wheel to the left to pass a semi-truck lumbering up a steep grade. He saw a turn in the road coming up fast. He slammed his foot on the accelerator, the van shooting forward, then he slipped back into his lane as an oncoming car roared past them.

"I'm no social worker either, Tom. It's just that I've been where this guy is coming from. Same side of the tracks and all that. Know what I mean? His family, everyone he knows, is caught up in this lifestyle."

"I don't buy it. Look at you, Garcia. You did just fine. Just because you happen to be from the poor side of the tracks, doesn't mean you gotta become a gang member."

"That's not what I'm saying." Hector struggled to express what he was feeling. "If you came from the same area I grew up in—gangs are more likely to be in your face. They're in your neighborhood, in your school, and in your home. Rich kids living on the hill are a lot less likely to have to deal with gangs messing up their lives."

"You trying to tell me that since I'm white, I can't understand what Mikio's world is like?"

Hector glanced over at Tom. "It's not that cut and dried, my friend. Sometimes life just doesn't give people all the tools they need to make it on their own. Particularly when they come from poorer neighborhoods. They stumble around, sometimes going down a wrong path, thinking that's their only option."

"Now you *are* talking like some social worker. I bet you started out with the same disadvantages Mikio faced. He chose one path—you, another."

Hector grimaced. "We all must accept responsibility for what we've done with our lives. But I think there has to be a measure of mercy, of understanding, granted them. After all—nobody's perfect. We all make mistakes."

"Now you're sounding like some Bible-thumping preacher. I didn't take you for a religious nut."

"Just call me Father Hector."

"Well, Father Hector. I hope you can get Ghost to confess his sins. It'll make our job a lot easier. Maybe if you tell him about coming from the same hood, it'll loosen him up a bit."

Hector glanced at Tom. "I've heard confession is good for the soul."

Tom's smile disappeared. "I'm not sure Ghost has a soul. I think he sold it to the devil a long time ago."

"Now who sounds like a preacher?"

A few minutes later, Tom settled back in his seat.

Hector punched the accelerator and pushed the car to its limits. It would be another long, twisty ride to Pelican Bay. If he was lucky, he'd make the prison before Tom woke up.

DJ eased himself onto the metal stool in the law library. A guard closed the door to his cage and marched down the corridor. DJ managed another trip to this place along with Snake, the NF general of the Pintas. The two men had manipulated library cells next to each other. It made communications that much simpler.

DJ pressed his face to the wall. "Snake. You there?"

"Hear ya. Loud and clear, homie."

DJ smiled. "The thing with Ghost is in place. His new cellie got a green light to transfer in a day or two."

He heard Snake move around in his tiny cell. *"Muy bien. Muy bien.* The sooner, the better. We don't want Mikio shooting his mouth off." DJ was about to answer when footsteps came their way. A guard wandered past. DJ pretended to read a law book until the guard was out of earshot.

"Yeah, but he has me worried, Snake. We all knew when he stepped away we couldn't let that happen without taking action. It would not be a good example to the young ones. And Mikio has too many secrets locked inside. He's a danger to our Family."

"I know, but we gotta be careful. Take care of Ghost for Mikio. That will buy us the time we need. To make sure there's no blowback when we take him out. Any idea how he might get that information to the canines if he bites it?"

"I got someone working on that. Once we know where he's stashed that information and how he plans to get it to the cops—we'll move on him."

A prison guard strode by and glared. The two men glanced down and feigned interest in their reading.

DJ was satisfied with the result of his trip to the library. The two of them had determined the fate of three men in one short conversation—the killing of Ghost. The killing of Mikio. And the lifelong loyalty of the soldier he had sent into the cell to end Ghost's life. Like a military general, DJ sat back to enjoy the rush of a well-planned strategy in which all his soldiers marched to his command.

Chapter 29

Pelican Bay State Prison

After a six-hour journey over winding spaghetti-like roads, Tom began to wonder if the trip might be worth it. Garcia drove faster than the law allowed, and Tom's stomach felt queasy from the twists, dips, and turns at high speed. He'd tried to take his mind off the road by listening to Garcia talk about prison life.

"This your first time to the Bay?"

"Yeah," Tom said. "Never had a reason to come up this far."

The burly agent drove with one hand on the wheel, gesturing wildly with the other. "From the ground or from a plane, this place is awesome," Garcia's gaze shifted from the road to stare at Tom. "A city within a city surrounded by miles of barbed concertina wire."

A big-rig truck lumbered toward them, and Tom's stomach tightened as their car wandered into the opposing lane. Garcia seemed oblivious to the danger.

"There are actually two exterior fences running parallel to each other. Between them lies a deadly—"

"Hector, a truck—"

"—string of wires carrying thousands of volts of electricity." Garcia did not lose a beat in the conversation as he yanked the wheel to the right as the eighteen-wheeler barreled down on them. "One touch of those wires and you'll be pushing up daisies."

Tom tried to relax as Garcia returned his attention to the road.

"And once you get inside, you'll see how easy it is to get lost, particularly inside the SHU."

Tom laughed. "We'll make sure not to lose you. We don't want you to wind up someone's girlfriend."

Garcia accelerated once again. "You'd better stay close. Prisoners would love to get their hands on a cop." He nodded off to the right. "There she sits."

Tom's first glimpse of Pelican Bay State Prison made him blink with awe. It emerged out of nowhere, looming through a lush coastal forest. The car had lulled him into a trance with miles and miles of towering fir, pine, and redwood trees whipping past in a steady stream of green. Crescent City, the last town of any consequence, lay behind them. Ahead, beyond the prison, Oregon's border awaited them.

Again, the prison shot into view. A pearl-gray concrete mountain, like an imposing military fortress, suddenly flashed in the corner of his eye. And just as quickly it vanished, the forest swallowing it up. For a brief moment, Tom thought he'd imagined it.

Then he saw the sign. *Pelican Bay State Prison.* Garcia abruptly turned off the highway and followed the exit. Tom scanned the walled city emerging in front of him. This place had a reputation as the toughest in the state and few in law enforcement ever ventured inside.

More than one criminal he'd interviewed told of serving time "in the Bay." They'd stare at him, haughty, arrogant, boasting they survived this place where criminal legends sat in cages and where exaggerations spawned stories as numerous as salmon.

Garcia pulled behind several other cars lined up at the main guard shack, their drivers waiting to be cleared.

"The prison is segregated into four smaller cities or yards. Yards A and B to the east contain several thousand inmates. These convicts are considered some of the worst. We're talking murderers, rapists, and an assortment of other predatory criminals, many of them gang members."

Garcia pulled the car forward, brakes squeaking. "They're separated by race or sexual preference, living out their sentences with an opportunity to walk on grass in their respective yards and enjoy the outdoors if they behave themselves."

His voice changed as he described another part of the prison. "To the west are yards C and D. We call this the Special Housing Unit. Each of these housing units consists of four walls, a ceiling, and a floor made out of concrete and cinder blocks. An occasional skylight might give a hint as to whether it's day or night. The SHU was built with one thing in mind—to isolate the worst of the worst."

Garcia paused as he brought the car alongside the guard shack. An armed guard in a green jumpsuit leaned out and peered into the car, squinting in the morning sunlight. He glanced at Garcia, a smile of recognition on his face. Slapping Garcia's outstretched hand, the sentry waved them through. The wheels of their car thumped over several speed bumps. Garcia weaved his way between rows of parked cars and steered them toward a building marked *Administration*.

"Within the SHU are gang leaders of all the prison gangs," Garcia eyed the building ahead, "and others considered so predatory that they can't be housed with the normal prison population."

Garcia glanced at Tom with a glint in his eye. "I hear one of these inmates practices cannibalism."

Tom rolled his window up as they neared the administration center. "Is he single celled?"

Garcia laughed as he pulled into a parking space. Beyond the barbed-wire fence was a mammoth building, whose gray walls jutted upward with an air of defiance. There were only a smattering of windows gracing the otherwise stark walls.

"That's the beginning of the SHU. From the air, it looks like a giant concrete X stamped into the earth, with small concrete boxes jammed together to form the four arms of the letter. Each arm has a series of pods segregated from each other by a series of gates, metal doors, and alarms systems." A look of exasperation crossed Garcia's face. "You know, it's like trying to describe a sunset to a blind man. I'll just wait and let you see for yourself.

"It's not the kind of world we wanted to create. It's just the way things need to be." The agent's voice seemed to shift from a somber tone to one laced with bitterness. "And trust me, they still manage to reach out from behind these walls and kill people."

Garcia parked in a space reserved for law enforcement. Tom leaned out his window and peered up at a guard tower that rose in front of them. Built on the other side of a tall wire fence, it stood like a small version of Seattle's Space Needle. It rose some twenty-five feet in the air, bulging at the tip with a circular bank of windows. A guard leaned out of one of the windows armed with a high-powered rifle. The tower afforded the guard a clear shot at anything that moved for hundreds of yards in any direction.

After stashing their weapons in gun lockers at the base of the tower, they returned to the car. Garcia popped open the trunk. "Okay. Dump your car keys, knives, cuff keys, tape recorders, cell phones, and any other kind of techno gizmos you might be hiding. None of that stuff's allowed inside." Tom followed the SSU agent's orders and Garcia slammed the trunk closed.

They made their way to the front counter in the administration building. "You need to show them your ID." Garcia reached into his own pocket while smiling at the woman behind the waist-high counter. "We're supposed to meet Terry Lentz from the IGI's office." He turned to Tom standing next to him. "He's the guy I told you about."

The woman walked over to a telephone and dialed. She briefly spoke into the receiver before hanging up. "IGI's been notified," she yelled over at them. "He'll be here in a few."

On the way up to the prison, Garcia gave him a little background on Terry Lentz. After clawing his way up the ranks—guard at Chino and Folsom, security squad at Pelican Bay—Lentz joined a small contingent of elite intelligence officers five years ago. These investigators became experts on the gangs—their membership, organizational structures, gang policies, and history. Most important, they tried to thwart any acts of violence these gangs might be planning.

With a slight chuckle, Garcia nudged Tom. "Watch when I call him General Patton."

Tom looked back, his brow wrinkled.

"This guy looks like some Hollywood war hero," Garcia said, "He's got close-cropped blond hair and deep-blue eyes the girls go ape over. A guard he'd worked with years ago started calling him General Patton because he is ex-military and his jumpsuits are so stiff with starch, I doubt he can bend over without cracking. Anyway, Lentz kept telling everyone, 'I am a Marine. Patton was...*Army*. But the more he fought it, the more the name stuck. He finally surrendered. Now, that's the only name I use when we cross paths."

The two men watched the gates open and close as people came through. Garcia tapped out a beat on the counter with his fingers as he watched one of the inmates cleaning the floor in reception. The inmate kept glancing at everyone coming and going.

"It's a different kind of animal here. A world where prisoners watch the guards, and the guards watch the prisoners. Nothing escapes notice. It's a world where the smallest, most insignificant event can capture their imagination and interest." Garcia's eyes twinkled. "Watching a female guard walk by can be the highlight of a prisoner's week."

Tom looked at him with surprise. "They have female guards in there?"

Garcia laughed. "Yes, my chauvinist friend. And I'd be the last person on this green earth to mess with them. They can handle their own."

Tom thought of the first time he met Garcia as the man drove up on his motorcycle and teased the SSU receptionist in the parking lot that day. Garcia was not above teasing anybody, including the female guards here in Pelican Bay. Maybe one of them hauled off and put Garcia in his place.

Grinning, Tom waited for Lentz to show. He would have given anything to see one of these female guards make Garcia squeal with pain. That would have been a sight to see.

Chapter **30**

PBSP Reception Center, Crescent City, California

Tom saw Garcia glance at the door leading into the prison and wave toward a man walking their way. This must by Terry Lentz. The man looked like he was under a lot of stress.

Garcia spoke first. "General Patton, I'd like you to meet my partner, Tom Kagan."

Lentz's jaw tightened for just a moment and then the investigator smiled. "Hector, you're getting uglier by the day." He extended a hand. "How ya' doing?"

After Lentz slapped Garcia on the back and introduced himself to Tom, he guided them past the guard station leading up to the Special Housing Unit.

"I'm glad this wasn't a wasted trip for your guys," Lentz said. "I wasn't sure until an hour ago whether Ghost would agree to meet with you."

"We appreciate the effort." Tom looked over at Garcia, who had a weird look on his face. "Something you want to tell me?"

"Yeah. There was one little thing I forget to tell you when we started this trip."

Tom waited for Garcia to continue.

"Ghost could've refused to meet us."

"How can he refuse? He's a prisoner."

"Yeah. Well, even prisoners have rights. One of those rights is to refuse to be interviewed. We can't force 'em."

"I don't believe it. Who's running this place?"

Garcia shot a glance at Lentz. "ACLU? Federal judges? Take your pick."

"Look at it from their perspective," Lentz said. "Everyone's suspicious of everyone else. The prison is full of informers. They watch each other like a hawk to see who leaves their cells under escort. All the gang members know there is only one reason a prisoner allows himself to be escorted to my part of the SHU. In their paranoid minds an inmate must be a rat. A snitch. He must be working for the Man. Just the perception is enough to scare them from leaving their cells. I've arranged for Ghost to have a medical escort, only he won't make it to medical."

Lentz pointed toward the door. "Come on. Let's see if Ghost will play ball."

Terry glanced at Kagan before ushering both men past a security checkpoint and through a door leading outside. They entered a galvanized wire cage, then traveled over a gravel walkway that channeled them to another security gate. It always gave Terry the sensation of being locked inside a dog kennel. This gate was controlled by a tower guard.

Terry looked up and waved. A guard, leaning out of a window high above, peered down from his perch, sunglasses jauntily resting on a bulbous nose. The man disappeared into his glass house. A moment later, a buzz sounded as the gate in front of them popped open. They walked through the gate and it rolled closed, clicking shut behind them.

They strolled into no-man's-land—a carefully graded stretch of ground between the inner and outer perimeter fences. Again, they found themselves confined inside an area best described as a kennel run. It stretched from the gate they just cleared to the final security gate on the far side of no-man's-land some forty yards ahead. This final gate was the portal through which they'd reach the SHU.

Between the exterior and interior fences, strands of high-voltage wires, one on top of the other, stretched out of sight. The wires looked lethally efficient, encircling them with their deadly arms of electricity.

Terry led them to the final security gate controlled by unseen hands. The gate clicked open and they passed through it, beginning a slow ascent as the gate snapped shut, prohibiting them from leaving.

"I like what you've done with the place." Kagan glanced at the barren, rocky ground. Not a shrub, plant, or blade of grass in sight.

Terry shot a look over his shoulder. "Wait until you get inside. We asked *Sunset* magazine if they wanted to do a spread on our decorating ideas. They declined."

Terry watched his visitors as they gingerly stepped into this dungeon-like corridor. A sense of amazement could be seen in their eyes—particularly first timers like Kagan. This was where sunlight and fresh air stopped, and total confinement began. As the doors slammed closed behind them, those who entered this domain inherently knew their freedom had just been snatched away. An eerie quietness settled on the men as they made their way into a concrete labyrinth, a maze that crossed and recrossed itself until visitors lost all sense of direction.

Terry winked at Garcia and pretended to hold a microphone to his mouth. His voice and tone mimicked Rod Serling's introduction of *The Twilight Zone*. "They've crossed the threshold into the Bay's war zone, where good and evil face each other in human form. In this place, these two sides stand only an arm's distance away. Will they survive?"

Garcia frowned at Terry. "Where did you come up with that garbage?"

Terry grinned. "A little spiel I've been working on. What do you think?"

"Don't give up your day job, pal." Garcia slapped him on the shoulder.

Terry shrugged. "Okay, enough with the jokes. From here on out you must do exactly as I tell you. It's for your own safety. Please do it."

Tom and Hector nodded as silence seemed to envelop them. Terry turned and led them deeper into the gray maze.

Tom followed Lentz down a corridor that fed into a small highway of concrete that ran to their left and right. Lentz led them to the IGI office. One of the other gang officers was in the office. He nodded toward another door. "He's in there...waiting."

Lentz nodded. "Okay, guys, let's go have a chat with Mr. Ghost."

Tom and Garcia followed Lentz through the door indicated by the other officer and found themselves in a windowless room with only one door, one table, and several chairs. Ghost was shackled to a table, his hands and feet still restricted by belly chains. The chains rattled as he leaned over in the chair to scratch his nose. The table was a solid block of concrete. The prisoner was tied down with nowhere to go, like a ship anchored to a concrete pier.

Ghost's gaze wandered from man to man as they entered. A glint crept into Ghost's eye as he stared at Tom.

"Where's your sidekick. Stevenson? Wasn't he invited to this party?"

Tom's muscles tightened as he glanced at Lentz. The IGI officer shrugged. "We didn't tell him anything."

Ghost had a smug look on his face. Score one for the bad guy. Let the games begin.

"Detective Stevenson couldn't make it." Tom sat across from the prisoner and opened his briefcase. Tom slowly pulled out several files and neatly stacked them in front of him.

Ghost eyed the files like a rat eyeing a piece of cheese. There was slight twitch in the man's cheek as he stared at the paperwork.

Tom studied the prisoner—a face lean and taut with a nose that hooked like a bird's beak. Ghost's thin lips looked dry and chapped and carried a harshness that matched his vacant, coal-black eyes. Tom had seen eyes like this before, in another place, another time. He tried to remember where but without success.

Tom saw the twitch again, slight and almost imperceptible. It was so fast, Tom's brain had to play it back to realize what he'd just witnessed. He smiled to himself. A telltale sign of stress. Something the man feared? The twitch was a weakness Tom might be able to exploit later.

"Mr. Hernandez, Agent Garcia and I drove all the way up here for two reasons." Tom pushed the files to one side and folded his hands. "First, I need to advise you that we believe the NF is going to kill you."

Not a muscle twitched, not one flicker of emotion crossed the other man's face. And then Tom saw it again, like a horse twitching its hide to dislodge flies. He'd struck a nerve.

"Secondly, we know that you ordered Paco to be killed and tried to have Mikio killed. You will be charged with those crimes."

A smirk crossed Ghost's face, but the gangster clenched both fists tight. And the twitch struck again.

"You will be facing the death penalty if convicted."

The smirk disappeared. The fists remained clenched. He stared back at Tom with dead eyes. And then it struck Tom like lightning. He remembered where he had seen those eyes before. It was the time he had taken Sara and his son to the aquarium in Monterey.

Sara and David had wandered off to one of the gift shops, and Tom wandered over to a large tank of seawater. Inside, a great white shark, recently captured, thrashed back and forth. Tom watched, fascinated, as the beast effortlessly sliced through effervescent green. Other sharks and marine life parted in his path, striving to put distance between themselves and this killer. Tom stared into the creature's eyes, captivated by their chilling deadness. It was the haunting stare of a killing machine. It was the look Ghost gave him now.

"So what ya' going to do? Convict me of another murder?" His gaze locked on Tom. "Who gives a rip? Look at my sheet. I'm already an LWOP—a life without the possibility of parole twice over. Two back-to-backs. Go ahead add a death sentence. I'll be dead before the courts ever get around to shoving a needle in my arm." Ghost glared at Tom. "Take your best shot, sport."

Tom matched the man's intense stare. He leaned forward and lowered his voice to a whisper. "You're right about one thing, Ghost. You'll be six feet underground before they ever get you to death row." A smile crept across Tom's face. "The NF knows you showed your cowardice in front of the enemy. An NF leader that the Mafia punked out. And they know you had Paco whacked to keep that secret from leaking out. You're history. You let Mikio escape and Rascal's still breathing. Now everybody's going to know. You got nowhere to hide. How does it feel to be hunted down by your own kind?"

Ghost erupted. He screamed as he furiously yanked at his chains trying to get at Tom. "You can't talk to me like that!" Ghost lurched forward with so much fury, Tom thought the chains might give. "You know who I am? Do you know what I can do to your family?"

Tom glared back, undaunted. "You are a little man in a maximum security prison. I'm not that worried."

"And what about your family? I heard through the grapevine that someone is shooting photos of her. The ones with your wife going about her business totally unaware she is being watched?"

Tom felt like the wind had been knocked out of him. "That was you?"

Ghost strained at his chains. "Show me a little respect, cop. Because you know what I can bring down on you. I'll have you hunted down like a dog. I'll have your family killed—piece by piece."

Tom shot to his feet and lunged at Ghost.

Garcia jumped in his path. "Whoa, partner. Trust me. It's not worth it."

Tom yanked himself free and stabbed a finger inches from Ghost's face. "I'm going to enjoy hanging a death sentence around your scrawny neck. And if you dare send anyone after my family, it will be the last order you ever give. Am I making myself clear?"

Ghost shot Tom a wicked smile and leaned forward, speaking just above a whisper. "Too bad about your little boy. Died in a car accident, right?"

Tom glared back, fighting for control.

"I heard there was a gang shooting just down the street. Since I'm stuck here for the rest of my life, I wanna to tell you a little secret about your boy." Ghost leered at him before continuing. "I was there that night— driving that car."

An icy hand gripped Tom's heart.

Ghost nodded. "The kid with the stupid baseball hat and his momma—now there was a fine, *fine* woman. I wanted to stay to say hello to *that*."

Hate paralyzed Tom.

The gangster gave him a sickly smirk. "But I had better things to do that night. Never looked back after I slammed into your family. Too bad

Daddy wasn't with them. I could have scored a home run—a cop and his whole family." Again, Ghost sneered. "Thinking back, I've wondered if the boy was still alive when I smashed into your car that night. When I ran off and left him to die. What do you think...oinker?"

Garcia grabbed Tom again. "It's not worth it, partner. You got him and he knows it. If you stoop to his level, you would be the only one getting in trouble."

Seething, Tom glared at Ghost. "See you in the gas chamber. I will be the one watching you die." He whirled around and stormed out of the room.

Ghost screamed, "You're a dead man, Kagan" just moments before Tom slammed the door shut.

Chapter 31

Tom felt wasted after the face-off with Ghost. He and Garcia checked into a motel late in the day before Tom realized his cell phone had been turned off all day. He activated it and saw he had one message from Stevenson asking for a callback.

That would have to wait. He needed to work off a little stress. After the raids in Santa Rosa last week, Stevenson remained behind on this trip to search for Tweaker. They were still sifting through the evidence, trying to tie pieces together from the series of attacks since Paco's murder.

Quickly changing into running clothes, Tom prepared to leave when a rap sounded at the door. Tom opened it to find Garcia running in place. The man's running outfit made Tom blink several times. Garcia looked like taggers worked him over with a rainbow-colored spray can. Tom stared at the stocky agent was wearing a bright-red T-shirt, shocking pink running shorts that were way too tight, and Halloween-orange socks sticking out of black tennis shoes. His hairy legs made the whole outfit seem more outlandish. "Come on! Time's wasting."

Tom shook his head. "I'm not going anywhere with you looking like *that*."

Garcia glanced down at his clothes and shrugged. "I forgot my work-out gear. The shop down the street catered only to women. I bought what I could. Come on, no one will notice."

"You gotta be kidding." Tom shut the door behind him. "Try to keep up, will you? I have a lot of energy to burn off today." Tom eyed Garcia's outfit. "And I just hope we don't run into anybody I know."

Garcia laughed, strutting down the corridor leading outside. Tom followed, trying not to stare at the man's pink shorts.

Garcia glanced back. "I know it must have been hard not to whale on that slimeball. Ghost had it coming."

As he walked, Tom moved his arms side to side to loosen up muscles in his lower back. "When he mentioned my family, it just set me off. And then when he talked about my son..."

"Hey, bro. Look on the bright side. If something happens to that snake, you will be in the clear. At least we went on the record warning him about the danger. And you gave the jerk a chance to cooperate."

A gray sky and salty air greeted them as they neared the beach. Tom felt a cool ocean breeze as he left the protection of the motel. A paved walkway, generously speckled with seagull droppings, led them through clumps of tall pampas grass waving in the wind. The harsh squawking of seagulls rained down on them as the hungry birds circled above, looking for garbage to feast upon. The path ended abruptly at the edge of a sandy beach. They began to jog, their footsteps laboring in the loose sand until they neared the wet runway of the seashore.

The two men matched strides as much as Garcia's shorter legs would allow. Tom's eyes scanned the oceanfront. "Ghost surprised me." Tom's mind replayed the confrontation earlier in the afternoon. "I thought once we let him know we knew about his little *secret*, he'd cave and want to deal. But it just set him off like a firecracker. He just exploded."

Garcia shook his head. "Oh, it got to him all right. That's part of why he got in your face. Not standing up for himself against the enemy, in that situation...it's not something the NF will forgive. He knows this is going to be brought out in the open. He knows it'll hurt him."

"Why is it going to hurt him? He was a victim."

"I guess Ghost is just going to have to deal with it."

"The way he was mad dogging you, Tom, you'd better hope he never gets out of prison."

"Why?"

"He blames you for all his problems right now. You're threatening to expose him. For my sake, watch your back. I don't want to attend your funeral."

"Well, I don't think I have to worry about him getting out anytime soon. Besides, he'll have no pull with the NF after this."

Garcia slowed down for a moment. "Tell me about the photos. What was that all about?"

Tom stopped running and leaned over to catch his breath. "This has to stay between us, Hector. No one—not even Stevenson—knows about this. If my boss finds out, he will yank me off this case and probably out of the gang unit."

Garcia nodded.

"For some time I have been getting these photos—of me, Sara, and other friends—anonymously mailed to the office with a note that simply says, 'We are watching.'"

"Jeez, buddy," Garcia said. "And you told no one?"

Tom shrugged. "At first, I would have them processed for prints by a friend at the lab on the QT. Tried to run down the paper stock, photo process, and locations from which it was mailed. Nothing came back that helped me identify who might be sending these warnings."

Standing up, Tom flexed his back, trying to stretch out a strained muscle. "After a while, I gave up. After I while, I just thought some guy was trying to mess with my mind. "And now that you know Ghost ordered it?"

"I've got all the letters and photos back at my office. I'll turn them over to you and see what you might be able to put together, see who's been Ghost's arms and legs out on the street. I don't think it was a gangster. They'd be too visible in some of the places those photos were taken."

"You bet," Garcia said. "I still can't believe you didn't tell anyone."

Ruefully, Tom nodded. "Yeah, I was caught between a rock and a hard place If I told Fat Louie, he'd just use it against me to justify dumping me out of the unit and back to patrol. I needed to be where I am right now for a number of reasons—including finding out who is doing this to me and my family. And more important, where I could mostly likely protect Sara. If they pulled me, I would have no eyes and ears into the gang unit."

"Which was why you went so hard and heavy on the gangsters."

"Exactly. Fat Louie and the others thought it was just about what happened to David. That may have been part of it, but I needed to find out who was watching me and my family—and why they were doing it. Now it all makes sense, at least in Ghost's screwed-up mind."

A beacon flashed from the mirrors of a lighthouse nearly two miles away. The light swept across the face of darkening clouds pouring in from the open sea. The beach ended at the base of the lighthouse's rocky foundation.

Tom pointed toward the flashing lights. "See that lighthouse?"

Garcia grunted and groaned in response, sweat beginning to create dark spots on his sweatshirt across his chest and beneath his arms.

"Last one there buys dinner." Tom kicked it into high gear and left Garcia in his wake.

Chapter 32

It was late before Tom remembered to return Stevenson's call. Garcia wound up paying for dinner while complaining that Tom cheated. The free meal just made the food more appetizing. They had just returned late to their motel rooms when Tom remembered his partner's message.

Mary answered when Tom finally dialed the home number. "I'll get Bill, and Tom—have fun in Tahoe."

Puzzled, he waited until he heard his partner come on the line. It sounded like Mary woke him up.

Before Tom could say anything, Stevenson said, "Hector filled me in on the interview with Ghost." His partner sounded worried. "I hear it got a little tense. Care to share?"

"Not much to tell. It was short and sweet—except I lost my cool."

"Don't let it get to you."

"I know. I've got to chill out. Not let this get so personal."

"Speaking of chilling out, we're all set up. We're going fishing, my friend."

"Bill, I already told you—"

"Hold on and hear me out. I've already cleared it with the DA's office and Sara. Got all the bases covered."

"No, Bill. We got a lot of follow-up to do on this case before we waltz it before the grand jury."

"Plenty of time. I've got everything we need and the jury doesn't convene for two weeks. All the reports are filed, witnesses tucked away, and evidence processed or in the lab getting worked on. Instead of twiddling our thumbs, let's take some downtime and head up to the high country. Here's the part you'll love—it won't cost you a dime."

"Bill, let it go. I'm not about to go fishing when we have all this work ahead. We need to be prepared for anything the defense might throw at us. So—thanks, but no thanks. Maybe another time.

Stevenson sounded disappointed. "Well, tell Sara I tried, will you? See you when you get back."

"Later," Tom said before hanging up. He stretched out on the bed and folded his hands behind his head. Tom traveled down a road he rarely ventured. His son's innocent face loomed in his mind and the memory still felt like salt poured into a fresh wound.

Tom turned on his side and stared across the empty room, memories finally driving him to his feet. He reached into his overnight bag, pulled out a bottle of scotch, and plopped several ice cubes from the ice bucket. He filled the glass to the rim and placed the bottle on the nightstand next to the bed. He held the drink up and gazed at the amber light filtering through the glass. He finally raised it to his lips and took a long sip. It burned all the way down. He grimaced as the smoky taste burned his stomach.

Across the room, he stared at his reflection in the mirror above the dresser. He knew he was not the man he was before everything turned bad. "Just let me get through another night," he said to the image in the mirror. He took another sip and wandered back to bed. He grabbed the bottle and refilled the glass once again.

The solitude of his motel room pounded in his ears, quietness looming in the shadows like demons. He hated this feeling, whether in the silence of a motel room or in a room full of people. This sense of loss gnawing at the very fiber of his soul.

Ice clinked in the glass as he drank. He glanced at the bottle. There'd be a lot less by morning. He intended to drink until the demons went away. Or until sleep came to rid him of this pain.

Chapter **33**

Pelican Bay State Prison

Terry Lentz came as close to insubordination as he dared. An order to allow Ghost to have a cell mate crossed Terry's desk that morning. The warden had authorized the move even after Terry warned of the consequences.

"Ghost is targeted by the gang to be hit, boss. We can't let this move happen."

"It's a done deal, Terry. Your information is wrong. I have it from reliable sources that everything is good between these two. And Ghost is not objecting, so why are you concerned?"

"Because they are going to kill him."

"Says who—you?"

Terry stormed out of the warden's office, afraid to say what came to his mind.

Even Ghost seemed blasé about the warden's decision. "Hey, what will be, will be." Terry was forced to sit back and watch.

Ghost intended to do just that. Watch and wait—for the right time to kill.

He did not have long to wait. It happened three nights after his roommate—a muscle-bound soldier recruited from the streets of San Jose—settled into his cell.

It came at three in the morning.

The first warning was the stench emanating from a handmade weapon the assassin quietly eased from his rectum. A shank! The second warning was the sound of his attacker moving slowly from his bunk. The creep was making his move. Just what Ghost would have done if he got the order to kill. Hit in the middle of the night when your victim was asleep.

Ghost coiled himself to make his own move. He saw his roommate's feet lower to the ground. The man hurled himself at Ghost, who quickly deflected the first blow intended to slice his carotid artery. He could not stop the less-lethal stabs to his head, chest, arms, and back. He struggled to roll out from under his larger opponent.

The attacker was able to get one more deep thrust into Ghost's chest, sliding the shank between two ribs and burying it deep.

Ghost gained footing and unleashed his own fury. Ignoring his wounds, he fought to survive, lashing out with his fists, striking the other man in the face, gouging his eyes in an attempt to blind him, and jamming his knee into the other man's groin. His attacker had lost the element of surprise and lost the shank still buried inside Ghost. The shank fell to the ground as the two men struggled.

Ghost blinded the attacker by tearing at his eyes, and the man screamed as Ghost slammed his head into the concrete floor. Blinded and stunned, the attacker clawed at his eyes in a futile attempt to regain sight.

With catlike quickness, Ghost worked his way behind his attacker and wrapped his arms around the man's throat. He squeezed his arms into a vise and began to choke the blinded cell mate, clamping down on the carotid to prevent blood from reaching the brain.

His attacker frantically pawed at Ghost's arms, trying to break the death hold. Ghost just squeezed harder. Within seconds, the bigger man slumped forward, temporarily unconscious. Ghost had only seconds to finish the job.

He yanked out the hidden wire behind the toilet and wrapped it around the unconscious man's throat. Using it as a garrote, Ghost heaved the man onto his back like a person pulling a large bag of grain. For a brief second, the man regained consciousness and clawed at the wire around his throat.

It was over in seconds.

Ghost used the man's own weight against him. The attacker's body went limp. Ghost continued to add pressure to the wire until he was sure the man was dead. As his cell mate slipped to the ground, Ghost grasped the shank and jammed the blade deep into his attacker's heart.

A few moments later, Ghost weakly sank to the floor as adrenaline from the fight dissipated. Guards came running to the door, alerted to the sound of the struggle. They found Ghost lying on the concrete floor in a pool of mixed blood—his and the dead man's. His attacker, eyes still open, lay sprawled on the concrete floor.

Ghost was still breathing.

Tweaker stood in the shadow of a large oak tree. Fluorescent streetlights struggled to illuminate the lawn where he stood, but the towering oak protected him from prying eyes. He studied people coming and going from the emergency room of the Santa Rosa Community Hospital. Too many people. He'd never make it past security. He began to circle the building looking for another way in.

Using shadows as cover, he worked his way around the sprawling complex until he saw an employee entrance. As he waited, Tweaker reached down and felt the bulge under his coat, a handgun he'd shoved into the waistband of his trousers. Several employees clustered together as they approached the door. One of them punched a code into a keypad. He was too far away to be able to see the sequence of numbers. He slid along the wall, waiting in the dark until the next employee arrived.

A nurse. It took her only a moment to activate the door. She swung it wide as she entered, and Tweaker was able to reach the door before it clicked shut. He pulled it open and poked his head inside. No one was around.

Halfway down the hall, he heard someone walking in his direction. Frantically, he searched for a place to hide. He tried several doors. Locked. The footsteps drew near. Unless he found a place, quick, they'd be on him in seconds. He grasped the handle of the last remaining door in the hallway and gave a pull. It opened to a darkened room.

Tweaker scurried inside and closed the door behind him, hearing footsteps pass on the other side of the door. Voices. A door opened and the voices disappeared.

He groped around the dark until his fingers touched what felt like a light switch. Flicking it on, he became momentarily blinded by the bright illumination from a fluorescent bulb. He was in a supply closet. He switched the light off and opened the door a crack to peer out.

His arm brushed against a fistful of keys hanging above the light switch. He closed the door once again, switched the light on a second time, and saw tags attached to each key. Printing on the tabs identified the rooms these keys opened. He smiled.

Across the hall, he saw a door marked *Employees Lounge*. He stepped out and dashed across the hallway. He pulled on the door but it was locked. He returned where he saw the keys, grabbed them, and flipped through each until he located what he was looking for. He slipped the key into the lock and felt a satisfying click as the door opened.

He glanced inside. No one. A television had been left on and a late-night movie about vampires played to an empty room. On one wall was a row of unlocked lockers. Tweaker tried several until he found one that contained an orderly's uniform left hanging on a hook inside. He quickly stripped and pulled on the uniform.

He took a peek into a full-length mirror attached to the door. The uniform came with an ID tag clipped to a pocket, however the pants were short and the shirt was tight in the chest. It would have to do. He slipped his gun into the waistband of his pants and cinched it up tightly, then pulled the uniform shirt over the gun. He took his street clothes and shoved them in the trash.

Now that he was dressed to blend, he searched for work tools that matched his uniform. He crossed over and entered the supply room. In one corner, he located a mop and bucket that moved on rollers. He filled the bucket with water and soap. Now he was ready to rock and roll.

Tweaker followed the signs to the Intensive Care Unit. The lights had been turned down to allow those who were conscious to rest. He pushed open the double doors and saw a nurses' station down the hall. One nurse was by herself behind the desk tapping away on a computer. No other staff members. Large plate-glass windows allowed visitors a view of each room if the curtains were not drawn.

He drew his mop out, wet it down, and pulled it through a ringer to squeeze out excess moisture. He pretended to mop the floor, working slowly down the edge of the hallway as he peered through each window he passed. The ICU was L-shaped, with the nurses' station at the bend in the hallway. He worked his way to the duty nurse without seeing the person he was searching for.

The nurse glanced up at Tweaker with a surprised look. Tweaker nodded at her, flashed a grin, and kept on mopping. Out of the corner of his eye, he saw the nurse shrug and return her attention to the computer.

His hands were wet with perspiration, and his face felt flushed. Footsteps came from behind him—another nurse passing. He kept his head down and appeared to be wrapped up in his work. The nurse entered one of the darkened rooms to his right without speaking.

Tweaker finally worked his way down the hall and rounded the corner. As he made the turn, he glanced down the hallway and nearly dropped the broom. A uniformed officer was seated in a chair outside one of the rooms reading a magazine. The cop glanced up and stared in Tweaker's direction. The gangster vigorously moved the mop across the floor as his arm brushed the gun in his waistband.

It seemed like an eternity before he dared to look up. The cop had returned to his reading. It surprised him that a cop was outside the door. At least this made his search much simpler. His target must be inside. It made his mission twice has hard.

Using the mop as cover, he gradually moved past the door until his back was to the officer. He glanced back to see the cop with his head down, reading. Tweaker slowly grabbed the barrel of his gun and eased it out. He dared not breathe.

In one whirling movement he spun and tried to bury the butt of the weapon in the cop's skull. The officer fell face-first to the ground unconscious. A woman screamed. Tweaker whirled around as a nurse fled down the hall. Security would be here in minutes.

Tweaker rushed into the room with gun drawn. His target lay on the bed. Rascal! The patient tried to pull himself to a sitting position, his eyes wide with terror.

Tweaker pointed the gun at Rascal's head and squeezed the trigger.

The explosion rocked the room. He fired two more times, watching Rascal's body twitch and then slump onto the bed.

Tweaker heard another woman scream after the last shot. He dashed past the nurses' station and out the ICU doors. More screaming and yelling erupted behind him.

He kept on running until he was outside. He slipped into the cover of darkness and entered a grove of eucalyptus trees. He paused in the shadows as sirens wailed in the distance. Police. He whirled around and fled deeper into the darkness.

Mission accomplished.

Rascal was dead.

Chapter 34

Fishing would have been a bad idea. Tom started running the moment he'd returned to Santa Rosa two weeks ago from Pelican Bay. And he was still running—from crime scenes to the DA's office and back to the streets looking for more answers. More witnesses. More informants.

Barely a couple days back from his trip up north, he received a frantic call from Terry Lentz telling him the bad news. "I told them something was going to happen. Ghost got stabbed up pretty bad, but not before killing his cellie. They airlifted him to a hospital near San Francisco. They put around-the-clock security on him."

At five the next morning, Tom was jarred from sleep by a call from Stevenson. Rascal had been shot to death in his hospital bed by Tweaker. An officer had been knocked unconscious. Security cameras captured the picture of the gunman as he fled ICU. Stevenson and other gang officers were scouring the city and county to hunt him down. It seemed Tweaker had crawled into a hole and vanished.

While the manhunt was going on outside, Tom had been trapped in Phillips's office for two days going over evidence, trying to see what could be salvaged since Rascal's death. An indictment had been handed down by the grand jury charging Ghost with Paco's murder, but prosecution had to put it on hold until he was cleared from the hospital. Fortunately, they videotaped the entire interview with Rascal. The video was now their best evidence.

Tom contacted Mikio by telephone and updated him on the latest killing and Ghost's injuries. "Now, make sure you and your nephew stay put. We'll let you know if anything comes up. Just stay away from Santa Rosa."

Mikio was not happy about the news, but he agreed to sit tight.

Garcia's unit was running ragged. They had split their time between searching for Tweaker and guarding Ghost in the hospital while trying to keep up on their other cases. The last two weeks had become a blur. And here he was stuck in the DA's office trying to save their case.

"I think that about wraps it up." Phillips pushed the last file in his direction. "I've looked at all the evidence, witnesses' statements, and facts of the case. I think we'll do fine. I'll be able to salvage the information Rascal gave us."

Tom reached for the file and tucked it away in his briefcase. Then his cell phone vibrated. Garcia.

"I've got some really bad news," Garcia said, his voice hoarse and angry. "Twenty minutes ago, Ghost jumped my guy at the hospital. He thought Ghost was sleeping, but the prisoner somehow slipped out of his restraints. Knocked my guy out cold. Thank God he didn't kill him."

Tom clutched the phone. Ghost out on the street—free! "H-he escaped? I thought he was barely alive." His stomach tightened as he remembered Ghost's face when they last met. The threats against his family. This could not be happening.

"Yeah, well he fooled us. Fooled the doctors. And now he's just vanished." Garcia paused. "And here's some more bad news—he is armed."

A chill swept through Tom as he closed the cell phone and slipped it into his pocket.

Phillips stared across the desk with concern. "Trouble?"

"Ghost just escaped from the hospital. And he's armed."

"How? I thought he couldn't walk."

Tom just shook his head. "The good news is that Garcia's man survived. Just a bump on the head and a major headache."

"I can't believe this guy is loose, Tom. What was CDC thinking guard-ing this creep with only one man?" She rubbed her temples with both hands. "I'm glad we moved Mikio and his nephew out of the area. We've got to let the other witnesses know, provide them protection if needed. Got to put together a full-court press to track Ghost down. Hector and what's left of his crew are coming up to hunt for this guy and to protect our witnesses."

He tried to adjust to the news. Ghost on the street—free—never fac-tored into Tom's plans as a possibility. The man had been locked up in one of the state's tightest security cells. He was not supposed to *ever* be free. And yet, here he was. Free and armed.

"Where do you think he'll go?" she asked. "If he's smart, he'll run as far away as he can."

"He might, but he's really got nowhere to run. He knows the NF and the cops are after him. It's not like Ghost, with all his tats, can set up shop in Montana or wherever. He wouldn't feel comfortable going south into Mafia territory."

"What about Mexico?"

"I doubt it. He's fourth-generation American, probably has no family ties on that side of the border. He would be a fish out of water down there. No, he's going to hide somewhere up here is my guess."

She looked up at Tom. "But why would he come here?"

Tom scratched his head. "Maybe he wants to tie up loose ends. Maybe reach out to people he knows for help." He stood and picked up his brief-case. "We've turned his world upside down with this investigation. He may even want revenge."

Phillips stood and walked around the desk toward Tom. "Most of the gang members I've prosecuted I haven't thought twice about, but this guy—"

"He won't get anywhere near this office." Tom tried to sound more confident than he felt.

She came close. Tom caught a whiff of her perfume as she looked up into his eyes. "This guy scares me." Her voice wavered.

"He won't get near you. I promise." Tom squeezed her hands, trying to give her the assurance he couldn't find inside.

As he walked out of the office, he tried to shake off a feeling that he was missing something that might come back to bite him. This case was as fluid as water. Witnesses killed. A suspect escaped. What else could happen?

He shook this off and focused on what he could control. He had to find Ghost before the killer hurt anyone else.

And then Tom thought of Sara. She would be just the kind of target Ghost might choose. Tom clenched his fist. He'd already lost one person in his family. He'd be damned if he'd lose another. Ghost would have to kill him first. That feeling about a pending storm came back to haunt Tom. That storm finally struck.

He braced himself for what was about to unfold. There was one more person he needed to talk to. When it was all over, he hoped he still had a job.

Fat Louie was still in his office when Tom returned to the station. He hesitated for a moment, took a deep breath, and knocked on Art Crenshaw's door. "Can I speak to you for a moment, Sarge?"

His supervisor looked up warily. "Yeah, take a load off." He motioned to a chair in front of his desk. "What's up?"

Settling himself in the chair, Tom started right in. "Did you hear our primary suspect, James 'Ghost' Hernandez, escaped from custody while in a San Francisco hospital?"

"Heard the BOLO go out earlier. Man, the guy escaped from maximum security. Who would have thought?"

"Yeah, go figure." Tom took another deep breath. "There is something you need to know, Sarge. Something that's not going to make you happy."

Fat Louie twisted his face into a grimace as if he was in pain. "And what might that be, Detective?"

"For some time now, I have been receiving surveillance photos of Sara and me mailed here to the office with a note that says, 'We are watching.'"

"How come this is the first time I—?"

"Because you'd bounce me from the unit. And this is the only place I could operate to try to protect my family. If you shipped me back to patrol,

I would be dumb and blind. No intelligence to work off. No informant to go after. I couldn't let you do that."

Fat Louie's face hardened, his eyes narrowed. "I should—"

"Before you fire me, Sarge, hear me out." Tom shifted in his seat as he tried to figure out exactly what to tell his boss that wouldn't get him fired. "I didn't see any other option. Spelling everything out to you would put you in a difficult position. Now I am asking for just a little more time to catch this guy and put an end to it. After that—"

"What? Fire you?"

Tom looked down at his hands. "After I catch this guy, boss, you can do whatever you want. I won't fight it."

Fat Louie ran his hand over his face and rubbed his jaw. He clasped both hands on the desk and leaned forward. "Just tell me this, Tom. Why couldn't you trust me?"

Tom stared at his supervisor for a moment and thought he saw a look of hurt in the other man's eyes. "Frankly, I couldn't trust anyone with the safety of my family. I had to take care of this myself." He paused. "I'm sorry I kept you out of the loop, Sergeant. I really am."

Fat Louie sat back in his chair, clasping his hands behind his head. "You are the best cop I know. But you are also my biggest headache." He straightened and leaned forward. "Here is what we are going to do. I want you to go after this SOB with everything you have. Let me know what you need and I will make sure you get it. Once you get this guy and the dust settles, we'll figure out the rest. Now, get out of here and get some sleep. I'll put a call to the sheriff's office and alert them to the risk out at your ranch—"

"Sarge, SSU is going to help out with around-the-clock protection until we nab Ghost. But a call to the SO would be great. Thanks."

Fat Louie nodded. "Just one more thing. If you call me Fat Louie behind my back one more time, I will personally see that you are patrolling Oakmont for the rest of your career."

Tom's face must have registered his shock. Fat Louie sat back and howled. "Oh, I wish I could have a photo of your mug, Tom. I'd have tacked that up on my board. Now…get out of here and do some real police work."

Tom walked out of the office, shaking his head. Maybe he was wrong about Fat Louie. And maybe he'd better start calling him Art Crenshaw from here on out. It was the only smile Tom allowed himself in days. It was time to get back to the hunt.

Chapter **35**

UC Medical Center, San Francisco, California

Ghost felt the thrill of freedom and the gut-wrenching fear of a hunted man. He quickly stripped off the clothes of the unconscious agent and dressed himself. He was armed with two weapons: one large semiauto and a small backup the agent had kept strapped to his leg.

He even stole the holsters.

Ghost slowed near the front doors and walked out into a sprawling parking lot near the hospital. He imagined staff had discovered his absence by now. It would take a few more minutes before the cops started his way.

A siren screamed in the distance. Had his escape been reported? This was a big city. Things took time. He sauntered through the parking lot. A man running through this place would draw attention, although his escape would depend upon getting away as quickly as possible.

A young woman edged her car into a parking spot right past him, inching it into the tight squeeze as if she feared damage at any moment. The car looked like it had just been driven off a sales lot. It must be brand new, and this driver must be suffering from new-car jitters.

The moment the young woman opened the driver's door, Ghost shoved a gun barrel in her face. He pushed her back in the car while covering her mouth with his hand. "Scream and I'll kill you."

She nodded, eyes wide with fear.

"Move over." He slowly removed his hand and waited to see if she obeyed.

"Please don't hurt me." Her gaze shifted between his face and the gun.

Ghost did not say a word. As he crawled in behind the wheel, he watched several black and whites in his rearview mirror, their emergency lights flashing as they screeched into the parking lot from several directions. One of the patrol units drove slowly behind him. The driver eyed those on foot and others climbing into cars as he drove by.

Ghost grabbed the nape of her neck. "Kiss me, and act like you love it."

Terror-stricken, she complied.

As they kissed, Ghost watched the patrol car roll past them. The cop glanced into their car and then moved on. He stopped near the hospital entrance, then jumped out of the car and ran inside. He was followed by other officers.

Ghost fought for control. *Slow and easy.* He eased the car out of the parking lot and onto the street. More police cars rushed past him without giving him a second glance. He drove several blocks before slowing down and pulling to the curb.

"Consider this your lucky day," he snarled, reaching over the frightened woman and opening the passenger-side door. With his right foot, he kicked her out of the car.

She fell half on the sidewalk and half in the gutter. She screamed as he drove away. He rolled down his window and could hear her screaming from a block away. He stepped on the gas.

He drove across the Golden Gate Bridge and traveled for several miles until he spotted an entrance to a large shopping mall just beyond the outskirts of Sausalito and Marin City along Interstate 101. The shopping center bustled with traffic and hundreds of vehicles were parked in the lot. He wedged the car into a tight parking space and got out.

He found a late-model Ford with its windows down. Next to this car was a truck. On the door panel was an advertisement for a building contractor's services. In the truck bed was a box of tools. Ghost grabbed the toolbox and threw it inside the open car. He started to look under the dash to figure how to hot wire the car when he saw a bulge under the passenger-side floor mat. He flipped the mat back and saw a spare set of keys.

Thank you for your stupidity. He inserted one of the keys and the car roared to life. He let the car idle as he grabbed a screwdriver and pliers from the toolbox. Within minutes he switched plates with another similar vehicle.

He was out of the parking lot and leaving the city within twenty minutes. By nightfall, Ghost crossed the Santa Rosa city limits.

He only had a few hours to take care of business before things heated up. He stopped at a gas station and used a telephone directory to locate the address of one of his contacts. With one phone call, Ghost was able to find out what law enforcement still could not find.

Tweaker's hideout.

He spotted an abandoned mobile home near the airport a few miles north of Santa Rosa. He parked the car and approached on foot. As he edged toward the trailer, gun in hand, he heard a dog bark and somebody tell the animal to shut up. He knocked on the door.

"Tweaker, I know you're in there. It's Ghost."

The door eased open. Tweaker peered out, a look of shock on his face. "Come on in, man. Heard 'bout your escape on the radio. Wow! My homie makes the pigs look like fools. I like it!" His words gushed out in a wave of nervousness, and he raised his clenched hand for a fist-tap.

Ghost ignored the gesture as he entered the trailer. He heard a radio squawking somewhere inside. The trailer was a mess: Kitchen counter piled high with garbage, a sink used as a dumping site for hamburger wrappers, and old milkshake cups and other fast-food wrappings strewn about the place. An odor of human sweat—mixed with rancid meat and putrid milkshakes—filled the trailer with disgusting smells. Ghost searched for a clean place to sit. He gave up.

A dog came out of hiding and sniffed Ghost's leg. The animal padded into the bedroom and sniffed the edge of an unmade bed. Ghost watched as the dog lifted his leg to urinate on the mattress. Tweaker seemed oblivious to what his dog was doing.

"A real honor, bro," Tweaker said. "Huh…why you here, man?"

Ghost tried to hide his disgust of this place and this man. "I wanted to thank you for following my orders, Tweaker. For taking care of business the way you did. You'll be looked upon with favor by the brothers. You have many friends inside."

Tweaker relaxed. Ghost let the younger man bask in the lies he fed him for a moment.

"Can you help me out with a little information?"

"Anything, bro." Tweaker gave him the same look Ghost had seen on the dog's face—a dumb animal trying to please its master.

"I need to know where Mikio is hanging his hat for starters. And the cops that are causing us problems—Bill Stevenson and Tom Kagan. I have some information, but I need to find out everything you can on these guys. And I need it now."

Tweaker gave him another puppy dog look. "This Kagan, the one who trashed my place, I don't know much about him. But the other oinker—Stevenson. He and the gang unit harassed me and my homies for years. I got a cousin whose younger brother goes to school with Stevenson's kid. We know where that pig lives."

Ghost listened intently, memorizing the street and description of Stevenson's house. "And Mikio?"

Tweaker looked at him like Ghost had caught him peeing on the bed. "I can't tell you exactly where he shacks up. Some apartment complex on the west side. Heard he took off—he and his nephew Gato. I'll ask around and see what I can turn up."

"Appreciate it. And what about the DA's office? Who is the prosecutor?"

The eager-to-please look returned. Tweaker nodded, lapping up Ghost's attention. "I'm not sure, but they have one lady who always seems to wind up slamming my bros, a broad by the name of Diane Phillips. She handles most of the gang cases."

Ghost turned as if to leave.

"Is there anything else I can help you with?" Tweaker edged toward him.

The older man smiled at Tweaker. "No, you've done enough. I'll take it from here. And you won't tell anyone about my visit?"

"No man, my lips are zipped."

Ghost knew a liar when he saw one. He extended his hand. "Put it there, brother. You are a true soldado."

Beaming, Tweaker reached out to shake his hand. Ghost grabbed his hand and tightened. In a flash Ghost spun the younger man around and wrapped his arms around Tweaker's neck like a vise. He jerked the boy's head to the left with a vicious snap. Ghost felt a pop as the vertebrae cracked. The young man slumped to the floor, never to rise again.

Tweaker would not brag to anyone.

The dog nosed Tweaker's body as if trying to wake him. The mutt whined as it stood over its fallen master, licking the dead man's face. Ghost kicked the dog away and rifled through Tweaker's pockets. He found a wad of cash in one of the pockets. Seizing the money, Ghost took one last look around the trailer. No evidence he had been here.

He stepped outside, closed the door, and made sure to wipe down any place where his prints might be found. Tweaker was no longer a threat. It was time to focus on the cop. Time to make use of all the lowdown he'd been given on Kagan.

Time to make the cop feel what it was like to fear.

Chapter 36

Ghost spent the rest of the night cruising Santa Rosa. It would be a while before anyone found Tweaker's body. And even if they did, they'd be hard-pressed to link the killing to him. If they did — he could care less.

Just one more body.

Thanks to the late Tweaker, Ghost easily located the Stevenson residence. He already knew where to find Kagan and his family, but Kagan would be watching and waiting. Better to hurt Kagan where he least expected it.

At sunup, Ghost bought some coffee and a breakfast burrito and parked his stolen car down the block from where Stevenson lived. A city park was a stone's throw from the cop's house, a tree-shaded two-story residence with a garage facing the street.

Ghost grabbed his food and strode deep into the park, where passing motorists and cops were unlikely to notice him. He stretched out on the cool grass, shaded by large sycamore trees. The leaves were just turning, autumn's first hint that winter's dance of death might be right around the corner.

Ghost lay back and began his surveillance.

A car pulled out of the garage and stopped several hours later. A woman climbed out of the car, walked up to the front door, and returned with a small boy in tow. They got into the car and drove away. Ghost watched the car until it turned a corner. *Detective Stevenson, you make this too easy. There goes Momma and son. Now, let's wait till Papa comes home.*

Ghost lay back in the grass and fell asleep. He awoke several times during the day, each time peering down the street to see if there were any new developments. By midafternoon, he had slept enough to watch the house continuously until dusk. Earlier in the afternoon he had seen the woman and child return. *Now, where is Papa?*

At about supper time, an unmarked police car pulled up to the front of the house. The car had the telltale all-black paint job with tinted windows and antennas sticking up like porcupine quivers from the trunk. Another unmarked cop car pulled up behind it. Both drivers climbed out and sauntered up to the front door, joking with each other.

Here comes Poppa Bear and a friend. Ain't that sweet.

Ghost smiled to himself as he recognized the second man. Kagan! As Ghost settled in for a long surveillance on the house, he remembered Stevenson's boy in the house and thought of a children's poem he once read a long time ago. A line from the poem seemed to fit as he watched Kagan disappear into the house. "'Will you step into my parlour,' said the spider to the fly."

Ghost added his own words to the poem. "Where you die and I'll live like a free man once again." A plan was already in the making as Ghost began to spin his web.

Tom followed Bill into the Stevenson home. As they entered the kitchen, he saw Sara standing at the sink washing dishes and Mary leaning over the stove. Mary glanced up and smiled. Stevenson walked over and put his arms around her, kissing her on the neck. Then he slyly reached around Mary, grabbed a spoon, and dipped it into a pan of sautéed vegetables.

Mary laughed and swatted his hand before he could take a bite. "Wait till dinner." She peered around Stevenson. "Do me a favor, Tom. Take my husband into the living room and keep him there until dinner is ready."

"You got it." He looked over at Sara, who was wiping her hands on a dish towel. She had given him one brief smile since they arrived. She seemed caught up in her own thoughts. "Come on, Bill, let's stay out of their way."

Stevenson followed him into the next room and plopped down in a gray-leather recliner near the fireplace. The arms of the chair were frayed from constant use. Tom settled on the sofa near the recliner when he heard footsteps running down the hall. Jonathan burst into the room and jumped into his father's lap. Stevenson hugged the boy and tousled his chestnut-brown hair. Jonathan glanced at Tom.

"Hi, Uncle Tommy."

Tom smiled and gave him a wave. Jonathan turned to his father. "Dad, can you read more of that pirate story to me? I left it right here near your chair." Without waiting for an answer, the boy clambered off his father's lap, found the book, and gave it to him.

Tom watched the boy's face as Stevenson began to read. He could tell the boy had entered the world of make-believe as the story unfolded. A story of pirates, battles at sea, and maidens held hostage in the clutches of evil. As he watched the boy's attentive face, Tom thought of a time when David snuggled next to him, father and son swept away by some adventure story he could no longer remember.

He shook his head as if he could somehow shake that memory from his mind and listened to Stevenson read. The battle had just ended and the maiden was saved when Mary poked her head through the doorway.

"Dinner's ready."

"Mom, just a few more minutes?" Jonathan gave her a pleading look.

Stevenson closed the book. "You heard your mom, Jon. We'll finish after dinner."

Apparently resigning himself to the inevitable, Jonathan slowly rose to his feet. They walked into the dining room, where dinner was already laid out on the table. Tom watched as the others bowed their heads and held hands while Stevenson prayed. Jonathan snuck a peek at him and Tom winked. The boy quickly shut his eyes. Tom glanced over and saw Sara watching them. She smiled and bowed her head.

After the prayer, Mary handed the first serving bowl to Tom. "Have you been able to find that convict who escaped from prison?"

Tom glanced at Stevenson before answering. "No, he just disappeared."

"Like a ghost?" Jonathan asked, a smile running across his face.

"Yeah, like a ghost." Stevenson smiled back, but his eyes were serious.

As the meal ended, Mary stood. "How 'bout Sara and I do the dishes, and you guys go finish that story."

Jonathan made a dash for the living room, scooped up the book, and delivered it to his father in a flash. "Here you go, Dad." The evening went fast as the pirates were finally beaten back into the seas, and peace and safety reigned once again.

After Jonathan dressed for bed, Stevenson read a Bible story to his son. Tom listened as the story unfolded. It was a story of good versus evil, the shepherd David battling the giant Goliath. Another story of good winning over evil, but not all Bible stories ended that way. Sometimes evil triumphed. Even in King David's life. Tom could see Jonathan loved this story. The women finished in the kitchen and took a seat in the living room, letting the story continue uninterrupted.

Stevenson finally closed the book. "Bedtime, young man."

"Uncle Tommy. Will you come say a prayer with us?"

Stevenson glanced at his wife. Clearly they hadn't expected this. Sara covered her mouth, trying to hide a smile.

Tom wrapped his arms around the boy and gave him a hug. "How 'bout I listen to your dad say the prayer. Will that be good enough?"

"Sure." He slipped from Tom's embrace and ran down the hallway.

It was like a parade of adults following the boy. Stevenson arranged the covers around Jonathan and sat on the bed next to him. The others stood and watched.

"Do you know the name of King David's best friend?"

His son shot Stevenson a smile. "Yeah. Jonathan."

"That's right, son. And Jonathan was a son of a king. Just like you are."

"Me? I'm a son of a king?"

"Sure. The Bible tells us that if we accept Jesus into our hearts, we become children of God. We're children of the King."

"You too, Dad?"

"Me too." Stevenson patted his son's head.

Tom listened as Stevenson prayed. The boy closed his eyes and snuggled under the covers. Mary stood with her back against the wall, smiling with closed eyes. Tom felt out of place. As if the others shared a bond in which he was excluded. It was a relief to hear Stevenson finally end with "Amen." The others opened their eyes.

Bill leaned over and kissed the boy on the forehead. "G'night, son. Sleep well."

Tom mumbled "good night" and slipped from the room. He returned to the living room, waiting for the others to join him. Sara and Mary paused in the hallway while Stevenson closed the door. Bill put his arm around his wife and they walked toward the living room together. Mary, resting her head on her husband's shoulder, smiled.

Sara trailed behind. She looked at the couple walking arm in arm. A wistful expression crossed Sara's features, a look that forced Tom to turn away. The memory of her face lingered in his mind as if she was remembering what used to be. Before... He forced himself to return to the here and now. Yet the happiness he saw in this home and the memories of his past seemed to merge together, creating a crack in the wall he built inside a long time ago to protect himself.

Tom grabbed his coat. "Hey guys, I'd love to stay and chat, but I've got to meet Hector in just a few." He turned toward his wife. "See you at home?"

Sara nodded without saying a word.

Tom turned and walked toward the front door. He had to leave, to get away from what he saw inside this home. And he had to do it quickly.

Before the damn broke and he lost control.

Ghost stood and shook off the leaves that clung to his clothes. He had seen what he came to see. Tomorrow was another day.

Ghost climbed into his car and drove slowly through the neighbor-hoods. He studied each block, its alleyways, paths, parks, schools, and major traffic arteries leading from the neighborhood. Once committed to memory, Ghost drove to another part of town, less desirable than the Stevenson neighborhood. He needed to find a safe place to roost for the night, a place where cops and the average Joe were not likely to venture.

It only took him a half hour to find where the invisible and undesir-ables lay their heads. A part of town that the city had given up on a long time ago. A place marked for destruction by developers. Tonight, it was Ghost's new home.

He parked his car in an apartment complex nearby, away from the prying eyes of patrolling cops. He walked down an alleyway until he reached one of the abandoned buildings that had caught his attention. He kicked in a plywood board covering what used to be a window. After climbing through the broken window, he propped the board back up to cover the hole.

It was dark inside the building, but some light filtered in from a streetlamp. He saw a room on the second floor that other transients used as a place to crash. Several dirty mattresses were strewn on the floor, a musky odor seeping from the mattresses, but they were softer than sleeping on the torn-up linoleum floors.

Ghost stretched out and tried to rest. He heard the clawing scratches of large rats near his head, like they were inside the walls, searching for whatever rats search for in the night. The gangster hoped he would not be on their menu.

It was a while before he could force himself to sleep. As he drifted into dreamland, Ghost heard the sound of rats still hunting in the night.

He was not the one to blame for all the chaos he'd caused. Society had always been out to get him, to slap him down, to keep him in place. Well, he was fighting back the only way he knew how. And if he was destined to die, if he was going out to meet his destiny, he'd take as many souls with him on his way down. They'd remember his name for a long time.

As he tried to fall asleep, Ghost traveled back to his childhood. To his mother, abandoned by his father. The string of boyfriends his mother paraded through their squalid home, each of them "playing horsey" with his mother as he watched from the closet. A toddler seeing them naked on his mother's bed. Many of the men couldn't tolerate a runt running under-foot. He remembered all the blows he'd endured as a child, all the slaps across his face by those who had no time for him. His mother screaming at him to leave them alone.

To leave her alone.

He finally learned to live alone. At a very young age he learned to fend for himself, to carve his little niche in life with his own hands. School had not been his thing. Students made fun of him when he was too slow to pick up what the teacher gave out in class. He had no one at home to guide him, no family but his whore of a mother. A mother who could care less about him. Life slapping her down, just like her son, until she looked at him like he was another bitter joke life had handed her.

And then he found direction, a purpose that would ultimately bring him respect and fear from others. It started at age eight, when he saw things in a store that he could never have. He started with the five-finger discounts and worked up from there. From theft to burglary, from burglary to robbery, from robbery to murder. The path had been preordained by circumstances.

It had never been his fault.

He graduated from his own schools. His first real school was juvenile hall. A few years later, he wound up in the California Youth Authority, a finishing school of young criminals approaching adulthood. And finally — graduate school. The California Department of Corrections became his home. At first, he was bounced between prison and parole for a relatively short period of time.

Each return trip to prison brought him closer and closer to a life sentence. And finally, his ultimate sin: a gang murder in the San Joaquin valley. The prosecutors slammed together a conviction for premeditated murder, actually an ambush killing, with a string of violent offenses. They tacked on a gang enhancement to his criminal history, and now he faced several LWOPs. Even the words made him shutter—Life With Out Parole. This was where the revolving door of justice finally slammed shut, never to reopen again. It was the end of all hope.

Or so they thought.

Ghost had pulled off the impossible—escape from one of the highest security prisons in the state. To run free until the canines caught up to him. Only the stupid ones got caught. Ghost was one of the smart ones. He stretched out in the bed, enjoying this life without bars. He was a free man. Freedom was worth everything he had. Even his life. He'd never go back.

Ghost finally drifted to sleep dreaming of where he would flee to when this hunt was over. He dreamed of cloudless blue skies, long sandy beaches, and the best brews money could buy. And women. Plenty of women.

He would run until he found this heaven somewhere on earth.

Chapter 37

The all-night diner at the edge of Highway 101, just north of Petaluma, was not Tom's favorite place to dine. A little pricey and the waitress expected tips. It was Garcia's idea to meet here—not Tom's.

Garcia had yet to arrive. Tom took a booth offering a view of the parking lot and an off-ramp from the freeway. Garcia had called to say he was on his way back from visiting Mikio in the safe house. He'd be at the diner in a few minutes.

Tom withdrew his wallet and counted the money inside.

"Dinner's on me, you cheapskate." Garcia was standing over him.

Tom slipped his wallet in his pocket. "Where'd you come from? I thought I had the parking lot covered."

Garcia slid into the seat across from Tom. "Always be unpredictable. Keeps everyone on their toes. I parked behind the café in the dark."

The diner was almost empty. Two truckers, caps pushed back on their heads, sat at the front counter trying to engage the sole waitress in conversation. The woman, a pencil buried deep in her brunette hair and with a tired expression, poured coffee for the two Don Juans. She moved away from the counter and worked her way toward Tom and Garcia.

"You ready to order?" Her expression of disinterest changed to a look of recognition when she glanced down. "Hey, I know you. Agent Garcia... Hector. Right?"

Garcia's eyes narrowed, trying to place the woman.

"Member me? Married to that no-good thief, Bobby Ray. You guys busted him on a third strike and sent him back for life."

Cautiously, Garcia nodded. "Yeah, I remember."

"I was the one who snitched him off, remember? Called your office and spoke to you about it."

The agent's face lit up. "Your name's Sally...Sally Spencer."

She beamed. "Yep. Best thing that happened to me. I never got around to thanking you."

"Things working out for you?"

The woman shrugged, pointing to the two truckers still seated at the counter. They kept glancing in her direction "You bet your rear end I'm doing better. I divorced the deadbeat the second he went off to prison. At least I'm a little smarter as to who I hook up with. You married?"

Tom choked as he tried to swallow his coffee. Garcia shot him a look that made Tom grin.

Garcia pointed to his ring finger. "Been happily married for twenty-five years."

Sally refilled their cups without asking. "Just my luck. All the good guys are taken. What can I get ya?" After taking their orders, she walked back around the counter with their orders in hand, poking her head through an open portal between the kitchen and dining area. She yelled to the cook to wake up and clipped a slip of paper to a revolving metal wheel.

Tom eyed Garcia. "You married?" He mimicked Sally's voice.

"Put a cork in it." Garcia scowled as he raised the cup of coffee to his lips.

"Hey. You're the one who picked this place. Now I know why."

The other man shrugged. "She must have just started working here. I'm surprised I remembered her name."

Their meal was delivered as promised, hot and quick. Tom only ordered a piece of warm apple pie à la mode. Dinner at Stevenson's house had filled him up. "Thanks for dessert. It tastes even better knowing you're footing the bill—again."

Garcia grimaced. "Oh yeah. I forgot. Enjoy it. You're picking up the tab on the next meal."

"How about Costco?"

"No, I mean a real restaurant. Someplace where the food is brought to you and you have to fork over a tip."

Tom smiled and returned his attention to the food.

Garcia put his fork down and watched Tom as he finished eating. "We're pushing hard trying to find Ghost, but he's simply vanished. We've contacted all his known acquaintances and associates, anyone who might have come in contact with this guy. So far, nothing."

"Can you have Lentz pull his files to see if there's anything useful? Family, friends, addresses of letters mailed to him? Anything?"

"I've already asked." Garcia picked up his fork, then put it down again. "That reminds me. Lentz came up with one thing of interest. Do you remember Rascal telling us about sending Ghost a letter after he killed Paco? He mailed it to the Bay using the name of a woman here in Santa Rosa. He used a local post-office box."

"Yeah, I remember. You got her name?"

"Better than that. Lentz's office sorts through all the mail going to the NF and records or photocopies the names and addresses on the envelopes. He pulled the file and found the name, Juanita Sanchez, and the post-office box number. I paid a visit to the post master and got the rundown on the box. They gave me the actual address where Juanita lives. I cross-referenced her name and address with our records. Guess who she's married to?"

Tom looked at the agent across the table. "I haven't a clue."

"Mikio's brother. And it gets better. Guess who her mother is?"

Tom waited for the answer.

"Maria Juarez, DJ's wife. Small world, no? Mikio's related through marriage to one of the most powerful NF leaders in the Bay."

"Why didn't DJ know about the communiqué, Hector? Something like that, I'd imagine she would send a copy to her father."

Garcia shrugged before taking another bite. "Maybe she didn't know what the message meant. Just passed it along."

Tom whistled. "Why didn't Mikio tell us this? About his connections?"

"That's what I want to ask him. I didn't bring it up when I met with him today. Thought I'd run it past you before springing it on him. I hate to do this turnaround, but I think we need to make contact with him tonight."

"I'll go with you." Tom folded up his napkin. "Makes me wonder what else Mikio forgot to tell us."

Garcia stood and placed several bills on the table, more than the cost of the meal. "That should make Sally happy. Let's get a move on."

Tom pulled on his coat. He looked down at the money on the table. "I'm telling you, Hector. Costco's a much better deal."

The other man laughed. "Bill was right. You are a cheapskate. Heaven help the guy who comes between you and your wallet."

The two men walked out of the diner and into the night. It would be a two-hour drive to the safe house. The news about Mikio and his family connections made Tom uneasy. "By the way, Hector. I came clean with Fat—er, Sergeant Crenshaw. He's going to let me continue to work this case. So, give me those photos and letters back and I will enter them into evidence like I should have done ages ago."

"I'm glad they didn't fire you, my friend. I am just getting used to your strange ways."

"My strange ways? This from a man who drives like a maniac and flirts with anything in a skirt? Gimme a break."

"Flirt! Only flirt. They know I'm all talk." Garcia held up his wedding band. "I'm a married man. If I stepped out on my dear wife—who I love more than life itself—she'd cut me so bad that I could never have little Hector babies. And I wouldn't want to deprive the world of that opportunity."

Tom shook his head. "Let's get out of here."

Garcia jingled his car keys in Tom's face. "Let's take my car. I want to get there sometime tonight."

Tom pushed the keys out of his face. "Depends. You going to let me sleep?"

Garcia started up the engine after they climbed into his car. "Of course not." He released the brake and shot across the parking lot. In minutes they were on the freeway toward Sacramento.

Chapter **38**

The attorney lifted a package across his expansive desk and waited for Maria Juarez to pick it up. In times past, she admired the dark cherry wood of the desk as it glistened in the afternoon light. A window behind the lawyer invited sunlight to filter into the law office. She liked the smell and feel of wealth this place gave off. Today, the package was all she had time for. Maria reached over and grabbed it.

"I don't want to know what's inside." The lawyer's fingers drummed the top of the desk as he watched her open it. Maria glanced up and saw he seemed nervous. So was she.

The words *Legal Mail* clearly printed on the outside of the yellow nine-by-twelve-inch envelope in large block letters told her the prison guards had not opened it. The attorney told her he hand carried it directly from Pelican Bay to this office after meeting with DJ. They had met under the protection of privileged communications, right under the noses of the guards.

She knew it was not the attorney's first visit to the Bay. He made regular trips to meet with DJ and five other NF leaders. He met with each gang leader under the pretense of representing them in ongoing legal matters. In reality, he was just a messenger. A highly paid errand boy.

Maria slit open the package with a pen knife and peered inside. It looked like a thick legal brief. She pulled the document out of the package and began to read. The first few pages were some kind of legal affidavit, listing DJ as the plaintiff in a civil matter. It had been handwritten, each line carefully printed in black ink. Five pages into the document, the language of the document changed. The writing was still clear and concise, but it had nothing to do with a civil-court matter. She knew exactly which page to search.

It was DJ's orders directing her to orchestrate the death of one man—Mikio Sanchez.

Maria gasped. She looked up at the attorney.

He quickly stood and walked toward the door. "I'll let you read this in private. Let my secretary know if you need anything. Please take it with you." He motioned toward the document Maria held in her hand. "I don't want something like *that* left here." He exited the room and quietly closed the door.

Maria glanced at the page in front of her. DJ was very explicit. Use whatever means possible to find out where Mikio had stashed information on the Family. Once this was confirmed, have him killed. And make sure everyone knew the NF ordered his death. *Blood in, blood out.*

She reread her husband's orders, hands shaking as she realized what she must do. He wanted to use family—his own family—to set the trap. The room seemed to shift and her breathing came in short gasps. Her stomach knotted and she started to look for a bathroom. It was the same kind of feeling she had as a girl when she'd traveled on a windy, dusty road with the windows rolled down. She was going to throw up—it was only a matter of time.

She sat back and waited until the sick feeling passed.

Leaning forward again, tears came to her eyes as she slipped the document back into the envelope and placed it in her purse. She pulled out her cell phone and punched a preprogrammed telephone number. The phone rang twice before another woman answered.

Maria struggled to regain her voice. "Juanita. We must meet. I can't talk over the phone. Come by the house." She closed the phone and put it back into her purse, knowing her daughter would obey.

Her hands still shook. *Family killing family.* A loneliness in the room pressed down and suffocated her. She put her hands to her face as tears streamed down her cheeks. She rocked back and forth, her cries muffled by the book-lined walls of the law office.

She thought of her daughter and the plans that must be set in motion. *Oh, Juanita. What am I getting you into?*

"Can we trust you, Mikio? If we can't believe you, how're we going to be able to work together?" Tom glared at the other man. They were standing in the driveway of the safe house on the outskirts of Sacramento. A jet screamed overhead, drowning out Mikio's reply. His eyes told it all.

As the sound waves rippled across the sky, a momentary quietness crept back into the neighborhood until the next aircraft took off.

"I told you the truth," Mikio said. "I just kept family out of it."

"It's that kind of judgment that'll get you and your nephew killed. *Trust no one!* You, of all people, should know the words to that tune."

Hector watched as the two men yelled at each other. Tom seemed to be carrying the lead here, so Hector kept his mouth shut. He'd probably wind up having to negotiate a truce between these two. They both had a point, but he would be hard pressed to make them understand that. He waited and watched.

"As far as I'm concerned," Tom said, "everything you've told us to date I'll have to question. And we haven't started on the debrief, our stroll down memory lane you promised. The agreement was to share everything you know about the NF."

Anger smoldered in Mikio's eyes. "I am a man of my word. I will give you everything—except for family."

Out of the corner of his eye, Hector saw Gato standing near the front door listening. Gato stared at his uncle with contempt before disappearing inside the house. Mikio's face blanched as he watched his nephew. A deep sadness settled across Mikio's face.

"I'll keep my word," Mikio said, almost to himself.

Tom waved his arm as if to dismiss Mikio's words. "And that is something I can take to the bank? I doubt it."

Mikio clenched his fists and took several steps toward Tom.

Hector stepped between them. "Hold it. Everybody cool down." He turned toward Mikio. "Are there any other family connections we need to be concerned about? I mean, your brother's wife is DJ's daughter. Gato is DJ's grandson. Did it ever occur to you we might need to know that?"

Mikio continued to glare at Tom, but Hector's words seemed to take some of the fight out of him. "There are no *other* family ties we need to worry about. I'm counting on this connection to DJ to keep Gato and me safe."

Hector patted Mikio's shoulder. "From now on, we won't take anything for granted. If push comes to shove, DJ will have you killed to save his own skin."

"DJ won't do that. I know too much."

Hector shook his head. "We'll keep that information under wraps for as long as we can, but some day, someway, DJ is going to learn you gave them up. Until then, do you really think you can trust DJ to protect you?"

Another jet took off in a furious roar of engines. The sound carried for several minutes until the jet became just a dot in the sky.

Mikio glanced back toward the house. "It's not about trust, Garcia. It's all about secrets." He walked back toward the house. "You'll have to excuse me. I've got to get back in there and put out a major fire."

Hector and Tom watched Mikio enter the house. They walked toward their car, and Hector glanced back at the house. "By the look on Gato's face, he just learned Mikio is cooperating with us. I hope he can control Gato after this."

Tom shrugged and climbed into the passenger side of the vehicle. "We've got bigger problems to deal with than worrying about how Gato feels about things. We are faced with an untrustworthy witness, Hector. I think Mikio's credibility might be shot."

Hector started up the car without comment. Tom just did not understand Mikio's world. Always living in the gray. Always one step away from disaster. He hoped he was not wrong about Mikio. Hector still wanted to believe. Wanted to think that someone like Mikio could change.

More than Mikio's credibility hung in the balance. Hector would never admit this to another living soul, but he'd always harbored a thought—a belief—that all this work, all this effort, might save others.

He hoped Mikio was on that road to salvation. Only time would make that known.

Chapter 39

Santa Rosa

Juanita Sanchez knocked twice on the door. She heard footsteps approaching and watched the doorknob slowly turn. Her mother stood in the doorway, her eyes red from crying. She held out her arms to hug her daughter.

"Mom, what's wrong?" Juanita stepped into her mother's embrace. Alarm set in as she felt her mother's hug. "Is there something I can do?"

"Come in. I have some tea waiting." She closed the door behind them, and with one arm around Juanita's waist, guided her into the kitchen. Two cups of tea had been laid out on the kitchen counter. Two stools had been pushed up to the counter. The women sat, Juanita looking with concern at her mother. A manila envelope lay near the teacups.

"I just got this message from your father." She pushed the envelope toward Juanita. "Read it. Page five."

Maria sat quietly, watching her daughter as she read. Juanita suddenly gasped. "Dad wants Mikio killed?" She looked at her mother. "He is…he's our family. And we're supposed to set this up?"

Tears pooled in her eyes as she searched the older woman's face. "Pedro, does he know about this?"

"Your husband is NF. It does not matter whether he knows." Her mother's eyes suddenly flashed in anger. "Mikio walked away and threatened to tell the cops everything. Your father cannot allow that. You know the rules."

"But Mikio is my husband's brother."

Her mother shrugged, stirring a spoon in her teacup and brushing the tears from her eyes. "Mikio trusts you. Your father wants to find out where that information is hidden. We expect you to do as you are told."

"How am I supposed to do that? We don't even know where Mikio is hiding. He and Juan just disappeared. All I know is what Juan's girlfriend told me. They're on some military base near Sacramento surrounded by cops and the military."

"Well, do you have their phone number? Give them a call."

"I tried, Mom. No one answered." Juanita gave her mother an incredulous look. "I don't know if I can do this."

"You have no choice." She reached over and brushed the tears from her daughter's eyes. "We have no choice, *mija*."

Another jet woke Mikio up the next morning. The boom from the jet's blast vibrated the house. *Now I know why no one else lives here.* He crawled from under the covers, the hardwood floor cold to his feet. Cold morning air added to his unhappiness. Clad only in boxer shorts and a faded T-shirt, Mikio wandered down the hall and pounded on the door of Juan's bedroom.

"Rise and shine."

Mikio continued down the hall and into the kitchen to make preparations for his first cup of coffee. A coffeemaker, heavily stained, had been left behind by the previous tenants. Much to his surprise, the ancient device still worked. In a few moments, the aroma of coffee filled the kitchen.

He opened the refrigerator to decide what breakfast was going to look like. His thoughts replayed last night's drama in the driveway. Garcia and Kagan finally drove away, leaving Mikio angry and uncertain. He didn't know whether the cops were going to write him off and feed him to the wolves or stand true to their word. Only time would answer those questions.

Juan had been no fun either. After Mikio stormed back into the house, he'd found his nephew sullenly watching television. He tried to talk to him, but Juan slouched on the couch without responding. His pinched face warned Mikio to back off.

Frustrated, Mikio had decided to turn in early. He hoped time would help Juan deal with whatever was whirling around in that young head. Several times Mikio tried to tell his nephew he was going to fully cooperate with the cops, but he never seemed to find the right time to have that conversation. Now it was too late.

He pulled out a carton of eggs and a container of bacon and laid them on the counter. He did not hear any movement from Juan's room. He walked back down the hallway and rapped twice on the door.

"What do you want for breakfast?"

Silence.

Mikio eased open the door and peered inside. Empty. He hurriedly searched the house.

Juan vanished.

He dashed outside and frantically searched the neighborhood.

Nothing.

Mikio shook his head as the reality of everything began to make sense. He had seen it on Juan's face last night when the young man overhead Mikio promise to reveal Nuestra Familia secrets. To become a rat for the government. It had been more than his nephew could stomach.

Juan was on the run.

Mikio felt sick to his stomach. His car was still parked in the driveway where he'd left it. Juan must be hitchhiking. He knew where Juan would run. He'd run to his old haunts, to those places and friend he felt safe with.

As he sat on the front steps, Mikio put his head in his hands, trying to figure out what to do next. He couldn't call Garcia. Not after the blowout last night. This was the last thing he wanted Garcia and Kagan to know. Mikio would have to handle this himself.

He went inside and picked up the telephone. He dialed a number by memory. A woman's voice answered.

"Juanita, this is Mikio. Juan has run away. He's probably coming back to you."

"Why shouldn't he come home, Mikio? He's not a traitor. He has nothing to fear."

"I'm sorry, Juanita. I was just trying to keep him safe."

"You can keep him safe by staying away from him. He's not the one who turned his back on the Family."

Mikio said nothing. He wanted to say he'd walked away *because* of his family, Juan and all the others. Juanita would never see it that way. To her, he was just a traitor.

"I didn't mean to say that." Her voice softened. "Look, I'm sorry. It's just that everything has me on edge. Juan almost shooting you. The two of you running away. All of this."

"I know. I'm trying to figure it out myself. He's got to be headed in your direction. I don't know what kind of head start he has, but I have the car and he's on foot. I'll start working my back to Santa Rosa. Once I get into town, I'll check in with you."

"Thanks, Mikio. Why don't you stay with us while you're here? We can look for him…together."

"I still have the apartment. I'll settle in there and check in with you once I know something."

"Okay. And there is something else I need to ask you. When you have the time." She sounded nervous, strained.

"What do you need to talk about?"

She hesitated before answering. "It'll wait until I see you. Be careful. I heard a whisper that Ghost's in town."

"Yeah. Well he's a dead man. I'm sure DJ's looking to take his wind."

Chapter 40

Santa Rosa

Bill stepped out of the warmth of his house in Rincon Valley and into a cold-gray mist. The air was brisk and fresh, bringing with it a salty cleanness from the coast. An overcast sky allowed just a hint of early dawn light to break through the blackness of the receding night, giving a lighter contrast to the mountains to the east. Streetlamps still burned their yellowish hue across the darkened streets. The briskness woke him up.

He wore Oakland Raiders sweatpants and a blue hooded sweatshirt. There was nothing printed on the sweatshirt, nothing to announce his affiliation with law enforcement. No need to advertise his line of work.

Looking up and down the street as he warmed up, Bill stretched out his leg muscles and bent at the waist to work out the kinks in his lower back. A car backed out of the driveway halfway down the block. He watched as the car's headlights came on. The driver carefully backed into the street, straightened out, and headed toward downtown. Another commuter heading for work.

He dropped down to the concrete walkway and completed as many push-ups as his tired arms would allow. Finishing, he stood and prepared to jog his way through the quiet neighborhood.

A car started up behind him, more than a block away. Another commuter, he thought, then crossed the street and cut through a small park the city maintained down the block.

He circled around the park, and began to run along a larger street that would carry him to a gravel pathway alongside a canal three blocks away. It was his favorite place to run.

Bill ran in the roadway, eyeing the entrance to the canal ahead. He approached an intersection and slowed when a car started to cross his path. He and the car were about to merge, so he ran in place to let the car pass.

The car slowed and the passenger-side window rolled down slowly.

Odd. He waited for the car to continue. The car rolled to a stop in front of him.

Maybe it was one of the neighbors wanting to chat. He didn't recognize the vehicle. As he stooped to peer inside the car, an overhead streetlamp suddenly illuminated the driver's face through the windshield.

Ghost.

Bill saw the barrel of a gun pointing toward his chest a second before the muzzle flashed. The shot struck him hard, slamming him backward. His world swirled. He knew he should get up, but his body refused to obey.

His world stopped spinning just long enough to see Ghost standing over him, a gun pointed at Bill's head. A muzzle blast and unconsciousness struck at the same time.

Tom climbed out of his car in the driveway. Sara stood in the doorway waiting for him. He felt no spring to his step, only a wooden deadness he could not shake. He had called her only minutes before, saying he needed to speak with her as soon as possible. When she asked what it was about, he simply said he'd explain when he got home.

Two SRPD marked units pulled up in front of the house, dispatched to leave the city limits and meet him at his house in the country. The officers parked their vehicles, got out, saw Sara, then quickly looked away.

Alarm swept over his wife as her eyes searched his face. He gritted his teeth as he approached.

"What's wrong, Tom? Please tell me."

"Let's go inside, honey."

One of Hector's men emerged from the house. "I'll give you folks a few minutes alone. I'll go check in with the officers."

Tom put his arm around her waist and guided her inside, then quietly closed the door behind him. He led her down the hallway and into the living room.

"Why don't you sit down, Sara."

"I don't want to sit down." She pulled herself from his arm. "Please tell me what's wrong?"

He tried to look her in the eyes. "Bill was shot and killed this morning. He's...gone."

"Oh no." Sara stared at him in disbelief. "How? Why?"

He moved in close and encircled her with his arms as he told her what happened. Her head rested on his shoulder. She wept softly at first, then with more intensity as the finality of his words became a reality. Her head fell against his chest. As he pulled her closer, Sara's cries filled the room and cut into his soul.

Tom wanted to scream out in anger. Instead, he shut down, holding his grief inside and gritting his teeth until his jaws ached. It was time to put all his feelings aside, to short-circuit his emotions until he found Stevenson's killer. Then, and only then, would he let loose.

For now, he needed to hold Sara and let her express the emotions he was afraid to let out. To be that shoulder she needed just like before.

Sorrow and grief once again dominated his home. Maybe it had never left.

Mikio heard the news over the car radio on his way back to Santa Rosa. He knew at once who pulled the trigger. Ghost had found his way to Mikio's neck of the woods. He stopped at a pay phone and called Juanita.

"You heard?" Mikio asked.

"The cops already came by asking if we know anything."

"We've got to talk. But not at your house." Mikio was only minutes from town. They agreed to meet at a diner south of town along the freeway.

"Make sure you're not followed," he said.

Mikio beat her to the diner. He parked his car in back. He entered the diner and selected a booth farthest away from the crowd inside.

"Mikio, what can I get you?" Sally walked up with a pot of coffee in her hands.

He turned and looked up at her. "Hey, you're looking fine, *chica*. Haven't seen you in ages."

She poured him a cup of coffee and stroked her fingers over the nape of his neck. "I've missed you, handsome."

"I'm sorry, hon. I've been kind of ducking trouble lately. As you know, I'm trying to go straight, but it's not easy."

"That's the only reason I agreed to date you. Knowing you were getting out and going straight. I'm proud of you. Don't be a stranger. Okay?"

Juanita walked into the dinner and searched for him. She spotted him and began walking toward him.

"I'll be in touch. Promise."

"I'll hold you to it, hon." Sally walked away.

Juanita reached the table and sat down, a wrinkle of concern crossing her brow, her mouth pinched. "Things are getting a little hot around here."

"Everything will level out once they catch Ghost," he said. "The NF must have put him in the hat by now. He knows he's a dead man, and he has no more power. Any hits he ordered on me—and your son for not following through—will be pulled back. The green light is on him right now."

Her face relaxed, but she sat rigidly at the table, her hands clasped together. "But what if you're reading this wrong? What if the Family is cleaning house, you and Juan as well as Ghost? How can we keep them in check?"

"What do you mean?" Mikio watched her warily, the friendliness in his voice dissipating.

She shifted in her seat. "Pedro always told me to keep a record of things, things other people did. He said it was kind of like having power over others. He said it was something you taught him."

Mikio clenched his jaw. He knew where she was going with this, and he did not want to take that journey with her. But this was his brother's wife; Juan was her son. She was family.

"You mean dirt on other people?"

She nodded, her face telegraphing her thankfulness that he understood. "Exactly. You must have kept such a record, all the years you were with them. Can you help us now? Give us information we can use to save Juan? To keep them away from our family?" She leaned forward. "To be honest, Mikio. I can't even trust my dad. That's how bad things are."

His words came out in a staccato cadence. "You don't know what you're asking, Juanita. They'll kill anyone they think holds this information."

"Not if they think you will pass it on to the cops if anything happens."

Mikio remained quiet, watching.

"Have you put information together in some way so we can protect the family?" Her eyes sought his face for a sign.

His face was rigid as a stone.

"I never thought I'd have to do it." His voice was quiet, almost sad. "If it becomes necessary, I'll do it to protect the family. But I don't think the family is in danger anymore."

"Are you sure?" She leaned back in her seat, watching him.

"I'm sure. And you always have your father to cover your back, to protect the family. He'll always side with his family. Right?"

"I suppose so."

Mikio saw the result of his words in the woman's reaction. She seemed to finally relax, as if she'd stumbled across the answer she was seeking. Juanita waved in Sally's direction, trying to get her attention.

"I'm famished. Let's order."

Mikio lost whatever appetite he brought into this place. Instead, a feeling of hollowness filled him as he watched his brother's wife order from the menu.

Sally glanced down at him, her eyebrows rising in concern. He shook his head and brought a finger to his lips. Juanita was too busy ordering to catch the look between them.

Sally's face reflected the pain in his eyes. In a moment, she turned to Juanita with a forced smile.

Mikio looked out the window and saw several cars pull into the parking lot. He watched as each occupant got out and walk toward the restaurant. He did not recognize anyone.

But then, when the moment came, the face of death would bear the resemblance of someone he loved or a stranger. He had a feeling the threat of death sat across the table from him. *Mi familia!* He thought of those words with bitterness.

He must wait to see if his worst fears would come to pass.

Chapter 41

Maria answered her cell phone on the first ring. It was Juanita. She told Maria she was so nervous, she could not wait until she got home to share what she just learned. "He has not recorded anything. He will do it only if the family needs it done."

Maria hung up without comment. She redialed the number. A man's voice answered.

"It's Maria. You have a green light to remove the weeds from the garden. I'll get your tools. Wait for my call."

She hung up. As she placed the phone down, she saw her hands shaking. Maria hugged herself, trying to rid herself of the chill that started deep in her chest. Fear. Remorse. Whatever triggered that feeling, she would never be the same. The future looked darker than a moonless night and a lot more dangerous. For her. For everyone she loved.

The explosions of rifle fire snapped Tom's mind back to the present. He stood next to Mary and Jonathan, the two of them seated with Sara. His blue Class-A uniform felt stiff and suffocating in the morning sunlight. The blue contrasted with the sea of green surrounding him as those from the sheriff's office came to pay their respects. Departmental rivalries ceased when a tragedy like this struck the community.

The honor guard had neatly and tightly folded the American flag that had been draped over Stevenson's coffin. The flag was presented to Mary by the chief, her hands shaking with emotion as she accepted it. Sara had her arms around Jonathan. The boy looked up at Tom with tears in his young eyes. He tried to give the boy a smile of sympathy, but it was contorted by the pain he felt.

Pastor Lawson stood over the grave, Bible in hand. "We are here today to honor a fallen hero. To some of us he was a comrade in arms, to others…a friend, a husband, a father. Bill Stevenson was many things to many people. And we are all going to miss the man who gave his life to protect and serve the people of this community."

Lawson paused and gazed over the crowd gathered around him. The sun had pushed the morning fog aside and spread its warmth over the rolling hills of the cemetery. A gentle breeze caused the flags, fastened to the standard nearby, to flap and swirl.

"This is a time of sadness and grief. We miss our friend. But I know Bill wanted a message of hope to be shared with you today as well. You see, Bill knew that someday he was going to a better place. A place where God will wipe away every tear; where we will no longer feel death's sting."

Lawson seemed to be looking directly at Tom as he spoke.

As he looked at the casket, Tom wondered if his friend had been right about the hereafter. *I hope you are at peace, my friend. I miss you. I mourn for you. I hope you have found what you believed in to be true. Take care.*

As Lawson continued, Tom's mind wandered as he tried to deal with the anger he held inside. He wanted to explode. To search for Bill's killer until he tracked the degenerate down. And then? How far would he take this manhunt to protect those he loved? It was a question that didn't need an answer. He knew what he must do. He fantasized pointing a gun at Ghost's smirking face and pulling the trigger.

A moment later, Tom realized his body had tensed and he was clenching his hands into fists. Wow. Maybe Fat Louie had been right. Maybe Tom could no longer manage the emotional baggage this job dumped on him.

Taking shallow breaths, Tom forced himself to calm down. To keep it under control. He listened to Lawson and watched Sara's, Mary's, and

Jonathan's faces as they sat huddled in their private grief. Mary and her son had become his extended family after his partner's death. It was now his responsibility to keep them safe. To keep evil at arm's distance from those he cared about.

Even in this sunlight, he felt darkness closing in, trying to suffocate him with its burden of hopelessness. He must try to pull free from this dark quagmire of loss if only to give others hope. They would be looking to him now to carry them through.

He must not waiver. His loss, his pain, must be thrust aside because if he failed, if he faltered, everything would come crashing down. It was not a time to wallow in his own grief. His own problems.

After the service, Tom led Sara and Mary through the cemetery. Jonathan tagged along at his side. They were joined by Garcia.

As Tom helped Sara and Mary into the car, putting the boy between them, Garcia tapped him on the shoulder and gestured with his head. "We need to talk."

Tom leaned inside the car. "I'll be back in just one minute." He closed the door and joined Garcia, who had walked over to stand beneath a large willow tree. "What's up, my friend?"

Garcia gestured toward the car. "It's not safe for them in Santa Rosa. We'll have to move them out of town. Now."

Tom turned toward the car, then back to Garcia. "I know. We put security on everyone involved after Bill was killed. But we can't keep this up for long." He watched those he loved talking among themselves. "I already have a place in mind. Just have to work out a few details. Tonight, I'll pull out enough cash to put them up in a hotel outside the city, down toward San Francisco. After that, I'm moving them way out of town until we find Ghost."

"Where you going to move them?"

"Let me check for sure, then I'll let you know. The less anyone knows, the better."

Garcia nodded. "You got that right. This guy is unbelievable. You would have thought he'd been hightailing it to the other side of the world. Not come back here and kill a police officer. That's sheer lunacy in my book."

Tom clenched his teeth. "I can't wait to get my hands on this animal. If I have my way, he'll never make it back to the Bay. I'll put him six feet under and let the worms finish him off."

"Just be careful, Kagan. Never know where Ghost will show up next."

Tom walked back toward the limo. Right now, he'd make sure his loved ones were taken care of. After that—the gloves would come off.

Chapter 42

Homewood, Lake Tahoe, California

Tom heard the sound of the lake's waves filtering through the darkness of the trees. He fiddled with keys, trying to get the right one to open the front door. He finally found it and heard the gratifying sound of a lock springing open. He pushed the door open and flicked on the lights.

This cabin was just as Pastor Lawson described. Beautiful and expansive. A smell of cold embers hung in the air. This was where Stevenson wanted to take him fishing.

A gut-wrenching wave of loss hit him again. His friend—dead.

A wave that first struck him years ago when David was killed. It was like those freak sneaker waves that came out of nowhere and wiped you off your feet. And now—Bill. This pain never seemed to go away. It only subsided for a moment to return when you least expected it.

Tom glanced through the cabin and saw a row of large-paned picture windows on the far side. Beyond these windows, the dark waters of Lake Tahoe were eclipsed by the harvest light of a full moon.

He heard Sara, Mary, and Jonathan's footsteps behind him as they entered the cabin.

"This is gorgeous," Sara gasped. "Mary, look at this place. It's so..."

"Perfect." Mary tiredly smiled at her friend.

Tom went out to the car and started to carry in their bags. He turned with an armful to see Jonathan standing next him.

"Can I help?" The boy gave him an eager-to-please look.

Tom saw the haunting similarity of Stevenson in the boy's eyes. "Sure, partner. Grab this," Tom grasped the smallest suitcase he could find, "and take it into the cabin. I'll show you where it goes once I get inside."

The boy trotted off, struggling with the bag.

Tom returned his attention to the rest of the luggage. He kept going over the events of the last few days in his mind as he worked. Before leaving Santa Rosa, Tom met with Garcia and they struggled to figure out Ghost's next move. Tom knew in his gut that it was only a matter of time before the killer zeroed in on someone else Tom cared about. Like a shark who already smelled blood. There were a lot of eyes and ears in the community willing to point Ghost in the right direction.

When Tom had first presented the relocation plan to Sara, she offered mild resistance. She had finally been offered a position with the Santa Rosa *Press Democrat* after many years away from her chosen profession—journalism. Tom had talked to the editor and asked that her position be held in absentia until things settled down. The editor agreed, and Sara seemed willing to wait.

Besides, Tom needed Sara and the others out of the way. He could not be distracted from the hunt while worrying about those he loved. The beauty of this hideaway was that nothing came back to Tom Kagan or the Santa Rosa Police Department. Nothing that would give Ghost an inkling Tom stashed them here.

He had pulled out a wad of cash from the bank before leaving the city. Everything would be paid for in cash. No credit or debit trails. Sara and the others had to be able to live comfortably up here without sending up any financial flares. Nothing that might lead Ghost to this secure part of paradise.

He had drawn Sara aside and warned her not to let anyone make any telephone calls. He would call her. If there was an emergency, call SRPD

Dispatch on a special line. He gave her that number. They'd immediately notify him.

The trip to the lake had been uneventful, almost relaxing, to everyone but Tom. On the way up, he would surreptitiously glance in the rearview mirror every few miles, memorizing the kinds of vehicles that trailed them, looking for that one vehicle that remained constant as they switched from freeway to highway, from highway to county roads. No one appeared to be tracking them.

He had crawled under their vehicles and looked under the hoods for portable GPS tracking systems. A part of him thought this was a waste of time since Nuestra Familia would hardly have access to this kind of technology that law enforcement, corporate America, the Hells Angels, or Russian crime groups might utilize. But Tom didn't want to learn the hard way that he might be wrong.

Look what Ghost already accomplished.

While the women settled in, Tom called the Placer County Sheriff's Office and asked to speak to a detective whose name had been recommended. The man wore several hats—violent-crimes investigations, intelligence investigations, and criminal street-gang enforcement. Tom quickly gave a thumbnail sketch of the threat to the investigator. He, in turn, gave Tom a number to reach him at any time and coordinated contact with a resident deputy working the west side of the lake—Deputy Dan Hoffman.

He dialed the deputy's private cell number and was surprised when Hoffman answered on the second ring. Tom explained who he was and the danger involved. "I don't want my wife and the others here to freak out. I want them to think everything is under control. I'll explain everything when I see you." They agreed to meet at the Homewood boat marina in about fifteen minutes.

Tom helped Sara move luggage upstairs and groceries into the kitchen. He glanced at his watch. "I'm going to take a walk. Be back in a few." She gave him a quizzical look, but kissed him on the cheek without interrogating him. He watched her walk up the stairs to help Mary and Jonathan settle in before leaving the cabin.

By the time he completed the ten-minute walk and stepped onto the wooden pier, Tom saw a patrol car pull into the marina parking lot. The deputy climbed out and glanced around. Then he spotted Tom and met him on the pier.

Hoffman introduced himself and thrust out a hand in greeting. He was slim but muscular, about thirty years old, with short sandy hair.

Tom shook the deputy's hand. "Thanks for meeting me so quick."

The deputy shrugged. "I called the detective you spoke with. He filled me in on your problem. I'm sorry about your officer. We got the teletype just the other day about the details. I hope you put that creep six feet under when you find him."

"That's the reason I wanted to check in with you," Tom said. "I've done everything to hide our trail up here. But I want to cover all the bases. Talk directly to you so you'd have all the facts."

Hoffman nodded. "I appreciate that. I'd hate to respond to something like this without knowing what I'm up against."

Tom laid out the design of the cabin and approaches to the property, and who would be staying in the cabin during his absence. He gave the deputy the access code to the gate.

Hoffman promised he'd pass the number on to Dispatch and have it entered into their computer system in case other deputies or emergency personnel responded. "I think I've been to your cabin once. It's really a classy spread from what I remember. I watched it being built. Lawson must have a few bucks."

The deputy handed Tom a business card with his home phone and cell number written on the back. "Can't always get hold of me in these mountains. But if you can get through, I will be here Code 3. Even Dispatch has a hard time keeping radio contact with me sometimes, particularly when I travel up some of these canyons."

Hoffman's portable radio squelched with a call from Dispatch. He had to respond to another call and the two men parted ways. Tom watched him pull out onto Highway 89 and head north.

There was a path leading to the water's edge on the south side of the marina. Tom walked through the parking lot and followed it down to the banks of Lake Tahoe. Stirred by the fury of winter storms and the range of temperatures in mountain climates, the lake's crashing waves scattered pebbles from the bottom up onto the beach. The stones lay in a mosaic of gray, black, and white colors, providing an uneven path for those treading along the lakefront.

Tom made his way along the beach with the lake to his left and cabins and trees to his right. Light from other cabins afforded him a glimpse into their lives. Wrapped in the darkness, he felt like a voyeur spying on them. He looked away to give them privacy.

He stared farther down the beach. He thought of ways a person could reach their cabin without traversing the highway. He saw one obvious approach—by boat. Another way, with little chance of detection, would be the beach he was walking on right now. Ghost could stay off the main highway along the waterfront, and come up from the water toward the exposed side of the cabin. Though there was a code-guarded front gate, the fencing failed to circle around and guard against intruders who might use the beach to gain access.

As he drew near their cabin, he saw Sara in the kitchen preparing dinner. Mary stood next to her, and they were engaged in conversation. Jonathan sat next to a roaring fire in the living room reading a book. There was a lot a person could see from this side of the cabin while standing in the darkness.

He walked onto the pier—belonging to Pastor Lawson—for a little peace and quiet. A chilling wind whipped up the lake and rustled the leaves above him. Tom shoved his hands deep into his coat pockets and stared out over the water. A rising moon outlined the mountain ranges along Nevada's side of the lake.

Running lights of several boats sparkled on the water. A sailboat was working its way off shore a few hundred yards, its billowing white sails now a grayish color in the moonlight. A gaggle of Canadian geese, a mother and her young brood, paddled their way from the lake onto the beach to his right. They searched for a place to spend the night. For some reason, his thoughts drifted to David, blending with images of Jonathan. Peaceful family moments that fathers and mothers spend with their children before the world intervenes.

Footsteps clacked on the pier. Turning, he saw Sara approach.

She stood next to him. "I saw you standing out here all by yourself. Thought you might like a little company."

He put his arm around her waist. "I saw you and Mary talking in the kitchen. Didn't want to interrupt."

"Thanks, but she's got the meal covered." She put her arms around his waist and laid her head on his shoulder.

He could feel her shaking in the evening chill. He took his coat off and wrapped it around her. The breeze bit into him but he just ignored it.

"So how're you doing?"

He looked out over the water. "I'm okay. I'm…I'm thinking about—"

"David?" Sara peered up at him. "I could see it in your face."

"You know me pretty well, Sara Kagan."

"That's why I love you. I know the kind of man you are."

"Remember the time we took David to the beach in Bodega Bay? He stayed in the water so long his lips turned blue."

She tightened her arms around his waist, laying her head on his chest. "I remember. I tried to get him to come out, but he wanted to stay. You had to go in and get him."

Chuckling, Tom circled her in his arms. "Sometimes I go back to those times and never want to leave. We were so happy."

Sara leaned back and looked up into his face. "And we will be happy again. We have to move forward while holding on to those kinds of memories. We…you have to, Tom. I don't want to lose you."

He hugged her without saying a word. She turned to face the water. They watched as lights danced from the shoreline around the lake. The wind pushed the waves higher and higher onto the beach as night settled across the basin.

There was nothing left for him to say, so he let the silence speak. As they embraced, he listened as the lake went about its business. This quiet moment with Sara at his side, Tom felt life finally allowed them a much-needed lull in this deadly storm.

He wondered how long it would last.

Chapter 43

Dawn cast a gray hue through the window as Tom rose early and began to pack. He needed a break. Ghost was out there, somewhere, and Tom needed to pull it together and track this killer down before he killed again. Yet as he zipped up his bag, Tom felt uneasy about leaving Sara and the others up here without his protection. He could not be in two places at once, and the greater threat lurked somewhere down below, closer to Santa Rosa.

He left Deputy Hoffman's name and number with Sara. After some hesitation, he motioned for her to join him upstairs away from the others. They walked to their bedroom, and he closed the door. "I am positive there is no way the killer can track you here. But I would feel better if I left you a gun."

Sara shook her head vigorously.

"Please, Sara. For my sake, take the gun." He reached into his briefcase and withdrew a small .40 caliber Sig Sauer pistol. "This is small enough for you to handle with ease but still powerful enough. You've been checked out on this before."

A look of indecision entered her eyes. "I don't know if I could use this thing."

He gently took her hand and held it firmly between his. "There is no reason to believe you'd have to ever use it. Take it for my peace of mind. I would feel more comfortable if I knew you had it available—just in case."

She nodded, finally.

He reminded her how to insert and eject the pistol's magazine and how to pull back the slide to house a round in the chamber. He watched her practice several times until he was assured she felt comfortable with the mechanics. He placed the weapon in the closet, high enough so it would not attract Jonathan's attention if he came snooping around the room. "I'll bring a small gun safe next time I'm here."

After saying good-bye, Tom drove along the west shore of the lake until he reached Tahoe City. There, he followed the gentle curves of Highway 89 as it ran parallel to the flow of the Truckee River. The road and the river went their separate ways just south of Truckee, near where the highway intersected with I-80.

He enjoyed this stretch of highway almost as much as Highway 50. I-80 meandered through the Sierra Mountains, giving motorists a glimpse of beautiful Donner Lake and the surrounding mountain ranges. At this time of year, the snow was gone and nature waited for the new winter to begin. From Donner Pass, the interstate gradually descended in elevation westbound as mountains and trees slowly changed.

Tom tried to focus He would have to start at ground zero—Santa Rosa—and work out from there. This would take some time and a little luck. Until he had this guy behind bars, he could never give up the hunt. Until he knew it would be safe for Sara, Mary, and Jonathan. Then they could return to their normal lives.

Normal?

They could never return to normal. Ever. All because of one sick, pathetic animal.

Ghost's day of reckoning would come.

Diane Phillips was just leaving the office in Santa Rosa when her cell phone chirped. She withdrew it, glanced at the screen, and smiled when she saw who was calling. "Tom, where are you?"

"Just pulling into the city. What's going on with the case?"

"Things are coming together. You get everyone settled?"

"Yeah, now I can focus on getting my hands on Ghost."

She heard what sounded like a semi roaring past in the background. For a moment, she thought they'd lost their connection. "Hey, I was just going to catch some dinner. Want to join me?" She heard him hesitate. "I'm having trouble hearing you, Tom…is that a yes?"

"Yeah. Sure. Where do you want to meet?"

"How 'bout my place? If you don't mind sharing the place with a cat."

Again, hesitation. "I'll be there in about an hour. Will that work?"

"Great, see you then."

She ended the call after giving him directions, then slipped the phone into her pocket. She'd just been thinking about him. It had only been a few days since the funeral. She'd wondered when he'd come up for air to let her know what was going on.

She was home in a few minutes, shooing the cat off the couch, and grabbing a dinner-for-two from the freezer, sticking it into the microwave. Diane slipped out of her work clothes and into a yellow blouse and blue denim pants. She remembered the times Tom tried to get her to come out to the ranch to ride horses. She had always begged off—too much work. She now wished she had taken him up on the offer. She was looking at herself in the mirror when she heard him tapping on the front door.

Tom looked tired and worn. He tried to smile, but his expression seemed drawn and guarded.

She saw a look in his eyes she could not interpret. "Come on in and make yourself comfortable."

He followed her inside and closed the door.

As she walked toward the kitchen, Diane said, "Dinner will be ready in a few minutes. Can I get you something to drink? Wine, coffee, anything?"

He followed her into the combination kitchen and dining room. He chose one of the chairs at the table that afforded a view of her and the kitchen. "A glass of wine, thanks."

She poured a glass for each of them and placed the bottle, a red cabernet, on the table. She handed him a glass.

He shifted in his chair. "You know, I don't think we've ever met outside work. I mean—socially."

She felt him watching her as she moved around the kitchen. She felt a little self-conscious, but in a pleasant way. It had been a while since she had shared this place with someone else, particularly a man. This had been her sanctuary, her retreat, but lately the sanctuary felt a little claustrophobic. "I guess we're just workaholics. No time to socialize."

He tasted the wine without comment. She had dinner on the table with a minimum of effort, and they ate quietly. They managed small talk and she filled him in on details about the cases he missed while relocating Sara and the Stevensons. By the end of the meal, they had run out of topics to cover with half the bottle left. She rose and began to clear the table.

He stood to help. She pushed him toward the living room. "This kitchen is too small for two people. I'll just be a minute."

She finished her chores, then poured herself another glass. After taking a quick sip, she carried it and the bottle with her into the living room. The wine made her feel warm and cozy. She sat next to Tom on the couch and after filling his glass, she placed the bottle on the glass coffee table directly in front of them. Diane glanced at him, pushing a strand of hair from her face. "Hey, you look kind of tired."

"I think we're both tired."

"Thanks for the compliment."

"No. I mean you look great, I just meant..." He stopped, apparently trying to backpedal from a precipice in their conversation. "Never mind. Let's leave it at *tired*." He waved his hand as if surrendering.

She laughed to let him off the hook. "How did it go moving Sara, Mary, and Jonathan?"

He gave her a quick update on the move and pulled out a notebook from his coat pocket. He jotted down the telephone and address of the cabin in Lake Tahoe and the contact numbers for Deputy Hoffman. "In case there's an emergency and you can't get in touch with me."

"Thanks. I can't imagine I'd ever need to use this. I'll put this in a safe place when I get back to the office." She turned toward him. "It seems Ghost has disappeared from sight." She gave a brief rundown on the search while Tom was in the mountains. "You know they recovered the car he stole, but he's still in the wind."

Tom nodded, taking another sip of wine.

"Oh, by the way," she said, "Hector called this morning. Said the police found Galen Roman's body—you know, Tweaker—in an abandoned trailer near the airport. Someone snapped his neck like a pretzel. So, that accounts for the third person to get a note from Ghost to do his dirty work. Rascal. Gato. Tweaker. And I'd wager Ghost is Tweaker's killer."

"That'd be a safe bet."

Diane shot him a puzzled look. "I wonder if he will hide now. After...Bill."

Tom leaned over and picked up the bottle of wine. He poured the wine into each of their glasses. "If he's got any brains at all, he'll run as far from here as he can." He put the half-empty bottle on the table in front of them.

The wine continued to relax her, its warmth spreading to her arms and legs. She watched as he took a sip, enjoying his closeness, his company. Feeling safe, comfortable.

The sound of a glass bottle crashing on the coffee table made both of them sit up straight. Her cat, its tail flicking back and forth, meowed as the wine bottle rolled off the table. The cat wanted attention and had sprung up on the table to let Diane know she was not getting enough. Red wine dribbled from the table onto the carpet.

Diane sprang up and ran to the kitchen and grabbed a roll of towels from the counter. She rushed to the table to begin mopping up the mess.

"I'm sorry. I should have let the cat out earlier."

Tom stood. When she glanced up, she found his eyes searching her face. "Is there anything I can do?"

"No, I've got this." She straightened up and smiled. "What timing..."

"I'd better be going. About that—"

"I've got everything under control. Don't—"

They both stopped trying to speak. Silence covered their awkwardness as they looked into each other's eyes. The cat rubbed itself on her legs as if begging for forgiveness. She glanced down and grimaced. "You know, when I first got her I really didn't like cats. She was a leftover from a friend who moved away."

He pulled on his coat. "To be perfectly honest, Diane, though I'm not fond of cats, I've learned to put up with them. They have their purpose."

She laughed. "Now you tell me." She glanced at Tom, and his expression made her smile vanish. She could not put her finger on it, but she could tell her friend was hurting. Maybe bringing out the wine was a bad idea. Once or twice in her office, she'd smelled alcohol on his breath during work hours. Something that never happened before. And she heard the problems he was having with his supervisor. "Tom..." She faltered as she tried to put it into words. "Are you okay?"

His guard went up. "I'm just fine. Why?"

She placed a hand on his arm. "You've been working a lot of hours—"

"We all have. After Bill died everything changed."

"Even before Bill died, Tom. Since the accident—"

"Diane, we're friends. Good friends." He turned toward her. "But there are some things I will not discuss—with anyone. Are we clear?"

She dropped her hand. "Forget it. I just wanted to let you know..." She stopped talking, not sure where to take this conversation. She felt hurt that Tom would shut her out.

He reached over and placed his hand on her shoulder. "Look, I'm touched you're worried about me. But I'll be fine. Right now, my only mission in life is to catch Ghost and put him back where he belongs." His voice softened. "I need to handle this my own way. Okay?"

She nodded, sensing this subject had been closed like a bridge across a moat rolling up to seal off the castle. Tom had put his invisible armor back on, and like knights of old, he would fight his own battle until the war was finally over.

She followed Tom to the door. He stepped outside before turning back to look at her one more time. "Thanks for dinner. I'll be in touch."

Diane nodded, watching him turn and walk away. She slowly closed the door, leaning against it as she heard his footsteps echoing in the night. She could not shake the feeling of foreboding.

Chapter 44

Diane cleaned up from the dinner. The more she worked, the more her mind returned to the case. By the time she finished the dishes, her tiredness had faded and she knew sleep would never come, though the wine made her drowsy. She made a strong pot of coffee and drank several cups as she thought about the case.

Reenergized, she hurried into the bedroom, dressed for work, and grabbed her keys. No reason to waste this burst of energy. She closed and locked her apartment door. The night breeze was exhilarating, and work would be the best thing to get everything else off her mind. Including Tom.

Diane parked her car close to the front entrance to the district attorney's office. She glanced around, aware of the lateness of the hour, and saw no one in the parking lot. She sighed and found her keys to the office and let herself into the building, then locked the door behind her. Another coworker was just leaving as Diane entered the lobby. She waved and hurried up the stairwell, intenton working until dawn or until her tiredness returned.

Work was her remedy for everything. She felt safe in this place. Where was Ghost hiding? And when would Tom and the others catch the killer so she could send him to death row?

She unlocked the main door of the DA's office and walked inside, again locking the door behind her. She jiggled the door to make sure it couldn't be opened. There was just enough night light to see her way down the corridor and reach her office without turning on any other lights.

Once inside her office, she flicked on the overhead lamps and made herself comfortable behind the desk. She powered up the computer and pulled out the first witness file. She had been back here every night for the last week. The office was quiet, and she could work without being disturbed. This was just another night. In minutes, she was focused on the upcoming trial. Everything else slipped from her mind.

After leaving Phillips's apartment, Tom drove to the police department. Once at his desk, he dialed up his voice mail for messages. There was one call from Lawson.

Tom punched in the number and put the receiver to his ear.

Lawson answered the call in less than ten seconds. "How did the relocation go?"

Tom filled him in on the details and thanked him for the use of the cabin.

"Glad to help. The reason I called was to invite you to stay at my place. I thought it might be safer for you while you're working here in Sonoma County. This city is big—but not that big. At least until Ghost is caught or you're sure he's moved on."

Tom vacillated as he mulled over the pastor's offer.

Lawson pressed on. "Look, you know it's not wise for you to stay at your house with this guy on the loose. He found out where Bill lived. No reason to believe he doesn't know your address. You can park your car inside my garage when you're there. This is the last place he'd think of looking. And...I'd appreciate the company."

Tom hesitated. On the one hand, the last thing he wanted was to have someone preaching to him and clouding his mind. He needed to stay focused on tracking Ghost wherever that might lead. On the other hand, Tom was not looking forward to staying in an empty house, one filled with sad memories. And there was a risk factor of Ghost finding out where he lived. After all, the gangster had found his friend.

"You got a deal. I'm not sure when I'll be checking in, though. I'll be coming and going at all hours."

"Don't worry. I thought a cop's hours were bad until I became a pastor. People are calling me all the time." He gave Tom his cell phone number and where his house was located. "I'll drop a key to my place in an envelope and leave it at the front desk. Just make yourself at home."

The next call was to Garcia. The SSU agent sounded tired and discouraged. "Man, we've hit every gang house in the county and then some. Ghost has vanished. No one is copping to seeing him. We've violated every paroled gangster we could get our hands on, but we've still come up empty."

"Hang in there, buddy. This wacko has to surface somewhere. And when he does, we'll find him." Tom updated Garcia on the relocation of Sara and the Stevensons. He told the agent he'd be staying with Lawson while in town and gave him the address and telephone number.

"I'm going to catch up on paperwork and then head over to his house for a little shut-eye."

He hung up and tried to clear his desk. A flood of reports and correspondence had been dumped there since everything hit the fan. It was almost midnight before he brought a semblance of order to his desk. He checked at the front counter on his way out. As promised, Lawson had dropped off a house key. Tom left a message on Lawson's answering machine, warning him he'd be over in a half hour.

Twenty minutes later, he saw lights on in Lawson's single-story house as he drove up. He opened the front door with the key. Lawson sat in an armchair reading in the living room. The pastor put his book down and stood. "I just got home myself. I made room in the garage for your car. Here's a door opener."

"Thanks." Tom walked back outside and looked up and down the street. Nothing roused his suspicions, so he activated the garage opener and drove his car into the open bay. Tom grabbed his suitcase and rejoined Lawson after closing the garage door.

Lawson waited in the kitchen. "Hungry?"

"No. Just tired."

"Let me show you to your room."

He followed Lawson down a hallway. Lawson turned the lights on in one of the back bedrooms. "Make yourself comfortable. Soap and towels in the bathroom. Let me know if there's anything you need. I'll be in the living room reading."

Tom thanked him and placed his suitcase on the floor near the bed as Lawson closed the door.

In minutes, Tom was unpacked and undressed. He lay on the bed and stared at the ceiling. He unhooked his cell phone from his belt and placed it on the nightstand to charge. He turned out the light and lay in the darkness.

What had he forgotten? His mind whirled through the events of the last few weeks. His thoughts jumbled. An image when he and Stevenson fished along the Klamath River up north grew in clarity. The event rolled through his brain like a movie camera until it froze on one specific frame—a snapshot of Stevenson gleefully pulling in a struggling trout. As usual, Tom had not enjoyed even a bite from a hungry fish that day. Tom focused on his friend's face toasting in the hot summer sun, reflections off the water turning Stevenson's features beet red. He remembered the look his friend shot at him. A large, goofy grin. Stevenson yelled out when he finally landed the monster.

Suddenly another face emerged. His young son, David, just before the boy died. David, grinning at his father during one of the few fishing trips they managed to take together. The boy alive, thrilled to spend some time with his dad. Tom remembered the hug of joy David gave him after snagging a whopper. The hug only lasted for a second, but it stayed with Tom forever.

The pain hit deep into his heart and the picture vanished into the gloom. Here he was alone in this bedroom, looking through the darkness at nothing in particular. The loss, the memories tore him apart. The ones he loved snatched away before their time. Stevenson. David.

Oh, God, why David? A father wasn't supposed to survive his son. That was not the order of things. He curled into a ball, trying to make the agony go away.

It seemed like an eternity until he slipped into another nightmarish sleep, a slumber that made him fight to wake up, to escape, to run.

A sleep without rest.

Chapter **45**

It had been a grueling day. One search after another. And now, after the rest of the normal world had gone home for the night, Tom and the other team members were out rousting gangsters, trying to get a lead on Ghost.

Tom eased into his black unmarked Crown Victoria and listened to the chatter between Garcia and another SSU officer on his encrypted handheld radio. A car had pulled out of one of the gang houses under surveillance. Garcia sat in the back of his own van, keeping eyes on the house.

"Our target is on the move. Moving southbound at a fast clip toward the fairgrounds."

"Roger that," one of Garcia's men answered.

Tom snatched up the handheld radio. "I'll take him, Hector. I'm a block away and can see him coming my way."

Headlights from the gangster's car swept past Tom's position. He fired up the engine, yanked the steering wheel to the left, and executed a quick U-turn. He caught up to the target vehicle moments later. The gangster began to speed up, heads bouncing back and forth as the driver and other occupants tried to see who was behind them. The driver's right-rear brake light was out. Tom had his probable cause to make the stop.

"I going to pull him over now." Tom knew SSU agents were on their way. He placed the portable next to him, grabbed the mike to his car's built-in radio, and advised Dispatch of his traffic stop. He called out the license number and location on channel one, then switched to channel two to request registration and history on the car.

In his rearview, he saw SSU units drawing closer. He flicked on his emergency lights to see how the gangster would react. *Stop or run?* There was a second of hesitation. Two in the front seat, at least one in the back. The targeted driver decided to pull over.

The gangsters had left a house in the South Park area and looped around the fairgrounds until they were heading north toward Highway 12 on Brookwood Avenue. The darkened fairground was to the left, a large, empty parking lot to the right. The car eased into the parking lot and rolled to a stop.

Heads in the suspect's car bobbed around as they tried to see where Tom might approach. He flicked on his left spotlight and flooded the back of the gangster's car with blinding illumination. The gangsters turned away from the light.

Once out of the car, Tom grabbed his flashlight and, using his right thumb, unbuckled the safety strap on his hip holster. He circled around the rear of his car, keeping the targeted vehicle in sight, and came up on the right side of the suspect's vehicle. Approaching on the blind side might give him an edge if guns were in the vehicle. Tom finally pulled out his own gun, carrying it low in his right hand.

He stood in the dark for a moment, watching the occupants as they kept looking over their left shoulders. They must expect him to come up on the driver's side. He smiled to himself, hearing two SSU cars pull up behind him as they announced themselves over the radio. He waited a few more seconds to give them time to take a position next to his own vehicle.

He started toward the car until a young man in the backseat reached down. A moment later, the glint of metal flashed from the floodlight.

"Gun!" He backpedaled to his own car. Dashing around the back of his car, he reached for the mike. He quickly identified himself. "Code 33. Man with a gun. Request two more units. Break."

The call went out, giving his location and the nature of the call. Several units answered up, and he could hear sirens coming from the other side of the fairgrounds.

"Santa Rosa, I need additional units. One unit to block off westbound traffic in front of the fairgrounds on Bennet Avenue. Break." A responding patrol unit answered up and designated herself to take the assignment. Tom wanted to prevent cars entering his field of fire if a gunfight erupted. "Santa Rosa, I need another unit to stop traffic on the south end of Brookwood Avenue as they come off Aston Avenue. Break." Another unit answered up doing that job.

Having locked down the area, he could concentrate on the gangster's car. The first two units dispatched rolled up and fanned out next to him, one on his left and one on his right.

Tom reached down and flicked on the PA system to allow him to give orders to the driver and his passengers. He aimed his weapon at the suspect vehicle with his right hand and activated the mike with his left. "Driver, roll down your window, and with your left hand, pull out the car keys and throw them out the driver's window."

The driver wavered for a moment. They seemed to be talking among themselves while reaching below the seats. *Furtive movements.* Maybe they had more than one gun in the car. The driver straightened up and the keys flew out the window.

"Driver, with both hands, reach out of the window and open the door."

Slowly, the driver complied.

"Driver. Exit the vehicle, face the sound of my voice, and let me see both your hands, palms toward me, above your head."

The driver climbed out of the car, waving his hands.

"Turn slowly around one turn and then stop, facing my voice."

The driver did a complete circle, finally facing Tom.

"Driver, okay, turn with your back toward me, your hands still raised, and slowly back up toward my voice."

Again, the driver complied.

When the gangster got within a few yards, Tom ordered him to stop and motioned to one of the patrol officers to approach, search, and handcuff the driver. Once that was competed, the driver was placed in the back of the patrol unit, and Tom repeated the same process with each of the other occupants.

After all the gangsters were handcuffed, searched, and placed in separate patrol vehicles, Tom and the others searched the vehicle. Two handguns and a bag of meth were found under the seats. In the trunk, they found a sawed-off shotgun, which the gangster in the backseat could access from a tricked-out panel concealed in the fabric. The occupant simply had to trigger a latch to allow easy access to the trunk.

"Transport them to the station," Tom said. "We'll be there in a few minutes." After all the evidence had been removed, he made sure the car was locked and secured.

Tom finally climbed back into his vehicle and headed for the station. It had been like this every night since he got back from Lake Tahoe. Every known Norteño member of importance had been placed under surveillance, stopped, and questioned—or arrested if they held weapons or contraband. Every gang house had been searched if probable cause existed, or if a gangster came with parole or probation conditions.

All this effort and they still had no clue where to find Stevenson's killer. No one wanted to talk. It was as if they were more scared of snitching than going to prison. Ghost was still out here somewhere, but no one wanted to point the cops in the right direction. Fear protected Ghost at the moment. Tom hoped something would break soon.

Common sense would dictate that the killer of a police officer would try to get as far away from the scene of the killing—as quickly as possible. Ghost hoped law enforcement would follow this logic and start looking for him farther and farther from Santa Rosa.

Ghost did not run. He simply returned to his hiding place.

The abandoned house he found his first day in Santa Rosa. He unleashed a firestorm by killing a law-enforcement officer. Before he pulled that trigger, Ghost knew that everyone with a badge would be hunting him down. But he also knew he would bring the wrath of law enforcement down on his former family—Nuestra Familia. For that, he was willing to take the risk.

Every cell would be searched, every inmate grilled, every gang house tossed until something turned up. The pressure would wreak havoc to the gang's criminal enterprises. Those things that made their financial world revolve—getting dope into the prisons and getting their soldiers on the street to do their bidding—would come to a grinding halt. All the things that made the gang so powerful—taxes and profits from the crimes their soldados committed—would dry up like water in Death Valley.

The Family will decree I should die. Okay, I'll bring the heat on them so bad, they'll think a giant blowtorch was turned on them. I'll cripple them until they rue the day they decided to move on me. I will take down as many as I can.

However, for the moment Ghost was stumped. How did he turn up the thermostat on this situation? How could he keep them off balance until he could permanently disappear?

The thought of Kagan in his face up at the Bay caused Ghost to grind his teeth into his bottom lip. Kagan was the one who pulled this all together, who brought the heat down. It was only right that Kagan feel a little of the same heat. Make him squirm.

Ghost had been unable to locate where the detective and his family lived. He made a list in his mind of pressure points in Kagan's life. Those who Ghost knew he could find. Those who worked with Kagan. Tweaker mentioned the prosecutor Diane Phillips. That gave Ghost an idea. It was easy to find a prosecutor. They were creatures of habit. And once he had her in his grasp, it would only be a matter of time before she would give Ghost the answers he sought. Pain was an effective tool.

As he visualized hunting Kagan down, Ghost felt the rush increase. The hunter once more stalking his prey. He felt like a forest fire out of control, burning up those trying to extinguish his flames, those trying to put him back in a cage or into the ground. He burned beyond their reaches. He wanted to keep on burning until he'd brought fear into everyone's life who sought him harm. Make them pay. Then—he would disappear. Vanish. Take a slow boat to China…whatever.

It would take money. He knew a couple places where the NF had stashed a "bank." The NF would not believe he had the *cajones* to rip off their organization's profits. One of those banks was hidden in Sacramento. The "banker" reported to him as regimental commander and word from the leadership that Ghost was no-good would take time to filter down to the streets. The banker would still report to Ghost until this confusion cleared up.

He had started with the bank held by gangsters in the North Bay. It worked just as he planned. Taking money off this banker had been too easy. The guy practically forced Ghost to take the money. The banker was so glad to give the responsibility to someone else. Before he disappeared, Ghost would hit one more bank located in the Sacramento/Stockton area before he disappeared forever.

Only a couple more chores before he slipped away. Time to really give Kagan the one-two punch and put him down for the count. Forever!

Chapter 46

Ghost sank down in the driver seat of his car, watching a man drive into the parking lot. One of Ghost's contact knew this man—a janitor at the Hall of Justice—arrived the same time each night to start his cleaning rounds. There was one thing the man had been entrusted with that Ghost desperately needed—keys to the entire complex.

After quietly opening his door, Ghost made his move.

Just as the janitor climbed out of his vehicle, Ghost crept up behind him and struck him in the head with a tire iron. The man collapsed, and Ghost stood over him ready to strike again if the guy struggled. The janitor lay motionless on the ground.

Grimacing, Ghost scanned the parking lot. No one nearby. No witnesses.

He knelt and fished out the janitor's car keys. He opened the trunk and tossed the unconscious man inside like a heavy sack of potatoes. He stripped the janitor of his uniform, including an identification badge attached to the shirt pocket and a set of keys to the Hall of Justice. He finished by binding the man's arms and legs with duct tape. For good measure, he put tape across the man's mouth to stifle his cries for help when he regained consciousness.

Ghost slipped into the janitor's uniform and attached the ID tag to his shirt lapel. He slammed the trunk closed, pocketed the keys, and tossed the tire iron into a nearby bush.

A quick visit to the local library had given him a good photo of the female prosecutor, which had been snapped by a local newspaper photographer. All he had to do was watch and wait.

He watched where she entered the building and then saw where the light in the DA's office came on. He even saw her standing at her desk before she sat out of sight. So the intelligence on the janitor paid off since he now had keys to the building.

Ghost stalked toward the building, staying in the shadows whenever possible. Once he got close, he edged toward a service door not commonly used. Fingering through the janitor's key ring, Ghost found the one that unlocked the door.

He was inside the Hall of Justice.

Diane's eyes felt heavy and the transcripts started to blur as she struggled to read. Days and nights running together as court dates loomed just ahead. She must be ready. Work seemed to be piling up since her meeting with Tom a few days ago when he returned from Lake Tahoe. She kept waiting for his phone call telling her Ghost has been scooped up. So far—nothing.

The light above her desk was the only one burning in the DA's office. Everyone else had gone home hours ago. They had a life outside of this job. Someone waiting at home. A door opened down the hall and someone entered the offices.

Diane returned to her reading. A crew of night janitors would be making their sweep. It seemed one of them got an early start. A trash container sat next to her, overflowing with discarded papers.

She glanced at the transcript before her, then peered at her computer screen. Using a mouse, she scrolled down to a witness list she had prepared for the James "Ghost" Herndandez murder trial. She compared the witness name on the transcript to the witness list. She looked to see if a subpoena had been prepared, ready to file at a moment's notice. Once Ghost was in custody, she'd fill in the date and time of appearance based on the court's schedule.

Again she heard someone shuffling down the corridor leading to her office. No lights had been turned on. Diane put the transcript aside, stood, and stepped out in the hallway. It took a moment for her eyes to adjust to the darkness. A photocopy machine sat in the hallway a few doors down from her office, giving off a lime-green glow indicating the machine had been left on, its feeble light overwhelmed by the darkness.

Why had no one turned on the lights? She walked as far as the machine in an effort to see who might be coming her way. The light from the copier failed to help her see any farther. She turned, feeling unsettled, and began to walk toward a light switch on the other side of the hallway. If she couldn't determine who had entered the DA's office, she'd give security a call and have them do a walk-through just to be on the safe side.

As she neared the light switch, an arm reached out of a doorway and clamped down on her mouth. A man's voice whispered in her ear, "If you scream, I'll kill you. Understand?"

Her eyes wide, Diane nodded. Her body remained rigid and tense, expecting the worst.

"All I want from you is to tell me where I can find Kagan and his family. You give me that, and I'll let you live. Understand?"

Again she moved her head up and down.

Slowly, the man moved his hand from her mouth and relaxed his grip.

Diane screamed and kicked.

The sound echoed throughout the DA's office. As she screamed, she tried to whirl around to face her attacker. The green light illuminated his face. Instantly, she recognized Ghost before his fist struck her in the face and fell to the ground. The first blow shattered her jaw. He followed her to the ground with his fists, repeatedly striking her face and head, raining blow after crushing blow.

Diane slipped into unconsciousness.

Ghost grabbed Phillips's arms and dragged her into the lighted office.

Once inside, he left her lying on the floor and walked behind the desk. He started searching through drawers and files.

He glanced over and a saw a blinking cursor on the computer screen. The screen saver had activated. He moved the mouse and a document emerged on the screen that Phillips had been working on. Ghost minimized the program and searched for her contact information. He saw Kagan's name referenced alphabetically. One click and all the detective's contact information popped into view.

He grabbed a pen and paper and wrote down the information about Sara, Kagan, and a Lake Tahoe address and telephone number. Following this information, Phillips had entered a notation that this number was not to be called unless it was an emergency. Next to it was a contact identified as Deputy Hoffman of Placer County Sheriff's Office. Ghost wrote this information down, exited the program, and turned the computer off.

"Well, Ms. Prosecutor, I don't need you anymore!"

Ghost pulled the semiauto from under his shirt that he stole from the SSU agent and grabbed a pillow from one of the chairs in her office. He walked toward the fallen woman when a door clicked down the hall. Lights flicked on in the hallway.

Startled, he lunged toward the switch in Phillips's office and smacked the lights off. He pulled the woman's body behind her desk. The footsteps continued in his direction. A deputy suddenly appeared in the doorway. Ghost crouched behind the desk and waited in the dark.

Using a flashlight, the deputy briefly illuminated Phillips's office. Ghost could see the deputy's shoes from under the desk. The lawman paused, then disappeared from the doorway, his footsteps continuing down the hall.

Ghost crept to the doorway and carefully peered around the doorjamb. The deputy worked his way, room to room, down the corridor, then came to a point where the corridor made a ninety-degree turn to the right. He looked back over his shoulder and then rounded the corner out of Ghost's sight.

Ghost looked back to where Phillips was lying. He heard her moan.

He couldn't risk a shot with this jerk in the office roaming around. And if he tried to choke her out, the deputy might hear the noise if she fought back. Reluctantly, he made his way toward the main lobby of the DA's office. He had only minutes to reach the lobby before the deputy circled back. With the hallways all lit up, the deputy would see him in an instant.

He was almost to the front door when he heard footsteps rounding the corner down the hall. The deputy was returning. Ghost heard louder moans. The deputy ran in the direction of the sounds. He paused in the doorway of Phillips's office and flashed his light into the darkened room. The man gasped and dashed inside.

Ghost scrambled for the front door and disappeared down the main hallway as he heard people running up the stairs. He reached the front lobby and picked up a metal chair. No time for keys. He hurled the chair through a plateglass window and dashed outside.

Once in the parking lot, Ghost ran. A block away where he hid his car, Ghost heard the first siren. Then others slowly built up until the wail of a dozen patrol cars headed for the Hall of Justice building.

He started the car and made his getaway before patrol units arrived. Ten minutes later, he parked his car and slipped through a break in the galvanized fence surrounding his hideout. He glanced around quickly to see if anyone was watching. No one spotted him. Once again, he disappeared into the darkened house by removing the plywood that covered one of the street-level windows. He replaced the sheet of wood against the window and propped it up from inside.

He ran up a flight of rickety stairs to the second floor, then made his way to an empty bedroom that offered a view of the street below. He peered in the direction he had just run.

No movement.

Ghost sat in the darkness and waited, getting his breath under control. The street in front of the abandoned house was illuminated by a few streetlamps. He listened carefully to the noises outside. The sound of crickets interrupted by an occasional patrol car screaming by with its red, blue, and white lights flashing.

He felt a warm, trickling sensation on his chest. Ghost reached under his shirt and felt liquid beneath his fingers. He pulled his hand out and examined it in the light from the street. Blood. His blood. Stitching from the stab wounds to his chest must have pulled apart when he was running or wrestling with that prosecutor. He pulled off his uniform shirt and put pressure on the wound until the bleeding slowed.

As the adrenaline rush from his night's activities subsided, the pain in his chest became more pronounced.

He watched a patrol car whiz by and then slow down and execute a U-turn. Maybe unseen neighbors had spotted him in the area and called it in. Another patrol car showed up. Police flashed their spotlights on the houses and yards on both sides of the street. Several teams of officers started to search on foot. Overhead, the whirling thunder of helicopter rotors churned the air with their fury. The helicopter team activated their powerful searchlights, flooding the night with the intensity of daylight illumination.

The cops must have gotten lucky. Someone's description might have matched his car leaving the Hall of Justice.

In the distance, he heard barking dogs, growing louder and louder. The sound of the dogs got his adrenaline pumping again. He had to move fast. Ghost quickly changed his clothes, still holding on to a bandage plastered over his chest wound.

He slipped out a back door and made his way through the abandoned neighborhood. He crisscrossed the streets leading toward the freeway, looking around for anyone or anything who might pose a threat. It took him more than an hour to safely navigate to the freeway.

Ghost paralleled the freeway for several miles, heading south away from the search. He followed an exit from the freeway that led into a large parking lot of a truck stop. A fleet of big rigs sat idle in the lot, their drivers getting a quick cup of coffee or a bite to eat inside the all-night diner.

He had his pick of transportation. Giving each one a quick look, he spotted one truck and smiled. Just the one! It was an empty cattle trailer that had not yet been cleaned up. He opened up the door and climbed inside. He made his way as far forward as he could get and lay down in the darkness, surround by manure left behind by cattle. Through the air holes, he watched for anyone who might be tracking him. Seeing no one, he settled back to get some rest. He waited for his chauffeur to move this tractor-trailer to a place where Ghost would be safe.

Once safely out of town, he'd head for the mountains and see a little of Lake Tahoe. A little high attitude and mountain air would do him good. And another killing or two would make him famous.

Chapter 47

Santa Rosa

Tom awoke with a start, cell phone ringing on the nightstand. The digital clock read two in the morning. A dispatcher, her voice brusque and businesslike, said, "Detective Kagan?"

"Yeah." He rolled out of bed.

"The watch commander wanted you to know first—Diane Phillips was attacked at the Hall of Justice. They rushed her to Memorial Hospital."

He struggled to clear his mind. "Why not Kaiser—? Never mind. What happened? How bad is it?"

"Pretty bad from what I hear. A deputy was checking a suspicious noise call at the district attorney's office and found her lying on the floor. Someone attacked her with his fists, they guess. She's still unconscious but they say she'll survive. Contact Six-Sam-Five at the hospital. Oh, there's a second victim. A janitor found locked in the trunk of his car outside of the Hall of Justice. He'd been knocked unconscious with a tire iron and tied up." She gave him the victim's name and a few more details.

"I'll be responding to the hospital."

Tom dressed quickly. He walked through the dark house and quietly closed the door behind him. Once he pulled away from Lawson's house, Tom activated lights and siren, driving Code 3 to the hospital.

The emergency room was a flurry of activity. A sergeant and several patrol officers had stationed themselves around the emergency ward, scrutinizing everyone who approached the examination room where Phillips lay. They were just beginning to wheel her upstairs for X-rays.

He followed the gurney as the patrol sergeant caught up to him. Tom tried to skirt around this guy as he trailed Phillips upstairs, but the sergeant latched on to him like a bloodsucker. "Hey, Tom, hold up one minute."

Irritated, Tom watched the elevator door close as the attendants took Phillips upstairs. He turned to face the sergeant. "What do you want, Hilby?"

Sergeant Dawson Hilby—a ten-year veteran who made rank last year after working patrol his whole career—found himself tasked to the limit. The last thing Tom wanted was to get caught up in Hilby's penchant for drama. He did not want to go toe-to-toe with a crusty sergeant from the sheriff's office over who had jurisdiction.

"Gotta call from Sergeant Harry Bristol at the SO handing me the case. I thought…"

"Forget it, Hilby. You need to work it out with Harry. I'm not involved."

"But I thought—"

"You thought wrong. The SO handed the case over to us per our jurisdictional agreement. Until this gets ironed out, this is your baby—run with it. Now, I have a friend I need to check on." Tom smiled at the thought of Hilby and the sheriff's sergeant duking it out. Hilby's gut hung over his belt and the man's arms were the size of a pair of chopsticks. The sheriff's sergeant, on the other hand, fought in the Police Olympics heavyweight division and won the gold medal three years in a row. Hilby would get creamed.

Rarely did jurisdictional issues between agencies come to blows. Supervisor to supervisor, these differences normally worked themselves out in heated negotiations that sounded like opposing litigants during a *Judge Judy* show. All talk. No action.

The sergeant faced a dilemma. Hilby's entire graveyard shift was tied up in providing security for Phillips, maintaining the crime scene, and fanning out in the city looking for her attacker. At least until the sheriff's office took over. The sergeant was motivated to pass this investigation over to the sheriff's office immediately.

It was no secret Hilby's mission was to make himself look good. He wanted to free his team up and get back to patrol so he might get a pat on the back from the watch commander. Tom's mission was simple. He wanted to get his hands on Ghost and protect Phillips and those he loved.

Hilby started in. "After the deputy called this in, we learned—"

"Save the speech, Hilby. I already got the lowdown from one of your men."

Hilby looked like a blowfish with his mouth wide open. "Who did—?"

"Does it matter?" Tom again cut him off. "I know you got problems. Frankly, I couldn't give a rip. That's my friend up there. That is all I care about."

Tom was walking a thin line of insubordination with Hilby, but the man just ticked him off.

"Now I know the assault on the janitor happened in the parking lot," the sergeant said, trying to keep up with Tom's fast pace toward the elevator. "But it seems apparent the assailant was intending to enter the county building to assault Ms. Phillips. So I think that the two cases are related and should be investigated as one continuous string of events. The most important event is the attempt on Ms. Phillips's life. She's an officer of the court, and the assault happened in their jurisdiction."

Tom lost patience with Hilby. "Contact the SO watch commander if you can't work it out with Harry. You guys make that call. Right now, my only concern is Ms. Phillips and the janitor and catching the animal who attacked them."

Irritation crossed Hilby's face. It seemed the patrol sergeant was going to make one last pitch. "I was hoping you could speak to the SO since you work closely with them. Tell them—"

"Not going to happen, Hilby. Your job. Your responsibility."

Hilby's shoulders slumped as he walked away. He was on his cell phone talking to Dispatch as Tom entered the elevator. Hilby might pitch a complaint about Tom's attitude to Art Crenshaw, but because of the race for lieutenant going on between the two sergeants, Tom's supervisor would back him up and let Hilby look bad in front of the brass. Or maybe, in light of his last conversation with Crenshaw, his supervisor would just want to do the right thing and back Tom's play. It felt strange to be seeing his supervisor in a different light. For the moment, it felt good to have the support of his boss.

The elevator door was about to close when Tom saw the same patrolman he talked to earlier walk by. Thrusting his arm to prevent the door from closing, Tom stuck his head out and motioned the officer closer. "When your boss gets off the phone, could you tell him I need him to start making calls to dayshift? Tell them to get their butts in here pronto. We'll need help protecting the deputy DA upstairs."

The patrolman gave a thumbs-up and walked away.

As the elevator door started to close again, the sergeant glared at him. Tom gave him a mock salute and positioned his other hand near his ear as if he was making a phone call. The door closed before Tom could hear what the sergeant yelled back. Probably just as well if the man's livid face was any sign as to what his words might be.

Another passenger in the elevator looked at Tom. "Man, that guy is mad. What did you do to tick him off?"

"I showed up for the job."

Tom had gotten a glimpse of Phillips as they wheeled her into the elevator just before Hilby cornered him. He could hardly recognize his friend. Only a few nights ago they were sitting around having dinner, chatting about the case. And now her face was cut and swollen.

Rage burned through Tom. David. Stevenson. Phillips. Who else would Ghost hurt or kill before Tom tracked him down? He clenched his hands into tight fists, frustrated that he seemed to be getting nowhere in this case. Just chasing his tail. Something had to give. And soon—before others died.

The daytime nurses just took over the shift. A nurse walked into the room as Tom sat next to Phillips's bedside, waiting for her to open her eyes. She lay there in the same position they left her in hours ago. Her facial features were hidden behind tightly wrapped gauze and bandages. The little skin that was exposed was mottled with black and blue bruising. He could only imagine what the rest of her body looked like.

A doctor had tried to close a deep gash on her forehead with stitches as best he could. After running X-rays and scans, the surgeon told Tom the outlook appeared *positive*, but he'd know more once she woke up. The doctor didn't need a medical degree to know that simple fact.

"Friend of yours?" The nurse gave him a smile as she walked around the bedside.

Tom nodded.

She glanced at the monitors near Phillips's bed, then gazed over at him. "You're a police officer, right"

Tom nodded again.

"Look, I'll be checking on her all day. Why don't you go get some sleep? Leave me your number and I'll give you a call if there's any change."

Tom was too tired to argue. He stood, wrote down his cell phone number on the back of his business card, and handed it to her. A police officer sat in a chair just outside the doorway. Tom spoke with him to make sure everything was being done to protect Phillips. The officer promised to call Tom if anything came up.

He stopped by a pay phone in the hospital lobby and made a long distance call to Sara. It was good to hear her voice.

"Hi, sweetheart," Sara said. "Glad you called. Sound a little tired."

"Can't hide anything from you." He thought about Phillips in the hospital bed above him and knew he ought to keep this information from his wife right now. "Just wanted to make sure you and the others are doing okay. Oh…Paul Lawson invited me to stay at his house while I'm down here." He gave her that number in case of an emergency.

"That was thoughtful of him. How's everything going?"

"Pretty intense." He tried to put Phillips's image out of his mind for the moment. "We're looking for this killer high and low. Sooner or later, we'll get lucky. Until then, I want you all to still stay put." He held his breath, hoping she'd drop the subject. "I'll check in from time to time to see how you're holding up. How's Mary?"

"She's hurting. It'll take time for her to come to grips with Bill's death. Right now, she's holding on and trying to take care of Jonathan." The mention of the boy's name choked Sara up. It took a moment for her to continue. "He misses his dad. It's like a part of him expects his father to come walking through that door. And the other part...well, you see the loss in his eyes. It's hard to watch."

Tom clenched his jaw and leaned his head against the phone booth. "I wish I could take their pain away. To turn the clock back and start over. If only I'd—"

"Don't do that, Tom. Don't beat yourself up for things you have no control over."

Tom's helplessness turned to anger. "I can't help but think if I'd made other choices, Bill would still be here."

"Please don't."

He slowly expelled a breath to give him time to answer. "Yeah. This thing with Bill just opened up old wounds. You're right, Sara. I need to leave it alone."

"I'm sorry, I just meant—"

"I know. I'll call you later, honey." Tom hung up the phone before she could respond, then walked toward his car.

He needed to get some rest.

He'd pushed himself too long, too many weeks with hardly any sleep. His body was starting to rebel, shut down. And no matter how hard he struggled, he could not get traction on this case.

As he pulled into Lawson's driveway, he saw the pastor waiting on the front steps. He parked the car and made his way to the front door.

Lawson stiffly stuck his hands in his jean pockets. "I heard about your friend. Is there anything I can do?"

Tom shook his head, too tired to carry on much of a conversation. "Thanks, but no thanks. I'm going to catch a few winks and start this all over again until it's done. He started up the steps when Lawson placed a hand on his shoulder.

"I have an idea, Tom. I have a few days off and I have a CCW for my firearm. I know you are worried about Sara and the others. How about if I head up to Tahoe and stay with them for a few days until you have a better handle on this case? Would that ease your mind?"

"That would take a big load off my mind, Paul. I can't tell you how much this means to me."

"Just consider it a friend helping a friend. I'm already packed. I'll head that way right now."

"Thanks. Stay in touch."

"You got it, brother. Now, go get some rest."

Tom made his way into the house and gratefully climbed into bed. Sleep was the only thing he needed right now. That, and the ability to turn his mind off and try to forget the past. Every time the past reared its ugly head, it brought guilt along with it like a long-lost twin.

He shuddered as he thought of the darkness in his life. How long could a man stand alone against this darkness, this evil, and still survive? He felt like he was standing in the eye of the storm, watching the darkness coming toward him with all its fury and force.

Time was running out.

Chapter **48**

Sacramento

Ghost had been a busy man after he attacked Phillips and took the ride in the cattle car. There was another NF bank in Sacramento he planned on hitting on his way up to Lake Tahoe. Before that, he must make a few more stops while in the state capitol. The cattle car, as expected, made a stop at a Pilot Travel Center off I-80 in the sprawling city of Sacramento. He rolled out of the trailer and used the showers at the center to clean up, then jumped into fresh clothes he bought off the hanger at the twenty-four-hour truck stop. He tossed the janitor's uniform into a trash bin.

Catching a bus into the heart of the city, his first stop was a hardware store where Ghost picked up a suction cup, duct tape, glass cutters, and the tools and wires he needed to hot wire his next ride. After these purchases, he searched the Capitol Mall parking structures. He located the ride of his dreams—or at least that met his needs right now—a small RV equipped with a bed, a little kitchen, and a toilet.

Ghost watched the owner park the vehicle in a metered parking spot and walk away with his family. They seemed to be headed for one of the large department stores. With two teenage daughters on the prowl for new clothes, Ghost knew the family would be gone for quite a while. Time to make a clean getaway.

Ghost popped the driver's door open, punched the key lock, and wired the vehicle to fire up with a turn of a screwdriver. He drove the stolen RV to the Arden Fair Mall farther north, where he quickly exchanged the license plates with another RV. Now he was ready to roll.

He purchased a disposable cell phone and phone card to make a few calls while on the move. He used this phone to make contact with a young NF banker living off Highway 50 on the way out of town. They agreed to meet at a public park near where the gangster lived. The exchange went quick.

Ghost eyed the man clutching the gang's funds. He appeared suspicious but unwilling to challenge Ghost's authority. Ghost knew the youngster had heard of him and was in awe of the power he wielded. Ghost was not someone the kid wanted to tangle with. Using that power, Ghost snatched the money—held in a gray gym bag filled with cash and ammunition—and praised him for his commitment to the Family.

Ghost intentionally let his shirt fly open in the valley breeze as they made the switch. The gangster's eyes widened when he saw Ghost had two pistols stashed in his waistband under his shirt. Then the kid's eyes widened even more. He must've seen blood oozing from Ghost's bandage.

The younger man also slid another bag toward Ghost. "Here are the tools you asked for."

Ghost unzipped the bag and peered inside. A Mossberg 500 with a pistol grip had been stashed inside along with enough shotgun shells to ward off a small army. He nodded his appreciation and zipped the bag closed. He stopped in a sport shop in Fulton, just off the freeway, and purchased a hunting knife, a powerful set of binoculars, camouflage clothing, and fishing equipment.

"Going up to the mountains?" The store clerk eyed him as she rang up the total.

"Yeah, I've been cooped up for too long. Want to get out and see a little nature." Ghost handed her the cash for the purchase and gave her a little wink. "You know what they say, all work and no play..."

He started to pick up his purchases. "Hey, by the way. I'm interested in doing a little animal watching at night. You got any night-vision scopes?"

The young woman shook her head. "No, we just sold out, but there's an Army surplus store up the road. I'm sure they have that kind of stuff." She gave him directions.

Ghost made two more stops on his way into the wilderness. First, he found a new and used boat shop off the highway between the towns of Fulton and Placerville. He purchased a small, thirteen-foot metal boat that could be easily carried upside down on the roof of his RV and a small outboard motor. He lashed the boat to the roof and stored the motor and an empty gas can inside. The second stop was the Army surplus store where he found night-vision equipment.

After climbing back into the RV, he began his ascent into the mountains on Interstate 50. Now he was ready to go hunting. He was ready to turn Tom Kagan's world upside down.

A law book was pushed through the opening into DJ's library cell. He and Snake had arranged a transfer to the Pelican Bay prison law library once again. The guard's footsteps echoed through the corridor as he returned to the book center.

"What's going on with your regiment, DJ? Word's gone out that everything is coming loose. The canines are hitting everybody. It's bad for business."

DJ wiped drops of perspiration from his forehead. He was screwing up in a big way. "I know, I know. Ghost ripped off one of our banks, and he has Five-O breathing down the necks of all our people."

"You're losing your grip. Handle it or we will handle it for you.?" Snake's voice bordered on disrespect.

This was an ultimatum that threatened his power. DJ must appear to be handling this. "I've got my people hunting that dog down. My guess—he's running scared like some coward. He can run but he cannot hide. Trust me. His wind will be taken soon."

"And what about Mikio?"

DJ held his breath before answering. "My source says he's bluffing about stashing information that could damage us. I gave them a green light to hit him. Hit him good, so everyone knows we're the ones who ordered it. Not Ghost."

"How is his family handling it? This thing...will his brother and the rest of the family accept your decision?"

"Not your concern, Snake. Not your concern." DJ gritted his teeth. He hated being questioned on how he took care of his own business. But the damage Ghost caused opened DJ up for all kinds of smut. It made him look weak. He knew that when they hit Mikio, there would be those in his family who might not accept it. He'd have to deal with them later. Now was the time to put out fires.

The ulcer in his stomach acted up again. The pain was getting worse, not better, even with the medicine he got from medical. He wished he could kill Ghost himself—with his bare hands.

Chapter 49

Santa Rosa

Hospital staff had just delivered dinner to the patients when Tom arrived in the ICU, at least for those who were in any shape to eat. He had not heard anything on Phillips's condition, so he decided to check on her status himself. A different police officer sat outside her room. Tom spoke with him for a moment and made sure his numbers had been passed on in case they needed to reach him.

He walked into her room. Phillips was lying in the same position she was in last night. A passing nurse told him there had been no change. The room was quiet except for the beeping of a monitoring system attached to her.

He sat back in his chair and made several phone calls. Garcia and his men were out running down leads, but no new information had surfaced. It was as if Ghost simply disappeared. He dialed his office for messages and spoke briefly to Art Crenshaw, bringing his supervisor up to speed on the case, including the status of Sara, Mary, and Jonathan.

Interestingly, Crenshaw remained unusually quiet. After Tom finished his report, the sergeant simply told him to stay in touch and to let him know if he needed anything. Maybe Crenshaw was finally coming around. Maybe. Still, the man's lack of input made Tom uneasy.

Running out of things to do, he pulled out a novel he picked up in the gift store downstairs and began to read John Lescroart's novel *The Oath*. From time to time, Tom would glance over and check on Phillips. He watched her as if expecting to witness her eyes opening in the next minute. Nothing. Finally, he returned to his reading, his ears alert for any sound that might give him hope that she regained consciousness.

Halfway through the novel, Tom became distracted by a noise in the hallway. Another officer had arrived to take over guard duties. Graveyard shift. Tom put the novel away.

He went out into the hallway. The new officer had just settled into a chair to begin his watch. Tom asked the officer to contact him if there was any change in Phillips's condition, then drove back to the Hall of Justice close to midnight. A chilling coastal breeze worked its way through the blackness of the night, and fog began to blanket the parking lot.

Tom contacted the sheriff's communications center and asked if the deputy who found Phillips could meet him downstairs and walk him through the DA's office. The deputy happened to be at the station finishing paperwork and met him outside the entrance to the courts. They walked upstairs and the deputy opened up the DA's office. "Tell me what you saw when you first entered."

The deputy rubbed his nose as he tried to remember. "I was walking down the main corridor when I thought I heard a muffled scream. I couldn't even tell whether it was inside this building or outside. I started to search every office to be on the safe side."

They neared Phillips's office when the guard looked over his shoulder, down the corridor. "I did a quick walk-through to see if anything was out of the ordinary. On my way back, I started to flick on lights. Everything had been turned off."

"Even in her office?"

"No, no lights. So I flicked on the overheads and flashed my light into each office. Still don't know how I missed her in there." He gestured toward her office.

Tom saw faint streaks of blood on the ground leading to where she was found. It would have been easy to miss this in the dark. The area had been cordoned off by the first officer on the scene. Although faint, blood spattered in the hallway, and then drops of smeared blood led to the office. Her attacker must have jumped her in the hallway and dragged her into her office. Phillips must have been working late and heard something. Why would she have turned the light off when she heard something? Or did Ghost turn them off?

Tom strolled into her office and flicked on an overhead light. He studied the desk. She was somewhat orderly, even though her desk always seemed to be piled high with files. Everything on her desk was in disarray. Someone else must have gone through these files. What was Ghost looking for? He must have been interrupted by the deputy coming down the hall. And he left her alive. Why? Maybe the deputy put a crimp in Ghost's plans for Phillips?

Thank God.

He continued to study the room. So she heard something and got up to investigate. She walked out into the hallway where she was attacked. He eyed the computer monitor on the desk.

"Do you remember whether her computer was turned on when you found her?"

The deputy scratched his nose again. "It was off. Nothing was on in this room."

The first thing most people did when they entered their office was to switch on the computer because it always took a while to fire up. Tom made a mental note to ask her if—no when—she regained consciousness.

A pillow had been left on the floor near where she was lying. What was this about? Maybe the deputy turned out to be her rescuer after all. Ghost would not want to leave witnesses behind. Something must have interrupted him before he could finish her off. The pillow would have made a cheap silencer.

"Tell me in detail what you did when you first entered the DA's offices."

The deputy walked him through the details, turning on lights, coming down this corridor, going to the far end, and hearing Phillips's moans on his way back.

"Did you hear anything other than her moans? Door closing, footsteps, anything?"

The deputy shook his head.

What was Ghost after? It wasn't just to kill Phillips. He could have easily killed her as she was leaving the building. He was after something else in this office.

Until Phillips woke up, he'd just have to try to figure it out on his own.

Tom used his cell phone to call Garcia while he walked from the DA's office to his car.

"Hector, it's Tom. Just checking in."

"I heard about Diane. I'm sorry. I feel like it's my fault, man. We should've had Ghost in custody by now. Me and my guys have never blown it like this."

"Hey, you can't blame yourself. There was no way of knowing he'd be well enough to attack your agent and escape."

"We should have been more careful." Bitterness weighted Garcia's voice. "Bill's dead. Diane almost killed. Sara and Bill's family in hiding. When's it gonna stop?"

"When we catch him," Tom said. "And we will."

"I've got some more bad news. Gato skipped out on Mikio. And Mikio came back to Santa Rosa looking for him."

"That's crazy. With Ghost floating around, Mikio is in even more danger."

"There's no reasoning with that guy. Once he gets something in his head, there's no turning back."

"Sounds like someone else I know."

"Yeah...you, Tom." Garcia laughed at his own joke and then stopped. "Hey, since Mikio's in town already, let's go pick his brain. He might know something that'd help us catch this whacko. Something we haven't thought of."

"Good idea. I'll meet you at his apartment in a few."

The lights were on in Mikio's apartment as Tom and Garcia knocked on the door. He peered through the security peephole before opening the door.

"What's up, Five-O?" Mikio glanced from Tom to Garcia. "I take it you haven't found Ghost."

"You guessed right." Garcia brushed past him as he made his way into the living room. Tom followed.

"Why don't you come in and make yourself comfortable." Mikio closed the door behind them, his sarcasm following them down the hall. He joined them in the living room where Garcia was pacing back and forth.

Tom had taken a seat in the recliner. "I'm going to be honest with you, Mikio. We can't figure what this lunatic is up to. Common sense would dictate this guy would run and hide as far away as he could get. Instead, he comes back here, kills Detective Stevenson, whacks one of his own soldiers, and breaks into the DA's office to attack the prosecutor. Then he just disappears. It doesn't make sense."

"He attacked the prosecutor?"

Tom nodded and gave him the details.

Mikio scratched his head. "Well, some of it makes sense. Once Rascal was killed, Tweaker was the only one who could really tie Ghost to Paco's and Rascal's murders—except for Juan. The others were just following orders from someone else. And he didn't come after me and my nephew because word on the street was we'd flown the coop."

"So where is Ghost?"

Mikio lowered his head for a moment before continuing. "He's trying to cover his little secret with the hits on Paco and me. But when the secret got out to the Mesa—the NF generals—he knew it would only be a matter of time before he got whacked. My guess is he decided to really stir up the hornet's nest in order to bring as much heat down on the NF while he sought his own revenge."

Tom rubbed his brow. "So he kills Detective Stevenson because Bill is working the case against Ghost, just to cause the NF problems?"

"Maybe. He figures he's already going to wind up on death row if he's caught, so he's got nothing to lose."

"So why didn't he kill the prosecutor?" Tom asked. "Why beat her up and drag her into the office? Why trash her place?"

"He needed to get something out of her." Mikio scratched his jaw. "Or he needed something out of her office. Sounds like he was surprised before he could finish whatever he was doing."

"But what was he looking for?"

"Your guess is as good as mine," Mikio said. "Witness lists? Addresses? I don't know. If I were him, I'd have flown the coop by now."

Garcia looked at the other two men, a look of frustration on his face, then finally focused his attention on Mikio. "Speaking of which, I wish you'd go back to the safe house and wait until we catch this guy. I don't want to lose another witness."

Mikio smiled. "Ah, you really care about me." His smiled disappeared. "Juan is running on the streets here. I want to try to pull him in, reason with him, before he does something stupid. Besides, I believe Ghost is long gone."

Garcia shrugged. "At least I tried."

"I've got information that won't make you happy," Mikio said. "Word is he ripped off the NF bank in Sacramento. He's running with a lot of cash in his pocket. He's sticking it to the NF where it hurts—in their pocketbook." Mikio flexed his arm where he'd been shot. The wound, still covered, reminded him of how close they got to him last time. Ghost was still out there—hiding. "Like I said before, this man has nothing to lose."

Chapter 50

Lake Tahoe

Ghost had never been to Lake Tahoe. He stopped near the summit of the highway, just before the road started its long descent to the valley floor, to stretch his legs. In the distance, he saw Lake Tahoe's dark-blue waters cradled in the arms of the Sierra Mountains, their gray slopes splashed with green patches of forest.

His gaze followed the road as it descended into yellow and green groves of trees. Off to his right, he saw the city of South Lake Tahoe's towering casinos on the Nevada side of the state line. The lake stretching for miles to the north. He looked at his map to get his bearings. He had to take the split to the left, Highway 89, to reach the west side of the lake.

In about thirty minutes, he was passing Emerald Bay. Up ahead, he saw a sign for a state park turnoff a few miles down the road.

There was one thing he needed to take care of before he faced off with the cops. He had been fighting it since he fled the hospital, but his body was tired and his wounds needed a chance to heal. His exertion at the Hall of Justice seriously tore many of the stitches loose as he ran, and the wound kept reopening. He needed to hold up someplace for a few days.

He drove for several more miles until he saw a sign identifying the state park between the highway and the lake below. He pulled into the park and found an unoccupied campsite. He slowly edged the camper into one of the parking spaces and unpacked. The other campers pitched their gear closer to the water or farther back in the park.

Ghost started a fire with dry branches from nearby trees. He pulled a folding chair from the RV and set it near the flames, stretching his legs out to bask in the warmth. The moon peered over the eastern mountains, sending its pale softness across the Tahoe basin.

It was the first time he really began to unwind since the Bay, since before he got the message that DJ wanted him to have a roommate. There had been a lot of bloodshed since then.

And there was more blood to shed in the future. But not right now.

Maybe he could have been a forest ranger in another life. Living outdoors appealed to him. He laughed at the thought as he stoked the fire.

Hunger gnawed at him. Ghost pulled out a camp stove from under the camper. He connected it to a butane tank, turned the knobs, and lit each burner. He put a pot on the stove and filled it with water. He opened several cans of vegetables, then pulled out some hot dogs, put them on a coat hanger, and dangled them over the campfire. He pulled out a beer and waited for dinner to warm up.

Once the meal was hot, he ate slowly and savored the freedom to choose what he wanted to eat and when he wanted to eat it. He finished the meal and cleaned up. The food and the beer took its toll as he sauntered back inside the camper. He closed and locked the door behind him, then fell asleep almost immediately.

The sun had moved high overhead when Ghost finally woke up, rays of sunlight flashing across his face through a window. He opened the door to find warmth from a late Indian summer that had descended over the campgrounds. He decided to start with the breakfast of champions and pulled another beer from the cooler. He stretched out in the chair and rested his legs on a picnic table that came with the campsite.

He was on his third beer when two girls walked by. He estimated they were in their late teens, probably traveling with Mom and Dad. He smiled at them. One of them smiled back.

"Where you girls from?" He tried to play the friendly camper. He eyed the older girl who was wearing shorts and a halter top.

"We're from Oregon," the older girl said. The younger one, probably her sister, hit her in the ribs with an elbow. They giggled. "Where you from?"

"I'm from LA," Ghost said. "I'm in the movie business."

The older girl's eyes lit up with interest. She took a few steps toward his campsite. The younger girl tugged at her arm, telling her they should be going. The older girl wasn't ready to leave. "What do you do in the movies?"

He took a swig of his beer, making her wait for his answer. "I'm a stuntman. You know what that is?"

The older girl nodded. "You take a lot of chances so famous actors don't get hurt."

"That's right. I flip cars over, jump out of buildings, and I've even been set on fire once or twice."

"That's *so* cool." She took a few more steps toward him. The other girl stared at her older sister and made head gestures in the direction of their campsite. She ignored the younger girl, who finally threw her hands up and walked away.

She returned her attention to Ghost. "My name's Nancy. What's yours?"

"They call me MacGyver." He saw the name slipped right past her. "Hey, you want a beer?"

"I'm not old enough. I'm only seventeen." She looked down to the ground, blushing. "But I turn eighteen in two months."

"Sounds to me like you're old enough to have a brew. Here, I'll get you one."

Nancy came closer and sat near him. She eyed his tattoos with interest. "Those are interesting. Did they hurt?"

"Like a mother." Ghost grinned at her, popped the top off the beer, and handed it to her. Nancy hesitated, then slowly reached for the bottle.

She brought it to her lips, took one gulp, and choked. "Oh, I'm sorry." She wiped her chin, white with suds.

"No problem. Drink slow, and you'll get the hang of it quick enough."

She put it to her lips again and took a smaller sip. This one stayed in her mouth. She looked at him with a look of confidence. Stubbornness.

"See, just takes practice." He watched her take another sip. "You ever thought of getting a tattoo?"

She giggled. "My parents would kill me."

"Don't you ever want to walk on the wild side? You know…do something your parents don't want you to do? Live a little dangerously."

Her eyes danced with a look of mischievousness. She took another sip and then another. "Yeah, I'd like to live a little on the dangerous side. Just do things for fun that I want to do."

"I know what you mean." Ghost looked her over. It had been forever since he'd been with a woman. Boys were good, but girls were better.

Something in the way he looked at her caused Nancy to blush. She took another sip of the beer, then another. He could tell she liked him looking at her like that. Like she was older.

She'd finished the beer. He handed her another.

"You trying to get me drunk, Mr. Hollywood?" Nancy giggled and took a deep gulp. Ghost read her face and knew he excited her in a way the boys back home never could. They didn't live on the dangerous side.

"Now why would I try to get you drunk, sweet stuff?" His chuckle sounded wicked. It caused her to giggle again nervously. She gulped more of the beer and finished it.

"MacGyver, could I have another?"

"Sure, sweetheart. You can have whatever your little ole heart desires. Here, let me open it for you."

Nancy snickered and moved closer. He handed it to her and let his hand rest briefly on her knee.

"Your sister coming back?"

"No, she'll hang around our camper over there. She pointed to another campsite in the distance, among a grove of trees. "My parents went to town for supplies. They'll be back in an hour or so."

Ghost moved closer. He tipped his bottle in her direction. "Here's a toast to those who like to live...dangerously."

Nancy smiled and took a long swig from her bottle. "I'm really starting to like this stuff."

Ghost smiled to himself and moved even closer. He watched her chest as she drank. His throat tightened. He reached over and put his hand on her bare leg. She jumped and sprayed a mouthful of beer all over his hand. He kept his hand where it was.

"Oh, look what you made me do." She peered at his hand resting on her leg.

"You want to see the inside?" He jerked his head in the direction of the RV. He watched her eyes as he stroked her leg. Her gaze darted from his hand to his eyes, a look of fear and excitement on her face.

A car pulled into the campground and drove to where Nancy had pointed out her family was camped. Moments later, he heard yelling in the distance and a car door slam. The driver put the car in gear, spun the tires, and headed in his direction. It screeched to a halt near his camper. Ghost quickly withdrew his hand from the girl's leg.

Nancy took one look at the driver and gasped. "It's my dad." She dropped the beer at her feet.

Ghost groaned. This was all he needed. Some white cracker of a dad bent out of shape because some guy made a move on his little girl. *It's not like she doesn't want it, Dad.*

A man leaped out of the car and glared over the rooftop. "Nancy, what are you doing here?"

She looked at the beer bottle lying at her feet, then back at her father, speechless.

The man stormed around the car, flung the passenger door open, and glared at her. "Get in the car—*now!*"

She made a dash for the car. Her father slammed the passenger door shut and turned toward Ghost. "I should report you. Giving beer to a minor. You should be ashamed of yourself. You're old enough to be her father."

Ghost let him vent. The party was over and there was nothing he could do about it. If he kept his cool, maybe this cracker would blow off some steam and then scram. The last thing he needed right now was for an irate dad to call the cops.

Ghost just stared back sullenly, showing nothing but contempt.

The father seemed to run out of steam. He stormed back to his side of the car, got in, and slammed the door. Then the car took the fastest route to Nancy's family's campground. The car slid to a halt, the father yelling at the girl as they got out. A woman's voice joined the yelling. It sounded like Nancy was getting it from both parents.

He stretched out his legs and savored the last drop of his beer. It would have been so much fun if Daddy hadn't come along. There would be other opportunities. After all, he was a free man and there was so much to choose from out here.

And then he thought of Tom Kagan. Once Ghost was in place, all he had to do was wait and watch until it was time for the kill.

Ghost leaned back and felt the warmth of the sun across his face. Once again, he felt like the hunter he was supposed to be, hunting those who dared to cross him, who dared to disrespect him.

Killing excited him. And the thought of killing someone Kagan loved made the killing even sweeter.

Chapter 51

State ranger Bob Kremer slowly drove his four-wheel drive Ford Bronco, through the campground. It was well past midnight and most of the campers had curled up in their sleeping bags, fast asleep. He checked the list of campsites and realized one of the occupied sites was unregistered.

He jotted down the license number and description of the RV. He'd run the plate later, noting the license-plate holder was from a dealership in the Sacramento area. *Nice setup.* He grabbed his green Smokey-the-Bear hat, climbed out of the vehicle, and put the hat on before venturing through the campsite and knocking on the door of the camper. "State Ranger."

No one seemed to stir, so he rapped on the door again and announced himself a second time. A moment later he heard someone mumbling inside and saw the camper shook. "Open the door."

A few moments later the door opened, and a disheveled man covered with tattoos peered outside with tired eyes.

Warning flags started to go off as Bob stepped to one side of the doorway. Something did not feel right here. He took a step backward, realizing he was already committed. Too late to backtrack to his car. The ranger lowered his hand to his gun belt, resting it on the butt of his gun.

"Sorry to wake you up, sir, but you failed to register. Need to see some identification."

The man nodded and rummaged in his pants pocket lying on a chair near the door. "Sorry about that. Came in late and didn't know where to check in. I thought I'd take care of it in the morning."

"No problem, we can take care of that right now. Just let me see some ID."

"Sure thing, Officer. Let me see, where'd I put that wallet?" The man pulled out a drawer near the doorway. "Ah, here it is." He reached into the drawer.

Instinctively, Bob unsnapped his gun belt and grasped the butt of his gun.

He was not fast enough.

The man in the camper suddenly pulled out a gun and fired twice. Bob was struck in the face both times. His body slumped to the ground.

Tom placed a call to Sara from the hospital on his way to check on Phillips. He thought he'd check in before taking up vigil at Phillips's bedside for the rest of the night.

"Still like the cabin?"

"This place is fabulous. If we had to hide out someplace, this is where I'd pick. Jonathan is really enjoying the lake. He goes swimming every day, even though it's as cold as ice. He keeps trying to get us to join him, but so far we've been able to make excuses."

"I'm glad he's enjoying himself. Got everything you need?"

"We're fine, Tom. I'm missing *you*."

"I miss you too." His words just slipped out, surprising him. He *did* miss her. He missed Sara's smile, her touch. Something inside him seemed to have changed, and for the first time in a long time, he *really* wanted to be near her. In that instant, he felt a sliver of hope.

"I hope this will be over soon and things get back to normal." He thought about what he had just said, feeling stupid. "I guess things will never be like they were…will they?"

"I have faith God will see us through this."

"I hope you're right," Tom said, unsure what to say next. This was not an area he wanted to explore right now—if ever. "I'm glad you're enjoying the cabin."

"We are. Any news on your end?"

"No. We're searching everywhere, but this guy's hard to find. Only a matter of time, though. Ghost can't help but screw up. And when he does—we'll be there."

"Well, it is good to hear your voice. Are you getting some rest?"

"Actually, I've never slept better. I'll take another trip up there soon."

"You sound good, even with everything that's going on down there."

"I am. Love you. Talk to you soon." Tom hung up and walked up to the ICU. The officer outside Phillips's door and waved as he passed. Phillips lay motionless on the bed just as he'd left her. Seeing her helplessness rekindled his frustration.

He took his novel out and began reading. Fifteen minutes later his eyes closed and he was asleep.

Chapter 52

San Jose

Maria Juarez knew her husband was worried because he'd never involved her in a murder before. She never carried messages like this or became personally involved in gang operations. He'd never made her take chances like this—not in all the years of their marriage. Not in all the years he brutally climbed the ladder of power until he finally sat on the Mesa. He was now one of the three most important leaders in the gang.

And he was fighting for survival.

Now Maria was headed to Salinas to make contact with a name her husband had slipped to her in the mail. She made two stops: the first to pick up two untraceable cell phones, paying for them in cash. And now, San Jose.

She knew enough about the second stop to be nervous—the residence of another gang member who owed DJ his life. The parolee flung the door open when she knocked, his expression one of annoyance and anger. Until he realized who she was, and then his attitude changed to respect. She knew this man had no regard for women, but he feared DJ and what would happen if he was disrespectful to her.

"My husband says you'd have two tools waiting for me, for a job we've planned."

"Wait here." His voice did not leave any room to negotiate. The parolee closed the door and disappeared inside. Maria waited, looking over her shoulder at anyone who might be lurking nearby. A woman, alone in this part of town, was begging for trouble to come her way. She kept glancing over her shoulder until she heard footsteps approaching the door again.

He opened the door a crack and handed her a paper bag that had been tightly folded and taped. She felt two heavy objects inside. "Is everything for the tools in here?"

He looked at her with impatience. "I put in two boxes of ammo. That should be more than enough."

She turned and left without saying another word. The door slammed closed behind her.

She caught the 101 South from San Jose, driving past the smaller cities of Morgan Hill and Gilroy. As she approached Salinas, Maria began to think about her husband and his power. With a sense of pride, Maria realized the land she had driven through, from Santa Rosa all the way down to Salinas, was controlled by her husband and other NF members. He was the general who controlled regiments in all the towns and cities north of the Tehachapi Mountains. He controlled an army. So why was he worried? All he had to do was say the word, and someone would be killed. He had control over large sums of money, all kinds of weapons, and hundreds and hundreds of soldiers. Each soldado stood ready to obey the command of the general.

A troubling thought suddenly sprang up that cast a shadow over all this power her husband controlled. If he was so powerful, why was he having his wife set up this murder?

This fear deepened as she continued south. And what would happen if she was caught? If some snitch traded knowledge about her to buy his own freedom? The thought of being locked up in a woman's prison for life made Maria shudder. Never to hold her children and grandchildren in her arms.

She shuddered every time she visited DJ. Those doors closing behind her with finality, her person and belongings searched on the way into that hellhole. And after the visit, locked inside until someone else opened the door and granted her freedom.

She could never live that way. Ever.

As she passed through Prunedale, she stopped and made a phone call. The contact gave her directions to a bar near the railroad tracks in downtown Salinas, where drug trafficking flourished. It was an area of town heavily controlled by the Northerners, hence the NF. All transactions taxed and controlled by her husband.

Maria suddenly recalled why the bar was so familiar. The NF had made very public example of what happened when taxes weren't paid. A tax violator had been brutally dealt with by the gang. The regimental leader for Salinas ordered one of his underlings to march into the bar and kill the violator point blank. The gangster had pumped a full clip into the victim. As the bar cleared amid the hail of bullets, the killer screamed out a warning. "This is from the NF." A security video camera in the bar captured everything. The killer played to the camera like he was on television.

Maria had dutifully carried back the information on this killing to DJ, including a news clipping from the *Monterey Herald,* with more intimate details not reported in the news provided her by the regimental leader. Several months later, the leader gave her a video tape of the killing as an added bonus. The tape had become evidence in the killer's trial. Now was she to be taped? Was her future sealed?

Neon lights flashed above the bar's entrance, illuminating a garbage-littered parking space a few car lengths ahead. She parked her car, grabbed her purse, and walked toward the bar. There were no friendly faces on this street, just men looking for their next drink or their next fix. The street population—prostitutes, drug dealers, gangsters, and victims—struggled to survive in the shadows of life here.

Maria took a deep breath and pushed open the door. At first, she could only make out figures hunched over the counter or sitting at tables scattered around a single pool table. It took a moment for her eyes to adjust to the darkness.

A pool game was in progress, players halfheartedly trading shots and killing time. Clouds of cigarette smoke mushroomed in the stale air in violation of California's no-smoking laws. It was clear no one cared about the law or anybody else. A jukebox vibrated the building with a rock-and-roll oldie. A few heads turned her way as Maria approached.

Her eyes finally adjusted. A figure rose from a table against the far wall. Overhead lighting above the pool table painted the person's face with just enough illumination for Maria to recognize him. She worked her away around the tables and along the bar until she cleared the pool table. The man sat down again, waiting for her to approach.

Maria clutched her purse and sat down, placing it in her lap. She stared at the man across from her, his eyes dark and expressionless, watching her like a cat watching a mouse in a cage.

He started in. "I got word that you had work for me. Give me the details, but be careful—lots of ears in this place."

She furtively looked around the room before reaching into her purse and withdrawing two envelopes, one larger than the other, and a cell phone. She pushed the smaller envelope toward the man. "Here is a photo of the customer. I've written down his address, his car and license number."

The man tore open the envelope and withdrew the photograph. It was a photo of Mikio the day he got out of the Bay. It was taken by Juanita as the family wandered along the beach at Crescent City.

Maria pushed the cell phone toward him. "Use this to reach me. No other contacts." She scribbled her burn phone number on a slip of paper. "We are never to be seen together again. Ever."

The man picked up the phone and placed it his jacket pocket.

Maria slowly pushed the second, thicker envelope to him. "For expenses."

The man took out a knife and made a slit near the folded flap, which had been heavily taped shut. The envelope burst open and revealed the thick stack of hundred dollar bills she had placed inside. By the man's expression, the money was enough.

He placed the money inside his jacket.

Maria hunched forward. "Call me on that phone once you're set up in Santa Rosa. We'll make a phone call and get him to leave his apartment. Once he opens the door, he's all yours. Don't miss."

The man leaned over until his lips almost touched her ear. She could feel his breath on her neck. It made her shiver.

"I never miss," he whispered, and then leaned back with a wicked smile. The look on his face frightening her.

She tried to speak, coughed, and tried again. "I have the tools you need in my car outside. Any questions?" Fear seemed to squeeze her words as they tumbled out.

The man shook his head.

They rose together and walked through the bar. A couple of men turned and watched them head out the door. No one followed. She moved over to her car and pressed a remote button. The trunk popped open. They walked around the back. Maria reached in and pulled out the folded bag she had just picked up in San Jose. "Here they are. Make them disappear after the job is complete."

The man clutched the bag tightly as he carefully looked around. She followed his gaze. No one watched.

She closed the trunk, opened the driver's side door, and climbed in. She started the engine and pulled away from the curb while adjusting her rearview mirror. The man still stood at the curb, watching her drive away. He did not move.

Maria's hands, wet with perspiration, clutched the wheel. Her heartbeat raced faster than she could accelerate the car. She wiped her hands on her skirt and regripped the wheel, watching with relief as the bar's neon lights slowly grew smaller and smaller in her mirror. As she sped away, Maria began to work out the details in her mind. Her daughter must handle the next part of the plan. Getting Mikio to leave that apartment at just the right time would be difficult. Particularly for Maria. Coaxing him out had to come from someone Mikio trusted, someone he'd never suspect.

If everything went as planned, Mikio's fate would be sealed and DJ could breathe easier.

She tried not to think of what would happen if things went wrong. What if Mikio survived? He'd survived before. This time he would know his own family set him up. Another kind of fear caused sweat to run down her brow. If they missed, he would come after them. He would take more than her freedom. He would take her life.

She shuddered at the image of Mikio standing over her, gun in hand. She pictured him slowly pressing the gun to her head and pulling the trigger with a look of hatred in his eyes. She blinked as if the muzzle flash had just flashed across her face.

She was shaking, cold with fear and sweat and worry. She hated this life.

Maria drove without looking, the dotted lines whipping past her faster and faster. This thing affected them all—her family, her friends. They each had a part to play; each with a life of limited choices. Either obey or die.

Maria could no longer remember how she had become trapped like this. It seemed like it had been this way forever.

She thought of her daughter, who might be implicated in the murder of another human being. She saw Mikio's face flash before her, a member of her family.

It suddenly became coldly real to her what they were about to do. Each of them had offered up their children, their loved ones, placing them on this sacrificial altar of the gang. Mothers helplessly watching as each of their children paid for the consequences of their actions. Trudging into the captivity of prison life or being swallowed up by the grave as death snatched up its victims.

There were no more tears for Maria to shed. There was no escape. The face of death loomed ahead for each of them. She had made her own choice a long time ago.

Chapter 53

Homewood

Paul's cell phone vibrated. He pulled it from his coat pocket and answered, hoping it was Tom with some good news. It was a woman's voice.

"Pastor Paul?"

It was Stephen Avery's mother. "Hi, Teresa. Everything okay?" His stomach tightened as he waited for her to speak. This did not sound good.

"He's dead. My son is dead." She seemed lost. As if she spoke the words to see if they might be real. Shock had kept reality at bay. Soon it would hit with a vengeance. "I'm at the hospital," she said, faltering. "The doctor…"

"I'm so sorry. I wish I could be there for you."

"I was just sitting there next to him, reading, when alarms and buzzers started going off. Nurses and doctors rushed in, but it was too late. He's…gone."

Paul remembered the newspaper article about the brutal assault on her son at the mall. Reporters followed up with a feature article about gang violence, and they'd interviewed Stephen's girlfriend, whose clothes had been torn off. Her words in the article signaled to him that the girl was still trying to come to terms with what happened. "We were so happy. Just looking in the stores and having fun. And then they attacked us. I don't understand...why?"

Teresa started to cry. "Why, Pastor Paul? Why did God let this happen? Help me to understand."

The mother's torment tore a hole out of Paul's soul, and his heart ached for her. Once again, words of comfort eluded him.

"The police said they found out who did this," Teresa said. "Some gang member called Juan Diego Sanchez. They said his street name is Gato. They got a warrant for attempted murder on this Gato. Now they can arrest him for murder, but that won't bring back my boy."

Her sobs echoed across the phone line as if she was standing in a empty room.

Oh Father. Why? Those words he kept to himself as he tried to comfort Teresa. Again, he could not give a reason. God seemed to keep His answers hidden for the moment.

Tom felt a hand gently shaking him. He opened his eyes and saw a nurse leaning over him. There was a smile on her face. He glanced toward the door and saw a swing-shift officer had come on duty. He checked his watch. Eight p.m.

The nurse jutted her chin toward the bed. "I've got a surprise for you, Detective."

Tom glanced over and Phillips looked back at him and smiled.

"Praise God," was all he could say.

Phillips's eyes registered surprise.

"How're you feeling?"

"I feel like a punching bag. And my face hurts all over."

"The important thing is you're alive." She did not need to know how close she came to dying. "We haven't found Ghost yet. But you'll have protection around the clock until we do."

He explained the scene at her office when the deputy found her. "It seems like he searched your office looking for something. But the place was such a mess, we couldn't determine what he was trying to find."

"Thanks for the compliment."

"No, I meant Ghost is the one who trashed it. Files were thrown all over the office. Drawers yanked out and its contents dumped on the floor. It's going to take a lot of effort to get everything back in order."

Phillips looked at him with eyes that broadcasted her pain. "The only thing I remember was realizing it was Ghost. And he could kill me at any moment." Her voice cracked as she tried to control herself, to concentrate on what needed to be shared. "He grabbed me by the throat and clamped his hand over my mouth. I can still smell his breath." Her eyes widened with alarm. "He said the only thing he wanted was to find out where you and your family were hiding. He said if I gave him that—he'd let me live."

Kagan felt like his body had become immobile, and an icy chill swept through him. "Did you tell him?"

"No! Of course not!" And then her anger changed. A look of pride crossed her face. "I let him think I'd cooperate. As soon as he slipped his hand off my mouth, I screamed and stomped on his foot as hard as I could."

Tom smiled. She looked at him as tears formed. "And then he beat me until I blacked out."

Tom reached out and took her hand. "You did a very brave thing, Diane. I am just sorry that we couldn't protect you."

"There was nothing you could do, Tom. How would we know he'd break into the DA's office? I mean…that's so bizarre." Something seemed to jar her memory. She glanced back at Tom. "What about my computer?"

"What'd you mean?"

"Was it on?"

"That's one of the questions I needed to ask. The deputy found your computer turned off. Is that the way you left it?"

"No." Phillips's eyes suddenly widened. "Oh no."

"W-what's the matter?"

"The computer was on when he attacked me. He must have turned it off."

"What could he have wanted on the computer? Witness lists? Case information?" He saw fear in her eyes. "What? Tell me, Diane."

"It's coming back. Oh my God."

Tom leaned forward. "What is it?"

"Oh, Tom. I'm so sorry."

His apprehension returned. "What's the matter?"

She began to cry. "I put the Lake Tahoe information there under your name. In case we needed to get hold of Sara and Mary. He must've gotten the address, phone number, everything. That's why he took the time to turn it off. He got what he came after."

Tom felt as if someone had hit him in the gut. Ghost knew where Sara and the others were hiding.

Ghost was going after his family.

Tom tried to reach Deputy Hoffman directly by phone, but his call wouldn't go through. The deputy's voice mail activated. Tom left a message and then frantically searched for the emergency phone number for the Placer County Sheriff's dispatch.

He found the number and spoke directly to Dispatch. They promised to contact the deputy and have him do a welfare check as soon as possible. They would have Hoffman call him with an update.

Tom thanked the dispatcher and left his contact number. The next person he called was Garcia. The agent was livid. "Man, that animal is sick. I'll get my crew together and we'll meet you up there—Code 3."

"Great. I'm leaving now."

He hated to make the next call. The phone rang five times. With each ring, Tom became more frantic until he heard Sara's voice. She sounded breathless. "Where were you? Where is Paul? I thought you'd never answer."

"I'm sorry, Tom. We were out near the lake. Stupidly, we left our cell phones in the cabin or turned off. It took a few seconds to get to the phone. I ran the whole way."

His breathing returned to normal. "Deputy Hoffman is on his way to check on you. He's going to stay with you until I get there."

"Something wrong?"

Tom hesitated for a moment. There was no way to make this sound good. "I think Ghost may have learned where you're hiding. Garcia and his team will be joining us. I want you to get that pistol I gave you and hang on to it until Hoffman arrives."

"Okay." A hint of fear crept into her voice. "Please hurry!"

"I'll be there as quick as I can. Let me talk to Paul."

A moment later, Lawson came on the line. "I was listening on this end. What can I do?"

"Just keep them safe until I or the deputy get on the scene."

"You got it. I'm locked and loaded. We'll be waiting."

Tom relaxed. "Paul, I can't—"

"Don't mention it, my friend. Just drive carefully." Lawson hung up.

Tom raced to his car and activated his lights and siren as he gunned his car out of the hospital parking lot. It was going to be the longest Code 3 run in his life. And he intended to torture the engine until he saw the lights of the Tahoe cabin.

Chapter 54

Lake Tahoe

Dan Hoffman received the call on his cell phone from Dispatch a few minutes after Tom phoned. He raced toward the cabin while still online with communications. The dispatcher had another message. "This just came over from El Dorado County. A ranger was shot and killed in a campground just north of Emerald Bay. The shooter was driving a camper registered out of Sacramento."

She gave him the license number and description of the vehicle. "The ranger didn't get a chance to call it in, but he wrote it out on a pad inside his car. They're assuming this is the make and model of the vehicle the killer is driving. Had a small metal boat tied to the roof of the camper."

Dan thanked her for the information. He activated his lights and siren and headed toward Homewood. He did not believe in coincidences.

Ghost had killed again.

It seemed like an eternity before the deputy saw the flickering lights of the Homewood market and marina. He cut his emergency lights and siren as he entered the hamlet and then cut his car lights as he approached the cabin. He parked alongside the roadway and walked up to the gate.

He quickly punched in the key code, and the gate silently swung open. He pulled out his firearm as he walked to the right of the driveway and into a grove of trees on the south side of the cabin. A bright full moon shone overhead, its silvery light filtering through the trees.

The deputy picked his path carefully, trying to step on soft pine needles and staying away from cones and dry twigs that threatened to give his position away. He edged toward the corner of the cabin.

There were only a couple of windows on the south side of the cabin, and none offered him a good view inside. Using the wall as cover, he crept around the southeast corner. There were many windows on the lakeside of the building, and he edged toward the corner of the closest living room window overlooking the lake. He glanced inside and saw wood brightly crackling in the fireplace, but he could not see anyone inside. The upstairs looked dark. No other lights were on in the house. Was Ghost already here?

He low-crawled under the windows until he got to the back door leading directly into the kitchen. He tried the door but it was locked. He frowned and continued around the perimeter of the cabin.

He tried the windows and another side door, all of which were locked. He finally reached the front door. The moment of decision. Break in or identify himself to those inside? If Ghost was already inside, that would give away his position. Unfortunately, there wasn't enough justification to take out a window and break into the house. For all he knew, they might be fast asleep.

He rapped on the front door with his night stick. "Police. Open up."

A light flicked on upstairs. A moment later a woman rushed down the stairs and ran to the front door. She flung it open. "Oh, thank God it's you." The gun shook in her left hand.

A man walked from the shadows holding a gun. Dan tensed for a moment. "Pastor Lawson?"

"Yes. Thanks for coming, Deputy. I'm putting my weapon away."

Hoffman reached over to Sara and gently removed the weapon from her trembling hand. "I don't think you'll be needing that." Dan began to breathe normally.

Tom answered his cell phone after the first ring. Hoffman.

"Everyone's safe. I'll stand guard until you and the others get here."

Tom prayed a silent prayer. "I owe you big time, Dan. Thanks for getting there so quick."

"Hey, I'm just glad I got here in time."

"I'm coming up I-80. Just passing Auburn. I'll slow it down, but I'll be there as fast as I can."

"No problem. I wouldn't slow down too much. I've got more information. Just came in from Dispatch."

Tom put his foot on the accelerator and picked up speed. "What is it?"

The deputy apparently covered the phone with his hand. "I'll be back in just a minute, Mrs. Kagan." It sounded like Hoffman had walked outside. "I didn't want your wife to hear this."

"Hear what?" Tom's chest tightened.

Hoffman relayed the information from Dispatch. "We've got every available unit responding to help El Dorado County in the search."

Hoffman paused. Tom heard Sara's voice from inside the cabin calling out to Mary that everything was all right. Everything was not all right. It was about to get worse.

"My guess is your guy is heading this way."

Fear left Tom almost speechless. "I know he's coming for them, Dan. Keep your eyes open."

Tom hung up the phone and flipped on the lights and siren one more time. He could smell burning oil from under the hood. He prayed the car would hold together long enough for him to reach the cabin.

Chapter 55

Homewood

Tom reached Garcia by phone. He quickly relayed the information Hoffman shared about the ranger. "Deputy Hoffman is standing by until we get up there."

"Great. We're an hour or two behind you. We'll meet at the cabin."

Tom hung up. A moment later his cell phone indicated he'd just moved into a dead zone. The rest of the trip would be torture for Tom as he tried to figure out Ghost's next move. There was just one deputy between Ghost and Sara.

Tom continued to push the car to its limit. He finally saw the lights of Truckee ahead and took the exit toward Lake Tahoe. Any other time, he'd be enjoying this ride. Tonight, only one thought was on his mind.

Would Ghost strike before Tom could get to the cabin?

Tom pulled into the driveway of the cabin and turned off the engine. The engine popped and shuttered before shutting down. The acrid odor of hot tires and spent motor oil stung his nostrils. The car survived.

The deputy met him at the front door. "All present and accounted for."

Tom relaxed for a moment as he shook Hoffman's hand. "I'll never be able to repay you. Thanks."

"Hey, we try to protect our own."

"Look. I know you guys need to be out looking for Ghost. We'll be fine until SSU gets here."

Dan turned to leave. "I'm a phone call away."

Sara ran to the front door and threw her arms around Tom. They watched the deputy pull out of the driveway and work his way south on the highway. She turned to him with a smile. "I'm so glad to see you. The deputy was so kind to stay with us, but I really couldn't let my guard down until I saw you. You got here fast."

"You can smell my engine a mile away. That car will never be the same. Thank goodness it belongs to the city."

Jonathan came bounding up. Tom knelt and wrapped his arms around the boy. "You taking care of the women while I'm gone?"

"You bet, Uncle Tommy."

Mary walked up to them. Tom stood and gave her a hug. "It's good to see you, Tom. I feel so much safer."

Tom glanced over at Sara for a moment. "Garcia and the others will be here pretty soon. Until they arrive, I want everyone to go upstairs and stay together. I'll be up in minute."

Mary and Jonathan turned to walk up the stairs. Tom reached over and touched Sara on the shoulder. "Honey, can you stay down here for a minute?" He let Mary and the boy get upstairs before he continued. "You have the gun with you?"

"I hid it in the kitchen after the deputy got here." She told him where to find it.

"Go on up to the bedroom and join the others. I'll get the gun and bring it to you." She nodded and went upstairs. Tom walked into the kitchen and located the firearm. He tucked it in his waistband and checked the doors and windows, making sure everything was locked up tight. Not that any of this would stop Ghost, but at least they'd hear if he broke something to gain entry.

Once he was sure the lower floor was secure, he climbed the stairs and joined them in one of the bedrooms overlooking the lake. He motioned Sara to follow him down the hallway.

He handed the weapon to her. "Put this up in the closet and wait with the others. Turn off the lights and keep the door closed. If anyone walks through that door without announcing himself—shoot to kill."

Her hands shook as she took the weapon. "Where are you going?"

He reached over and embraced her. "I'm going to make sure Ghost never sets foot in this house. Once Hector and his crew get here, we'll relocate you."

"Watch yourself, Tom." She squeezed him tight, then turned and walked back into the bedroom. Tom followed her into the room. The boy was sitting on the bed watching the adults. Tom walked over to him and sat down. "Jonathan, let's pretend we are camping out in the woods and there are no lights. Now, you hang with your mom while I'm checking on things, okay?"

The boy nodded. "Where will you be?"

"I'm going to be outside until the other policemen arrive." He saw a flicker of fear cross Mary's face. "Everybody will be just fine. Just stay as quiet as you can until I return. Paul will be here in the house standing guard." Tom stood. "See you as soon as the others get here."

Lawson met him as he walked out in the hallway. "Where do you want me?"

"Stay by the top of the stairs. Don't let him anywhere near their room." Tom thrust his chin toward the room where Sara and the others were hiding.

"And where will you be?"

"I'll cover the grounds outside in case the creep tries to approach the house. If you hear glass breaking—it won't be me."

Lawson nodded. "Stay sharp."

Tom turned and walked down the stairs, making sure all the lights were turned off. The only light came from the fireplace.

He grabbed the house keys and slipped out the back door leading to the lake, making sure it locked behind him. He worked his way along the side of the house, dashed across an open area and into the shadows of a grove of trees north of the house. He crouched down, watching and listening. From this position, he could see anyone approach either side of the cabin, the front door on the west, or the lakeside door from the kitchen. Silver moonlight filtered through the trees and cascaded across the blackness of the lake.

Tom tried to imagine from which direction Ghost might attack. He worked out a tactical approach to the cabin if he were Ghost. The highway along the estate was too open, too easy to be spotted. The lakeside offered more cover and concealment. He could almost make it to the edge of the house on the north and south sides without being seen using trees and brush to camouflage his movements. However, anyone who risked sneaking through the woods would most likely step on dry underbrush alerting anyone listening for movement. Still, the lakeside offered a better approach.

Tom decided to stay concealed where he was until SSU arrived. He nestled in the brush and remained motionless, listening and watching,

Tom heard engines winding down the highway. He knew it was the cavalry before they arrived. He stood and walked to the front gate, activating the gate to allow them to drive through.

He was standing in the shadows when Garcia leaped from his car. "Don't shoot, Hector. It's me."

Garcia wheeled around and peered in the direction of the voice. He relaxed as Tom stepped into the light. "And I thought I was sneaky. Everybody good here?"

"Now that you're here."

Garcia slapped Tom on the back. "Man, it's good to see you still alive and breathing. I thought we might have to come in here—guns blazing."

His crew silently filed past like a small army, noiselessly spreading out around the building and setting up their own protective perimeter. The men blended with the night. Ghost would have a hard time getting to the cabin now.

"We talked about what to do before we got here. At least until we heard your plan."

Tom gratefully nodded. "I've got a big favor to ask."

"Anything, my friend."

He quickly laid out his plan to Garcia.

"I like it. But I get to watch your back, right?"

"Wouldn't have it any other way."

Tom went upstairs and knocked on the bedroom door. "Sara, it's me. Everything is all right." He opened the door and flicked on the light. A row of worried faces stared back at him. They were all sitting on the bed. He crossed the room and pulled up a chair next to them. "I've got a plan and I will need everyone's cooperation."

They all nodded, even Jonathan. As he told them his plan, Sara shook her head. "I don't like this, Tom. It puts you in too much danger."

Tom gently closed his hand around hers. "Honey, we have to stop this guy. We have to stop him before he disappears again. We know he'll try to hit this place. And we will be waiting."

Sarah gazed at him with fear in her eyes. He knew she would go along with the plan, albeit, reluctantly. "Just be careful. Promise."

"I will. We have him outgunned. He doesn't have a chance." He wished he felt as confident as he sounded.

Lawson joined him as Mary and Jonathan gathered their belongings. "I'd thought I'd head back to Santa Rosa unless you need me here."

Tom turned and thrust out a hand. "No, we'll take it from here. I can't tell you—"

"Forget it," Paul said. "You want me to check in on your friend — Phillips?"

"Thanks. Just let me know how she's doing, would you? I'll clear it with the watch commander since they have a twenty-four-hour guard on her."

"Consider it done." Lawson walked away to get his belongings.

Tom turned toward the empty highway in front of the cabin. There was no traffic at this hour, and the trees above him seemed to be standing still, watching and waiting—just like him. A killer lurked out there in the darkness. He must turn his attention on capturing this two-legged animal. Put an end to this hunt before Ghost vanished forever.

Ghost heard a caravan of vehicles roaring in the distance and suspected that the cavalry arrived. They must have figured out what he gained by assaulting the female prosecutor. And killing the ranger only advertised the fact he was in the area. SSU and that cop were coming to the rescue.

He had been listening to the night sounds, like a bird of prey listening and watching for its victim. Sounds carried great distance in the high mountain air. When he heard the vans near Homewood, he slid behind the wheel of the black Mercedes—compliments of another unknowing lakeside resident who must have taken a long trip someplace and left his car behind. In the trunk was all the equipment Ghost would need.

The hunter was ready to hunt.

He parked the car in the shadows of a business on the west side of the roadway and waited for movement. He positioned himself between the downtown of Homewood and where he guessed the cabin might be situated. He was not disappointed. Just as he killed the engine, headlights emerged from one of the cabins along the water. It was the approximate address where they stashed Tom's family. Several vans pulled out of the driveway, turned north, and approached at a high rate of speed.

Now he knew exactly where the cabin was in the dark.

The two vans flashed past. He did not think the drivers spotted his location, two agents in the front, both looking forward, never once looking in his direction. He could not see inside the van.

He grabbed the night-vision scope with one hand and turned on the engine with the other. He eased onto the roadway without turning on any lights and followed the taillights of the van ahead.

Ghost looked through the night-vision scope with glee. This was too easy.

Most of the cavalry must have stayed behind to protect his prey, and these guys must be going to get some rest at a motel and set up operations. Just needed to follow them to find out where they'd be operating from so he knew where to hit them when the time was right. It was good to know the enemy.

The van neared Tahoe City and turned toward Truckee on Highway 89. He continued to follow the red taillights until they turned into a parking lot of a restaurant and hotel alongside the Truckee River. He flicked off the night-vision scope and switched on his headlights. He continued down the road without glancing over. He did not want to appear too interested. He traveled a half mile and made a U-turn to see what he might be able to spot on his way back.

He passed the parking lot more slowly and saw one of the agents removing equipment from the van. The other agent must be inside the hotel. No one else was around the vehicle. Ghost continued past the hotel and kept driving.

Time to return to the cabin where Kagan's loved ones were stashed. Time to start planning his attack. They probably thought they were safe, now that the cavalry was here.

They had been so careless, so...unprofessional. They would make more mistakes. And he would be there to take advantage.

Chapter **57**

Santa Rosa

Gato entered his mother's house through the back door. He opened it quietly, slowly, straining to hear if anyone might be at home. Mikio was back in town looking for him. He wanted to stay clear of his uncle.

He heard a woman's voice coming from the kitchen. He crept to the door and looked through the crack. His mother was talking to Grandma Maria. The older woman was leaning on the counter, watching her daughter pacing back and forth.

"Juanita, would you sit down. You're making me nervous."

"We've a lot to be nervous about, Mom. What if my husband finds out we helped set up his brother? Are you sure this plan will keep us in the clear? When they…you know, take care of Mikio?"

"I've set up everything," Maria said, calm and steady. "Honey, we've been over this a million times. Your father is not giving us a choice. It has to be taken care of."

Juanita continued her nervous pacing across the tiny kitchen. "Okay. I am supposed to call Mikio and ask him to meet me in the park near his apartment tomorrow night. At 8:00 p.m. sharp. I tell him our houses are being watched by the cops and we don't want to draw attention to ourselves.

I need to tell him something DJ passed on. Something important. Right?" She stopped for a moment, wringing her hands.

"That's right, honey. Only you won't be there. Everything is taken care of. You'll stay with me until it is over."

His mother started pacing again. "But what if they miss? They've tried to kill him before and he always escaped. And what about Juan? I mean, I know he thinks Mikio is a traitor, but he's still fond of his uncle. Still looks up to him. If my son finds out…"

Maria pushed herself away from the counter and walked over to her daughter. "Hush, hush." She held her daughter in her arms. "Once this happens, we forget everything. No one will know anything if you do this right. Nothing can be traced back to us."

Gato froze. A sick feeling in the pit of his stomach surged upward. He was going to throw up. It was the same sick feeling he felt the time he read the note from Ghost ordering Mikio's death. He had to get out of this house, out of this place.

Gato turned and crept toward the back door. He opened it and started to step out when the door squeaked on its hinges.

His mother yelled, "Who's there?"

He dashed through the doorway and disappeared into the darkness. Gato was running once again. At first, he didn't know where he might run. He just knew he had to move. As long as he ran, no one could catch him.

And then it hit him. He knew where he had to go.

With the speed of a deer running from a pack of hungry wolves, he ran through the night to escape the sounds of his mother's voice echoing in the recesses of his mind.

Mikio was sitting on the sofa when the phone jingled. It sat on an end table next to the sofa. He picked it up.

"Hello?"

"Mikio, is that you?" It was Juanita's voice.

"Yeah."

"Look. Something's come up. DJ wants me to pass something on to you. But not over the phone. Can we meet?"

"Sure. Where?"

She paused for a moment, as if thinking of a place to meet. "The cops are watching my place. I'm sure they have an eye on yours too. Can you meet me in the park near your house, the one on Fourth Street?"

"Why don't I just pick you up and we can drive someplace?"

"I don't think we should be seen together. I'll be over there in half an hour. Okay?"

"See you there." Mikio hung up the phone. He turned to face his visitor. "You were right, Juan. They're setting me up. Just like you said."

Juan looked crestfallen. "So what are you going to do about it?"

Mikio stood. "Nothing." He walked back to his bedroom.

His nephew tagged along. "What do you mean nothing? They're setting you up to kill you. You have to do something."

"Juan. Sometimes the best thing you can do is walk away. That is what I'm going to do."

"Where're you going?" He followed his uncle into the bedroom.

Mikio pulled a large gym bag from the closet and emptied the bureau. He hadn't brought much back to this place, just enough to get by.

"I'm heading east." He quickly finished packing, zipped up the bag, and walked back into the living room. He turned to the younger man. "You can walk away too, Juan. If you'd like, you can travel with me. We can start over."

Juan looked at him and shook his head. "There's no reason why I should split. Now that Ghost is as good as dead, I'm all good. My grandfather is a shot caller for the NF. I'm protected."

Mikio shook his head. "Do you really believe that?"

"You bet I believe that." His nephew stared back at Mikio with a look of belligerence.

Mikio put his bag down. "Listen to me. DJ screwed up. First, DJ was responsible for Ghost, and look what happened. Ghost had Paco killed, a member in good standing with the NF. He tried to get DJ's grandson to carry through on that killing. Then Ghost wanted you to kill me. After all that fell through, Ghost ripped off the NF and brought all kinds of heat down on the organization. All that was DJ's responsibility to handle"

Mikio waited for his words to have some effect on the young man. Juan's face showed no emotion.

"DJ was supposed to take care of me, but they held off because of the information I hold over their heads. DJ sent your mother to find out if I had that information hidden somewhere. I purposefully told her I might do that in the future. I could tell by her expression that she was relieved to find out I had not written down anything. Then DJ ordered them to arrange for my death. I am going to disappear and DJ is going to be held accountable."

The young man said nothing.

"Sooner or later, the organization will turn on your grandfather for his screwups. Where's that going to leave you? Now DJ is using his wife and daughter to set me up. He can't even get his own people to take care of business. He has to use women to clean up his mess. Family!"

Juan listened to his uncle, but a hint of belligerence still lingered. "You turned on the NF, Tío, and you ratted them out to the cops. I can't forget that." He stared down at the floor, his face contorted by the turmoil raging inside. "On the other hand, I can't just stand by and see you get killed by your own family. That's not right."

Juan began pacing the room. Mikio watched the younger man in pity. He suspected where this was going.

"But I'm no snitch. I'm all good, as far as they're concerned. The farther I can get away from you, the better. You're just gonna have to go it alone."

Mikio tried to keep the hurt from showing. Further argument would be pointless. "You're wrong, Juan. You're not all good with them. They'll pull you in, use you up, and then spit you out. They'll kill you to get what you've earned, or they'll kill you for what you were not able to do for them. Or they'll kill you because they want to make a point. No matter what, you'll end up dead and wasted. I beg you. Think about it."

Juan raised his hands to cut his uncle off. "I've heard enough. All I hear is the whining of a has-been, a person who's gone over to the other side. As far as I'm concerned, we're no longer family." He walked toward the front door.

"Stop!"

Juan froze, then whirled around. "What now?"

"If you walk out that door, you're a dead man," Mikio said. "Didn't you just listen to what I was told to do? They are expecting me to walk out that door and walk toward the park. Do you think I'll even make it to the park? Think about it. Anyone who walks out that door, they'll think is me. It's dark out there. There are probably two or three guns already drawn out there. Use your head."

Juan glared back at him. "So what are we going to do? Sit here until they go away? Come on."

Mikio struggled to be patient. "I'm going out this back window and over the back fence. My car's two blocks away. I'll drop you wherever you want. Just don't go walking out that door. For my sake."

Juan seemed to mull over what he had just said. The pride in his face changed when he must've realized Mikio might be right. "I'll go as far as the street. After that, you're on your own. We're through."

"Have it your way," Mikio said. "But before we go, I just want to tell you I love you. I don't want you to waste your life like I did. You can walk away from them. Maybe not with me, but you can walk away and start over. It is all up to you."

"This is my life, Tío. It was your life too, until you gave it up. You got soft in your old age. Running is not what I'm about."

Mikio let the insult wash over him. His love for the younger man allowed him to take this abuse. In times past, he would have killed men who spoke to him this way.

He picked up his bag and headed for the back window. "Let's get out of here before they kick in the front door."

They crawled through the back-bedroom window and dropped to the ground outside. The temperature had dropped and the night air felt crisp and sharp. Lights from adjoining apartments glowed just enough to provide light to the back fence. They scrambled over the fence, Juan helping Mikio get his bag to the other side.

They walked through another backyard, finally working their way to the street behind Mikio's apartment.

He extended his hand. "Here's where we part ways, Juan. Take care of yourself."

Juan took his hand and started to shake it. Mikio brought him in close and put his arms around him. "Keep your head down, and watch your back."

His nephew shook his head, his voice muffled with emotion. "Take care, Tío. I love you."

Mikio reached over and cupped his hand behind Juan's shaved head. "I'm going to miss you. *Vaya con Dios.*"

Juan turned and walked away into the blackness of the night.

Snake leaned forward in his seat, telephone receiver pressed against his ear. He glared through the separating glass of PBSP's visitor center at the defense attorney on the other side. James Chancellor shifted in his seat, beads of sweat collecting on his brow.

"Listen to me, you shyster. And listen well. We own you. We paid for you. We gave you clients. We gave you money. Now is time for payback."

Chancellor's eyes bulged. His hands shook as he held the receiver to his ear, looking pale. "Snake, I can't do this. If I'm caught, they will lock me up and I'll be no good to you guys."

Snake laughed at the attorney's outburst, but his eyes had the look of death. "You don't have a choice. We *will* have you killed if you walk away from this one."

"But my name will be in the records as having set it up."

"They can't prove anything," Snake said. "All you got to do is get him moved to a place where we can take him out. Understand?"

"Yeah, I understand," the man said weakly. He could not refuse. They had him. They knew it. He knew it.

"There's been a vote. DJ violated his trust to the organization. He let things get out of hand, and the heat is on. He was supposed to take care of Ghost and Mikio, and he has not been able to do anything. He has dishonored us."

Chancellor listened intently as if he cared.

Snake watched the other man as if he might be Snake's next meal. The attorney squirmed in his seat.

Were there ears in the walls to this conversation? If guards were listening, nothing they heard could be used against him. It was a privileged conversation between attorney and client. Worst-case scenario, the guards might learn of the gang's plans. Snake had covertly put out the word he sought a vote. It had taken only a few days before the vote of a select few filtered in. It had been unanimous. Thumbs-up.

Snake very carefully laid out what the gang expected Chancellor to do. Surprise showed on the lawyer's face. "You had this planned from the beginning."

Snake slapped his hand on the glass. "Keep it down, you idiot." He glanced around to see who might be listening.

The other man just shook his head as if suddenly wakening from a long sleep. He seemed to not understand Snake's warning. "You knew Paco was going to get killed, you knew—"

"Yeah, I knew." A sneer crossed Snake's face as he glared. "Paco told me years ago 'bout Ghost's weakness."

"But why? Why all these killings?"

"Use your college-educated brain and figure it out."

The attorney leaned back in his seat as if slapped. "Power. It's about... power."

A smile emerged as Snake stared at the attorney like an entomologists studying an insect. "The shyster figures it out. Yeah, idiot. Power is everything."

"But you made me give up information that got people killed. For what?"

Snake shot him a look of boredom. "So that I can control this organization and push it where it has to go. So I can have power over the likes of you."

Realization seemed to finally sink in. The attorney numbly shook his head.

Anger flashed through Snake. "Listen. Get a grip! You knew what you were getting into when you got in bed with us. Now it's time to pay the piper. If you don't wanna play ball, we'll have you taken out and have another shyster step in. And believe me, having you whacked will be a lot easier."

Chancellor sat back in his seat, sweat pouring down his neck and into the collar of his shirt. Snake saw how damp the man's shirt had become in just a few minutes. The attorney's face reminded him of a man about to die.

Shakily, the attorney looked across at Snake. "I'll start things rolling as soon as I get back to the office."

The gang leader leaned back with a sneer creasing his face. "I thought you'd see it my way, *counselor*." The word *counselor* sounded dirty in the gangster's mouth. "Now get out of here until I need you again. I'm tired of your sniveling face."

Chapter 58

Santa Rosa

The thrill of danger zipped through Gato's body. He held a gun in one hand and a black ski mask in the other. He sat next to the driver, and his backup sat behind him. After tonight, they'd get respect. It had not taken much to get him to join his homies. One quick score would fill their pockets with green. His pockets were getting pretty empty.

They drove through the neighborhood slowly. The all-night market's floodlights shone down on an empty parking lot. The night clerk sat behind the counter, watching a television attached to the far wall.

Gato and the others drove by twice and circled once more through the neighborhood. No cops had shown up for the last thirty minutes. It was in a perfect location, only three blocks from the on-ramp to the freeway. A straight shot to freedom.

The building had been poorly planned for security. The parking lot wrapped itself partially around the market, but the exterior cameras only captured those who entered through the front door. Their getaway vehicle would be off screen, and they would be masked when they hit the place.

Gato patted the driver on the shoulder. "Pull in on that side of the parking lot and away from the front door." He pointed where he wanted the driver to go. "Pull in slow and keep the engine running."

The driver nodded. Gato and his partner yanked on their ski masks. Even before the car came to a stop, Gato and the other young man leaped from the car. "Follow my directions," Gato said, "and watch my back. We don't know if there is someone else in the back room."

They rounded the corner and rushed through the front door. Gato pointed the gun at the clerk's face and glanced at the cash register. "Open it up or die!" The clerk froze for a moment. Gato screamed, "Do it now, *puta*, or you're dead."

The clerk frantically clawed at the register, trying to follow Gato's orders. It took him several swipes at the register to hit the right key. The cash drawer rolled out.

"Get outta the way." Gato leaned over the counter.

His partner had swept through the store. "Store's clean."

Gato grabbed all the cash he could clutch in one hand while pointing the gun in the clerk's face. He shoved the cash into his jacket pocket just as a rear door squeaked.

As the door swung open, another clerk leaped out and tried to point his .22 caliber revolver at Gato.

Gato got the jump on the other clerk, firing three shots in rapid succession. The clerk fired off two. Gato's partner did not fire any. He ran out the door toward the waiting car.

Gato's first two shots killed a Bud Light cardboard cheerleader. He nailed her in the chest and the head. His third shot put a bullet hole in the squeaky door.

The clerk's shots took out the glass of the front door and put a hole in a small refrigerator stuffed with ice cream bars. The two clerks dove for the floor. Gato dashed through the broken glass of what was left of the front door and sprang toward the getaway vehicle.

The car was moving before Gato rounded the corner. He grabbed the handle. The door would not open. He slammed his palm against the window. "Unlock the door, you idiot!"

Screeching to a halt, the driver put the vehicle in Park and the door unlocked, allowing Gato to leap inside just as the driver hit the accelerator. Smoke bellowed from the tires as they burned their way across the asphalt.

The vehicle rocked back and forth as the driver tried to compensate. Once on the street, the car grabbed traction and leaped forward.

"Oh man. That was close." Gato pulled off his ski mask. He rolled down the window and felt the cool night air on his face. "That guy came out of nowhere."

The man in the backseat leaned forward to join the conversation. "Man, I never saw him coming."

Gato turned in his seat. "How could you? All I saw was your fat ass heading out the door."

The other man leaned back in his seat. "Hey, what was I supposed to do, man? It was time to split."

"You were supposed to have my back. Not run out of there like some girl." Gato breathed deeply, trying to get his anger in check. Gato reached into his jacket and pulled out a fistful of cash. "Look at this. At least we didn't leave empty-handed."

The other men laughed. "It's party time," the driver said, before glancing in the rearview mirror. "Uh-oh!"

Gato and the other man whirled around and stared out the rear window. A patrol car's lights and siren suddenly came alive, four car lengths behind.

Gato grabbed his seat belt and stared ahead. A new kind of fear gripped his chest. "Where did they come from?" He kept glancing over his shoulder as the threat behind them drew closer. A second unit pulled in behind the first as they headed toward the freeway.

Gato hit the driver on the shoulder. "Punch it, man. Get us out of here."

"I'm trying, I'm trying." The driver pushed the accelerator to the floor. The engine screamed its complaint as it careened around a corner and onto the freeway on-ramp.

Gato braced himself on the front dash. "Get us out into the county, away from the city. Less cops and more places to hide if we have to ditch our ride."

The driver nodded as he fought for control.

They pulled onto the freeway and raced north. The city lights slipped from view minutes later, but they could not outdistance the cops. Gato glanced behind them and the night lit up with flashing lights from a dozen police vehicles. Both lanes of traffic filled with red, blue, and white lights flashing in the darkness as they kept pace with the gangsters' vehicle.

Gato looked ahead. "Take the first exit we come to that takes us out into the county. We need to try to lose some of them. We have the whole damn police department behind us. And here comes a sheriff's deputy."

Seconds later, an exit loomed in front of them. Gato slapped the driver's arm. "Take that one. It'll get us to the river."

Without answering, the driver wrenched the steering wheel. The car hurled toward the exit. As they left the freeway, the roadway gently sloped downward in elevation, ending at a stop sign some twenty feet below the surface of the freeway. A two-lane county road intersected with the off ramp, running beneath the freeway.

The driver shot through the intersection and viciously yanked the steering wheel to the left. The car slid sideways as its tires tried to grab asphalt. He braked to try to control the car, but it only made the slide worse, fishtailing on loose gravel.

The driver punched the accelerator. The surge of power helped the car's tires to straighten out and regain contact with the road. They hurtled under the freeway and out into the blackness of a rural roadway.

Gato turned to watch their pursuers. The flashing lights spread out in single file as the patrol units followed each other.

"Do you guys know where this road ends up?"

No one answered.

Gato peered ahead, his view limited by whatever the car's headlights illuminated. "Let's see if we can outrun 'em. If not, pick a spot to ditch the car. If we gotta run, spread out and head in different directions. Maybe we can get away from them in the dark."

The driver pushed the car to its limits. The chase continued for more than two miles without any change, but they picked up a helicopter hovering above, its searchlight bathing the car in bright light. They led the cops in a chase that seemed like it might continue forever if nothing changed.

They were wrong.

Gato was the first to notice something up ahead. He wasn't sure, but he thought he saw a car illuminated by headlights. A deputy's car? Then—only darkness. He glanced out the rear window. "Hey, the cops are falling back."

As he turned to look out the front window, the driver said, "What the—?"

Gato saw a deputy's patrol car parked at the side of the road, all blacked out. Then the tires hit something in the roadway, making loud popping noises.

The car shuttered and began to fishtail. The driver screamed as he fought for control. The steering wheel seemed to fly out of his hand as the car plowed off the asphalt and hurtled out into blackness. A second later the car's nose smashed into the ground and tore through a vineyard. The car ripped out several rows of grape vines before grinding to a stop.

All three gangsters hurled forward, heads smashing the steering wheel, windshield, and each other. Dazed, Gato straightened. Before he could react, flashlights illuminated the inside of the car.

"Put your hands on your heads. Now."

Flashlights blinded Gato. His ears alerted him to the blood-chilling sound of several shotguns being racked as officers forced shells into the chambers. An attack dog barked close by. Overhead, glare from the helicopter bathed them in cold light, giving the whole scene a Hollywood-like feel of surreal sounds and figures dancing to a deadly script. Gato and his friends slowly raised their hands.

Officers ordered Gato and his friends, one by one, from the car. Each was searched, handcuffed, and individually placed in the backseat of a patrol car. It was over. They were headed for some serious time behind bars.

Within an hour, Gato and his partners sat in the sally port of county jail. Again, they were stripped, searched again, and then given jailhouse uniforms to wear, their personal items inventoried and stored away.

A female correction officer interviewed each new arrival. When the officer got to the part of the intake form about gang affiliations, she looked at Gato and glanced at the tattoos on his arm.

"Who you claiming?"

Gato just glared at her.

"Look, these questions are for your own good. I need to know who you're going to be safe with—Norteños or the Sureños."

Gato looked away. "I run with the north." His words were terse.

She filled in the box regarding his gang affiliations and noted his tattoos displayed on both arms and chest. Another officer photographed his tattoos. After the intake questions and photographs, another correction officer escorted Gato to a floor where Norteño gang members were segregated.

Gato walked out into the main room, around which individual cells had been built to accommodate two prisoners. Due to lack of funds and a growing jail population, the county was forced to house four to a cell. He glanced around him. There were some seventy gang members standing, sitting, or lying on the floor in small groups. All heads turned his way as Gato was escorted from the elevator and into the large holding tank. He recognized some of the gang members, one or two from his own gang. The others—strangers. A few of them were getting on in years.

He walked toward a small group who he recognized from his own neighborhood. They opened up their circle to receive him. One of the gangsters stood and greeted him. "Hey homie, what's up? What did the canines get you for?"

"Murder and armed robbery." He listed the charges against him with pride. These crimes would gain respect with the others.

"That's heavy, man. Welcome to the house, homie." The man sat down and offered Gato a seat.

"Yeah. If they get me on this one, I'm going to the *pinta* for a long time." The stoic look he gave his friends did not match the fear clutching his heart.

"Well, you put in the work. They'll watch your back when you hit the big house."

The small group opened up to allow an older gangster to approach. The man was in his late twenties, shaved head, with an upper torso covered with prison tattoos. One of Gato's friends leaned over and whispered, "He's Nuestra Raza—from the Bay. Just violated his parole. Word is the NF is about to pull him to their membership for the work he did."

Gato eyed the older man with as much aloofness as his face would allow. He showed his respect, but not much else. The man motioned to Gato's friend to move over. He sat next to Gato and smelled of sweat and alcohol.

"You Gato?"

He nodded.

"Heard your uncle's no good. Snitched to the cops."

Gato nodded again, trying to keep his temper in check. "He's no good. So what?"

The man tensed, eying the younger man without emotion. "Are you a snitch?"

Gato jumped to his feet, fists clenched. The man remained seated and slowly smiled.

"My father and grandfather are all good. Maybe you heard of my grandfather. DJ, up at the Bay?"

The other man stopped smiling. "Yeah, I've heard of him. I also heard that there's lots of changes coming down. I'm waiting to see who winds up on top. Y'know what I mean?"

Gato stared at the OG, unsure as to what he should say. "All I know is that I put in work for the north. I am down for the north. And I'll do whatever it takes, whatever's required."

The other man nodded his approval. "Watch your back, homie. Just watch your back." He stood and walked toward one of the cell doors. The man's walk was a flat-footed swagger Gato had seen so many times before.

Gato slowly released the air he'd trapped inside, heart still racing. His hands—clammy. Trying to relax, he took deep, even breaths to calm his heart.

The winds of change were coming. Was he going to be caught up in these winds, this storm from the north? Would the work he put in be enough to keep him safe, to keep him alive until he was free again?

He no longer knew who to trust. Who his enemy might be. Even his friend could be his enemy in this war without borders. He would have to watch his back. And then Mikio's words of warning came back to him. Gato fought the tears that threatened to appear. If only he had listened.

Now, he must travel down the road he had chosen. How long might the road carry him before he faced a dead end with no place to turn?

Chapter **59**

Homewood

Ghost awoke just as dawn spread a pink glow across the eastern sky. It would be a while before the sun poked its head over the mountain ranges. Just enough time for him to get on the lake. By the time he moved into position, the sun would be in their eyes.

He dressed the part of a fisherman, grabbed his fishing gear, binoculars, and weapons, and walked down to the pier. Ghost loaded his gear into the small aluminum boat, then looked up and down the beach for anyone who might be suspicious. No one in view.

Satisfied, he untied the boat, pushed away from the dock, and leaped aboard. He positioned himself on the small craft before twisting around and pulling on the starter cord. After a couple yanks, the engine sprang to life. With one hand he turned the bow toward deeper water, carefully guiding the boat due east until he was a good half mile from land.

He cut the engine down to trawling speed and dropped his fishing line, replete with lure, into the clear lake water. He let the line out until it was a significant distance from the boat, set the line, and turned the boat due north.

The sun had just crested the mountain ridges, shooting blinding rays across the lake and into the eyes of anyone standing on the western shore.

All they'd see would be the silhouette of a little boat with a single fisherman against the backdrop of a rising sun.

Ghost brought up his binoculars and studied the shoreline. He located the cabin where Tom had stashed the women and the boy. They must be late sleepers. He could not see anyone walking around.

Wait a minute. He readjusted his glasses, trying to get a closer look. There was a woman walking from the pier back to the cabin. He only saw her for a moment as she swished her way inside. He scanned the property but did not see anyone else.

Fantastic. It must have been Kagan's wife or the other woman. Maybe they haven't put things together after all. They must think he couldn't find this place. That they'd be safe here from him.

Before the sun reached much farther in the sky, Ghost turned the boat around and made a wide circle to the south. A half hour later, he edged the boat back to the pier.

By this time tomorrow if everything went well, his job would be done. He would be off to who-knows-where, leaving a trail of bodies in his wake.

Garcia couldn't stop laughing. "You are the ugliest woman I've ever seen."

The youngest male agent, still in his early twenties, had been recruited by Garcia to wear a dress. Disgust written across his face, he pulled the lady's hat off his head and threw it down on the floor. "Help me with this bra, will you?"

Garcia just roared louder. "Hey, you wanted to work undercover, hombre. If you're going to be James Bond, then you'll need to figure out how to get in and out of your own disguises."

Tom, feeling sorry for the young man, stepped forward. "Here, let me give you a hand. It's the least I can do."

Garcia turned his attention to the lake. He scanned the water with a powerful set of binoculars he'd purchased out of his own pocket. The lone fisherman had caught their eye earlier in the morning. They had been following his path since he became visible by the light of dawn. After the feminine masquerade across the lawn, the fisherman circled to the south out of sight.

Garcia's Nextel crackled as one of his agents on the south end of the property called in. "The fisherman has landed about five cabins south of us. Can't be sure which one from this angle."

Garcia turned to Tom. "Do you want to try to move on that location now?"

Tom shook his head. "We're not positive it was him, although I'd bet the farm that's our guy. We might spook him since we don't know exactly where he landed or where he's headed. Let's stick to the plan. We've set the bait. Let's see if the rat will come looking for the cheese."

"Your call, Tom."

Tom telephoned Deputy Hoffman and let him know they may have spotted Ghost. He told the deputy of their plan to capture the fugitive. Hoffman appeared to have doubts.

"Man, you guys have guts. You sure you don't want us to come in and search the area? You're taking a big chance."

"I know. But this guy is very elusive. I believe we have him thinking there are only women here...that we aren't smart enough to figure out he knows where we hid them. If he doesn't make a move tonight, we call in the troops and do a search—cabin by cabin. That'll be a lot more dangerous, and I don't want one more officer getting hurt because of this gangster. If we can't get him by dawn tomorrow, go ahead and shut down the highway—north and south. That RV of his is probably hidden in one of the garages near us. If he runs, he won't get very far."

Hoffman wished them luck. "I'll check in with you tomorrow before sunup."

"I'm hoping you'll hear from us before then." Tom closed the cell phone and slipped it into his pocket.

Tom glanced at Garcia. "How about I fix us some lunch?"

Garcia sputtered and choked. "How about I fix lunch and you clean up? I want to survive this thing. I've tasted your cooking. I'd rather not experience that horror again."

"Well, don't sugarcoat it, Hector. Don't worry about hurting my feelings."

"I didn't know you were so sensitive, pal." Garcia made his way into the kitchen. Tom followed.

"How about I supervise?"

Garcia pulled out a skillet and several pans, then he shot Tom a look of impatience. "Instead of supervising over something you know nothing about, tell me more about this great plan of yours. How're we going to make sure this thing works?"

Tom looked down at his hands. "You'll have to trust me on this." He paused, catching Garcia's eye. "I think this is the only way to catch Ghost without getting anyone else hurt."

"Hey, I trust you. I just want to be clear on the plan."

Tom laid it out one more time in more detail than he had shared earlier. Garcia's eyes widened and he let out a slow whistle. "You're taking a big chance, my friend. Are you sure you don't want backup a little closer than that?"

Tom shook his head. "This animal has hurt too many people, people near and dear to both of us. Trust me, he's the one who'll need help when I get through with him."

"So, you're sure he'll fall for the trap?"

Tom shifted in his seat. "I don't know. But is seems like our best shot. He is not going to give up—until he is captured or killed."

Gato's public defender shook his head as he read the charges filed against his client. He whistled under his breath at something on the page. Gato leaned forward to see through the plate glass at what had caught his attorney's attention.

"What's the matter? What kind of lies did they put down there?" Gato was worried. He'd spent a week in county jail awaiting his time in court. The hearing was continued twice due to his attorney's unavailability, and he had been forced to waive time. A hearing was set for tomorrow.

"I didn't realize you had a violent felony conviction as a juvenile." The attorney made a note on a yellow legal pad. "They'll use that against you as an adult."

"They can't do that, can they? I was just a kid. I just beat up a punk at school and took his school jacket."

"They call that robbery a felony. Says here you were fifteen years old when you were convicted of robbery. That is a strike against you. Three strikes and you go away for life."

"Okay. What am I looking at?"

The attorney continued to shake his head as he read further.

Gato pounded on the glass, making the man jump in his seat. "Tell me what's going on? I'm growing old here."

The attorney straightened his glasses. "I need to study this a bit further, but here is what I see so far. On the second-degree murder charge, normally you're facing fifteen years to life. That means you're eligible for parole after serving at least fifteen years. But since this murder was conducted in the furtherance of gang activity, they've charged you with 186.22…uh, a gang enhancement that gets you an additional ten years. That means, you can't get out on parole until you've served twenty-five years."

Gato's heart sank. He'd be an old man before he would ever see freedom.

The attorney coughed. "I'm afraid it gets worse. That robbery conviction when you were a kid. They can use that strike to double your twenty-five-years-to-life sentence. And I haven't even started to calculate what the current robbery charge will get you."

Gato felt sick inside. He'd sat down a few minutes ago thinking he was going to hear some good news. That he'd get out in ten to fifteen years—tops. His world was crashing down on him and the trial had not even begun.

"Here's what I see happening, worst-case scenario. If you're convicted on this armed robbery at the market, they'll give you a determinate sentence of fifteen years, five years for the aggravated term and ten years for personally using a firearm. When you finish serving that sentence, then you start serving the indeterminate term of twenty-five years to life."

Gato's head was swimming. "What does this mean in terms of me ever getting out?"

The attorney shook his head. "I would recommend that we try to cut a deal and throw ourselves on the mercy of the court. If they can prove all these charges against you…"

The attorney could not hold Gato's gaze. He glanced down at the papers in front of him before speaking again. "It means if the court throws the book at you, you will die in prison. You'll never be free again."

Gato clutched the edge of the counter and stared at the attorney through the glass. The room began to swim as the words hammered into his brain. Deep inside, Gato knew he would never be free again. Society had never been merciful to him before.

Why would they start now?

Chapter **60**

Ghost reached the dock and tied up his boat with little effort. The morning calmness of the lake made visibility crystal clear, as if he could reach down and touch bottom. He had not enjoyed one bite from his fishing excursion, but the trip had been extremely profitable.

At least one woman staying at the cabin. Probably Kagan's old lady. The target's still in place. He entered the vacated cabin and made his way to one of the bedrooms to catch a little shut eye. Darkness was a long way off and it was going to be a long night.

He laid out the equipment he would need when night came. He pulled out the arsenal of weapons he'd stolen from the SSU agent in the hospital and the dead ranger, broke down the weapons and began cleaning them. Once this was completed, he carefully rebuilt the weapons and lubricated those parts that needed to be friction free. He slid the slides back and smiled with satisfaction as each shot forward when he hit the release button. He was ready.

Next Ghost laid out the rest of his tools: a glass cutter, leather gloves if needed, a flashlight, and plenty of ammo. He carefully wrapped this into a backpack he could sling over one shoulder.

He set the binoculars aside and peered at the night-vision equipment he'd already used. He could stalk them at night and they wouldn't even know he was watching them. Ghost packed everything away in a backpack. Once he had taken out the guards, the women would be all his. He'd love to see the look on Kagan's face. With any luck at all, he might be able to arrange for Kagan to watch.

He relived the moment he pulled up alongside Bill Stevenson as the cop was just starting his run. *Perfect timing!* That look of surprise when the cop saw his face. Oh, that was so sweet. Moments before he sent the cop into eternity with a squeeze of the trigger.

And now to finish the job. Kagan's wife. Stevenson's wife. Even the kid. He relished the look on Kagan's face after Ghost was done with his wife. Just a little emotional twist of the knife into Kagan before he ended the detective's life. Ghost imagined the look of horror and pain.

He smiled as he stripped down to his shorts and climbed into bed. The thrill of the killings and the anticipation of new prey tonight would make it hard to sleep. His mind began to wander, retracing the events of his life that led to this moment.

It was not his fault he'd ended up like this. He was not the one to blame for all the chaos he'd caused. Society had always been out to get him, to slap him down, to keep him in place. Well, he was fighting back the only way he knew how. And if he was destined to die, if he was going out in one fiery ball, he'd take as many souls with him on his way down. They'd remember his name for a long time.

Ghost finally drifted to sleep, dreaming of where he would flee to when this hunt was over. He dreamed of cloudless blue skies, long sandy beaches, and the best brews money could buy. And women. Plenty of women.

He would run until he found this heaven somewhere on earth.

DJ nervously popped the knuckles of each finger. His messages were not getting through, and he felt as if he'd been cut off. He paced in the tiny cell trying to figure a way out. His week had not gone well.

Maria had paid him a visit. She only brought bad news.

"Mikio slipped through our fingers." Maria watched the storm brewing on DJ's face.

"And your grandson…arrested for murder and robbery. There's no way he's going to beat it. It looks like he's headed your way."

He just glared at Maria. "I could care less about Juanita's little snot-nosed kid. It's Mikio that I told you to take care of. He's gone?"

She nodded.

DJ slapped the wall of the visiting booth. "Can't you do anything right? It was all so simple. All you had to do was follow my instructions."

Maria looked back at him with fear in her eyes. "Baby, we followed your orders. Everything was set. Juanita made the phone call—but something spooked him. One minute he was inside his apartment. The next minute he's gone. They kicked in the door to his apartment and went in after him. He left practically everything behind. The back window left wide open."

"I want you to go back there and finish the job. Whatever it takes." He was screaming into the phone. Several people in the adjoining booths leaned out to see what the commotion might be. A guard walked over and told them to keep it down and then strolled away.

Maria looked at DJ, her voice quaking. "What if I can't find him?"

His eyes bore into her with a hatred she had never seen before. He had just answered her question without saying a word.

A guard was about to return DJ to the SHU when another guard stopped them. He handed DJ's escort a paper. The first guard looked down at the document and turned to the prisoner. "DJ, looks like you have another visitor. Your attorney."

DJ sat back down and waited. He was confused. He did not have a planned legal visit until next week. In a few minutes, James Chancellor sat where Maria had warmed the seat, the man's forehead wet with perspirations, his collar soaked. The attorney gave DJ a worried look.

DJ picked up the telephone receiver and waited until the attorney had his receiver in hand. "I thought you weren't coming here until next week."

"Plans changed." Chancellor fidgeted. "I've been retained to represent a client in Fresno. A…cousin of yours. Up on first-degree murder charges.

They're claiming he's an NF member and that the murder was directed by the gang."

DJ rolled his eyes. "So?"

Chancellor coughed, struggling to get his words out. He wiped his brow with a white handkerchief wadded up in his hand.

DJ eyed the attorney warily. "What has this got to do with me?"

He leaned forward. Couldn't look DJ in the eye. "I am going to need you to help us out in the case. To be a character witness."

"What are you talking about? A character witness? I'm a gang leader. All I'd be able to do is help the DA hang this guy."

Beads of sweat ran down the attorney's face. His gaze shifted to the guards and back to DJ. "You don't understand. I need you to get on the stand and tell them that he is not an NF member. That the NF is just a group of friends in prison who get together to protect themselves."

"And who do you think will buy that?"

Again, the attorney glanced at the guard and then back at DJ. "It doesn't matter. As long as we can get just one person on the jury to fall for that argument, we'll get a hung jury. It only takes one."

DJ laughed at him. "You got to be kidding. And what if I refuse?"

The attorney's face turned white. "I was asked to take on this case by other clients here at Pelican Bay, other clients you're familiar with. They indicated to me that this was what they had decided. I am just following orders. They—voted."

DJ felt as if someone had punched him in the gut like a boxer who receives a punch below the belt. Other *clients* in the SHU had decided he needed to go to Fresno. "You can tell your clients to go to hell."

Chancellor glanced back down to the floor. "I'm afraid they insist. I am going to issue the subpoena. You are going to be transferred whether you like it or not. We don't have a choice. Do you understand?"

"Who put you up to this?"

Chancellor just shook his head. "I can't tell you. They...decided."

DJ erupted from his seat and screamed. The attorney dropped his open briefcase and papers fells to the ground. He scrambled to gather them up, shoving them into his briefcase. He clicked his briefcase closed and hustled toward one of the guards. "I'm ready to leave now." His eyes pleaded with the guard.

DJ's screams of fury filled the room. Guards forcibly removed DJ from his visitor's booth and returned him to his cell. NF leaders had him boxed in with no room to move. He knew his transfer was inevitable, just like his future. It was over just that quick, that silently, a vote taken in secret. He had orchestrated just such a vote in the past on other men, other lives.

His hands were not clean of the blood of others. They dripped with the killings of many, many people. He had even forgotten some of the names he'd given a thumbs-down to when the secret vote came around. Or the many votes he had self-initiated in the interest of building up his own power structure.

Now his blood was required. Blood in, blood out.

The organization would move on, and his place in the gang would be snapped up by someone else, another man willing to raise his hand and run the risk DJ had accepted many, many years ago.

It would always end the same way.

DJ had not lived honorably. He had not lived a good life. And now it was time to pay the price. He sat in his cell, head in hands, a broken man. When they got to him—and they *would* get to him—they'd only be killing a shell of what he once was. He had been broken in the space of one day. One visit. A lifetime of struggle over in the blink of an eye.

He was a warrior who had somehow lost his way, lost his bearings, his honed ability to sense and elude danger. He saw this coming but refused to believe his people would take these steps against him.

His people? What a laugh. He should be worth something to the organization, but to them he was now a useless piece of garbage to be cast away as others scrambled over his grave, grabbing what he once possessed.

To some in the NF, he was just a coldhearted killer who'd lost his edge, an old man who needed to be removed from the seat of power to make room for others.

New blood coming in. Old blood being spilled.

Change within the gang was always inevitable, and it came without remorse or pity. Like a machine that just grinds away, chewing up things in its path and tossing them away. The allegiance of brothers had been broken. Maybe deep down inside each member, there never was a true allegiance to the brotherhood. Just an opportunity to grasp power.

DJ began to prepare for the end

Chapter 61

Homewood

The fluorescent dots on the face of Tom's watch read four o'clock in the morning. He began to harbor doubts. The moon, bright and silvery, had illuminated the lake and cabin most of the night. It began to work its way over the western slopes of the mountains, its light brightening the eastern shoreline.

Once the moon traversed the tip of the mountains, the cabin would be in the full shadows of night. This would make their job harder. The fire in the living room had burned down to smoldering embers, and cold night air spread throughout the dwelling like a premonition.

Tom had left a light on in one of the bedrooms. He hoped the light would draw Ghost to the second floor, like a moth drawn to a lamp. Garcia and the other agents had spent the night in the woods surrounding the house, motionless, silently watching.

So far—nothing.

He sat with his back to the wall, the bed between him and the open door to give him a straight shot. Off to the right, beyond the door and across the hallway at a diagonal, was the trap. The door had been left partially open to let the light from its single lamp trickle from the room and down the hallway. Ghost's night vision would be blinded, and he would be standing like a silhouetted target in the hallway.

This was the hardest part. Waiting for the trap to spring.

Then Tom heard something. At the same time, a Nextel phone—switched to person-to-person chatter—came alive. "I think the eagle has landed," Garcia whispered. "One of my guys saw movement coming from the lake."

"Yeah. I just heard something." Tom kept his own voice low.

"I guess he is not a ghost after all."

Tom heard glass being cut and the door latch unlocked. Ghost must have slipped past the outer security ring. He was inside the house.

"Garcia, he's in. Keep your guys on the perimeter. I'll try to take him here once he reaches my location. Shoot anyone who leaves—it won't be me. I'm turning off the phone."

"Got you covered, brother."

Tom turned his Nextel off. If the trap worked as planned, Ghost would be in his sights in just a few minutes. Tom pulled his weapon out and double-checked to make sure the magazine was shoved all the way in and locked. He'd only have one opportunity to fire. He wanted to make sure it counted.

After several minutes, panic began to creep in. There was no sound. Had he imagined the sound of glass breaking? If Ghost was in the cabin, where was he? He should have worked his way up the stairs by now.

He listened for anything that would warn him where Ghost might be lurking. It seemed hours before he heard the telltale creaks on the stairs. *Here he comes.*

Tom's hand felt sweaty as he gripped the pistol. He now held the weapon with a two-handed grip. His breathing echoed in his ears along with the pounding of blood. He struggled to control both. To make a good shot he had to breathe even and steady.

Could Ghost hear his breathing? *Calm down, Kagan.* It seemed like this moment was never going to happen. Ghost had to be in the hallway. Then Tom heard another creak. First at the top of the stairs. He imagined

Ghost carefully picking up each foot and quietly setting it down. Calculating. Controlled.

He heard the squeak of wood again as the killer worked his way down the hallway. Then the sounds stopped.

Tom held his breath, waiting for the next sound, the first glimpse of movement. Nothing. Just silence. Silence so loud it screamed in his ear. Maybe this guy was a ghost.

He heard the rustle of someone walking across carpeting. And then he saw a silhouette.

The killer crossed his doorway and looked into the room where Tom sat crouched. He froze, hoping the shadows concealed his position, waiting for Ghost to move. Then Ghost turned and crept toward the lighted bedroom across the hall.

Tom slowly raised his weapon, his finger pressed against the trigger. He must give this killer one chance to give up. To surrender. Just as Tom was about to call out—Ghost disappeared. Vanished! Something had spooked the gangster. Instead of heading toward the stairs to retreat, Ghost moved to the right, farther down the hallway out of sight.

Tom cursed to himself. He'd not acted fast enough. Why didn't he just squeeze the trigger and end it right here? Who would know? It was just him and the killer. It was not as if Ghost played by the rules. Why should he? The killer had broken into this house to kill Tom's family. In Ghost's world there was only one rule—kill or be killed. But Tom knew he had to play by the rules. And his hesitation caused an opportunity to slip away into the shadows.

He eased himself off the floor, gun in hand, and crept toward the hallway as quietly as his weight would allow, his hands drenched in sweat. The weight of his weapon felt like he was trying to hold up a ton of bricks. His breathing became irregular.

As Tom inched toward the door, a floorboard squeaked beneath him. He froze and groaned to himself, holding his breath. He could not hear the other man's movement.

Maybe Ghost was waiting for him.

What seemed like minutes clicked by. Sweat ran down Tom's face as he waited. His ears strained to pick up the faintest of sounds.

Nothing.

He moved forward once again, gun held in front of him as he sighted down the barrel. As he got to the doorway, he began to slice the pie, to slowly move from right to left, using the sight of his gun to direct his line of vision. What his eyes saw his weapon pointed at. Once he spotted his target, Tom had only to squeeze the trigger.

His target had disappeared.

Tom worked his way to the left, still standing inside the room, ending up with a clear view of the hallway. Ghost was not there.

Fear squeezed his lungs. The prey had sensed the trap, moved out of the kill zone into the shadows. Tom lowered his weapon for moment. The weight of the gun rigidly held out in front of him caused the sights to bounce to the beat of the blood that was pounding through his veins. He had to give his arms a rest. Just for a moment.

Tom took a deep breath, trying to control his breathing. His eyes searched back and forth, looking for the target.

The hallway was empty. Ghost slipped into one of the other rooms or continued down the hallway? Maybe to the large game room at the north end of the hallway? Tom had to walk through the kill zone to get to his target. The tables had been switched. Ghost waited somewhere in the darkness ahead. The killer had the advantage.

Tom had to make the playing field even. The light had to go.

He stepped out into the hallway and glanced in the direction Ghost had disappeared. No one. He dove across the hallway and into the brightly lit bedroom. No shots rang out.

Tom scrambled across the room. It took him only a second to reach the light switch. In a moment the room was bathed in darkness, Tom momentary blinded by the absence of light. He would stay crouched in the corner until his night vision came back.

He expected Ghost to pop out from the shadows to try to nail him as he scrambled across the room. Or maybe the killer was waiting in the hallway shadows for Tom to commit himself.

It was several seconds before he started to see images around him. Now, time was on his side. Garcia and the others had the cabin sealed off from the outside. No way could Ghost escape. Tom needed to settle down and take his time. Room by room. Shadow by shadow.

Filtering moonlight became his friend. It entered through the windows on the west side of the cabin, lights and shadows dancing together across the carpeted floor. But his "friend" would go dark any minute as it crested the ridge and continued west. Tom would have to cross the threshold of the bedroom once again and reenter the kill zone.

Ghost would be waiting.

Tom stood and raised his weapon with two hands, controlling his breathing. He sliced the pie to the hallway from this doorway, gun sight slowly working its way to the right.

No movement.

He searched the moonlit hallway for any sign of the life, knowing the killer lurked somewhere ahead.

Ghost had the edge. He knew Tom had to come to him. Not like before.

And then he heard a faint squeak as Ghost shifted his weight. A floorboard in the game room gave Tom the break he needed. Tom edged along the wall, staying in the shadows, until he came to the game room doorway.

Ghost had finally made a mistake. He had slipped into a room with plenty of moonlight. Windows to the west permitted light to stream inside. Just long enough to finish this hunt.

There was no escape.

Tom had one problem. He didn't know precisely where Ghost might be hiding in the room. He could sit back in the shadows and fire when Tom came through the doorway. The gangster had a better than fifty-fifty chance of nailing Tom.

Tom didn't like those odds and waited for another squeak. *Come on, Ghost. Give me one more sound. One more mistake.*

He waited. Hoping.

And there it was. Ghost moved one last time. The creak came from the left side, toward the west windows. Ghost was between him and the incoming moonlight. With any luck, Tom would get a silhouetted Ghost in his sights.

Tom had only a few seconds to make his move. Ghost might shift his position.

Tom dove through the doorway and rolled to his right. A muzzle flash ripped through the room. More flashes. A sting struck his left arm as he rolled. He came up in a kneeling position ready to fire. The sting throbbed.

He swung his gun's muzzle in the direction of Ghost's muzzle flash. Tom fired repeatedly. Move. Shoot. Move. Shoot. His first muzzle blast blinded him. The gun recoiled in his hand from each blast. He fired five more shots. Glass shattered. The window frame seemed to collapse.

No return fire.

Tom waited for his vision to return. From his angle, he could not see if Ghost landed inside the cabin or fell through the window. He could not hear a sound inside. Outside, he heard pounding feet. Someone running. Ghost? Maybe Garcia and the others had broken the perimeter and moved in to back him up. Slowly, his sight returned and he pointed his weapon where the body should have dropped.

No body. Ghost had disappeared.

Tom quickly scanned the room, looking for where Ghost might have crawled. Nothing.

Garcia was the first one to reach the doorway. "Tom, you okay?"

"Yeah. Don't come in. Can't find the suspect. Flick the light and cover the doorway. Ghost is still loose."

Light filled the room. Tom's eyes began to tell him the story. The gunman had smashed through the cabin window at the same moment Tom squeezed the volley of shots. A trail of blood led to the window and over the windowsill to the ground below.

"I hit him but he's gone."

Garcia walked into the room and holstered his pistol. His face hardened. "Hey, bro. You took one yourself."

Droplets of blood fell from Tom's fingertips to the floor. His own blood mingled with the killer's. A pounding in his head began to dissipate. His brain shifted into a slower gear and recorded what the rest of his body was trying to tell him. Tom grimaced as pain worked up his left arm like a swarm of angry wasps. The bullet had ripped through his left bicep without hitting a bone. It hurt worse than a dozen yanked teeth at the dentist, but he could still move the arm.

"It can't be that bad. I didn't feel it until now."

Garcia shook his head. "Who gave you a medical license? I'm going to call an ambulance."

"Not now, Hector." Tom tried to keep the frustration out of his voice. "We need to get to Ghost before he disappears forever. This can wait."

Garcia's look told him the agent did not agree. "I'll tell the others to keep an eye out." He raised his Nextel and gave out a warning.

Tom pointed down the hallway. "Grab one of those sheets from the bedrooms and help me patch this up."

Garcia scrambled out of the room. Tom heard him pulling and tossing things in one of the bedrooms. He reappeared a moment later, ripping a bedsheet into strips. He firmly tucked the strips around Tom's arm and snugly tied it off. "There. That should hold until we can get you to a hospital."

The bandage appeared to do the trick. Tom was thankful his gun hand went unscathed. A doctor would have to patch the left arm later. "Call Hoffman. Give him an update, and tell him where I'm going. And make it fast. We're running out of time."

Tom had to make sure Sara and the Stevensons were safe. The only question in his mind right now—did Ghost know where they were hiding?

Chapter 62

Ghost felt a flash of pain and knew he had been shot. He had crashed through the second-story window, and as he fell shards of glass surrounded him. Miraculously, a tree bough broke his fall, and he was able to hit and roll the moment he touched the ground without breaking a bone. Rising on shaky legs, he heard running feet toward the cabin and saw glimpses of at least two shadows approaching from the north.

He froze for a moment, watching and waiting. The running shadows told him the perimeter had been broken and they seemed confused. He assumed they were cops or SSU agents. Two men broke through the brush and scrambled for the cabin's rear door, then disappeared around the corner. They must be rushing inside to see if Kagan had shot him, not knowing Ghost just fell through the window.

He could not figure out how they could be so stupid, but he just found an avenue of escape. He took one step and his leg almost gave out. Pain raced up his leg. Twisted ankle. Ghost limped toward the tree line, testing the strength of the ankle. He could walk on it. Edging his way along the lakefront, he tried to stay concealed under the shadow of tree branches.

It was then he began to feel a different kind of pain. Touching his side, he felt the oozing warmth of blood. He had been hit.

Ghost turned and swiftly worked his way through the trees until he reached the marina. He couldn't stop now. Later, he'd patch himself up. Right now, escape was the only thing on his mind.

He reached his car, left parked between two trailered boats behind the marina office. He turned on the engine and squealed the tires over gravel until he reached the highway. He drove north toward Tahoe City. The cops might hear his car leaving, but he needed to put some distance between him and the cabin before the cavalry wised up.

There was one more place to check before he disappeared forever. Maybe the SSU agents had stashed the women and the boy at the hotel he'd seen the other night. If he moved fast enough, he just might make this happen. One more chance to hurt his enemy before he disappeared forever.

Tom pounded the steering wheel with his fist. Perspiration stung his eyes as he peered into the night. The car's emergency lights pierced the darkness like strobe lights across a darkened dance floor. Broken yellow lines on black asphalt blended into a blurry, solid line as Tom's car gained speed. All lights, no siren. He wanted to make this run in silence. The only noise was the howl of an engine being pushed to its limits.

The blast from the gunfire still rang in his ears. It had been more than ten minutes since he squeezed off a half-dozen rounds at the intruder. The killer had loomed in his gun sight for a brief second. It had been impossible to miss. And yet, once again he was chasing this shadow, always one step behind.

Ghost shouldn't know about the hotel where Sara and the others had been stashed. Two SSU agents were protecting them until Tom reached the hotel. Garcia phoned ahead to put them on the alert while the remaining agents searched around the cabin where Ghost disappeared. The hotel was miles ahead. The distance seemed to stretch out in front of him, each minute an eternity.

His mind played its own kind of wicked game. The chase forced Tom to the edge of complete exhaustion. As he raced through the night, Tom felt evil crashing against the very foundation of his life. As if Ghost were some kind of prince of darkness, trying to snatch from him those Tom fought to save.

Then he saw the face of the woman he loved. Sara's smile and gentle touch coaxing him back into this life, into the light of her love. The thought of Sara brought fear crashing down upon him. Ghost was after her and the Stevensons. This time, Ghost would not win. Tom pushed the accelerator to the floor and the engine howled into the night with its own kind of fury.

Ghost pulled off the highway a quarter mile from the hotel. The cops back at the cabin must have called ahead to alert those at the hotel. They probably drew their protective net even closer, trying to keep him from reaching his goal.

He would just have to play smarter.

Climbing out of the Mercedes, Ghost slipped down a dirt embankment that emptied onto a bike path paralleling the Truckee River. The hotel lights flickered through a grove of trees ahead. The gentle splash of the Truckee River changed at this point, its banks closing in and creating rapids that churned over jagged rocks. The water deadened the sound of his footsteps on the asphalt bike path. As he neared the hotel, the noise of the water increased. The river curved around the grounds of the two-story hotel in a rushing torrent of water.

Ghost was a betting man. He bet they had not left more than one or two guys to guard the women, while the others tried to corner him at the cabin. He slipped into the role of a strategist as he stalked the hotel. If he was running this show, he would have put both men upstairs, outside the women's rooms, as the last line of defense.

As he neared the hotel, Ghost reached down and buttoned up his coat to hide his injury. The blood had slowed to a trickle. He would only need a moment of time to get the attention of whoever was in the lobby. He pulled a hunting knife from a sheath at his side and slipped it into his coat pocket.

He slowly pushed the lobby door open. No one seemed to stir. A young man behind the receptionist's desk was slumped forward as if he might be asleep. No one else in the lobby. He quietly closed the door behind him and walked to where the young man rested.

Ghost eased around the desk until he stood next to the clerk. On the desk in front of him, a computer monitor had slipped into sleeping mode. With a click of the mouse, the computer screen awakened. Pulling out his pistol, Ghost raised the butt of the gun and brought it down on the back of the clerk's head in one vicious blow.

He lowered the unconscious clerk to the ground, then sat down and searched the computer for the rooms where his victims might be hiding. Scrawling through the registration list, he came across the names of two parties—one a single woman and the other a woman and child. They had been housed next to each other, and an SSU agent had authorized the expense to be paid by the California Department of Corrections.

Noting the room numbers, he found a map of the hotel and saw how the rooms had been laid out. He would start with the single female. That had to be Kagan's wife. He assumed the cops were upstairs in the hallway, guarding each of these rooms.

He would outflank them and kill any agent who came through the door to rescue them. After that, it would be a walk in the park.

Slipping through the lobby, he came to a small restaurant—now closed and dark—that opened up onto a patio overlooking the rapids beyond. Thick wooden trellises, supported by sturdy four-by-four beams, attached to the wall of the hotel just below each bedroom window. It was a ladder to the second floor.

He studied the windows and located the one he sought. It had been left partially open. Ghost reached behind him and pulled out a pistol. He racked the slide to ensure a round was in the chamber and tucked the gun back in his waistband.

Ghost began to climb the thick trellis, gritting his teeth as pain from his gunshot wound to his side from Kagan and the stab wounds to his chest by his attacker in Pelican Bay tormented him.

He quietly climbed to the open window and peered in. The room was dark with just enough moonlight for him to see the shape of a figure on the bed. It appeared to be a woman, her back to him. He inched open the window and eased himself inside while watching the woman for any sign of movement. If she moved, he would just shoot her and be done with it. Her breathing was steady and slow. He pulled out his gun and made his way toward the bed.

This is too easy. He carefully leaned over and reached for the woman.

Chapter 63

The illuminated hotel loomed in the distance and Tom cut his lights. He eased to the side of the road to park. He opened the door and stepped out, closing it quietly behind him.

A black Mercedes was parked alongside the roadway ahead on the opposite side. The car seemed out of place. There were no houses nearby and the car faced the wrong direction, its nose partially in the opposing lane of traffic. His gut told him who used this car.

Ghost.

He drew his weapon and walked briskly toward the hotel. He began running as fear gripped his heart and caused his legs to feel weak. He swung around the front of the hotel and tried to hug the side of the building until he got to the front door. He peered inside. No one at the desk.

Tom pushed open the lobby door, searching the room over the muzzle of his weapon. As he neared the front desk, he leaned over and saw a young man lying unconscious on the floor. He rushed to the man's side and felt for a pulse. Still alive.

Sara.

A chill swept through him as fear fought for control. "Oh God, please…" He edged up the stairs, grimacing as several of the steps creaked under his weight. The place was built like a tiny European hotel, tiny steps and dimly lit hallways. Once on the second floor, he glanced down the long hallway before pulling back for cover. Two agents, both sitting in chairs reading magazines. They seemed oblivious to any danger. It was clear the agents had not heard any suspicious noises.

Where was Ghost?

Tom holstered his weapon and slowly stepped into the hallway, extending his open hands to show them he was unarmed. The agent nearest him suddenly lurched forward, realizing someone was walking down the hallway toward him. Dim hallway lights must have made Tom hard to see. The other agent leaped to his feet and began to draw his weapon.

Tom paused and waved at the agent to stand down. He put his hands to his lips to motion for silence. The agent recognized Tom and nodded. Tom pointed to Sara's room and mouthed her name. The first agent again nodded. The other agent farther down the hallway did the same. The two men stood stiffly, waiting for Tom to make the next move.

Tom motioned to the second agent to try to kill the lights in the hallway. The agent turned, disappeared down the far side of the narrow passage, and a moment later the lights went out.

Tom quietly stepped to the door leading to Sara's room and raised his foot—gun raised.

Ghost froze at the side of the bed. Out of the corner of his eye, he saw the light under the door disappear. Someone had turned the hallway light off.

He slowly raised his weapon and pointed it at the door. His ears strained to pick up the slightest noise.

Silence!

He eased his way around the bed to the doorway leading into a small bathroom. If he could position himself in the bathroom for cover, he could take out the agents as they came through the door. Their first glance would be toward the bed to make sure Kagan's wife was still alive.

He started toward the bathroom. Something caused him to glance back at the bed. Kagan's wife woke up. Instinctively, he swung the gun toward her to silence her scream.

It was at that moment wood splintered, and he realized he was trapped between the bed and the bathroom. It was too late to make a dash for safety. He swung his weapon back toward the doorway.

He fired even before the muzzle reached its target.

Tom raised his boot to the door just as he heard Sara scream. He kicked the door open and peeled to the left as he entered. Seconds seemed like an eternity. He frantically searched the darkness trying to focus on a target. There was a muzzle flash to his right. Sara screamed again as Tom fired a microsecond after Ghost fired.

Tom kept firing.

As if in slow motion, he watched the impact his rounds made on the target. Ghost seemed to jolt with each shot. He staggered toward the window as Tom continued to shoot.

Tom's last shot struck Ghost in the head, causing the man to lurch backward through the window. Tom dashed to the window to see Ghost lying on the bricks below.

The killer did not move.

Tom motioned to the agents in the hallway. "Get down there and make sure he's dead. This guy seems to have nine lives." The two agents disappeared from the doorway.

He turned to the bed for the first time. Sara was sitting there, looking up at him in shock. "Are you okay?"

Sara barely nodded.

He sat on the edge of the bed, reached over, and took her into his arms. Her body shook as her sobs were buried in his shoulder.

"It's over, honey. He's dead." He stroked her hair, trying to give his strength to her.

Mary and Jonathan raced into the room, alarm on their faces. "We heard the shots and screaming," Mary said, clutching Jonathan to her.

"Everyone's fine," Tom said. "This nightmare is finally over."

Mary hugged her son and walked over to Tom. Her smile turned to concern as she saw his bandaged arm. "You're hurt."

Sara pulled back and saw his arm for the first time. "Tom, what happened?"

His gaze followed hers. "Just a nick. Something to brag about later."

She didn't say a word, just clutched him in a tight embrace. Tom held her close, not wanting to ever let go. It felt good to be this close, to be safe, to be together once again. Tiredness swept over him as the tension of the night drained from his body.

It was time to go home.

Chapter **64**

Santa Rosa

"The defendant will rise." A black-robed judge peered over his reading glasses at Gato, seated at the defense table. Gato stood slowly, his legs wobbly.

Several weeks ago a jury convicted him on all counts—second-degree murder, armed robbery, three strikes, and gang enhancements attached to these charges. All that was left was to hear the pronouncement from the judge at this sentencing hearing.

Gato steeled himself, expecting the worse.

"Son, this court has given you every opportunity to mend your ways. You have chosen to ignore those chances. You have continued a life of violence and this court finds you to be a threat to the community. On Count 1, I hereby sentence you to the maximum sentence..."

Gato phased out the rest of the judge's utterances. He was headed for prison for the rest of his life. That was all he'd waited to hear.

There'd be no leniency. No mercy. He didn't really expect any. As far as the rest of society was concerned, it was time for him to pay the price for his actions. To lock him away from the rest of society.

A court-appointed psychologist, angry over Gato's failure to cooperate, had bluntly told him, "As far as I am concerned, you're a threat to

society. You're like a malignant growth contaminating everyone you touch."
So much for an unbiased opinion.

Gato spit in the man's face, an act well documented in the report to
the judge.

A bailiff approached and took Gato's arm to escort him from the
courtroom. Gato turned and saw his mother sitting among the spectators.
His grandmother sat next to her—watching. His mother's eyes filled with
tears as she watched him being led from the courtroom. His grandmother
hung her head.

Gato's knees felt weak as he entered confinement. He forced himself
to appear unaffected by the sentence. He would have an audience to play
to when he returned to jail awaiting transport. He would be tough because
he had to be. He knew his role. Softness in this place got you hurt, preyed
upon—dead. Only the strong survived.

And he was going to survive. He would do whatever it took.

The steel door clanged shut just behind him. The urine-soaked floor,
the dirty gray walls, the screened-off light shining above would be his world
for as long as he breathed air.

As the bailiff escorted more and more prisoners to the holding tank,
Gato scrutinized each new face trying to determine whether that person
might be an ally or enemy. There were no friends here.

Even the way you looked at someone was dangerous. He had been
told by one old-timer: "Never stare, boy. It only invites trouble." It was
always a quick look. If you stared or held the gaze of another for more than
a second, it could be a sign of disrespect and an invitation to fight. He had
begun to learn the rules of survival. None of which anyone bothered to write
down. All of which had to be learned and adhered to if one was to survive.

His fight for survival had just begun.

Mikio's ears hurt when the cook yelled out her name over the phone.

"Sally, phone call."

He heard footsteps approaching.

"Hello?"

"Sally, it's Mikio."

She gasped and then giggled. "I was hoping you'd call me. Where are you?"

"It's better you don't know right now. Maybe later."

"Can I count on that?"

"I promise." Mikio waited a second before continuing. "How're you doing?"

"I'm doing okay."

"Were you able to get in touch with Hector?"

"Yeah, I gave him that package. He sure looked surprised when he realized what you sent him. He almost fell out of his chair."

"Will they be able to use it?"

"Oh yeah. That female prosecutor Ghost attacked just got out of the hospital, and Hector said he'd hook up with her and Detective Kagan. He said they were going to be busy for years thanks to you. The NF will never know what hit them."

"I honor my promises," he said. "And you told him I will testify?"

"Yeah. He practically had a heart attack. He'll leave a message with me whenever you check in again. It will be a while before that happens."

"Good. I have no desire to return to California anytime soon."

"You on the road?"

"Yeah, you could say that. Let's just say I'm far, far away."

"Can I come with you?" She sounded almost shy. Tentative.

"Maybe someday soon, hon. There are some things I need to do. Things I need to figure out first. Thanks for taking care of that thing with Hector. I didn't know who else to trust."

Sally laughed. "You know how you could show your appreciation?"

"I can guess."

"No you can't, Mikio. Just let me know how you're doing from time to time. And maybe someday—when you figure out the secrets of living—you'll give me a call. I'll come running."

"That sounds good. I'll stay in touch."

The traffic whizzed past Mikio as he climbed back into his car. He had pulled off the highway, somewhere east of Denver, Colorado. He still had a long drive ahead of him.

He felt good that Garcia had the package. He felt good that Sally might be a part of his life someday. Mikio looked on his map and found the route to his ultimate destination. *Windy City, here I come.*

He thought of his nephew on his way to prison. It hurt to think of what Juan would face, what he'd have to do to survive. As Mikio drove east, he thought of what lay ahead. He figured out one thing. He would never go back to his old life. Whatever he was looking for did not lie in his past. It was in the future. And he had a long way to go.

Chapter **65**

Truckee River in California

Tom's fly cast looped across the river and settled in front of a large granite boulder. A deep pool of water swirled and lapped against the boulders as he allowed the line to lie for a moment. There had to be a big one just waiting down there in those shadows.

He glanced upriver and watched Jonathan making his first cast of the day. The boy intently watched his line as it slipped through the air and landed midriver. Just the way Tom taught him. The boy was a quick learner. Jonathan glanced in Tom's direction looking for approval.

Tom gave him a smile and a thumbs-up.

Behind him, Sara and Mary sat in the shade of trees beyond the beach. Their voices carried over the water from time to time. He even heard them laugh. The sound pleased him.

The early summer brought warmth and sunlight to the mountains. Above, patches of snow were still visible along the peaks and in the shades of some of the mountain passes. Nearly eight months had passed since Ghost had darkened their lives. At first, Tom wasn't sure whether to suggest they return to Tahoe for a vacation. The place held some bad memories.

Interestingly, Sara thought it was a great idea. "For me, Tahoe is where we stopped running, Tom. Where we became free from the past. I think we should go back—together."

Sara was right. This place was where their lives changed for the good. Were they began to heal. And there were good memories here too.

Tom looked at Jonathan and thought of David. The hurt was still there, tucked away in a corner of his heart, but it was not like before. Sadness over his loss remained, but he felt comfort at the same time. And Tom knew over time he would slowly heal, never completely, never fully…but enough.

He looked at Jonathan and knew the loss this boy would carry. He pictured Jonathan reading to his own son someday, remembering his father, remembering the good times they shared.

As Tom worked his line across the water, he knew there must be a reason why he was still here. Maybe he could help Jonathan grow to become a man. To live a life—like Bill's—of honor and courage. Mary and Sara could teach the boy about God. Something Tom felt ill prepared to share with the boy. At least at this point in his life. Mostly, Tom hoped the boy would someday look up to Tom as a substitute for his father.

Tom looked forward to that day. And he intended to make this a priority in his life.

Tom watched the river flow past his legs, the cold current pressing against his waders. There was still a lot to learn.

Today was a good day. A peaceful day.

It would not always be that way. Sometimes, life just got dirty and downright nasty. An ongoing war would always be waged between good and evil. He had seen it up close and personal. And he hoped there really was a God who would bring down final judgment on all of mankind. That mankind would finally be accountable for their actions here on earth.

Maybe God would be merciful and let this old cowboy cross over heaven's border into the Promised Land, where David stood with open arms and his son's laughter would fill the air.

Until that time, Tom would try to do his best here on earth.

After reeling in his line one more time, Tom rhythmically whipped his rod back and forth, listening to the line whistle and slice through the mountain air. He waited until the fly reached almost across the river, next to an outcropping of granite, before he let it settle on the water as gently as a hummingbird, landing in that special place every fisherman seeks. Those dark pools of water where the big ones lay —hungrily waiting and watching.

Maybe his luck would change today.

Author's Note

I have tried to keep this novel as factual as I can—given this is fiction. The scenes at Pelican Bay State Prison are as I remembered—the Special Housing Unit, the law library, and reception. There is one deviation that takes place in the visitor's center and where prisoners meet their attorneys. I have changed this to meet the needs of my story. So those of you who have visited PBSP and know the areas I have described—don't shake a finger at me and say, "That is not the way it is." This is called literary license, my friend.

Lastly, I have termed SRPD's gang investigation unit as the Organized Crime and Intelligence Section (OCIS), a name I was familiar with during my stint in that unit. If you search the SRPD website though, you won't find any mention of this unit—but at one time it did exist.

OCIS produced phenomenal intelligence gleaned from investigations like Operation Black Widow and many other cases. Police were able to prevent a number of crimes from ever occurring—homicides, robberies, and even an escape from a federal prison in central California. They were able to solve hundreds of cases in which investigators had been stymied until OCIS investigators turned up leads that blew these cases wide open. OCIS investigators I worked with were outstanding, and what they achieved still amazes me today. (See the Acknowledgements section of this novel for some of the names I credit with this success.) So, for the duration of this Tom Kagan series, this unit will continue to be called the OCIS. Finally, I will always remember the folks from OCIS. I am proud to have been counted among their number.

Made in the USA
San Bernardino, CA
23 October 2013